HERE'S TO FALLING

CHRISTINE ZOLENDZ

DEDICATION

For my real J.
*I miss you **every day**.*

This story was
Inspired
By
True Events

Author's Note

It took me over twenty years to get this story out. Little by little, over the years I wrote, trying to get everything down. My readers will probably be able to tell the difference between the things I wrote long ago and things I wrote more recently. Honestly, this is probably the first story I really ever wrote. Trust me when I say it was very hard to do. It's inspired by events that I have lived through. You'll know the events when you read them. I weaved fiction through the story to make it a story. Just realize I'm giving you a piece of me on these pages.
I hope my words are strong enough.

PROLOGUE

*I*t was the edge of forever ago.

I could see my young self. Fingertips curled tightly around a worn-out paperback book. White-knuckled and clenching it with the intensity of the words, I was *devouring it, burning* through the pages like I was a blazing inferno. The off-white pages were wrinkled and dog-eared; the smell of them, like any true die-hard-reader would admit, was *heaven.* Hea*VEN!* In my nine-year-old mind, Judy Blume was the most talented writer ever created, and *Blubber* was the most brilliant collection of words giving life to my imagination between the covers of a book. *The book was a classic.* Joey, my best friend in the *whole entire universe,* sat next to me, flipping through my latest sketchbook and sighing loudly and, let's face it, *way too* dramatically. He knew my reading rules though - thou shalt not bother me until I finish the chapter. He had felt the wrath of my book upside his head one too many times already—he knew better than to chance fate—again.

Lying back against the dark grey pillows of my bed (because pink was for silly girls), Joey tossed my drawings aside, grabbed one of my Barbie dolls, and swung it around by its platinum blonde hair. It was a newer one that my father's secretary gave me. She thinks I'm like five *or something*. My dad never bothered to tell her that I hated Barbie dolls or any sort of baby doll. I hadn't yet chopped all of Barbie's stupid hair off or gave it permanent marker tattoos. As she launched through the air, she made a small whizzing sound and smacked up against the wall. Poor Barbie fell onto my rug; her head completely decapitated from her body, and bounced against my feet. I *wanted* to laugh, because it *was* funny. But, I *wanted* to read more. I had to bite my lip. Rules are rules. Chapters need finishing.

"Whoops," Joey giggled.

I reluctantly lifted my eyes off the last sentence of the chapter and narrowed them at him. *Oh, his Teenage Mutant Ninja Turtles were going down!* It was definitely going to be a microwave-his-Ninja Turtles kind of Friday afternoon.

"Charlotte!" my mom's voice hoarsely called through my bedroom door. Her wild, dark-haired head poked in, her rumpled clothes not hiding her daylong nap on the couch. "Looks like someone bought the house next door. There's a moving truck outside, and it looks like they have a kid," she said through a yawn.

Joey jumped off my bed and ran out of my room, "It better be a boy,"

What? No way, Jose!

Are you there, God? It's me Charlotte... Please, pleeeeeaaasssee, let it be a girl. Not one of those girly-girls, like the **ONLY** other girls on my street, the Jenson sisters (I'm still a little angry with you about them). Rebecca and Rachel Jenson wore pretty, pink, frilly dresses to school every day with shiny patent leather shoes. Shiny, *like I-could-see-my-face-in-them shiny!* They looked like porcelain dolls that came to life, *zombie-Chucky-dolls*, and they scared the stuffing out of me with their glossy, *red lipstick lips* and their sparkly glitter that **always** got in my eyes, even when I was ten feet away from them. Have you ever had glitter in your eye? It hurts! *I think it's a form of torture from the olden days.* No, God. I need a nice, normal, quiet, smart girl, who loves to read and is not afraid to play with smelly boys (like Joey: *best friend extraordinaire*), just like me. Amen.

My mother, with her red and glassy eyes, leaned her small frame against my door and pulled out a cigarette from the pack she kept in her shirt pocket. It stuck to her lip as she lit it and she laughed, inhaling deeply. She gave me a wink as I walked past her.

Joey and I quietly watched from my front porch as four huge men carried a large, brown couch into the new neighbor's house. A woman, a lot younger than my mother, sat almost motionless in a wheelchair that slowly buzzed itself up the sidewalk and up the neighbor's front walkway. Slightly moving a small lever on the armrest, the woman controlled the chair with one of her stark white, delicate hands. As she rolled by us, a small, tight smile passed her lips, but was gone instantly. Her body looked strange, kind of *scary strange*, because her legs looked really tiny compared to the rest of her. I shivered. And before you say anything, *I know* that's not nice, but I had never seen anything like that before, so it just...it just scared me a little. And remember, I was only nine and quite impressionable. I still slept with a nightlight, but uh, don't tell anybody that, okay?

Behind her, bouncing a basketball, was a tall kid with shaggy, dark brown hair that whipped up wildly with a passing breeze. His face was focused intently on the ground as he bounced the ball against the back of the woman's wheelchair, catching it with both hands each time it flew back at him. That bothered me, because isn't that a **mean** thing to do to someone in a wheelchair? The ball bounced

3

against the chair and onto the cobbled stones of the walkway three more times before Joey whispered, *a bit too loudly*, next to me, "Uh-oh."

The kid's head snapped up instantly, locking his eyes directly on mine. My body flinched back. This kid had the meanest look on his face, but that wasn't the part that made my belly feel sick. It was the strange color of his eyes. I had never seen such a color. Eyes that shade of blue couldn't be real. I never knew such a light shade of blue like that even existed until his eyes stared down mine.

I think he's an alien.

My mind immediately went all *Star Wars*, and for a minute, I, Princess Leia, was going to befriend this alien being so he could teach me how to use the force. Not the dark side, though. I was gonna be a Jedi!

Then, the kid stuck his middle finger up at me and walked into his house.

He did!

He just stuck his alien **middle finger right at me** and **walked away**. I gasped out loud. I didn't even know what that gesture meant, but I knew it was really bad, because I've seen my dad do it while he drives and curses at people who cut him off. *Oh God, it meant he wanted to kill me, didn't it?*

Oh. My. God. The alien-kid hated me. And he stuck his middle finger at me! It was the worst thing in the world to ever happen to me. I really, really, really mean it. It was the worst thing ever. My eyes burned with tears.

Sweat broke out all over my forehead as I stomped back into my house and into my bedroom. Joey was right behind me, closing my bedroom door and running to my window. "That kid is trouble," he whispered, peeking through my curtains.

Opening and closing my hands into fists, I paced in front of my bed. "That was just so rude! What? Why? And, I don't get what *that finger thing* means!" I stammered, sliding in front of my window and nudging Joey out of the way.

"It means he hates you and wants to poke you in the eye really hard with his finger. Duh," he said, nervously raking his hands through his dark hair.

From my bedroom window, which faced the alien-kid's **stupid** house, I could see right where the **stupid mean** space-jerk was standing. He was in a room full of boxes, standing on one of them, taping up a poster. *I hope he falls. I hope he falls and breaks his dumb stupid mean finger, so he never gives it to me again!*

Squinting my eyes, I tried to make out what was on the poster. Some stupid group of superheroes. That's when I realized: *that's his bedroom!* That mean stupid finger giving alien-kid was going to be in a bedroom right across a small alleyway from my bedroom. *Oh, snapdragons! This is the worst day ever. **WORST DAY EVER** in the history of ME!*

Joey stepped in between my curtains and me, flipping them **wide open**, which, *of course*, made the stupid alien-kid notice we were at my window **STARING** at him. He narrowed his eyes at us and started quickly opening a box, looking for something. I wanted to duck down and hide before he zapped me with his laser eyes and toasted me into a crispy pile of ash on the floor, but Joey was in my way, peeking his own head up from where *he was hiding* on the floor.

"This morning, when I went with my mom to the store, I saw that kid taking candy and sticking it in his pocket without paying for it," Joey said, pointing to the stupid mean alien-boy who was now writing something on a large piece of white paper. "He's a criminal," Joey whispered. "And he lives right next to you! What are you gonna do?"

I didn't dare take my eyes off the mean kid as I answered Joey, "I'm definitely not playing with him. I hope he's not in our class this year. Do you think he's the same age as us? You don't think he'll be in *Freddie Krueger's* class with us, do you?"

Before Joey could answer, we watched as the mean alien taped a drawing of a **horrible** skull and crossbones to his window. Above the skull were the words, "**YOU MESS WITH ME,**" and below the crossbones were the words, "**YOU DIE!**"

"Holy Cheese-whiz, he's gonna kill us," Joey yelped. "I bet there are lots of dead kids' bodies in those boxes. We should call the cops!" His big brown eyes looked to me for my *brilliant wisdom and guidance.*

I crossed my arms over my chest and stared down the mean boy with his *horrible* drawing of a skull and his *stupid* threat. He wasn't even cool enough to be an alien with *that dumb drawing*; he was just a **stupid boy**. Stomping over to my stack of sketchpads, I lifted up my largest one and thumbed through the pages until I found exactly what I needed. Grabbing a thick black marker from my *Fantastical Cup O' Markers*, I wrote the mean kid a little note back. And then I taped my own picture of a skull and crossbones to my window with the words: **THAT'S NOT SCARY BUT THIS ONE IS!!!! YOU STAY AWAY FROM ME!!! Thief.**

Oh, did I tell you I could draw? Like, really well. My skull looked like an actual skull; it even had blood dripping out of its empty eye sockets. And there was an eyeball rolling away in the background. The mean boy looked shocked at my *AWEsome* drawing. Then he looked back at me. And that's when I gave him *my* middle finger and shoved the curtains back over the window.

"That *was so badbutt!* I bet you could beat him up if you had to!" Joey said, jumping on my bed.

I climbed up on my bed next to my best friend *in the entire universe* and started bouncing with him. "Well, I hope I never have to see him again, because I just might have to beat him up if he bothers us!" Secretly, I hoped I didn't. There were two boys in our class that were always mean to Joey, Slate Marshall and Drake Fischer. I fought with Slate and Drake all the time, so they wouldn't bother Joey. But I had never had to beat one of them up, so I didn't think I really knew if I could. *I hope I never have to find out, which made me kind of sad that the mean kid wasn't an alien. I could really use the force or some cool Jedi mind tricks when people teased Joey.*

We bounced on my bed for about an hour. Yeah, you definitely can't ever get tired of bouncing on a bed, can you? No way. Never. The government should make it an Olympic sport; Joey and I would probably win all the medals for it. We stopped only because it was five o'clock, and we were hungry.

My mom was back to sleep on the couch with a completely burned down cigarette still between her fingers. There was a long line of ash that dangled from its tip—just about to fall. Joey and I stood over her, laughing to each other. I poked her in the belly. "Mom, when's dinner?" I asked, loudly.

Blinking her eyes open, it took her a minute to focus on me. "Oh, sweetie, sorry. What time is it?" she yawned, flicking her cigarette into the ashtray that she kept on the floor.

"It's 5:06. And my stomach is rumbling," I said, watching the cloud of ash puff up from the ashtray.

Joey made growly rumbling noises beside me. He was hungry too.

She let out a long sigh and scratched at her scalp full of curls. "I don't feel like cooking; I'm not feeling too well today. There's ice cream in the freezer." She lowered her voice and smiled, "It'll be our secret, okay? Ice cream sundaes for dinner with all the fixings. You know where everything is Charlotte. Just make sure to clean up any mess, so your father doesn't see. He'll probably be working late *again* tonight." Then, she rolled over and tucked her arms under her head, falling back to sleep almost immediately.

Ice cream sundaes for dinner. Like I was going to complain about *that*! *My mom rocked!*

High-fiving each other, Joey and I ran for the kitchen and pulled out everything we needed for the **best dinner ever**. All my thoughts of the mean stupid boy fell away with the excitement of secret ice cream sundaes, and my worst day ever quickly turned into my best day ever.

Five whopping scoops of vanilla ice cream landed in each of our bowls and were immediately covered with sweet, sugary, caramel syrup. Joey poured extra nuts over mine while I threw extra cherries on top of his. Rainbow sprinkles for me, chocolate for him, and some in both of our mouths.

Cleaning up quickly, we grabbed handfuls of napkins and ran out the back door and into my yard.

In the right-hand corner of my backyard, right next to the stupid mean boy's back yard, stood the tallest tree on my block. *And* up in the branches of the tallest tree on my block, was the biggest and best tree house to have ever been built by human hands. And it was all mine.

Joey and I climbed in and ate our delicious dinner, both getting brain freezes, and howling and laughing in the pain. It was okay. *I'd rather have a brain freeze than be a brain fart like the stupid mean boy next door.*

We spent the rest of the night there, like we usually did, looking for dragons and hiding from zombies and monsters, like Slate and Drake, and of course, Jason Voorhees from *Friday the 13th* (the best movie in the universe).

※

THE MEMORY WAS SO real and vivid; I felt like I could just

reach out and touch us. I could still feel the cool breeze that blew through the tree house windows, still smell the watermelon lip-gloss that I smeared daringly across my face, and still taste the blueberry *Hubba Bubba* bubblegum that Joey and I both chewed after finishing our sundaes. Cue in a cheesy 1999 ballad, something along the lines of *Iris by The Goo Goo Dolls*, and the memory came to life.

Tears sting my eyes and my breath turns into a hard, thick knot in my throat. We were the best of friends, like Charlotte and Wilbur, Pooh and Piglet, Calvin and Hobbes, or any other amazing literary friendships I could have come up with when I was nine.

I wish there was a device implanted in our brains to record memories, so we could play them back and watch them whenever we wanted, like old home movies. Because sometimes, I think the things we remember pale in comparison to what was real, and I would love to see the *real* images instead of just the thin, pallid ghosts of them.

It's so funny to me as an adult, the things that I remember, or the strange things that spark a memory. A memory that had been buried deep under a lifetime of days that followed and left behind can suddenly spring to life on a whim. Once, I tried to write all the memories of my childhood down in a journal, but all I accomplished was to ruin them, making them cold and unfeeling.

Lifeless.

Sometimes, the memories attack me like a fever, and all I want to do is hide my mind from them, hide my heart; protect what's left of it.

I've heard some people say that what you remember is not the whole truth; it's our thoughts of what we wanted things to be remembered as. They believe that we change our memories, that we just fabricate them into pasts that we can live with. *Do I believe that?*

9

No. I believe I remember everything, every little detail.

My memories are true. They may be just from my point of view, but I could never embellish my recollections to make them more or less than what they were. My memories have a heavy, tangible weight to them. I've felt their burden for so long; they have become almost bearable to carry. They don't pull me under any longer.

Not to say that they don't still hurt

Or give me joy...

They have just become what's made me stronger

They are what have made me...

Me.

Damn, I went all poetic on you, didn't I?

CHARLOTTE

*B*ren stood on the corner trying to hail a cab, once again too drunk to drive or even remember where he'd put his keys. The only thing he cared about was getting back to his place in time for his nightly never-ending party. "You're coming over, right?"

"I have an early day tomorrow," I said, looking down at my watch. I ran through more excuses in my head in case I needed them. *I have cramps, a headache, food poisoning, another chapter to read...* He always asked; I always refused. I don't enjoy spending my time with a bunch of drunken slobs.

A cab pulled over to the curb and Bren yanked open the door. "What is wrong with you? Everybody's asking where you've been. People think I have an imaginary girlfriend," he said with a curt tone.

He placed a hand on the small of my back, a gesture that used to send warmth through my body. Now it did nothing but make me cringe.

"Bren. It's eleven o'clock. I'm exhausted. I worked all day," I said.

"Oh, I get it," he snapped. "I do nothing all day, right? Suddenly, I'm a bag of shit." His breath was heavy with the tang of beer and his eyes were bloodshot.

"Yep. Those where the exact words that came out of my mouth," I hissed, shutting him up.

No words passed between us in the cab. All I did was scream at him in my head. About how sad and shitty he seemed to always make me feel. How much he messed up everything. How much stress and tension he had filled my life with for the last few months. How the only time I felt better was when he was gone. But we owned a business together, and it had been years since I really let myself believe I deserved to be happy.

When the taxi pulled up in front of his building, he slammed the door without a goodbye or a glance back in my direction.

When I got home, I stripped down to my bra and panties, not even bothering to put on pajamas, and fell right into my bed. The minute my body landed, I was asleep.

Sometime around the ass-crack of dawn, I felt a warm body stumble into the bed and snuggle up behind me, wrapping strong arms around my stomach, embracing me in a tight hold. "Mmm, babe. You up?" Bren whispered, moving his hand heavily to my chest and squeezing. I swear I saw stars; he never has any clue how heavy-handed he is when he drinks. Nuzzling his face into my hair, his warm breath tickling my ear, he whispered again, "Babe?"

"Well, I am now that you almost ripped my boob off."

You want to know what the sad part is about all this? I could tell you word for word, exactly, what was going to happen before it even happened when Bren and I were alone. I could write the script and sell the rights to it. Bren had, like three moves, that's it. He'd tweak my nipples two or three times, rub his fingers over the place he *thought* was the most important spot on a woman's body, but wasn't (he missed it by an inch so he always ended up playing with my inner thigh), then he'd pull himself out of his pants and pump his hand up and down himself, waiting until I can get myself undressed. Then, he'd jump me.

Or, even better, is what had been happening for the last four months: **nothing**. As in, his man parts just didn't work, no matter how hard he tugged on it.

Hello whiskey dick. At that point he usually fell asleep, limp dick in hand, snoring loudly.

God, it was so sad.

I used to love sex, everything about sex. I loved the anticipation of it, the flirting and teasing. I loved the kissing and tasting that goes on, the fun, the laughter and dares. I loved the way a man looks at you, like you're the only one in the universe to make him feel like this. I loved the slow, hot caresses *and* the fast hard need. I even love the angst, the fighting, and the make-up sex. What *I didn't like* was how detached and disinterested we both became toward each other.

Bren was like a complete stranger lying next to me in that bed; a two hundred pound dead weight beside me, holding me down.

I tried with Bren, I really did. In the beginning, when we were just friends and I knew how he felt, I wanted it to be love. But right now, it just feels like a burden; some obligation that I'm stuck with; an albatross around my neck that I just cannot shake. I knew it would never be that crazy-love they wrote about in those angst-filled books I loved, but I've been through that kind of love and when it's gone, you're just never the same. You know the love I'm talking about, right? The one with kisses that spark fires, touches that ignite your soul, and the whispers, *God the whispers*, that make you believe you can *fly*. The problem with that love is I was still left in ashes, burnt little embers, charred remains of things that *could have been*. I needed to just settle for one of those loves that was mild and tepid against my lips, and non-flammable to my heart. I didn't want to be singed again. I'd never live through it.

Bren didn't fall asleep with his dick in his hands this time, though. He just lay next to me, our backs turned away from each other. Neither of us wanted to seek warmth from each other's bodies in the dark room, because, I don't know, maybe it would take too much effort. Or, maybe, neither one of us wanted to feel as rejected as we already did.

I was completely exhausted with my life, and I was only twenty-four.

We were both silent for a few minutes when Bren let out a low sigh. I wished he'd just fall asleep so I could climb out of bed and get the hell away from him. But, I know I can't—won't. I'm chained here, to him, to obligations and promises I can't ignore—won't ignore.

"Come over here, baby. Put your mouth on me," he slurred.

I climbed out of bed, laughing angrily, "Bren, I'm not wasting fifteen minutes of my sleep to suck on a limp dick that's too drunk to get hard. Besides, you're gonna pass out any minute."

Grabbing my cell phone off my nightstand, I walked to the door and turned to start yelling at him.

Bren was already snoring.

I hated to think that there was not one part of him I liked anymore.

Not one.

Suddenly, the walls of my small apartment felt suffocating

to me, and I needed some sort of escape. The choking, overwhelming feeling of hopelessness clamped its knotted claws around my heart; was there any way that we could ever fix the indifference, resentments, and silence that had become our relationship?

I didn't want to look at him any longer. He disgusted me.

With my messenger bag slung over my shoulder, I walked out of the apartment, down the street, and into the crowded coffee shop. Tapping my foot impatiently, I waited in line for ten minutes to order my crack. *I mean my coffee.* Oh, all right, *hello...my name is Charlotte Stone and I'm a coffeeholic. It absolutely is my crack, just like my books.*

God, I wished my life were more like my books.

I was practically frothing at the mouth when I got up to the register, so I ordered two. And right about now is the time where you think that Mr. Right swooped in from behind the counter, the gazillionaire who owned the store, no, *the chain of stores*, and I was his new infatuation. He yanked me into the back of the café and licked every spot on my body while promising me enough free caramel lattes that I could bathe in them, right? Just like in one of my romance novels.

Ah, no.

A pierced up, pink-haired teenager theatrically told me how much I owed her and smiled her perky, wide smile, while bouncing around extremely way too happy to serve me that early in the morning. I waited for the rays of sunshine to burst forth from her ass cheeks as she handed me my coffees.

Yeah, that didn't happen either.

I walked away from the counter a little more depressed than when I got there. My books were so much better than my reality.

A huge, yellow, neon sign boasting free Wifi service hung

over the front doors. Smiling at my own foresight to bring my bag with my iPad inside, I decided to sit at a table and read. Sipping at my coffee, I tried blending in with the everyday working people frantically ordering coffees and the moms with the SUV sized strollers wearing giant mom bags that matched in size to the ones under their tired eyes. I was an expert in blending in. People didn't look at me anymore; they just looked *through* me. Complete invisibility. Some people suffered in their lack of being noticed; me, I knew the worth of people NOT weighing and measuring you and forming their opinions of you the minute they saw you.

After a few chapters of my book, and one whole coffee devoured, my phone buzzed softly in my pocket. I opened the text and smiled.

J: Hey you. How's life?

Me: Can't complain. How are you?

J: Crap night at work, just got in. Needed to see your little smiley face on my phone.

Me: Well then...

And just like that, my mind went back and stood right over the ledge of *what ifs* that have attached themselves like heavy chains around my thoughts through all the years. Someone sitting at the table next to me was eating a blueberry scone and I'm nine again, walking to the first day of school with my best friend Joey, each of us chewing on three pieces of blueberry bubble gum—even though my mom said that it would make us choke.

Fourth grade, room 404, Mr. F. Krueger's classroom (we called him Freddie Krueger, and it might have been his real name. We never did find out).

For the first day, all the classes lined up in the schoolyard, behind smiling teachers holding up their class numbers—all except for Mr. Krueger, who was frowning, probably because he hadn't eaten enough kids for breakfast that morning.

As we made our way through the crowds of screaming and crying students, Joey yanked on my school bag, hard, and I stumbled back, arms flailing. Turning my head quickly, I saw Joey's eyes were wide with fear, "It's that kid, look!"

He was right. A few steps away from us stood my evil alien neighbor, right next to our new teacher. *Great.* This was going to be the worst school year EVER! I think I may have stomped my foot on the ground for emphasis, but I still looked cool, because nobody noticed me anyway.

"Come on, Joey. Let's just get in line and ignore him."

Smiling at Mr. Krueger, I lined up behind Ava Marie

Trebisky. The alien boy narrowed his laser beams at me and stared. It wasn't a normal stare either, because he didn't look away at all. He just looked straight into my eyes. So I stared right back at him until the first bell rang, and we had to follow Mr. Krueger into our new classroom. Where, to my *horror*, Mr. Krueger assigned the alien (whose name was Jase Delaney, probably from the planet Uranus) to the seat **ACROSS** from me. That meant that we would **HAVE TO** work together in reading groups, math teams, and all the other team building sharing/caring/Kum-ba-ya-la-de-da stuff they had us do.

The whole first day of school, whenever I looked at him, his eyes squinted at mine, and his mouth did this mean, twisty thing. I hated him. *I hated him so bad*. I hated this class, this teacher, and even dumb Rachel Jenson who sat next to me digging up her nose, collecting her little yellow-green treasures, and sticking them lovingly on her gold-glittered star pencil.

Even worse, Joey had to sit next to Slate Marshall, the *worst* and **MEANEST** kid in the whole school, no, *the whole state of New York*. **I DID NOT** understand either, because every year that Slate Marshall had been in my class (since kindergarten), our teachers pulled his seat to sit next to the teacher's desk, far away from the other kids. He was **THAT** bad. I heard his father was in prison or something. I guessed Mr. Krueger didn't know that—yet.

By the end of that first day, Slate managed to "accidently" put gum in Joey's hair, steal all of the girl's snacks (it had to be him even though no one saw him do it. He went to the bathroom, like five billion times, and every time he came back with a ring of cheese around his mouth!), and Jase Delaney and I got stuck being partners in relay races in gym.

Are you there, God? It's me, Charlotte. *Do you hate me?*
Yes, I think you do!

Because for the rest of the month of September, the same things happened EVERY DAY! Slate "accidently" stuck gum or sticky peppermint candy in Joey's hair. It happened so many times that his mom had to give him a buzz cut. All his long, floppy, beautiful, black hair was completely shaved off. Slate started "accidently" sticking gum in Juliana Crispin's hair next, and her haircut was just awful. I thought she was a new boy in class! And Jase Delaney still made faces at me every day, but refused to talk to me. And he was **just as bad as** Slate. He always acted out in class. He never worked with anybody. He stole snacks from the lunchroom (and Mr. Krueger's jar of chocolate bars, which was only for the **GOOD STUDENTS**), and he even visited with the counselor! Not only was he bad, he was **CRAZY!**

Plus, each day he bounced that stupid ball against my fence, making a huge racket while I was in the tree house trying to do my homework. I'd never even seen Jase Delaney turn in homework! And if he wasn't slamming his basketball loudly, he was playing his music really, really, really loud.

I hated him!

I know I keep repeating it, but honestly, I can't say it enough. *I think I need to make bumper stickers.*

Then, three weeks into the school year, was the dreaded 'Meet the Teacher Night,' where you go to school **at night** with *your parents* so they could meet your teacher! All our parents filed into our classroom and crammed their adult-sized bodies into our kid-sized chairs and listened to Freddie Krueger talk about student goals, correct behaviors, and state standardized testing. My classmates either stood next to their parents, or hung out in the back of the classroom where we stuffed our faces with the goodies Mr. Krueger left out for our parents. I ate four chocolate glazed donuts, and Joey ate three. I was immediately sick to my stomach.

My mom sat in my seat and kept pulling out her mirror

to reapply her lipstick—see how boring my teacher was? He couldn't even keep the adults entertained. Jase Delaney stood next to both of his parents. His mother sat in her wheelchair with a far-away look in her eyes, and his father was dressed in a fancy suit. He had the same color alien eyes as Jase. Both of his parents looked so much younger than all the other parents. *Maybe they really were an alien family!*

Even Slate's mom showed up. She had a crying toddler on her lap that she kept on telling to *shut the hell up* and had a tattoo of some man's face across her entire chest (she wore a really low cut shirt, one of those ones that had all the other mothers *tsking* about and shaking their heads).

But Slate didn't go near his mom; he stood off to the side, staring at Joey and cracking his knuckles, trying to scare everybody away from the donuts. Well, no matter how sick I felt, I wasn't moving away from the donuts, and if he tried sticking gum in my hair, I would hit him in the **you-know-what** with a cream stick!

When Mr. Krueger was finished putting our parents to sleep, they were asked to sit in the school auditorium, so Mrs. Beverly, our principal, could speak with all of them. Some of the students followed their yawning parents and some of us just roamed around the hallways, looking at the displays and bulletin boards. I mean, come on, we were in school at night. We wanted to look around!

Joey and I walked past the main office and into the music room, my eyes zoning in on the upper grades' band drum set. I always wanted to play the drums, but everyone told me they were way too loud.

"Hey, Drake, look who it is. It's *Piss Pants* and his girl-friend, *Four Eyes!*" Slate's voice echoed with the acoustics of the music room. *Oh no.* I felt Joey stiffen next to me.

When Joey and Slate were in preschool, Joey couldn't get to the bathroom fast enough, and he had an accident.

Slate still teased him about it. Slate teased anyone about anything. He called me four eyes because I had to wear glasses to see what the teacher was doing in the front of the classroom. I didn't care though, because last year in third grade, when I first got my glasses, my teacher, Mrs. DeMarco, told me about a surgery I could get when I'm older to fix my eyesight. So, I won't always have to wear glasses, but he'd always be mean. Slate Marshall and his little sidekick, Drake Fischer, were the dumbest, meanest jerks ever.

The two boys moved closer to us, each of them walking and circling to the side of us. "Nice haircut, Piss Pants. What are you guys doing in here? You going to try to kiss your *girl-friend?*" Slate teased.

I stepped in front of Joey, pushed the sleeves of my sweat-shirt up my arms, and crossed them in front of me. "First of all, I'm not his girlfriend. I'm his best friend. Second of all, you both need to leave us alone or else I'm going to tell on you!" I knew I was about to die, but I was going to make sure I got at least one good kick at him.

Slate shoved me out of the way and grabbed Joey by the collar of his shirt. I tried to kick at him as I flew back, but all I managed to do was get him in the back of his leg and fall on my butt. Next to me, Drake started laughing so hard he had to bend down and grab at his stomach while loud hiccups belched from his stupid mouth.

Slate raised his fist and held it in front of Joey's face like he was about to punch him. I jumped up off the floor and moved forward, grabbing at his fist to hold it back. Drake still rolled on the floor, he was laughing so much.

"I don't think it's *that* funny," a voice called from behind us.

The four of us turned our heads at the same time to see Jase Delaney looking at us with that mean ugly scowl. Oh no, now there were three boys against us. Joey and I were *so* going to die.

Slate let go of Joey, who slumped down onto the floor with watery eyes, and walked up in front of Jase. "I don't care what you think," Slate said.

"I think it'll be funny if she beats the crud out of you for pushing her. That's what I want to see," Jase said, pointing toward me and stepping closer.

"Get out of here, loser. Go back inside to your *freaky mommy* and daddy."

"At least I have a dad; one who isn't in jail," Jase said.

"Yeah, well, at least I have a mom with legs that work!"

Jase's eyes scanned over to me, then to Joey, and the corners of his mouth lifted into a smile. It was pure evil. *I'm not kidding.* Then, his fist came out of *nowhere* and punched Slate square in the nose.

"Hey, did having a mom with legs help you out at all when I hit you? Nah, it didn't help you one bit, did it?" Jase snarled angrily as he stood over Slate.

Slate was screaming and crying and blood gushed from his nose.

Coolest thing ever.

Hearing all the noise, Mr. Krueger came running in and demanded to know what was going on. Fighting in school was an automatic weeklong suspension. And not one of the fun ones where you got to stay home all week; nope, you had to go on a special bus to attend another school for the week. I didn't care about Slate getting suspended. He deserved it, and it would be great to be in school without him for one whole week. But, Jase Delaney just punched Slate in the face for bothering Joey and me. The alien just saved our lives.

I was so confused.

"I'm waiting for an answer!" Freddie Krueger screamed at

us while he held a white handkerchief to Slate's face. *Eww, is that the handkerchief he used to blow his nose?*

I stepped forward, "Mr. Krueger, Slate tripped and hit his face against the edge of the...desk." *Oh my God, I lied.*

Mr. Krueger's eyes tightened into thin little slits as he looked at me. "Is that really what happened?"

Everybody nodded.

"Okay then, let's get you into the nurse's station, shall we?" he said to Slate, walking him to the door. Drake followed right behind him. "The rest of you, go find your parents and go home."

Jase, Joey, and I were left in the music room alone.

"THAT was the COOLEST THING EVER!" Joey yelled, jumping up and down in front of Jase "Where did you learn to punch like THAT?"

"My mom," Jase said, walking out the door without saying another word to us.

Later that night when I got home from school, I climbed into my tree house by myself to sketch. Leaning up against my beanbag chair, I closed my eyes and tried to picture the tiny fireflies I noticed on my way home, and how they glowed their bright little bodies as the late summer sun set.

Something made a heavy thud against the wooden floorboards of the tree house, sending vibrations along the planks. I opened my eyes and Jase Delaney was right next to me, his alien eyes watching me.

"How'd you get up here? I pulled up the rope ladder, there's no way..."

"I climbed up to the roof of my garage and jumped over," he said quietly.

I ran to the open window and stuck my head out, "But that's like a million miles away!"

"Yeah, I know. For a minute I thought I might die, but I jumped anyway," he chuckled. "I just ah...wanted to say thank you, for you know, not saying shit to Krueger. That was pretty cool." He talked like someone who was much older than me.

"Thanks," I answered quietly, not able to look in his eyes.

"You know, you don't look like a Charlotte," he said.

I snapped my eyes to meet his, "Yeah, I know. I was named after my father's grandmother. I hate it. It reminds me of *Charlotte's Web* and I hate spiders."

"You're always reading...books like *Charlotte's Web* and shit."

"Yeah, I really like to read."

"I'm not gonna call you Charlotte, since you hate spiders. I'm gonna call you Charlie."

That made me smile. Charlie. I liked it. "Did your mom really teach you how to punch someone?"

"No, she taught me how important it is to block someone," he whispered.

The memory slowly faded as the sounds of the coffee shop poured through my ears, and the sweet smell of pastries attacked my other senses. My last thought as the young images of us vanished from my mind, was wondering if we'd still be able to recognize each other, or had life left its mangled scars on us and the kids we once were could no longer be seen.

I sat up in my seat a bit straighter, kicking the cobwebbed thoughts out of my mind, and noticed that the person sitting at the table behind me was reading the screen of my iPad over my shoulder. The woman even had the nerve to clear her throat to get me to turn to the next page. She was so close to me that I could smell what her flavor of coffee was - Pumpkin Spice.

Mischievously, spurred by thoughts of Jase, I felt my lips tug up at the corners of my mouth, quickly swiped my screen to my favorite photos, and pressed on my slide show of black and white erotic pictures.

The woman gasped loudly behind me, and her coffee spilled across the table. I stood up to leave, smiled wide, and gave her a little wink before I left.

Slowly making my way back to the shop, every step I took closer to the place I've called home for almost ten years made my smile falter, until I felt it turn into a straight, tight line.

All because the closer I walked to my future

The further I was from my past.

And sometimes your past just doesn't let go

Of you.

POLICE REPORT

Investigation: Criminal Sale of Controlled Substance
  Date: September 17, 2014
  Time: 1634 Hrs.
  Location: Corner of Bleecker and Barrow Street
John Doe "Doc" [CASE SUBJECT] Male/Caucasian,
Approx. 25-30 Yrs. Old. 5'11 -6'2", 200 LBS. Wearing: Black
suit jacket, white dress shirt, and black suit pants.

On September 17, 2014 at approximately 1634 hours,
while in a long term operation in an undercover capacity
under the supervision of Lieutenant Masterson who was
conducting a case buy operation in the confines of the 16
Precinct, I Undercover (UC) #C5192 picked up approximately 25 grams of alleged cocaine from John Doe "Doc"
for the set price of $880.00. The circumstance to the above
is as follows:

Prior to Meeting my subject John Doe "Doc" [Case
Subject] at the above location mentioned, I had spoken
and made arrangements yesterday via cell phone to pick
up the above amount of cocaine from John Doe "Doc."
When I reached above location I again called John Doe

"Doc" via cell phone and told him that I was there. "Doc" stated, "You're here already?" I replied, "Yeah, get down here." After waiting approximately 2-3 minutes, I observed "Doc" walk out main door of building # 420 towards my direction. Once "Doc" approached me we shook hands. At that point "Doc" wanted me to follow him upstairs. But I told him "Let's do it the way we always do it." "Doc" pointed to cameras on ledge of building as we walked towards Bleecker Street. Once we reached the corner of Bleecker and Barrow I observed "Doc" take out one clear plastic twist bag white powdery/ rocky substance, from his right pants pocket, which I believed contained cocaine and handed it to me. In return I handed "Doc" $880.00 USC/PRBM which he placed in to his front pants pocket. I then mentioned that I had a big party that weekend, like the last time (100 gram pickup) and I asked for Oxycontin also. "Doc" stated that for the pills it would cost me $2000. I told "Doc" that I would call him the next day to confirm. I also invited him to party. I then shook his hand and informed the C.O. what transpired. No arrest made-Case Buy.

CHARLIE

$\mathcal{S}$lipping off my glasses to rub my tired eyes, I stepped past the gothic style painted glass doors of the shop. The cool, air-conditioned room brought a prickle of goose bumps along my skin, and a small shiver rumbled across my shoulders.

The raspy voice of Austin Winkler, lead singer of Hinder, was pouring out the lyrics of "Better Than Me" through the gallery's state-of-the-art sound system, and the sterile smell of bleach and lemon filled my nose.

I glided my fingers against the long, smooth marble of the countertop, lined with delicately decorated gothic portfolios, containing the most talented works of art by the best tattoo artists in all of New York City. Hell, we were the best in the country. I wasn't being biased because the shop was mine. We were actually coined, "the best in America," by *ForeverArt Magazine*. Stone Caresses Tattoo Gallery was way more than your traditional tat studio; it was a 5,000 square foot art gallery of the best female tattooists to ever live.

Ever.

My girls and I treated the studio like a fine art museum.

The shop had cathedral-like ceilings and elongated walls of exposed brick, which were entirely covered from floor to ceiling by photographs of tattoos, original drawings, and oil paintings. Some tourists even came in to browse through the walls and snap photos of themselves with the girls. We'd even seen our fair share of celebrities in here.

You usually didn't come to Stone Caresses when you wanted a tiny ladybug inked on your ankle, even though we had my girl, Sky, there to do just that. You came in to get an intimate experience with a talented artist, and you left with a piece of authentic, original, fine art on your skin, *forever*. We usually had a two-month waiting list for appointments, except for the handful of walk-ins that just came to meet with Sky and her little ladybugs or skulls.

The shop wasn't always this upscale. Before it was handed down to me six months ago, it was called Under The Gun— My New Addiction, and the greatest woman to have ever lived, Auburn Tequila Rose, owned it. Auburn wasn't her real name, but Tequila Rose was, which always made me wonder about her parents and what crap they had to have been smoking when she was born.

Tequila nicknamed herself Auburn, because of the deep, brownish-orange color of her eyes. She nicknamed everybody after the color of their eyes or hair; that's why everyone called me, "Sage," now. I was seventeen when she saved me; and she *did* save me. She saved me from the world, from my demons, but mostly from myself. *"Give me a cooler nickname, like Jade or Hunter Green. Something badass,"* I said.

"No, baby girl. Sage it is," she said, smirking at me.

"But, Sage makes me think of an old wise woman with saggy boobs, who says profound stuff and knows the meaning of life. That ain't me."

"Sage fits you, Charlotte, you'll see," she said.

Walking through the main gallery of the shop, I headed

for my private studio. It was only ten o'clock, and I still had two full hours before I had to officially open the shop's doors. I figured I'd pound on my heavy bag for a while.

Making my way down the long, back hallway, I noticed Hazel's studio door open and poked my head in to say hello to her. Four sets of red-rimmed, tear-filled eyes looked back at me.

Holy crap, did somebody die?

Throwing my bag on her counter, I crossed the small room and headed straight for Violet, who stood in the middle of the other three girls, sobbing the loudest. Her face was streaked with tear-soaked black mascara; her long, midnight black hair (with violet streaks) was pulled back into one of her flawless frizz-free ponytails. I really wondered how she did that; my hair had so many split ends they flew all over the place.

"Oh no, what happened? Whose ass am I kicking?" I asked, taking her chin into my hand. One eye and her cheek-bone looked swollen, and it was just beginning to turn a sickening purplish-blue color. Anger flashed through me.

Hiccupping and gasping for air, she just about got out a full sentence before covering her face with her hands. Unfortunately, the sentence made no sense to me, something about a surprise pig's tail wrapped in sheets.

"Can someone translate?" I asked, sitting heavily onto one of her chairs.

Blowing out a long breath next to me, Hazel gave Violet a sympathetic smile and sighed, "She went to surprise Matt last night, and he was hiding a naked girl wrapped in his bed sheets in his room. Vi was there, messing around with him for a good fifteen minutes before she heard a noise in his bedroom and had to push him out of the way to get inside his room."

Sitting on the floor next to Violet was Ginger, looking up

at me with her big brown eyes, "The little slut had pigtails in her hair, held up with hot pink bows, and a school girl outfit was crumpled up on the floor. When Violet flipped out on the both of them, he *punched* her," Ginger said, looking at Vi with sympathy. Shaking her head, she added, "I say we kick both their asses right now, and then call the cops." With her pixie haircut and tattooed arms, she looked like a badass fairy; all Ginger needed was black wings.

Violet sobbed louder and slammed her fists against her thighs, "Two years, Sage! Two years I gave that cheating son of a bitch! And instead of getting a proposal, I have to be thinking about getting tested for sexually transmitted diseases!" She took a deep, shaky breath and started bawling again. "What am I going to do?" she wailed. I noticed, *we all did*, the big pink elephant of him hitting her in the face wasn't what she was upset about. Truthfully, I'd had a sneaking suspicion for a while that he sometimes knocked her around, but whenever I tried to talk to her about it, she would just deny everything. Even though we all worked together, I wasn't very close with the girls. I was more of a loner.

"We *could* kill him," Sky shrugged, smiling at me. Her perfectly sculpted, dark eyebrows were arched, waiting for my response.

Putting my fingers around Violet's wrists, I gently lifted her up off the floor, "Come with me for a sec, Vi."

"How am I supposed to forgive him?"

"*Forgive him?* Ah, no way. Vi, you've got to *forget him*. You don't forgive someone who physically hurts you. They don't deserve it, and they'll just do it again."

I pulled her into my studio and handed her a lollipop out of my candy container. I always run to food when things go wrong.

Or go right.

Or just go.

Shut up; don't judge me.

Anyway, while she was unwrapping the candy I grabbed my boxing gloves off the hook that hung from my workout corner next to my punching bag. I dangled them in front of her face and smiled at her.

She held up the round, pink lollipop, looked at it, and started crying again, "Lollipops always remind me of having sex with Matt."

"What? Seriously?" I laughed. "What? Does he have a really round, tiny dick?"

"No. It's just that he's not going to be around anymore for me to, you know, have his lollipop. I was used to having a lollipop at least four nights a week," she whined, the honesty dripping from each word.

That's it, right there, that sentence comes out of Violet's sad, little mouth, and my poor lonely girl parts start fantasizing about strangling the horny bitch. Four nights a week! I never got it four nights a week from Bren, *ever*.

"Hey, you know my favorite thing about having a lollipop is biting and gnawing off the edges of the sucker and crushing them with my teeth. Especially if it's cheating and domestic violence flavored," I growled out a sarcastic joke.

Violet looked at me and laughed. "I just feel like such a loser, like I lost the popularity contest. I wasn't better than the hooch dressed up like a school girl."

"Vi, there are no winners in relationships—there are just survivors. Now, I'm going to show you how to punch that bag like it's that jerk's face, because if he ever hits you again, I want you to know you have the power to hit him right back."

I shoved my sparring gloves over each of her hands and tightened the Velcro on them while she crunched the sucker to pieces in her mouth. Yes, I know not many normal women have a punching bag and sparring gloves on hand, but it's one of the things I do to de-stress and work out. And someone showed me a long time ago that every girl needs to learn how to throw a punch. And throw it well. With rage and vengeance behind each blow.

"Okay, Vi. Ball your fists up tight and do not bend your wrists." I demonstrated with my hands. "Hold your hands in front of your face, like this, and give me a little slow jab like this..." I punched the bag softly with my right hand, keeping my left hand blocking my face.

Violet mimicked my stance and punched the bag gently.

"Now, punch a little harder, Violet."

She punched the bag again with the same gentleness and sighed, "I can't do this, Sage; I'm not a mean person. Matt didn't mean to hit me, and he's been asking me for so long to dress up like a little school girl, but I haven't and...this has got to be a mistake..."

I watched Violet turn the whole messed up situation around and place all the blame on herself. I desperately wanted to grab her in my arms and shake the stupid right out of her. "Cheating on someone is a choice, not a mistake, Vi. Matt *chose* to have sex her. But that's not why you should forget him. Forget him because he also *chose* to hit you. You were nothing more than this punching bag to him."

She looked at me wide-eyed.

"Hit the bag, Vi." I got close up to her face. "Don't pretend this was the first time. You deserve flowers and candy, Violet, not punches and bruises."

She hit the bag harder, and a small whimper escaped through her lips. "He's a bastard," she sobbed as she hit it over and over, landing punches harder and harder each time. "I HATE HIM!" she screamed, slamming her gloved fists against the bag.

I threw a punch alongside her. "You know, Matt doesn't deserve you, Vi. It hurts to be cheated on, and I know you feel alone, but don't spend any more tears on a guy who doesn't love you like you deserve to be loved. It's going to take some time, but trust me, you'll forget about him, and someday, it won't hurt so badly anymore..."

Then she went all Rambo on my bag and kicked the crap out of it. I stepped back and let her get it all out. The vibrations of the bag against the chain it hung from resonated against the walls, and all the little knickknacks on my shelves started jumping around and falling. I cheered her on, screaming her name, until a loud crash of a falling picture broke her from her wrath.

"Oh crap, Sage. Sorry," she said, picking the frame up off the floor. Strangely enough, the glass hadn't shattered. "I always wanted to ask you about this picture," she said through heavy pants.

I scanned the old photo in its pewter frame, and a thick band of steel tightened around my chest. It was the last full day of summer vacation before sixth grade, and we were sitting in the tree house, all three of us. We were all ten and inseparable. On one side of me stood Jase, sticking up his middle finger at the camera, and on the other side of me was Joey, with his eyes crossed and tongue sticking out. My arms were around both of their shoulders—a giant goofy smile plastered across my face. The photograph captured us perfectly, full of fierce affection for each other, always laughing and joking together. There was an awe-inspiring relationship between the three of us, as it always is with innocent children, before there is any darkness in their lives.

The day that picture was taken my father took us to an amusement park in Long Island, something called Adventure Land, or some other clichéd amusement park name. My father, *being the greatest dad in the universe*, handed us ten (ten!) twenty-dollar bills and sat on one of the benches at the front of the park and told us to have a blast. He said to meet him back there in four hours and shooed us away with his hands.

Four hours and two hundred dollars to three ten-year-olds was the same as hitting the lottery. We started at the rollercoaster and went on every ride—twice. We ate popcorn, corndogs, funnel cakes, cotton candy, and went back on the Tilt-A-Whirl. Joey puked. A lot. Then, we climbed up under the bottom of the Gravitron, and Jase pulled out a pack of cigarettes that he stole from his father and taught us how to smoke. Poor Joey puked again, but he didn't care. He put the cigarette to his mouth once more.

"You're an idiot! Stop smoking it if you're going to barf all over," I laughed.

Joey tried to blow smoke rings like Jase had taught him, but he was laughing too hard. Laughing *and* spitting up.

God, sometimes boys were so gross.

"Hey, Charlie," Jase called to me as he expertly flicked his cigarette between his thumb and middle finger, "you don't ever curse."

"Yeah, well my father would kill me if he heard me curse," I said, pulling a tiny drag from my cigarette. My head started to spin.

"Well, then don't curse in front of him! Say *shit*," Jase chuckled.

"No way," I shook my head.

"Say *asshole*," Joey giggled along with him.

"Nuh uh."

"Say *fuck*," Jase said, stalking toward me and pouncing, grasping me on my sides. "Come on, Joe, tickle her!"

Laughing and screaming, I ran away from them. "Shit-asshole-nuts-stupid-fuck-shitpie-asshand-crapstack!"

Joey froze in mid-run, laughing, "*Asshand and shitpie?* Coming from your mouth, Charlie, you make cursing all girly and pretty,"

It was the first time I remember anyone ever putting the words 'pretty' and 'Charlie' in a sentence together, and I felt my face get all hot and sweaty.

I immediately pretended it didn't happen. Strangely, I wanted to hear that *I* was pretty and not just the words I said. I blinked away that awkward feeling.

After almost three hours, a whole pack of cigarettes, winning a seven-foot tall giant, blue, stuffed giraffe, and a sudden thunderstorm, we ran to find my father at the front gates. We all fought over who would keep the monstrous giraffe; neither boy wanted to be seen carrying it, and personally I was glad, because I absolutely loved the ugly thing.

At first my dad wasn't where we left him, but within two minutes, he came walking from the parking lot and through the front gates. "Hey, did you guys have fun?" he asked, out of breath.

"Yeah, but we wanted to ride the big coaster again before we left; it stinks that it's raining," I pouted.

My father smirked and started walking toward the roller-coaster like he owned the park. We followed him wordlessly. He rapped his knuckles against the entrance of the roller-coaster line to get the attendant's attention. "Excuse me, my daughter and her friends want one more ride, is that okay?" he called to the older man through the pouring rain.

"Sorry, sir. We have to stop the rides during electrical storms."

We watched my dad reach into his side pants pocket and pull out his wallet. He handed the guy two fifty-dollar bills, "How about just one small, quick ride?"

The rollercoaster man smiled, winked at me, and looked up at the sky. "Looks like it's letting up a little anyway. It's probably just a passing shower."

I tried to hand the giant giraffe to my dad, but he told me

to take it on the ride. So I did. Joey and Jase sat behind me, while I sat next to my gargantuan blue stuffed giraffe in the first car of the rollercoaster while lightning lit up the sky.

"Your dad is the coolest," Joey screamed from behind me as we plunged into the first loop, screaming. *Yeah, he was.*

My dad took us home after that; the entire ride was spent with him listening to us talk over each other about all the fun we had.

He dropped Joey off at his house and then drove down the block and pulled his car into our driveway. Jase hopped out, thanked my father, and high-fived me across the hood of the car.

"Charlotte, you feel like ordering a pizza with me?" my dad asked, unlocking the front door.

My hand clenched the load of amusement park bricks swimming around in my belly, "Ugh. No thanks, Dad. I think I ate way too much at the park. I'm just gonna go out back and sketch some of the things I remember seeing today."

He smiled at me with what looked like pride and nodded his head. "Okay, but if you decide to sleep out there, remember to shut the window. I'm not running out there at six o'clock in the morning to kill another spider," he chuckled.

"I couldn't help it! The spider was trying to kill me, and my sonic cry was part of my self-defense!"

"Ah, you've been reading science-fiction lately, I see."

Nodding my answer, I skipped out the back door and headed to my tree house. Climbing up the rope ladder and pulling it in, *so no kidnappers or horror movie characters could climb up to get me,* I turned on my small drawing lamp and made myself comfortable on my beanbag chair. Propping my sketchpad against my knees, I closed my eyes and unconsciously wobbled my pencil between my fingers. Laying my head back, I listened to the just audible sounds of distant cars passing on the streets and a few crickets calling out to each other in the settling darkness.

When I opened my eyes, my hands slid across the blank white paper and lines formed under my fingertips, dancing themselves into images of rollercoasters and lightning. My head cleared, not one thought passed through; just the feathery light grey lines of my imagination coming to life on the paper.

A door slammed somewhere outside. Voices with harsh tones broke into my consciousness and my hand stopped drawing.

"Where did you get the cigarettes from? What have I told you? And don't lie to me and tell me you didn't have a cigarette, you smell like an ashtray!" Mr. Delaney's voice was harsh and unrelenting. "Stop shrugging at me like you don't care! I'm not putting up with your immature antics anymore, Jase. I *WILL* put you in military school. You know what I want for your future; don't be a screw-up!"

Crawling over to the window, *which of course I left open*, I peeked my head up to see Jase and his father in their back-yard. Mr. Delaney always took Jase outside to scream at him, so his wife wouldn't get upset. Every night. Every night Jase was outside getting screamed at. And it some-times ended with Jase getting smacked or shoved. I hated Mr. Delaney. My mother said that he screamed at Jase because he's so young and doesn't know how to handle a pre-teen, especially when his wife couldn't help him at all. Jase's parents had Jase when they were like sixteen or something, and his mom had to drop out of school and stuff. But his dad didn't; he went to college and law school, and now he was this big hotshot lawyer. That's what my mom said anyway. She also said Jase was so bad that he deserved to get spanked, but I didn't see it. Then again, I'd heard my mom also say Mr. Delaney could spank her anytime, because he was so good looking. I didn't get that either.

My gut twisted as I watched Mr. Delaney raise his hand and shove it hard into Jase's shoulder. "What? What is wrong with you? You're crying like a baby now? If you don't want to get punished, then don't do stupid things!" His dad pushed him again and stormed into the house, leaving Jase all alone in the backyard.

He leaned back heavily against the outside of the house and stared up into the night sky.

"Psst," I whispered down to him. I poked my head out and made a stupid face at him. "Get up here you shitpie!" I watched as he climbed his garage and jumped over, landing on the tree house with a loud thump.

"Are you okay?" I asked, leaning back against soft material of the beanbag.

Jase snorted and climbed through the open window. His brilliant blue eyes, reflecting the storm within, looked at me and he shook his head. He threw himself on the beanbag chair next to me and snorted again.

"Did you forget I have a door here?" I giggled.

"Yeah, but I never do what I'm supposed to do, haven't you heard?"

Reaching up to the shelf above my head, I grabbed a bag of barbeque potato chips, ripped open the bag, and handed it to him. Taking the bag, he set it down on his lap and met my eyes.

"Can't you tell someone what he says and does to you, Jase? Can't you tell your mom?" I whispered, wanting desperately to help him.

"It won't change anything," he said, eyes filling with hurt. "They both think he's God. Besides, my mother used to get it much worse than me; I'd rather it be me he takes his anger out on and not her."

"It's just not fair. You're nothing like what he says you are, and he's your dad, Jase. Dads are supposed to protect their kids and take care of them. I just don't get it. Why is he like that to you?" I felt the rage twisting deep in my belly, my heart aching for my best friend.

"It doesn't matter why someone does bad things. It's not going to stop them if you understand the reasons or not. You're not like him, Charlie, so you can't understand him," he said in a soft voice. "Besides, I'll take whatever he gives me as long as he leaves my mother alone. He's done enough damage to her already."

"He's the reason why your mom is in a wheelchair?"

Jase crunched a few chips into his mouth, looked away, and shrugged. "The only thing I can honestly tell you about my parents is that I'm never going to become the monsters that they are, *either* of them."

He twisted his shoulders and looked back at me. When his shoulder softly touched mine, he looked down and stared at my drawing. "Charlie, you're really good at that. You're going to be a famous artist one day."

Bumping his shoulder with mine, I agreed with him, "Yeah, thanks. What do you think you want to be one day?"

"I'm going to be a superhero," he laughed.

"You're such a dork."

"I thought you said I was a shitpie," he smiled at me.

"A huge, dorky shitpie with a load of shitcream on top," I giggled.

"Hey, call Joey on the walkie-talkie and tell him to come over. Us shitpie superheroes need to protect our future famous artist from the tiny little legs of spiders."

The both of them always protected me from scary spiders. They also teased me mercilessly about my fear of them, but that's what best friends do, don't they?

❦

BEFORE I RETURNED the picture to its spot on the shelf, I stared at it for a bit, tears stinging my eyes. Violet stood next to me waiting for me to explain the picture to her. I guess she just wanted something gossipy to take her mind off her breakup. What I hoped was her breakup, anyway. You never can predict what anyone was willing to put up to avoid being alone. "This is just a really old picture of my best friends and me when we were kids. I think we were ten."

"You don't keep in touch with either of them anymore?"

I swallowed the thick lump that knotted itself in my throat and placed the picture back on the shelf it came from, right next to the bulky album of letters that I never let anyone ever see. "Nah, sometimes the past is best left there, you know?"

Violet shrugged her shoulders and took off the boxing gloves, "Thanks for…trying to make me feel better, girlie."

I took her in my arms and hugged her. "I promise you, you'll be better off without him, Vi," I whispered.

Silently, she hung up the gloves and walked out of my studio. I felt horrible not having the right words to say to her that would make her feel better, but my words now aren't going to help her heal. Only time away from Matt would help her recover and get on with her life without him. *That much I knew for sure.*

Grabbing my own lollipop, I walked to the back of the shop and climbed up the stairs to my apartment. I barely got the little plastic wrapper off before I shoved the whole sucker in my mouth. Bitter sour apple burst onto my taste buds, making the bottom of my jaw ache all the way up to my ears while tears burned in my eyes. Quietly, with pursed lips, I tiptoed into my bedroom. My light was still on, and Bren was in the same exact position I left him in five hours ago.

Five hours! I wanted to laugh, but I was too disgusted. Here's my lesson to you: Don't wish for a knight in shining armor. You'll just end up spending most of your time doing lots of polishing. And that armor tarnishes faster than any other substance on earth; instead, spend that time on yourself.

I jumped in the shower to get ready for work. I blew my hair dry, played some Avenged Sevenfold at about the same decibels as a space shuttle liftoff, and sang even louder. Bren still didn't wake up. I bet if I opened a can of beer, *that* noise would get him up.

Frustrated, I opened the shop and took my first appointment of the day, which was a very dear piece of art to me - the back of Michael Storkes. As soon as I saw the man's determined smile, my frustrations melted away and calmness stole over my body. Michael and his wife had visited Stone Caresses for over ten years, maybe even more. When Auburn ran the shop, they would spend the day here, catching up and drinking together.

Two months ago, after a painful six-month battle with Stage IV breast cancer, Michael's wife, Susan, passed away. The day after he buried her, Michael came to the shop in tears, burst into my studio, collapsed on the small couch, and asked me to draw up a portrait of Susan to go on his back. With shaky fingers, he handed me an array of photos of her and got up to leave. But I gently placed my hand on his shoulder and pulled him back.

Every tattoo tells a story. Whether it's a silly story from a drunken night that you'll never remember or the story of the memory of the love of your life, there was *always* a story.

I pulled up a chair next to my drafting table and asked him to sit down and tell me some of the best memories he had with his wife. Because that's the story I wanted to capture and etch on his back, the love he had for her. He told me how they met at a dance in high school while he played in the high school band, and she danced with her date in front of him. He laughed as he told me she left her date at that dance and let him drive her home, instead. He reminisced about how they had an intense courtship and then he left to fight in Vietnam. He told me that right before he left, Susan looked at him and said, "True love always comes back."

By the end of his story, Susan Storkes looked up, breathtakingly beautiful, from my paper, surrounded by everything that was ever dear to her. "Oh, my God," Michael whispered over my shoulder. "I haven't seen her look that alive in such a long time. Sage, she's exquisite. *I knew.* I knew you could bring her back to life for me."

Today, I finished her portrait on his back with a strange sense of triumph. Cancer would never affect her there; not in his memory, not in my picture. Screw you cancer, you don't win everywhere.

Michael hugged me tight as he thanked me. With his fatherly arms around me, I wondered what it would feel like to be loved like that. To feel a love that waits through a war for you, that loves you enough to want to marry you, a love that battles cancer with you, one that walks by your side without ever judging or trying to change you. A love unlike Matt's, with his cheating and hitting, and definitely unlike Bren's, with his indifference and resentments. Truthfully, I couldn't believe I just coupled the words "love" and "Bren" in the same thought. We hardly even tolerated each other anymore.

I knew real existed. I saw it in Michael's eyes, and I'd also felt it, once, long ago. But, like I told Violet before, some things are best left in the past. Hidden deep alongside your secrets. *And don't tell me you don't have secrets; everybody does. We just all have different levels of severity to them, and different ways we deal with them.*

When I looked up, Bren was just walking into the shop.

He looked perfect in his dress shirt and designer pants. Only his hair looked disheveled, but Bren always pulled that look off like he'd just mussed it to death.

He sauntered through the shop, saying hello to the girls and holding a half full bottle of water to spit in, a huge bulge of chewing tobacco wadded up under his lips. He walked over to me and squeezed my shoulder in a friendly-hey-buddy-how's-it-going way. "Can I talk to you for a minute?" he murmured into my ear.

I had about thirty minutes before my next appointment, so I followed him into my apartment. He walked me right into my bedroom.

I must admit that I had a bit of the butterflies twirling around in my lower abdomen, thinking maybe I was going to get to whip out my girly parts and have some fun.

When Bren and I first decided to try for a romantic relationship, we'd set a slow, lazy pace of intimacy that I thought was sweet and cute. There was never any crazy-lusty-passion, or angst, no slamming me up against a wall. Everything was just…nice. Easy. Safe.

Right about then, I wanted to slam myself up against a wall and show him how it *should* be done.

I practically threw myself on my bed, yanking off my clothes like I hadn't had sex in four months. *Oh, wait—I hadn't. And looky there, I ripped my own damn shirt. Damn, I was good.*

Bren licked his lips.

That was a damn good sign, wasn't it?

He crawled himself over me with a devilish smile, opened his pants, wrapped a condom on, pumped himself with his hand, and dove in.

Yeah.

Read it again. Go on.

Dove right in.

No nipple twists this time. No rubbing the spot two inches from my fun-button that might have eased my *complete dryness*. No. Nope. Nothing like that. The idiot just dove in.

If I had one, I would have screamed my goddamn safe word then, because of the sheer pain. "Gah!" I yelped.

"Oh, yeah, it feels real good, right?"

What the hell parallel universe did he get sucked into?

And then he was done.

Done.

Finished.

Three pumps, an '*ahh*,' and he was climbing off me.

Holy crap. Four months. It'd been four months since I had sex. *Four sexless months.* And he gave me, literally, two seconds to have a chance at an orgasm.

My girl parts were very angry and very neglected. Angry, neglected, and dry.

"Seriously, go screw yourself Bren."

"Huh? Why?"

"Because that's exactly what *I'm* going to have to do!"

Bren held the tip of the condom, so none of "The God's Juice" got out, and with a disgusted face, he tied it in a tidy little knot, buried it in a handful of tissues, and dropped it in the garbage like it was contaminated with the next apocalyptical-zombie-causing virus. Then, he looked up at me with sad, tired eyes. "Look, Sage I'm sorry about how it's been lately. I'm under a lot of pressure. Come here."

I let him wrap his arms around me. Let him touch his lips to mine.

My eyes closed tight, and his cool minty lips moved from my mouth and pressed against my forehead. That's when I realized he hadn't even bothered to spit out his tobacco; he never even planned on kissing me. I felt pushed aside, like an autumn leaf blowing against a hard, unmovable stone.

What happened to Bren?

He looked like he was so successful; wore the perfect clothes, always has the perfect hairstyle, but he was just a shell. I could recognize a shell of a person; they have the same emptiness as me. Bren once had a plan for his life. Maybe the issue he was facing was that his plans weren't going according to what he wanted. I knew all too well about plans that turned horribly wrong. I knew what being shattered and torn down felt like.

Right about now you think I'm a pushover, don't you? You think maybe I'm staying with Mr. Moneybags because of his bank account, or that I'm not confident enough, or whatever the hell it is you're thinking. Don't judge me, because really? Come on, your love lives are so perfect? Are there always flowers and candles lit when you come home from a long day at work? Was there always lust and amazing multiple orgasms and a gorgeous man who would rub your back for hours? Yeah, I didn't think so. Bren *was every guy*.

This wasn't a Disney fairytale. Bren was no Prince Charming, and I never pretended he would be. I may have loved to read my romance and smut novels, but I was not blinded by the 'fiction' part of it all. I knew the difference between what was real and what came from a hopeless romantic's imagination.

Reality was the toilet seat would always be up. Dirty socks would be strewn carelessly about on the floor, while toothpaste and shaving cream were caked all over the sink.

And the saddest reality of all
Was there would never be any more
Fluttery butterflies in your belly
Or in your heart.

POLICE REPORT

Investigation: Criminal Sale of Controlled Substance
   Date: September 21, 2014
   Time: 1634 Hrs.
   Location: Bleecker Street and Barrow Street
   John Doe "Doc" [CASE SUBJECT] - Male/Caucasian.
Approximately 25-30 years old. 5'11 -6'2", 200 LBS. Wearing: White dress shirt and navy pants.

On September 21, 2014 at approximately 1634 hours, while in a long term operation in an undercover capacity under the supervision of Lieutenant Masterson who was conducting a case buy operation in the confines of the 16 Precinct, I Undercover (UC) #C5192 picked up approximately 100 grams of alleged cocaine from John Doe "Doc" for the set price of $1500.00. The circumstance to the above is as follows:

Prior to Meeting my subject John Doe "Doc" [Case Subject] at the above location mentioned, I had spoken and made arrangements yesterday via cell phone to pick up the above amount of cocaine from John Doe "Doc," When I reached above location "Doc" was waiting outside door of building # 420. "Doc" shook my hand and inserted one clear plastic twist bag white powdery/ rocky substance, from his right pants pocket, which I believed contained cocaine. In return I handed "Doc" $1500.00 USC/PRBM which he placed into his back pocket. He told me of a delivery of Oxycontin he was getting and he'd get in touch when his contact pulled through. I then shook his hand and informed the C.O. what transpired. No arrest made-Case Buy.

CHARLIE

losing the shop that night, I found Violet standing stiffly in the corner of her studio with *I'm not only the President of the Douche Club for Men, I'm a Member* Matt blocking her doorway into the gallery.

Violet's eyes were huge, and the punch that Matt had handed her the night before had, in the last few hours, blossomed into an angry mess of red and purple busted blood vessels along her beautiful cheekbone. She looked terrified and seemed to be frozen in that emotional state, glued to the damn floor. What is it with us women that when we see someone who looks stronger than us, we cower from fear? My adrenaline kicked in and flooded like an electrical current of heat across my chest and down my arms. There was no way I was going to let him hit her again.

Matt stood tall and imposing. He wore a typical muscle shirt that let him brag about how mighty and strong he was without having to say a word. Yes, Mr. Douche President, Sir, you have some mighty big muscles there, but I'm going to kick you in the junk real hard if you touch her.

And then, *it* spoke its venom.

"If you just did what I asked of you, then I wouldn't have to look elsewhere, Violet. What did you expect me to do?" he questioned with an air of superiority in his voice, making him the victim and not her. "She was offering everything I was begging you for, baby. Everything and more. You were getting boring, baby. You work too much."

He slid his hand over his nearly shaved head and down his face. "You. You act like you're so much better than me, but you ain't, girl. You ain't. You ain't nothing but a trashy runaway who got lucky. You're nothing but shit and a bad lay and I've…"

I watched as her shoulders dropped forward and her head hung low with each cut of the words, taking every one in like the blade of a knife. Making her believe it was all her fault. She bent over, clenching her eyes, holding her stomach with the physical pain of what he spit from his mouth.

"Get out of my shop," I said as I took out my phone and dialed a *9* and a *1*. I let my finger hover over the last *1*.

Both of their heads snapped up to look at me. Violet's eyes widened even more; I swear I feared they'd pop right out. But Matt's ugly scowl just got uglier, which I didn't even think was possible–but it did. Did you ever meet one of those guys? Those muscular juiceheads you see in the gym; beautiful, tanned, toned, spandex-wearing bodies, with the tiny creepy face of a hairy little bat, and you wonder how they could ever find a girlfriend. *That's Matt.*

Matt's beady black eyes narrowed at me, taking a long look. One of those once overs from head to toe like a rapist would do to his next victim. "Fuck you, Sage. What are *you* going to do to me?"

"Matt, sweetheart, all I have to do it press another little number one on my cell phone and the cops will come here. Then, it will be up to you to explain to them why Violet's face looks like she went a round with Mike Tyson."

His jaw clenched and his hand flew across Violet's drawing table, whipping up a frenzy of fluttery drawings and sketches across the floor. "What-the-fuck-ever!" he yelled and stormed out the door.

I followed him out the front door and locked it as soon as he was outside. My hands were shaking from the adrenaline rush. I slumped myself up against the wall and slid down until I hit the floor.

Violet slid herself down next to me and laid her head on my shoulder. Tears streamed down her face and fell against my skin.

"Vi, you should stay here with me tonight."

"Okay," she sniffled.

"Please don't believe the crap he said to you. You're none of that stuff and you sure as hell didn't make him do everything he did to you," I whispered.

"Yeah. Easier said than done," she murmured between her tears.

"I know, Sweetie. I know," I said, squeezing her hand softly.

"Would you really have called the cops on him?"

I looked down at my phone. The screen was still on the keypad screen waiting for me to press the next 1. I closed the screen and saw an alert for a new text message. "Of course I would have called the police if I needed to. I wouldn't let him hurt you, Vi."

I pressed the text message.

J: Going in to work. Sweet dreams C

C: Stay safe

I ran my thumb over the screen and wished, wished with all my heart, that things could be different. That my past didn't have to stay so far away from me. I wished that people didn't need to fear other people, and that words didn't hurt as much as they did.

🐚

MY BOOBS FOUND me in September of sixth grade. And even though all the girls in my class were amazed by my overnight C cups (yeah, can you imagine?) the boys (read as Slate Marshall and Drake Fischer) labeled me *fat*.

And with the sudden growth of the aforementioned 'boobage,' my sixth grade year in school became renamed "The Worst Year EVER,"

Sixth Grade, *The Worst Year Ever*
By Charlotte Stone
Chapter 1: Colossal FAT Knockers
Chapter 2: Slate and Drake
Chapter 3: The Terrible Split
Chapter 4: Did I Just Poop My Pants?

Need I go on?

Okay, fine. I'll give you a little more, but I'll hate you for it.

In the middle of September, our teacher Ms. Spittsman (aka: Spitball), announced to our class that our sixth grade performance would be a stage play of *The Suessification* of *Romeo and Juliet*. Okay, so I had a bit of a false start of the year, because *Romeo and Juliet* was one of my favorite stories. *That month, anyway.* I say a false start, because I thought since we were doing a play on one of my favorite stories, the year was going to be amazing.

Fat chance.

I was cast as Juliet, and Slate was Romeo! For the first week of practice after school, I walked around holding one of the school's metal garbage cans in case I needed to vomit when he touched me.

After three weeks of practice, during our dress rehearsal, in front of my entire class, Slate snapped my bra. Not the back strap, but the front one! Yes, in front of *every-*

one, he reached his dirty, creepy hands up and touched between my newly-developed *secrets*, that I had been trying to **hide**, and hooked his fingers around the little space between the cups and **snapped**. Then he said, right into one of the microphones, "Oh, my God, Charlotte has colossal, fat knockers!"

Everyone, but Jase and Joey, laughed.

This crap still gives me nightmares.

After that, all the boys in the class called me, "Fatty Knocker," I thought about all the ways I could kill Slate Marshall without ever getting caught, but I couldn't come up with anything. I planned on asking Jase. I knew he'd help me. He'd probably chopped up a few kids before.

Anyway, the night after the dress rehearsal, Joey, Jase, and I were in the tree house playing with my Ouija board. It was our new obsession: trying to contact the dead. And I know it's completely my fault. I had just finished reading this scary book (Joey's new favorite genre was scary stories and horror…WOOOOOO!) called *The Ghost of the Isherwoods* by Carol Beach York, and we were OBSESSED. It petrified me in such a *good way* that I read it out loud to Jase and Joey, who then became just as, or maybe slightly more, obsessed with talking to the dead as me. So, we sat in the tree house every afternoon until sunset, and tried to contact the people who had passed on.

We'd been trying an entire week before the dreaded dress-rehearsal-fat-knocker-day, and I was in such a horrible mood that I decided to get a little creative. Okay, so maybe I'd been planning it all week long, but whatever. Jase and Joey watched me carefully as I ripped the little fuzzy foam pieces from the plastic planchette that you push around the board to communicate with the ghosts. From out of my pocket, I pulled these tiny little magnets I had from one of my craft kits. *You know the one*, the make your own refrigerator magnet kit; my father's secretary bought it for me. *Again, she still thought I was like, five.*

I stuffed the little magnets into the three legs of the planchette, and when I felt they were in securely enough, I put it down on the game board.

"What are you doing?" Joey asked, hovering over me.

"I'm making this stupid game more fun."

"Wait, do magnets attract the ghosts?" Joey asked excitedly.

Jase's eyes narrowed, watching me. I loved those guys right then, because they were the only ones that hadn't said anything about my colossal fat knockers. They didn't even notice them. They were only concerned with how I would find a better way to talk to dead people.

I placed the Ouija board on my crisscrossed legs, and both boys moved in closer to me, our knees touching. I reached my right hand into my back pocket and grabbed the last and biggest magnet, but I didn't let either of them see it. Then, with it closed tightly in my fist, I placed my hands under the board.

"Okay, I just want to try something," I said seriously, looking them both in the eyes. "Just keep your hands on the edge of the board and don't touch the planchette. Just try to concentrate on talking to someone, okay?"

"Okay," they both said in stereo.

"Spirits of the afterlife. Is there anyone here in the tree house with us?" I whispered all spooky-like. Then, I pulled both my lips between my teeth so I wouldn't bust out laughing, because I knew the next thing to happen was going to be written about in the history book of our friendship.

Under the Ouija board, I gently touched the bigger magnet I held in my hand to the bottom of the board right beneath where the planchette stood. Then, I slowly slid the magnet up the board to the word, "yes," The planchette moved along, attracted to the magnet that was unseen, and it looked like it had answered us, *all by itself.*

Jase was the first one up, flipping the board off his knees and trying to get up and scoot away so fast that he fell right on his butt. Joey screamed like a girl.

I laughed and almost peed my pants.

"See boys; that is how you play the game."

Joey was at the corner of the tree house, desperately trying to get the window open to climb out, and Jase had squashed himself flat up against the wall.

Joey was yelling, "Charlie! Charlie! You *have* to have the ghost say goodbye or else it will possess your body! Hurry up! It's gonna be like *Poltergeist,* stay away from TVs!"

I was laughing so hard that I started hiccupping and yes, I peed a little in my pants. It took me a full five minutes to finally be able to explain to them what I did and another five minutes to talk Joey into believing me while pulling him back into the tree house.

When they both realized my prank, we went laughing into my house so I could change my undies and get some dinner. It was another *make our own ice cream sundae* night, because I had no clue where my parents were. Since I was only ten, I couldn't cook, and we were out of those little *cup of soup thingys.* Three bowls, five scoops each of chocolate and vanilla, extra nuts for me, extra cherries for Joey, and chocolate syrup, not caramel, for Jase. We had a rainbow sprinkle fight and left the mess. Nobody was there to see it anyway.

"What the hell?" Jase's voice caught my attention by the front window. "The Jenson sisters are walking up to your door."

"This feels like the beginning of a bad horror movie," Joey whispered. "Someone hold me; I'm scared," he chuckled.

"Oh, God, what Disney princess drama is this?" Jase whispered as I opened the door, while clutching my giant bowl of ice cream dinner to my chest.

Rebecca and Rachael stood next to each other, smiling their creepy, lip-glossed, identical smiles. A clone of each Jenson sisters flanked the sides of them; ironed, pin-straight hair, lips glossed to a sparkling shine, all four standing in the same exact posture, heads all creepily tilted in the same way.

"That's just creepy," Jase whispered next to me. "They look like four of the same exact people." I nodded my head, thinking the same thing.

"Uh, hi?" I said.

"Hey, Charlotte. We came by to see if you wanted to hang out," *Um. What?* Crap-on-a-stick, my ice cream was going to melt.

I opened the door to let them come in. I may not have been in my right mind; I'm not sure what my thought process was. These girls never paid attention to us, and honestly, I never paid attention to them, so let's call it curiosity.

The four Jenson droids filed in, all walking the same way, all using the same strange dramatic movements. I spooned a heap of ice cream into my mouth, waiting for the punch line to the joke.

Joey sat himself at the edge of my living room, on the small loveseat, and Jase folded his arms across his chest and stood next to me, feet spread wide (I called this his *Law-man* stance, because it was exactly how our school safety officer stood by the front entrance to our school).

"So," I said after swallowing the mouthful of ice cream and shoving in another spoonful (excuse me, but I was starving), "what's up?"

Rachel looked around my house and then back to me. Her eyes scanned my face, but ended right on my chest. "Are your parents home?"

I narrowed my eyes at her. Then, I noticed all four droids staring at my chest. "Nope," I replied.

"And they let you have boys in the house while they're not home?" Rebecca asked.

I shrugged my shoulders and ate another spoonful of my quickly melting sundae. "It's just Joey and Jase. My parents don't mind."

All four identical mouths smiled their identical smiles.

Jase leaned in closer to me and nudged his shoulders against mine. And I knew exactly what he was thinking. Because I swore I could communicate with my best friends without having to use any words. *Way better than I could communicate with the dead.*

The nudge.

Hey Charlie, the creepy girls are planning something.

Yeah, Jase, but what?

Don't know. But if you start painting glitter all over your face like that, I'm revoking best friend rights.

Ha-freaking-Ha. Let's have them play the Ouija board with us.

I knew you were my best friend for a reason.

Are you going to finish your ice cream?

Ah, that would be a, "Hell yes."

Mine is getting all melty.

You can't have mine. Just eat yours faster.

Forget the ice cream! Let's scare the crap out of the Jenson Droids.

Yeah! But you still can't eat my ice cream.

It took all of twenty minutes, and then three of the girls ran out of the tree house, screeching. Rebecca fell halfway in her mad dash across my backyard, and Joey climbed down to help her up. That left Rachel, Jase, and I alone.

Pursing her still glossed up lips, she stood up and planted her hands on her hips. "Well, *that* was interesting. I don't know how you did it, but that was scary-cool. Anyway, Charlotte, I was wondering if I could ask you a question, *alone*," She looked at Jase, smiled, and batted her eyes like something was stuck in them. Jase's cheeks turned all red, and I wondered if he thought she might be pretty.

"Alone?" I asked.

Her dark eyes glanced at me and then back to Jase. His stupid face got even redder. "Yeah, well it's like, a private—girls only question."

Jase held up his hand and walked to the door, "I'll wait outside."

Rachel stared at the door even after Jase left. "He's really cute, isn't he?"

"And he can burp the whole alphabet after drinking soda. He's the best. Now what's this girl thing you want to ask me?"

She looked at my chest then at my face, and my stomach flipped. "Are they real, or do you stuff?"

"Is. What. Real?" Oh, God, I just wanted to crawl in a hole and die.

She leaned heavily on one leg and jutted her hip out awkwardly. I wondered if it was painful to contort her body in all the unnatural poses she kept moving it into. "Your chest, Charlotte! Is it real?"

Then, the *b-word* poked me with her finger, because I guess maybe I took too long to answer her or something.

Her eyes bulged when her finger touched my chest.

I smacked her hand away. "You touch me again I will beat the ever-loving crap out of you. Yes, they are real. Why, do *you* have to stuff?"

Her face turned bright pink, "No. I have boobs. I'm just not as FAT-chested as you. Slate was right!" She stormed out of my tree house, which was the perfect time, because then she couldn't see my stupid tears.

I heard her gasp right outside the door and the murmur

of Jase's voice. Jase probably stood there and heard the whole thing. That just made my tears come faster. I swiped at my eyes and turned to face the back window, watching Rachel stalk through my yard. Jase's arms were around me before my next thought; his blueberry bubble gum breath fanning hot against my cheeks, "You're perfect, Charlotte. Don't listen to what anybody else says."

Later that night, way after Jase and Joey went to their own houses, I tiptoed into mine. It was ten o'clock and every single light in my house was on. Strangely, my mother and father sat at opposite sides of the living room; a weird, tense air between them.

My father stood up from where he sat, and my mother, with her tear-streaked face, suddenly grabbed her precious crystal vase from the middle of the coffee table and hurled it across the room where my father stood. It crashed into the wall—two inches from his head.

"You are one crazy bitch," my father said, like he was telling her the time.

"Charlotte," my mother said, ignoring my father, "your father is leaving the both of us for his slutty, little whore. The one he's been sleeping with every night for the last year. Say goodbye to him, because he won't have any time for you anymore."

Without looking at me, she got up from her seat and ran into her bedroom. She didn't come out for days after that, and when she finally did, she didn't speak to me at all unless it was to tell me that it was *all my fault* for being born. *What? Like I asked for that?* It was like the hole my father left behind when he walked out on us had swallowed her whole, and the mother that I had always known was gone. I had two parents who left me that day.

My father shook his head and sighed, "Don't listen to her,

Charlotte. Of course I'll have time for you. She's just upset and saying hurtful things."

"But, you're still leaving and I'm staying here, right?" Without waiting for an answer, I walked right into my room and slammed my bedroom door as hard as I could. My father didn't bother to chase after me; I guess he didn't think it was important to let me know why he was destroying my life. I locked my door and pretended it would be my fault for locking it that he didn't come in, but I would always know the truth was, because he just didn't bother.

When you're ten and both your parents abandon you, physically like my dad or mentally like my mom, it changes you. It becomes *you*. Within those ten short minutes of my life, standing in the living room with my parents, I was completely altered. I no longer felt loved. I no longer had the answers to all the world's questions. And I no longer believed that I was worth explaining something to or had any value. But like I said, I was only ten, and I couldn't formulate those logical thoughts in my head. I was confused and angrier than I had ever felt in my life.

My walkie-talkie buzzed around fifteen minutes later, and Jase's voice echoed through the speakers. "Can't sleep?"

I swept the curtains aside and waved to him as he sat on his windowsill; he must have seen my light still on. I brought the walkie-talkie up to my lips and tried to explain without crying, "My dad just left us."

Jase stood up and stared at me strangely for a minute, then spoke into his end of the walkie-talkie, "Meet you in the tree house in five."

I walked out of my room, into a dark, empty house, and padded into my backyard in my black skull and cross bone pajamas and matching skull decorated slippers. I climbed up the ladder with tears in my eyes and pulled it up after me, so no one else could come up and see me.

"Come here," Jase said, reaching out both of his hands and pulling me into his arms. He wrapped them around my waist and squeezed me gently. Then I cried so damn hard that my chest hurt when I tried to take a breath. I told him everything ugly about me; I told him all my little secrets, my angers, my fears. And he didn't tease me, he didn't make fun of me; all he did was hug me tighter.

And that's exactly how I woke up the next morning when Jase's watch alarm went off for school; wrapped up in my best friend's arms, clinging to him like he was my air.

Without talking, we both went to our houses and got ready for school and met up with Joey on the corner. A little bit of nervousness danced in my belly, not because of Jase hugging me all night; *that was the coolest thing one of my best friends ever did for me.* No, I was nervous, because that day was the play.

First period started with Ms. Spitball having to move Joey's seat to the back of the classroom, because all of Slate's spitballs that were aimed at Joey kept landing on her desk. Well, at least he got to sit next to Jase and me.

Second period, we lined up and walked silently through the hallways. Slate and Drake threw spitballs at the back of the teacher's head. Her long blonde hair was infested with them. I swear you could see the saliva dripping off one of them. I gagged back vomit.

We piled into the auditorium and began getting everything ready for the play. The stage was set, lights flashed, music sounded, and then costumes were put on. Slate and Drake were in rare form, cracking their knuckles and calling everyone names.

As the girls got dressed behind a curtained off area, Slate came waltzing in. His eyes zeroed in on me while I was changing my shirt. His eyes brightened and the shitstorm started.

"Whoa, Piss Pants girlfriend's tits are huge! Kissyface. Four Eyes. Fatty Knockers. Loser. Dog. Butterface. Trash. Lesbian. Freak. Shorty. Fat Ass."

The minute the words left his mouth all that I felt was the burning sting of the tears that I tried to fight against pouring from my eyes. A constant question in my head... *Is that true? Is that true? Is that true? Is that true?* My mind bounced to my father. What did I do that he left me? Why didn't he take me? Why wasn't I enough? You carry that feeling with you, forever. I don't care what anybody says about it, "Oh, it'll be different when you're older," or "Oh, sticks and stones..." That feeling of being walked away from doesn't ever go away. The names that little shitpie called me never got erased.

Ever.

No.

They helped a young, impressionable girl form opinions of herself. Because, really, I didn't feel awkward enough in my own skin, please make me feel worse about myself. See the sarcasm dripping thickly off those words? And you know it's true too, right? If you have ever heard anyone call you something, the first thing you ask yourself - *is that true?*

And so it happens, when you're filled with so much anger and *anguish*, you just have to let it out or your head and heart might just frigging explode. I screamed a string of profanity and rage. Then, I tried to grab at the little toilet-head's throat. I wanted to shake the words from his mouth, shake out those thoughts about me from his head. I didn't want to be the names he said I was.

Jase and Joey were in front of me in an instant; Joey wrapping his arms around me to cover my chest, and Jase all up in Slate's face, whispering threats to his life. But, to hell if that stopped me from going utterly crazy. My thoughts were simple: rip his tongue out so I could no longer hear his *vile words.* Rip his brain out through his nostrils, ancient Egypt style, so he wouldn't think those poisonous thoughts about me.

Joey could not calm me down, so he just shoved my shirt back over my head and hugged me tight.

Then, the teachers came.

The play was delayed.

And of course *that* was the main issue. Oh, and that it was *entirely my fault for my sudden, unprovoked outburst.*

I was hauled off into an office; my lower stomach was literally writhing with sharp pains, like I was being stabbed from the inside. Ms. Spitball held my crying snot-nosed face in her hands. Jase was banging on the other side of the door where he was being spoken to, screaming Joey's name and mine over and over. I had no clue where Joey was.

NOBODY ASKED ME WHAT HAPPENED.

Nobody asked me what was wrong.

Nobody tried to help me.

Then the teachers spoke...

"What's going on with her?"

"She's usually so quiet, so smart."

"Jase Delaney. The boy is such a misfit."

"And why does that Joey always get caught up with Slate?"

"Doesn't he know how Slate is?"

"Misfits."

Inside, the words caused bruises that nobody but me, could see. And that stupid rhyme repeated in my head. *Sticks and stone may break my bones, but words can never hurt me.* Screw that, they do. They did. They hurt so damn much. Because when others say them, you believe them. The words, the names, are like bullets that *tear* through your skin and burn so badly going in, you wonder if they're the truth, and you wonder if they'll kill you.

Me?

Was I a misfit?

Because I was friends with Joey, the most brilliant, sweetest boy ever created, and Jase, the toughest protector to ever live? Then, I'd rather be a misfit than be whatever *they thought was normal.*

Screw them. Screw all of them.

Slate, Jase, and I were forced to shake hands and go on with the play.

We did, but only after Jase taped a large white paper to Slate's back that read: **KING of SHITPIES**.

The audience gasped and tsked.

But the play went on.

After our performance, Ms. Spitball told me how disappointed she was in my actions. And only then was I allowed to tell *my side* of the incident. She screamed at me about how I should have gone to her (sure, half-naked) if Slate was bothering me. And she would need to place a call to my parents. I didn't care. She could call my home all night; nobody would answer.

We all ran back to class.

I felt like I was running with a stick of dynamite, lit at both ends. Waiting for the BOOM. *And, I need to stop and tell you here–it does come, that BOOM. It's so harsh and explosive that it does rip me into nothing. It destroys everything.*

Back in the classroom, I sat with my hands clutching my aching stomach as folded up notes were passed around the room. I sat, rigid in my seat, holding back the angry tears, belly twisting, watching the notes as they traveled closer and closer. Quietly received hand to hand, quietly read, and quickly passed on. The first was a naked drawing of me with enormous boobs. It looked nothing like me; stupid shitpie couldn't draw. The second was of Rachel Jenson, also naked, with tiny little bumps for boobs. The words MOSQUITO BITES were written with an arrow pointing to her chest.

The third note was of Maria Carrington with a huge fat belly and a boy's *you know what* hanging from her private area. Written under it was "SHE'S A BOY!"

Note after note, Slate and Drake attacked every single kid in the class, until I took all the folded up pieces of paper and stood up on my shaky legs.

"Charlotte, what are you doing out of your seat?" Ms. Spitball demanded, her face turning red with anger.

I slowly walked up to her desk with a wad of crumpled papers in my hand. Jase was behind me, grabbing the other papers that he saw other people reading and walked up to Ms. Spitball's desk next to me. He slammed them down in front of her with the palm of his hand.

"Well, Ms. Stone? Mr. Delaney? What is going on here?"

I held my head up and looked my teacher in the eye, "Just wanted to let you know what's happening while your back is turned to write on the board. This, I think is harassment, and if Slate Marshall isn't removed from this class, I might sue the school. Jase Delaney's father is an important lawyer in Manhattan, he'll help me."

Slate was only suspended for five days.

I was scarred for life.

After school, I sat in my tree house with my sketchpad on my knees, pencil motionless between my fingers, and nothing coming to life for me on the page. I felt too sad to draw. For the first time ever, I wondered why I even bothered drawing. Maybe I wasn't even good at it. So, I exchanged my pad for a candy bar and my pencil for an entire large bag of Doritos. A gourmet meal, right? Well, to a ten-year-old it is. And let's just be honest with each other, if you had the metabolism of a ten-year-old, you'd be eating that crap for dinner every day too.

Jase and Joey came over as the sun was setting, and a strange thing happened as the three of us silently swung our legs off the roof of the tree house. A large group of fireflies slowly lit up the backyard.

Without having to say a word to each other, we ran into my house and grabbed three clear, glass cups to catch the insects. And slowly, as if we were somehow warped into a land full of magical blinking lights, we walked through the enchanted backyard. The fireflies surrounded us. Hundreds of them, probably shining their little bodies for their last performance on earth, before the cool autumn weather set in.

We spun and twirled around the blurry, blinking lights, capturing a few to keep for a while. Maybe hoping their magic was real.

Then, we laid ourselves out on the roof of the tree house, holding our magical friends tightly to our chests, making wishes.

Under the darkened sky beside me, the boys smelled of Dorito chips and sweat. I could barely see them in the moonless light, except for every few seconds when the fireflies lit up their bodies; only then the soft yellow glow of the magical bugs lit their faces with a pale shine.

Joey sat up and pulled his feet in, tucking them under his body. "I wish I was a lightning bug. I could light up the whole night, you know? Nobody hates a lightning bug."

Jase sat up and scooted closer to us, "Yeah, I get it. I wish I were a firefly too. I want to light up the sky, set the whole world on fire with my shine."

"Me too," I whispered sitting up and touching my knees to both of theirs. I could feel the warmth of their legs against mine; it made me shiver.

Joey chuckled and nudged his finger into my forehead, "You already do that, Charlie."

Staring down into my clear glass, I said nothing, because Slate's words, Spitball's words, and my parent's words were louder than Joey's. Even though his words should have been the only ones that mattered to me.

Joey and Jase both shifted away from me and stood, letting their fireflies out of their prisons and into the night sky. I watched as they slowly floated away.

My firefly sat still on the bottom of my glass cup, her tail dimly lit, her wing looked bent. "Oh, no. I think I broke my firefly!" I shook the glass gently and the bug rolled out and crawled onto my hand.

Joey climbed off the roof and down the ladder, "Night guys. Smell you later, gater."

The warmth of Jase's hand touched over mine, and we both held the little broken bug in my palm. He softly pulled on my hair with his other hand, and then let it fall to the place where my neck meets my shoulder, and his strange blue eyes looked into mine, the soft glow of the firefly dimly lighting up our faces. "Charlie. If someone ever breaks your wings, you just got to find some other way to fly. Show them what you're worth, Charlie. Nobody should set your value but you."

He slid his hand slowly down my neck, and something in my insides fluttered. It felt like I was hit with a pillow, filled with tingly fairy dust, and immediately my stomach was twisting with sharp pains. "Life knocks you down. It's going to, and you got to just turn around and get back up, hold on to me if you have to, but always get back up. People will just walk all over you if you leave yourself beaten on the ground."

And then, he jumped off the roof and landed on his garage, just like a real superhero would do. Instead of the tiny broken firefly in my hand, I wished I could have captured *that* moment in my glass cup. I would have given anything to have held onto it forever.

I looked up into the sky and felt like such a little girl, gazing up at the stars. Looking out at everything that I was too insignificant to touch, and seeing how impossible everything was, all I could think of that very minute was that if I looked into the mirror, I wouldn't recognize the little girl staring wide-eyed back at me. Not after that week.

When I looked back down into my hand, my firefly was gone. I didn't know if it flew away or was just blown from my hand with the sudden wind, but I hoped that it found some other way to fly, just like Jase said.

You think that's enough for a ten-year-old girl for a while, right?

Hold on a second, my sixth grade year was not done crapping on me quite yet.

Because then, I went into my house, changed into my pajamas, and used the bathroom. I saw crap all over my underwear.

Yes, crap.

Now, I know it had been a hard day, but I think I would have felt myself having an accident in my own pants. Then, I wiped and realized it wasn't crap. It was dried blood.

I'd read books.

This. This was my period. *Um. Okay.*

Um.

Sweat broke out all over my forehead and chest. It tingled of heat, and I felt faint. *Can I bleed to death from this?*

I wadded up a bunch of toilet paper and shoved it between my legs and stood, pulling up my dirty panties to hold it in place.

I ran to my mother's bedroom door and knocked lightly. I knocked harder. Finally, I was pounding my fists against the door. *It was locked, and she was not coming out.*

My vision blurred, and with the room spinning, I grabbed the house phone and called Joey. Thank God his mother answered.

She came running over to help me and then told me I

should celebrate becoming a woman. So I absolutely did, with a whole gallon of Butter Pecan ice cream, that I ate so fast I couldn't feel my tongue for the rest of the night.

Yay for periods!

And for my swift kick in the ass into becoming a woman.

I wish I could have stayed

A kid forever.

POLICE REPORT

Investigation: Criminal Sale of Controlled Substance
  Date: September 25, 2014
  Time: 1830 Hrs.
  Location: Cross Streets Bleecker/Barrow
John Doe "Doc" [CASE SUBJECT] - Male/Caucasian,
Approx. 25-30 years old. 5'11 -6'2", 200 LBS. Wearing:
White dress shirt and tan pants.

On September 25, 2014 at approximately 1800 hours,
while in a long term operation in an undercover capacity
under the supervision of Lieutenant Masterson who was
conducting a case buy operation in the confines of the 16
Precinct, I Undercover (UC) #C5192 picked up approximately 100 count Oxycontin in large clear container. Each
Oxycontin cost $20.

In return I handed "Doc" $2000.00 USC/PRBM which
he placed into his back pocket. I then shook his hand and
informed the C.O. what transpired. No arrest
made-Case Buy.

CHARLIE

*I*t was a Friday night and Bren was holding court on his couch; all his loyal subjects surrounding him. As always, I felt the unyielding desire to jump out of one of his windows.

Bren was actually sitting in the middle of his couch in a tuxedo, drinking an enormous goblet of brandy, and covered in a cheesy, dusting of Dorito crumbs. There were about half a dozen cheesy handprints on the pant legs of his tux. *He better not ask me to take those filthy things to get dry cleaned tomorrow.*

Next to him was Jett, son to a famous, washed out, bad-boy rock star. So washed out, I didn't even remember his father's name or what 90s hair band he was the front man for. Both idiots were balancing their drinks in their hands while holding X-box remotes and playing some sort of crazy fighting game with lots of guns, while their drinks spilled mindlessly and carelessly all over the floor.

I sat across from them, front row for the train wreck.

Added to my entertainment was a barely dressed woman named Lola, who sat next to me and repeatedly rubbed her thighs together and giggled like some demented horny cricket. Supposedly, she was a district attorney. Wow, I felt safe with her crickety pheromones running rampant.

"You are the luckiest girl on earth," she said to me. "You know, to have someone like Bren. He is so *hawt*."

I pitied our justice system.

Then Bren jumped up, arms waving in the air, doing some idiotic victory dance, while Jett grimaced, cursed, and threw the game controller at the wall.

Disgustingly impressive, he threw it so hard that it stuck right in the drywall.

Violet sat silent on the other side of me, frozen, with that deer caught in the headlights look. She may have been in shock; she had never seen Bren act like this. Plus, Bren (the *wonderfully thoughtful* guy he was) thought it was a terrific idea to invite Matt, so the poor girl was crapping a pill the entire time.

"So," Lola said, placing her hand on my knee. "Is Sage your real name?"

Shaking my head, I gave her my typical Groucho Marx answer, "Nope, it's not mine. I'm just breaking it in for someone else."

Her eyes crossed in confusion.

"Didn't you say she was a district attorney?" Violet whispered next to me.

Lola finally laughed. "And what is it *you* do for a living, *Saaaggggeee?*" she asked, purposely enunciating each letter of my nickname. "It sounds a bit like a stripper's name."

Yeah. That's original and not at all bitchy. Nope, I never heard *that* stereotypical remark before.

"I'm an artist, and I was asked to teach a few classes this semester at the School of Visual Arts," I said, quietly. My mind was done with the conversation between us and was steadily watching what Bren was taking out of his pocket and setting up all along the coffee table.

Bren looked up at me through his pretty little lashes, his lips in a pouty expression, already asking me for forgiveness for what he was going to do in front of me. His hands spread out a mountain of fine, white powder, and then divided it up into smaller straight lines. It was like something you'd see on television or in one of those horrible 80s movies about disco and drugs.

His eyes shifted to Lola and then back to me, "Sage is a tattoo artist. Best one in the whole city,"

Bren bent over the table and snorted a long line of whatever the hell it was in front of him. What was it, cocaine? I knew nothing about drugs, but I knew all about vomiting, which was exactly what I felt like doing. He lifted his head to continue talking to her, but only looked at me, "I've been working my ass off to get her shop on the new reality show, *Forever Inked*. She doesn't need to be some stuffy art history professor in some stupid-ass college she went to. She's gonna be a star."

A wave of hatred and disdain surged through me. Was I the only one who thought that what he just did was nasty and vile? And why the Hell are the things that are important to me to do with my life, like my dreams, easily swept aside by him? Who the Hell was he to judge my dreams and tear me down, like my feelings about my life were insignificant, and that *he* had the final say?

Bren turned his glassy eyes away from me and smiled stupidly at the ceiling. Matt leaned on the couch behind him with a menacing look directed toward me. He'd been watching us the entire time we were there.

"Oh, what a cute little job," Lola smirked at me. Then the *district attorney* bent over her side of the coffee table and snorted double the amount of cocaine that Bren did.

"Holy shit," Violet whispered next to me.

Bren's head wobbled back and forth as his chin sank into his chest. "Sage, I'm going to marry you one day..." he slurred lazily. His glazed eyes seemed to crawl over my body, repulsing me so much that bile burned in the back of my throat.

"You're not the marrying kind," I shook my head, stunned. Was this why Bren was the way he was? How long had he been doing this stuff? How often? How could I have not known? Sometimes, people only take the time to see what they want to see, I suppose.

His head lolled heavily against his shoulder. "I'll never let you leave me, Sage."

Grabbing Violet's hand, I tugged her off the couch, "Let's go." I gently pushed her in front of me and practically shoved her out of Bren's living room. When I got to the door, I felt a pair of heavy hands grabbing the back of my arms; fingers digging sharply into my skin and pulling me back in. Whoever it was twisted my arm, meaning to cause me pain. "Where do you think you ladies are going?"

The meaty hands gripped harder, spun me around, and shoved me roughly against the wall next to the door. Violet screamed out next to me, when a thick, fisted hand hit the wall next to my head.

Without even thinking, I balled my fist tight and swung, hitting my assailant, hard, along the bridge of his nose. A spray of blood spurted across his face as he grunted and fell backward.

Matt.

I gently pushed Violet out into the hallway and turned to face him head-on.

Holding his broken nose in one hand, he grabbed me with his other hand, "You stupid cunt! I'm going to kill you!" Pain tore up my arm as he squeezed my flesh and tried lifting me up off the floor.

With an open hand, I shoved my palm straight against his bloody nose; he dropped to the floor with a sickening crunch, out cold. Then, everything seemed to move in slow motion; everything quieted, dulled down like time had stopped.

Bren still sat on the couch, watching through dull, empty eyes.

Lola giggled, slowly snorting another line of cocaine.

Jett laughed silently, slowly slapping at his knees.

A few people I knew, Bren's friends, pointed, laughing at Matt, like insane, scary-ass clowns at one of those freak-ass carnivals.

One man stood to my left; he stood out like the summer sun on a cold winter day. Sandy blond hair, blue eyes, crouched down low, hands reaching into the back waistband of his pants, waiting to jump in and help me, the only one ready to defend me in a room packed full of people.

Violet was yelling my name, pulling me out of my trance. I winked at the gorgeous blond, who immediately straightened up, smiled at me, and looked around to see who was watching him.

Then I walked out the door.

Bren didn't follow me. Didn't check to see if I was okay. Didn't jump in to defend me—not that I needed it—but still.

It was easy to walk away from Bren's apartment that night. And *I knew Bren*; he wasn't someone you could expect more from. But what hurt me was that I wanted more from him. I needed more from him.

And he wouldn't give more.

I wanted to punch myself in the face. I didn't want to be one of those girls who needed to be rescued. I didn't want to be one of those girls who *wanted* to be rescued. I wanted to be the heroine of one of those books where I rescued myself. I didn't want to be one of those girls who stood FOREVER and waited until some dumbass knight in shining armor just happened upon me. I wanted to be the hero of my own story. I didn't want to be saved by someone else.

But still, it would have been nice for the guy who was supposed to be in love with me to make sure I was okay, or stand up for me in some way.

"Oh. Oh. Oh. My GOD!" Violet freaked as soon as we hit the sidewalk in front of Bren's apartment building. "You just kicked the crap out of Matt! What the Hell?"

Looking straight ahead, I kept walking down the block, not answering her. Well, I couldn't really. I was wound up tight; pure adrenaline surged through my arms, anger boiling just under the surface of my skin. I walked faster.

At the corner, Violet jumped in front of me, arms up, hands waving in front of my face. "Charlotte! Holy crap!" She held her hands out to stop me from walking. "I have never seen you go all animal like that! You knocked him out. How *did you do that?* Is that from your karate classes? Because I think you need to sign my ass up!"

Taking a deep breath, I stopped trying to move forward, "No Violet, it's from seeing too many people being bullied and pushed around in my life to let anyone ever again hurt me...or someone I love."

Wordlessly, I continued to my apartment; Violet trailed quietly behind me. I didn't know how much she really knew about me. No one really knows what other people know about you, what has been said about you behind your back, what secrets you don't realize you've let slip. But, she walked so quietly behind me, I wondered if she knew, if she understood why I was the way I was. Or maybe she was just reflecting quietly on her own life. Nobody ever really knows.

Once in my apartment, I headed straight for my bathroom and ran the water until it was icy cold and splashed it over my face.

I looked up at the mirror and stared at the reflection. My arms were already bruised with purple handprints. It was okay, I thought; I defended my friend and myself before he could hurt either one of us. I stared at my bruises. Okay, before he could *seriously* hurt one of us.

I might be twenty-four years old, but all I could see in my own reflection was a scared little girl.

Sometimes, I wish I could sit down with that seventeen-year-old girl, hold her hand tightly, and tell her everything would, one day, hurt *less*. Tell her she needs to be strong. Tell her she *will* get knocked down, but for every time it happens, she'll come up swinging.

Just like tonight.

When I look back on all the past chapters of my life, I see all the pain I have endured. I see the mistakes and heartbreak, the horror and loss. But when I stand in front of the mirror now, I see all my scars and the strength I've found from them. I see the lessons I have learned about life and the wisdom I've gained from each of my experiences. *I will be fine*.

I used to wonder, second-guess myself constantly, about the decisions I made in my life; if they were the right ones for me. In my teens, I had all the answers—don't we all when we're that young, and have the world open like an unwritten book in front of us? Then life shit on me, changed me forever in ways that I can't even put in to words. I wish I could just whisper to that little girl of my past, just once. Give her a little pep talk before the big bad wolf came in and just screwed it all up.

Wouldn't that be helpful? You get what I'm saying, right? Being able to have a little heart-to-heart with the person you were before the world crashed down on you.

And, it will.

Mark my words, one day you'll feel like your world is crashing, spinning out of control, whatever the Hell that is to you, whatever storm that comes, whatever tragedy floods your life. And, believe me, you'll have them; we all get touched by some tragedy in our lives. You better hope you've got the strength to swim, before it pulls you under and you drown, or become nothing more than the storm, forever moving across the waters, stirring up trouble wherever you touch down.

Somewhere in my small kitchen, I can hear the sounds of Violet looking for some sort of alcohol in my cabinets. All I have are the ingredients for a Mad Hatter shot, and a bottle of wine that Bren brought over one night when he was trying to be a *real* boyfriend.

Bren.

Maybe you think I'm weak, or a bitch. But, I've just proven to you that I'm far from being weak or a bitch. I guess that I haven't told you enough about me; please don't form those opinions about me, yet.

Not yet.

Not until you've heard it all. And I'm sorry, but I *have* been going slowly. Taking my time with my sweet memories, and trying to bury the bad ones. However, you can't be selective and only bury the ones you choose to bury; I know firsthand.

They don't stay buried.

Only the things you **don't** want to be buried stay buried.

But to say what it took to get *here*, Hell, to put it down in words, *damn it*, it deadens everything. It makes it seem *unreal*, easily swept under the rug, and it's not.

It's not.

I'm so worried about missing something, of not doing justice to the emotions, to the people, to the heartache, and to the happiness. Because I don't want my words to just be *words*. Every one of them has a history behind it, an emotion so strong that they changed me, touched me, killed me, raised me, made me.

Everybody has a dark side. Some are riddled with guilt about it and hide from it. Me? I needed to embrace mine, because I won't let anything ever tear me down again.

Violet and I vegged out on my couch for the rest of that night, drinking the wine she found. Then, I mixed up some Mad Hatter shots for her.

I held my phone in my hands the entire time. But Bren, of course, didn't call. Matt, on the other hand, called Violet at least twenty times. The last time it rang, she walked into the bathroom and took the call; I wanted to throttle her.

Looking down at my own phone, I swiped through my contacts and typed a text.

C: Hey. Had to use my mad Karate skills tonight!

J: WHAT?!
C: Yep. Gathered up my Chi and kicked some A$$
J: Glad now we took lessons?
C: Wax on!
J: Wax off!
C: Think I'm getting pretty buzzed.
J: You alone?
C: Sort of. Wish I wasn't

J: Are you trying to sext me?

C: You effing wish!

J: You know, a beautiful girl sexting from thousands of miles away that she's getting pretty buzzed ALONE, is the same as a dish of fettucine alfredo texting me it's yummy all the way from Italy.

C: LMAO. Shut the eff up.

J: You still can't curse right.

C: :P

J: Is that...your tongue wagging at me?

C: You are such a dork still.

J: Text me a curse. Come on. Text dick.

J: Come on.

J: Do it.

J: I dare you.

J: Chicken.

C: DICK! Cock, schlong, pecker, willy, shaft, rod, gut buster, flesh flute, soul pole, beef bus, el presidente, taco warmer, blue-veined junket pumper, 100% all-beef thermometer, Alabama black snake, anaconda, anal impaler, baldheaded, yogurt slinger, pocket rocket, skin flute, disco stick, man meat, meat popsicle, wanker, Johnson, and Russell the Love Muscle!

J: God, I miss the shit out of you.

C: Shut up.

J: You forgot penis.

J: But I'm impressed.

I couldn't text it, but I missed the shit out of him too.

❀

MY VERY FIRST kiss happened when I was twelve.

Jase, Joey, and I were invited to Ava Marie Trebisky's thirteenth birthday party, and just like in any boy-girl birthday party, our horny hormonal bodies immediately started a rowdy game of *Seven Minutes In Heaven*. And don't even say that thirteen year olds don't do crap like that, because *I was at the party*! I saw what they did. And honestly, I couldn't WAIT for my turn!

Quickly, I hid the book I secretly took to the party, *just in case* I was bored out of my skull, in my purse. It was an old, beat up copy of Lewis Carroll's *Alice's Adventures in Wonderland* that Joey had bought for me at a yard sale for a quarter, and I'd been reading it to the guys out loud in the tree house every night that week.

As I slid my hands out of my purse, they started to sweat. I was so nervous. Would I actually get kissed? Would it be a romantic, closed-mouth kiss? Or would his tongue touch mine? How long should we do it for? Do we use the full seven minutes, or talk a bit before and after? Would I run out of breath? How would I breathe if he's sucking the air out of my lungs? Where would my hands go? WHAT IF I BIT HIM? Did my breath stink? I slathered on a bit of my watermelon lip-gloss. Oh, God, would his lips slide right off mine? What if I burped? Or sneezed? What if he bit me? What if I did it all wrong?

What if he *didn't want* to kiss me?

Thousands, no, millions, of thoughts flooded my brain. Insane. *All kinds of crazy.* So crazy that I started mumbling to myself as I sat between Jase and Joey, both of them looking at me like I was *full* of crazy.

Who was I going to kiss?

Oh, my God, the anticipation was going to give me a frigging heart attack, and I was going to die NEVER KISSED. My first kiss would end up being with the big, stinky, old paramedic that would come to give me mouth-to-mouth resuscitation! He'd probably even have a long, hairy mustache. And a beer gut.

While I sat hyperventilating, Ava Marie handed each girl in the room a different colored balloon, and when you popped your balloon, it contained a folded up piece of paper with a boy's name on it.

I popped mine, and Joey jumped a million feet in the air from the sound. I laughed so much from my nerves, Jase had to unfold my paper for me.

Aaron Henley.

Oh my GOD! I was going to have *seven minutes in Heaven with Aaron Henley!*

Black spots formed in front of my eyes; I had a sudden fear of eating his entire mouth off his face. Okay fine, that wasn't likely to happen, but what if we had one of those freaky accidents and somehow my mouth got stuck on his and we COULDN'T separate?

Aaron Henley?

I had *never* even *spoken* to Aaron Henley. I mean, maybe I said hello to him if I saw him outside of school with his mom or something, but I didn't remember ever talking to him in school. And, I only had one class with him in our middle school, *Advanced Placement Mathematics*, so it's not like I could talk or *flirt* with him during *that* intense class. Oh, who was I kidding? My idea of flirting was peeking at a cute boy millions of times, like I had some sort of nervous tic, and then hoping that he had more guts than me to talk to me first.

My sort of flirting hadn't been working for me.

Ava Marie quietly walked up to Joey and showed him her paper with his name all swirly with hearts all over it. Oh cheese-and-crackers, this had to be a set up! On the other side of me, Rachel Jenson showed Jase his name on her folded up piece of paper. There were no hearts on hers, just Jase's name with a giant pair of red lip prints, as if she kissed the paper herself. *Yep, that was the taste of vomit I was swallowing back down.*

I looked down at my paper again. It just said Aaron Henley, with nothing else on it.

As I stood up on my wobbly legs to walk over to Aaron to show him my paper, I watched a strange look pass between my two best friends. Jase ripped the paper out of my hands and shoved it into Rachel Jenson's hands. Then, Jase took her folded piece of paper with his name on it and shoved it into mine. "Sorry, I think there's been a mistake in your little *set up*," he smirked. Then standing up, he gently walked me into one of the empty rooms with a sign on the door that read *HEAVEN* and had cotton balls for clouds decorated all over it. Ava shoved Joey into the one next to us and slammed the door closed.

A small table lamp in the corner dimly lit the room. Inside was a washing machine and dryer, but no place to sit. In the middle of the floor there was a basket full of dirty laundry we had to climb over. The smell of decaying socks surrounded us. The laundry room; *how romantic. Heaven, my butt.*

I shoved him on the shoulder. "Why the heck did you do that, Jase?"

"I was saving your life! Aaron Henley has razor-sharp braces; he'll scar your mouth for life."

"Really, dork? That's what you're going with?" I pulled myself up to sit on the edge of the washing machine and hung my legs off the sides, swinging them slowly back and forth. *Ugh. Now I'd have to wait and see what name I'd get next.* I hoped like mad there was another round to this game. I was not leaving this party without kissing *someone*.

Jase's face reddened and he looked down at something on his shoes. "No. That's not what I'm going with," he said, combing his fingers through his hair. Lifting his eyes to mine, he slowly stepped closer to me, brushing the front of his shirt against my knees. The warmth of his body seeped into my skin.

My heart skipped a beat then just stopped. I think I may have died a little. *What was Jase Delaney thinking?*

He moved his body in between my legs and leaned the palms of his hands on the edge of the machine on either side of me. He lowered his face two inches from mine, and *I was lost*, floating somewhere helplessly in the soft blue waters of the Bermuda Triangle in his eyes. Then he smiled, a spark of something so honest and true, so utterly *Jase*, it completely stole my breath away. "Come on, Charlie, come with me down the rabbit hole," he squeaked in an unsteady voice.

His words, whispered so dark and beautifully, caused my heart to stutter wildly in my chest. Then I thought to myself, this–*this feeling right here*–was what grownups wrote those great love stories about. That one breathtakingly beautiful moment that you will remember forever is happening right now. I mean, come on, my best friend just asked me to kiss him with a quote from one of my favorite books!

Before I could think another thought, Jase's trembling fingers were cupping my chin. With the lightest of pressure, he tilted my head gently back and slowly lowered his face closer to mine. "I want to be your first kiss, Charlie," My belly filled with fire, and my cheeks flushed with heat. I could barely breathe from his whispered words.

"Then kiss me," I whispered nervously.

As if a breeze, his warm lips brushed against mine. Jase's hand trailed feather-soft fingers down my neck, making my skin tingle with what felt like flames. The outside sounds of the party grew faint, and all I could hear was our quick, shallow breaths as his mouth moved against mine. Heat traveled down my neck and across my chest, tightening my skin and coiling my muscles. I never knew such a feeling existed in such a simple touch of lips. The heat from his body up against mine, the smell of the shampoo he used, the press of his lips against mine, and there was nothing and no one else in the world, but us. In my head, the written words of Lewis Carroll whispered in my ears, *"In another moment, down went Alice after it, never once considering how in the world she was to get out again."*

When the tip of his tongue hesitantly brushed over my lips, I lost myself in his taste and his touch. Warm and wet, soft and sweet, our hearts were crashing and pounding together like a thunderstorm beneath our chests. I could feel his heart beneath his shirt, pounding so hard and fast against me that I imagined it bursting right out to meet mine.

I reached my hand up and softly curved my fingers around the back of his neck and threaded them through the silky strands of his hair. It was one of those touches that I had read about in a few young adult books, and I'd always wanted to see how it felt. Whoa...it felt good...it felt really good. He moaned quietly, and his fingers pressed into my skin, fisting into the material of my shirt.

It felt...*beautiful*.

"Time's up!" Rachel Jenson's voice screeched from the other side of the door.

Both of us jerked away from each other, eyes wide. Seven minutes was way too short of an amount of time.

"Crap-on-a-celery-stick," I whispered.

He shook his head, "Hell no. Uh-uh. No way. Curse if you have to, Charlie, but don't pull that crappity-crap shit with me. *Tell me.*"

"Oh, my God. That was *awesome*," I giggled.

He leaned in and kissed me again on the lips. "Yeah, Charlie, it was. Just like I always thought it would be," he murmured softly to me before walking out the door. And slowly, like I was made completely of jelly, I slid down the side of the washing machine until my butt hit the floor, and I completely melted into a puddle of Jase Delaney goop.

Of all the kisses in the history of first kisses, that had to be the most perfect one—it just had to be.

Rachel Jenson came stomping into the laundry room, dragging a crazy-eyed Drake Fischer. "Charlotte, it's my turn for seven minutes now!" she giggled.

Drake Fischer? I thought she was supposed to go to heaven with Aaron Henley.

Wait a minute.

If Drake Stupid Fischer was here, that meant…

So was Slate.

Jumping to my feet, I ran out of the laundry room and slammed chest-first into Slate Marshall. Stumbling backward, I (like a brainless dork) grabbed onto Slate's shirt to try to steady myself. Instantly, I realized I had broken Slate's "No One Comes Ten Feet Near Me" rule when he smiled that evil, satanic smile of his and pressed his body *closer* to mine.

Immediately, I let go of his shirt and dropped my hands away from his chest.

He flicked a folded up piece of paper in front of my face and opened it for me to read.

Charlotte Stone.

My body went numb. Could someone get paralyzed from a look that someone is giving you? Because, I swore that Slate's look was freezing me to the spot. Heavily, he dropped both his hands on my shoulders; the stupid folded paper fluttered silently to the floor.

His ugly, evil lips curled up higher, "I just popped a balloon with your name on it." Lowering his face closer to mine, he whispered, "Now, I'm going to pop your cherry in seven minutes."

Shrugging his hands off me, I stepped back, but only managed to back myself into the wall behind me. I looked around for help, but everyone seemed paired off, kissing or talking or *living*.

Me? I was dying in the corner.

I moved closer to the other kids in the room, sliding myself along the wall. I only made it about a foot before Slate's arms were blocking my way to safety.

"Slate, there is no way I'm going anywhere with you for seven minutes!" I hissed.

"Those are the rules of the game, Charlotte," he replied, wrapping his hands around my wrists and pulling me closer to a room with a "HEAVEN" sign hanging on the door.

I leaned back away from him, but he just dragged me harder, my sneakers sliding along the floor.

"Let me go!" I yelled, twisting my body away from his.

Slate was stronger than me, though, and his hands still stayed clamped around my wrists as I tried to break free. My bones bent in ways they shouldn't as I tried to yank my hands back from him.

"Let go of her," Joey's voice growled next to me.

One of his arms swung around my waist, while his other pushed against Slate's chest. "I said let go of her. She doesn't want you to touch her," he hissed.

Slate dropped my hands, laughing. "Relax, *Piss Pants*. I was just playing around with her." He stepped closer to Joey and laughed louder in his face. Spittle flew everywhere and Joey flinched back, blinking it out of his eyes. "What were you going to do about it, anyway?"

"Whatever it takes to keep your hands off her," Joey said.

Oh. Crudcakes.

Ava Marie chose that moment to run upstairs to get her parents, or the police or whomever. At the same time, Jase slammed his body in between Slate and Joey. "Okay, enough. This is a party, and Charlie doesn't want to play the game anymore. Get over it."

Thank God Ava Marie's father came downstairs then and herded us all out into the backyard to cool off.

Swinging my arms around both of my best friends' shoulders, I squeezed them tightly against me. *What girl in the world had two real-life superheroes, huh?*

Joey knocked his head against mine, "Let's just get out of here and go hang out in the tree house," he whispered, shakily.

So we did.

And right after we walked into the tree house, Jase picked a thick black marker from my *Fantastical Cup O' Markers* and carefully climbed on a stack of my hardcover books to write the words *Rabbit Hole* above the door.

Joey read the phrase with a raised brow. "What's Rabbit Hole mean?"

Jase's eyes grazed past Joey and landed on mine. "From *Alice's Adventures in Wonderland*, you know...down the rabbit hole, where there's a whole different world. And it's only ours. Our safe place to go from the jerks like Slate."

He jumped off the books and swept his hand through his hair, throwing the marker back into the *Fantastical Cup O' Markers*. It landed perfectly inside the cup. "Oh, and tomorrow...the both of you are coming to Sensei Satuo's dojo with me. You're going to learn how to defend yourselves."

"Dowho?" Joey chuckled.

"Dojo, *Piss Pants*. It means 'training hall' in Japanese."

I shook my head at Jase. "You know my mom doesn't have any extra money for me to take fighting lessons. She barely has enough money to feed me," I complained. I may have sounded like a whiny brat, but it was true. Since my dad left us, my mom had to get a job working in an office all day answering phones *and napping*. I knew this because I had visited her office a total of nineteen times so far, and *every* time I had to wake her up! The job was okay she said, but it only paid her minimum wage and had no benefits (whatever that was). She couldn't get anything better, because she never went to college. *Her second job* was going out every night to a singles' bar, dressed like one of the Jenson sisters, looking for the next guy who could help pay the mortgage. Her second job seemed really important to her, because she was really good at bringing new friends home and keeping me up all night with their loud music and nasty smelling cigarettes. It was so annoying that I just started sleeping in the tree house every night. Her weekends were spent on dates, or I-Need-To-Get-Married-Like-Yesterday.com sites, searching for someone who could give her a sense of stability instead of just finding it in herself.

I tried to help her by getting her a college application from my counselor at school, but she told me that was too much work for her. She wanted to do it the fun way, like my father had.

I didn't understand.

So, I just left her to do whatever she did and ate lots of SpaghettiOs and ice cream. Ice cream always makes you feel better anyway.

"Sensei takes donations, he's the real deal. Just come and I'll handle everything," Jase said.

And the next thing I could remember was wearing a stiff white *Gi* and walking barefoot into a large room where I had to bow, submissively, to some old *Mr. Miyagi* looking character. Joey chuckled next to me and whispered, "Ah, Danielson, you must wax on and wax off."

Jase stood next to the Sensei in a black *Gi* and a purple belt. His smile was infectious, and I got really excited about learning lots of ninja moves.

Yeah, excited.

I was giddy with stupid, ignorant anticipation, until I found myself sweating like a fountain and stuck in a headlock under the smelly armpits of another student. Jase was trying to help me, telling me how to bend my knees and fall forward to get myself out of the hold, but I was seriously passing out because of the kid's armpit stench.

The kid finally let go of me, raising his hands in surrender, and Jase took over. Walking behind me, Jase placed his right hand around the front of my chest, right under my neck, and pulled me close against his body. His left hand gripped tightly onto my hip. It was the same exact headlock that I was just in, but with Jase's body flushed up behind mine it felt...different.

Why would that make my insides tingle?

"Okay, first you need to bring up your right hand and grip onto the collar of my *Gi*."

I slid my hand up and accidently mushed him in the nose.

"Holy ninja-crap, I didn't mean to do that," I laughed.

"Yeah, *sure* you didn't. Doesn't matter, try it again, and grab my collar tight. Get a good grip on it." He pulled me tighter against him, but this time leaning his cheek softly against my ear—so close that all I could hear and feel were the soft, warm sounds of his breaths.

He slowly went over the steps and movements for me, but the only thing I could think about was how warm his body felt up against the back of mine.

How tall he was compared to me.

How softly his fingers slid over my skin.

How hot his breath felt, blowing against my skin.

The smell of his soap and whatever laundry detergent his father used on his clothes.

Turning my head slightly, all I could see were his lips *so* close to me. *So close to my lips*. The sound of his voice just rumbled against my skin; none of his words made sense to me when all I could see were his lips. They were confusing me. This was Jase; we'd hugged millions of times and wrestled and played. But, in that moment, I felt every inch of his body against mine, and I tingled from head to toe. My scalp even burned. *What the heck was that about?*

Then, my feet were airborne, and he was slamming me down on the mats that covered the floor. "Charlie, if you don't try to do the moves, someone will be able to take you down," he said, hovering over me. All I could think about was him hovering over me.

Okay. I had to focus.

Jase was one of my best friends. Yes. He kissed me. *And God, it was the most perfect kiss in the world, like, I could **still** feel his lips on mine a day AFTER!* But, and this is a huge BUT, Jase didn't like me like that. We were best friends. Best friends; forever. He went into Heaven with me for seven minutes so he wouldn't have to go with Rachel Jenson...and I wouldn't get mouth massacred by Aaron Henley's braces.

"Come on, Charlie, get up. Let's try again."

I stood up and brushed my uniform pants off, and without even giving me a minute, he looped his arm around my neck and pressed his body hard against my back. "Come on, Charlie. Kneel on one leg and pull me over with your..."

So I *did*.

I dropped down on my right knee, curled my body forward, and yanked him by his *Gi* over my right shoulder.

Jase flew over me and landed flat on the mat in front of me, slapping out in a perfect fall.

Power.

Strength.

Pride.

I was hooked.

He looked up at me from the mat, blue eyes blazing, lips spread in a huge smile. "Not bad. Get up! Let's try it, again."

Hundreds of times. Stances. Punches. Kicks. Again and again.

The three of us, in the dojo, in my backyard. Over and over, Jase taught us to defend ourselves. "You don't start the fight, guys," he would say. "But you don't let anyone push you around. Because once they push you, even an inch, they'll keep doing it. Teach them that *nobody can ever hurt you.*"

Jase didn't kiss me again after our seven minutes in Heaven, and we never spoke about it. But sometimes…sometimes, I would catch those blue eyes on me, and when I did…

I would look

Right back at him

And he *never*

Looked away.

JASE

*W*hat the hell was I doing?

You don't even have to ask me, *I'm* asking me. *What the hell was I doing?*

I was in her apartment: Day *Three*. The floors and table were littered with dozens of bottles of wine, pillows, and empty condom wrappers.

Yeah, I was screwed.

Brooke was sitting across from me, *in my damn shirt*, lifting a forkful of the greasiest Chinese food I've ever tasted to her mouth. Her eyes lifted to mine as she opened her lips; her tongue slid along one of the hanging sesame noodles and seductively glided it into her mouth.

Yeah, I was so screwed. I didn't want a relationship with Brooke, but she wouldn't listen. It was almost as if she didn't care what I said. She was wearing my shirt, eating take-out after work with me, and there was a mess of sexual evidence strewn about the apartment. Sure as Hell looked a lot like the relationship I didn't frigging want. Not now, not with her. Nope, wouldn't hold up in court. I'd get thrown in some khakis and tied down with a ball and chain wrapped around my neck and secured to my nuts.

Brooke flung her fork back into the little takeout cardboard box our food was delivered in and crawled on all fours over to me. "You're *so* sexy sitting there. Now I'm hungry for something *else*," she purred.

Who the hell was I to say no, right? She was *hungry*, she just said it, and me, well,—I was horny. Again. I *am* a man, and we were two consenting adults. I didn't want to think about how screwed I was. I didn't want to think about how this was someone I worked with. I always tried not to shit where I eat, but hell, when the food was free, and she didn't mind the smell, screw it. And I'm going to. *Screw it*, again.

"You're so sexy," she murmured, in probably what *she thought* was an erotic tone. It wasn't. "Just so, so, *so* sexy," she repeated. Yeah, I got the memo; I'm sexy. Awesome. *Let's just have a quickie so I can get the hell out of here*. I hadn't been home in three days, and I started to feel a little smothered with what I like to call the *bridal gaze* she was giving me. You know the one. After a few nights of sleeping with a girl, and she starts staring at you like she's listing the names of babies in her mind at the same time she's redecorating your apartment with little, smelly-ass candles and her personal belongings.

Like a box of those *tampon-pad-things*. Hell, I don't even know if I'm saying that right.

Why would I ever need a box of *those things* next to my damn shaving cream in the bathroom cabinet? Or one of her glittery tubes of lip puffer-upper-whatever-the-hell-that-stuff-is. And all because you've stuck a part of your body in a part of her body? What in the world makes women think that means we want to *marry* them?

Her hands drifted to my bare chest and she slowly traced the lines of one of my tattoos with her index finger. Every muscle in my body went on alert as she gave me a slow, sexy smile and straddled me. She lazily trailed her finger between the two names I had inked over my chest; her eyes questioning everything they saw. Lowering her mouth to my skin, she gently flicked her tongue along the pathway of the two names.

My hands closed into fists against my thighs; my body coiled tight with tension, waiting for her to ask me about crap I had no intention of telling her about. Ever.

"I always wondered about your tattoos," she murmured, licking and teasing my skin. "Who are Joey and Charlie? And what's the story about the tree and rabbit hole?" she asked, skimming her tongue along the lines.

Hell, it was making me *sick*. Having someone else's tongue on me *saying* their names. The tension twisted my muscles and strained against my skin, my fists clenched tighter.

Charlie. *Charlie*.

That was a hell of a shit story. I leaned back against the edge of the couch and chuckled to myself. This conversation was a fight waiting to happen. That's another thing I don't get about women. Why do you ladies want to know about the girls *before?* It's not going to make you happy, especially when we explain to you our first great relationship, the one you'll never live up to. Ever.

I wasn't going *there*.

I needed a quick fuck and a quicker getaway.

Slumping my head back against the cushions of her couch, I loosened my fisted hands to open the button to my jeans and unzipped them. I tugged myself out, stroking, squeezing; then letting it spring free. "Don't want to talk," I said, tangling my fingers through her hair and spreading a hand across the back of her neck to push her mouth over my cock.

With a low moan, Brooke took me all the way in and gagged. Setting up a slow pace, she bobbed her head up and down, softly raking her teeth against me.

Man, I needed it faster. And what was with the teeth? Damn, no teeth. Ever.

I had to get the Hell out of there.

I tightened my grasp on her hair, twisting the strands through my fingers—pulling and pushing, quickening her speed, pressing her deep, getting the rhythm I needed.

She pulled her mouth off me with a small whimper and looked up at me. "Tell me who they are," she whispered, running circles over me with her tongue.

Big turnoff. I hate the sexual power games women try to play.

One of her eyebrows lifted. Her hand wrapped around my shaft, and with perfect pressure she continued to try to torture the truth from me.

Another small swirl of her tongue and both eyebrows lifted up as she tilted her head to the side.

Brooke was waiting for my answer. She was looking at me with those giant blue eyes, her wild, sexy hair framing her cute face, and she looked like a life size Barbie doll. Any man would probably cut off his left nut to spend a night with a woman like that, and I'd be a fool to tell her anything about my past. So as always, I kept my thoughts to myself. I kind of liked my manhood in one piece, and since it was in her mouth at that moment, I was feeling if I started talking about Charlie, she might bite it the hell off.

And what the *hell* was she thinking, asking me that stuff when I was in her mouth? What did she think—she could suck and slurp the answers out of me?

One long swipe of her tongue, from bottom to top, "Tell me, Delaney. Or do you want me to stop?" she teased.

But I didn't want to think about that shit.

I tried to forget. I tried to forget how everything happened, how the whole damn Charlie-Joey-fuck-my-life-situation played out. About how I tried getting it all back, but I couldn't bring back shit.

I couldn't do anything.

So, I always kept my thoughts about everything in my head. I didn't give a voice to them anymore; it was just a wasted effort.

I just stopped trying to get everything back.

Everything.

Everyone.

Was gone.

Sometimes, when I'm working, and I see a woman with that long, silky chestnut colored hair standing in a crowd, my body freezes, and I stare at her until I know for sure it isn't Charlie.

It's never Charlie.

No one had that cinnamon colored hair; nobody held a cigarette the same way Charlie did. Nobody ever had a book clenched tightly to her chest, and nobody's laugh sounded anything like hers. *And* no one ever looked at me the way Charlie did.

It had been years, and no one had ever come close to being anything like Charlie. And Joey, well that was a whole other different level of shit.

"You seriously won't tell me about them?" Brooke asked, leaning back.

"Nothing to tell," I said after I climbed up off the floor and walked away with just a small, backward glance.

Her mouth was still open; my cock just left her hanging.

I tucked myself back in my pants and buttoned up. Total loss of wood.

Now, don't go thinking about me like I'm a grade A asshole, I'm really not. I wasn't trying to be a jerk to Brooke, but I'm not the sort of man that can be forced into shit. I don't like games, and she just tried to play one with me. You saw what she just did.

Why didn't I just tell her? Of course, you would ask that.

There are just some things in my life I don't want to relive. I don't want to feel them again or have anyone else know about the worst and hardest parts of my life. Guys don't want to rehash and talk something to death. And, if us guys talked about our stuff, it would be with someone we chose to do it with, not with someone who forced us into it. I didn't want to tell Brooke.

I didn't want to be that close with her.

I wouldn't be that close to her.

I laid it all out on the line with Brooke when we first met for drinks after work one night—over a month ago. I told her point-blank I was not looking to get into a monogamous relationship. It's not that I was a guy who messed around, because let's face reality; I don't have a bunch of different beautiful women jumping into my bed every night. That's just frigging unrealistic. That crap only happens in movies and in girl porn, it just doesn't happen in real freaking life. And, let's face it, I'm just a normal guy. There's nothing wrong with me, but I'm not anything special either. I'm not a player. I don't have money falling out of my pockets. I'm not a rock star, movie star, cutter, drinker, drug user, bipolar, card-carrying man-whore club member, or anything else that's trending right now. And what the hell are these things trending for? I'm just a city cop who doesn't have mental or emotional issues; I see the filth of life firsthand, working day-to-day, and I try hard not to take that crap home with me.

Brooke and I had a deal. This girly talk and getting to know each other's deep, dark secrets was not part of the deal. And I've known Brooke since she got on the job about four years ago; she was always a serial dater. I know at least three other guys she's been with and I've never held them against her.

Brooke slithered up and ran after me. "Okay, okay, sorry, Delaney," she said, pulling on my waist to wrap her arms around me. Yeah, I didn't like that crap either. "I just wanna know you better. Just tell me who they are."

"What the hell *Brooke-Lyn*? Stop with the personal inquisition of my life. You're smothering the Hell out of me."

She stepped in front of me, long, tan legs posturing, fist planted on her hip, the hem of my shirt she was wearing riding up over her thighs. "It's just that we've been together for a few weeks, and I kind of was hoping that you'd…"

"*What?* Change?" I asked.

"Well…a little, maybe…" she mumbled, looking down at something on the floor.

"What is with the female population of New York City? There's nothing WRONG with me. I like who I am, and I don't want to change."

"I just wish we could, you know, maybe talk or…"

"What the Hell do you need to hear from me? All of a sudden, you want to be my shrink and listen to me cry about my messed up childhood friends. What next? You going to ask me what it was like when I went overseas? Want my body count?" I walked up real close to her face. "Stop looking for something more in me, when I'm telling you, I can't give you anything else."

"It's not that you can't. It's that you WON'T!" she yelled aggressively.

"That's right, because *I don't want to*," I said, calmly.

"Alrighty there, Detective Dickhead, I don't even know why I bother!"

"That makes two of us."

With a frown, Brooke started pacing in front of me,

blocking my way out of the apartment. Yeah, that's not a game either, right?

I'd been nothing but honest with her.

She started pacing faster, getting more agitated. Then—here's my favorite part—she ran at me and shoved me with both her hands, hard against my chest.

Don't worry, I'm not a little punk who would hit a woman back; I just stood there and let her get it out. After a while, I had to admit, it kind of annoyed me, but I didn't have the heart to stop her.

"You!" she screamed, shoving me a last time. "You don't even know my middle name. You don't even know my favorite food, or color, or movie. And I know NOTHING about you, except for how big your dick is!"

Well, now. You heard her say BIG, right? *Just making sure.*

"Your middle name and *favorite color?* What the Hell does that have to do with fucking? Because that's all we've been doing. And don't get high and mighty with me Brooke, you don't know shit about me. I don't know shit about you either, because we both agreed it would be just fucking."

"My God, Delaney. Whoever broke your heart ruined you for every other woman after her, huh? What are you afraid of?"

"Clowns, mostly."

"*What?*"

"Yeah, clowns kind of freak me out."

"You are the biggest asshole I've ever met!" she screamed.

"Then you definitely shouldn't waste any more of your time on me."

"YOU have an answer for everything! Can you talk to me seriously for a minute? Fuck, Delaney." Then she added in a low whisper, "I think I'm in love with you."

Okay, so that statement caught me a little off guard, especially when she looked as if she were wiping away a tear from below her eye.

And for a small moment, a very small one, I considered what she said. Then, I watched her expression carefully; defiant stance, hand on hip, the other hand swiping at a pretend tear, eyes fixed on mine, and a daring smirk across her face. I read people for a damn living, and she was lying her ass off. That's not love. I've seen love. And if that's the kind of shit Brooke thought was love, I didn't want any of it from her.

"Brooke, five minutes ago you told me that you know nothing about me. How can you say you love me if you don't know me?"

"Delaney..."

"You don't even call me by my first name."

"Jase..."

"Did I forget to tell you about my wife and kids? That's okay; I didn't mention my herpes, either—did I?" I said, annoyed.

"You better be kidding around!"

"The point is Brooke, you don't know. You don't know *me*; so don't tell me you love me. If you don't want to continue with the way things are, that's fine. But Brooke, I'm not offering anything else. I can't."

"Jase, I'm standing here crying in front of you. I want to know you better."

"No. You're pretending to cry in front of me, and I told you I'm not offering anything else. It's your call."

"Are you going to be sleeping with someone else?"

"Here comes the crazy," I mumbled, grabbing my boots and stomping my feet into them. My own damn hand made for a better relationship than anything I've had in the last few years. Looks like I'll be hooking up with that every night from now on.

"Okay, fine. I'm sorry I asked about the stupid tattoos." She took a deep breath and gently put her hands over my chest. "I just want to know if maybe someday we could talk and get closer, maybe...I don't know."

"Whatever, Brooke. I gotta go."

"You think you could find someone better than me?" she whispered as I walked out the door.

"Nah, Brooke. I'm not looking for anything or anyone," I said, closing the door behind me.

And that was the truth, because for the last few years I've Googled Charlotte Stone and have never found her, so I just stopped looking. Every search came up empty, like she had just disappeared. Being a cop isn't like it is in the movies. You can't just run someone's name and find his or her location. We aren't allowed to run a name through the department's computers unless it's part of a case. Besides, if she never committed a crime, her name wouldn't turn up in our criminal databases.

I just wish the memories could have gone with her, because I can still see her in front of me.

I don't remember exactly how old we were, maybe thirteen, I don't know...I remember it being the second or third week of eighth grade and sitting in the back of Honors Literature. "Jase? Jase..." Mrs. Kaplan called out from in front of her desk.

I pretended not to hear her. I was too busy staring and daydreaming about the back of Charlie. She had curves all over. Even from the back of her, I could see the swell of her breasts, the curve of her hips, and the slope of her neck... I could even tell the crazy thoughts that were probably running through that head of hers as we sat there reading through *Romeo and Juliet*. She'd probably read that damn play over a thousand times.

All that *beautiful crazy* just sitting in her head. Her glasses were pulled back over the top of her long, silky, reddish-brown hair, and she was wearing her vintage Metallica, cap sleeved T-shirt. My little bookworm.

That Kaplan lady didn't give up though; she started banging on the top of her desk with one of those long ruler torture devices while she screamed, "Jase Delaney! I know you can hear me calling your name!"

I looked up and gave her a small wink. Of course, I could hear her banshee scream; the damn bodies in the cemetery across the street were covering their decaying ears with their decaying hands trying NOT to hear her.

"Sorry, Mrs. Kaplan. What was the question again?"

"Mr. Delaney, I asked if you believed it is plausible that a love story of this magnitude could take place so quickly?" she chirped.

Charlie swung her head around and smiled at me. *Man, she was so pretty.*

"Nope," I answered.

Mrs. Kaplan leaned her back against her desk and knocked her knuckles against the wood, "Please elaborate on your feelings about this subject, Mr. Delaney."

I huffed out a long breath, and Charlie turned her body more to watch me.

"I just don't see this play as being a *love* story. Maybe a lust story, but not love. I mean *come on*; it's three days long! It's a three-day relationship of a thirteen-year-old girl and a seventeen-year-old guy. That's lust and statutory rape. *And*, he was banging some other chick in the beginning—or wanting to bang her, before she decided to become a nun. But don't even get me started on that," I joked as a few chuckles filled the room. "I get it when you explain to us, Mrs. Kaplan, that it's supposed to be intense and by squishing all the things that happen into just a few days, Shakespeare adds a heavy importance to each event. Yes, it helps to show that shit is flying out of control; it heightens the pressure of the emotions. But, it's not real, not plausible at all. Six people die because two kids want to hook up and..."

"Mr. Delaney!"

I stopped my rant, but I ignored Mrs. Kaplan and watched Charlie laughing in her seat. We had this argument about *Romeo and Juliet* all the time. "Yeah. Yeah. I know, do you want me to go to the Dean's office?"

"No, Mr. Delaney. But I would like you to write your feelings down on a piece of paper and hand them in for me to grade."

Son of a bitch.

"Yeah, I'll get right on that," I smirked.

But I was tired and didn't write a word, and all I wanted to do was watch Charlie.

I was on my third night of wet dreams that week, all starring Charlie, my best friend. I didn't think she even knew I'd been in love with her since, well, forever. It was a heck of a lot longer than three days, that's for sure. I don't remember exactly why or how, I just remembered when I discovered that I did love her. One day, I was just watching her on the roof of that old tree house, and I remember her green eyes sparkling as she spun her body, laughing and twirling in the summer sun. That day, I knew I never wanted to live without her in my life.

...that she was more than a friend.

...that I wanted to be the one who kissed her lips.

...the one that she wrote about in her diary.

...the one she ran to when she had trouble.

Damn, I think we were only in fourth grade.

Anyway, how the hell was a guy like me supposed to be able to concentrate when Charlie was in front of the classroom? There was no frigging way.

There was never any way for me to concentrate on anything but her; she was the world to me.

Right after school, Joey and I would shoot baskets while Charlie sat on the grass with her head in a book. She had a stack of books next to her, and every now and then, she would pull the pencil that she had tucked into her ponytail out of her hair and underline things to tell us about later on. I never cared too much about what the words said, but I didn't think there was anything better than listening to Charlie's voice reading to me. I didn't say shit to her—I just listened. I guess that's how I got stuck knowing crap about *Romeo and Juliet* and being placed in an AP literature class.

I always listened to Charlie. She had this strange spell over me that I never quite figured out a cure for. Never even wanted to, either.

When we were in fourth grade, the three of us becoming quick friends, we used to walk to the candy store right after school, and every day, before we'd get to the cash register, I'd shove whatever shit I could into my pockets and walk out. I never got caught either, but Charlie made this big stink about it. Charlie always had these serious rules about what was right and wrong. She always did what was right. Me, I always seemed to choose the wrong direction. But I could still see her face the last time I grabbed three candy bars for us; she stood there, green eyes blazing, arms crossed and refusing to let me out of the store.

"You are better than that, Jase Delaney," she said. "Stop trying to prove your father right. You're one of the best friends a girl could ever have…But, I will call the cops on you if you ever do that again! And I won't be visiting you in prison, either."

She even sat me down and read some book to me, about a kid that shoplifted and a superhero that came along and made him stop stealing to help fight crime with him. It was the coolest story I had ever heard, and it was the first time Charlie ever read a story to Joey and me. I was really interested in being a superhero back then, especially when she looked at me with those eyes, as if she really thought I could be one. She *made me* believe I could be one.

She made me want to be a better kid. She made me feel invincible. She made me feel like I could do anything, be anything. She made me feel powerful, strong, funny, brave, and just *normal*. She made me *feel*.

She would take me on adventures
With those books
She killed me
And brought me back
But *just knowing Charlie*
Was my best adventure…
Until it wasn't.

CHARLIE

I had to talk myself out of eating an entire box of chocolate covered pretzels, two-dozen white chocolate dipped strawberries, and a five-pound box of some expensive, decadent, milk chocolate crunchy pecan *things*. Because *that*, and two-dozen red roses, was what Bren thought he should buy me to *help* me to *forgive* him and *forget* about his messed up drug party. You know, because *that* crap will make me want to stay with him.

Stupid much?

I sat in front of the wilting flowers and the chocolate-covered crap, and went over the night before in my head.

An hour before closing, Bren stormed into the shop with all his idiotic gifts, looking nothing like a coke-head and everything like the beautiful GQ guy he once was. The girls and I ignored him and continued with our *deep, meaningful* discussion about opening another business in the empty storefront across the street. Violet wanted a revenge shop for jilted lovers, and Hazel thought it would be best if we bought the space and made it a slap and tickle kind of a bar. Me? I wanted it to be an ice cream shop. One of those old-fashion ice-cream parlors where you have special names for all the flavors, like "He's Not Worth It Vanilla," and "Instant-No-Strings-Attached Orgasm Chocolate," maybe even a "He Had a Small Penis Pistachio."

Bren interrupted our laughter by saying, "And you girls always say that us guys are bad..."

"No, Bren. We usually say you guys are douche rockets," I snapped.

"Shit," Bren whispered, turning pale. "Sage, *please* come inside and talk to me."

I know! I'm a glutton for punishment; I let him walk me into my back studio as he balanced all the crap in his arms.

He placed all of his guilt-laden-get-out-of-jail-free presents on one of my tables and slowly walked up in front of me, "You haven't answered any of my calls. You haven't let me apologize. You haven't..."

"Just stop. Let's not make this about what *I* have or haven't done. The only way to fix this is if you go get help, Bren. If you don't, like I said to you before, there is no us. Hell, Bren. There's barely an *us* now, anyway."

"Shit, Sage. You know how much I love you, right?"

"How often do you do that stuff?"

"What stuff?" I watched him tense with the question.

"That's it, then. I'm done. You either own up to the crap or I bounce," I turned my face away and started for the door.

He gently embraced me and buried his face in my neck. "I promise, I won't do that shit anymore, especially if it scares you. I've only done it a few times, I swear. I don't have a problem; I don't *need* to have it, okay?" Leaning his head back, he looked in my eyes, "Sage, I've just been really stressed out with trying to get you on television and make this place famous. I have the producers of *Forever Inked* flying here next week to scope out the place..."

"But that's not what I want and you know it. I never

agreed to any of that. I told you I didn't want this place to become a cheesy reality show."

"Sage, it's a tattoo parlor. It isn't a fine arts museum, and you're not some stuck up art history professor, so just face the facts. You are hot, baby. Me and you, we belong on a hit reality show. Do you know how much money we're talking about, Sage?"

I tried to pull away from him. "So, you don't think I can hack it as a professor, huh?"

"Give that a rest, okay? I know you. We've known each other for years; you're too wild, Sage. Stay where you belong, with me. We used to have so much fun together," he whispered, still trying to cling tightly to me.

"Yeah, well. I've done a lot of growing up."

His fingertips brushed across my chin, and lifted it toward him. "Where's the girl that used to be the life of the party, huh? Where's my girl? You used to wear those little tiny skirts, stay out all night with me, drink all my friends under the table, and ride me hard until morning. Hell, you used to shave that sweet pussy of yours bare; you don't even do *that* anymore. Now you're all grown-up and don't have time for any fun."

Panic quickly filled my body. *What the hell did he just say to me?* Stepping out of his arms, my back hit the wall, hard. "Bren, if you can't handle me at my hairiest, then sweetie, you don't deserve me when I'm waxed." I seriously did not want to do *this* anymore.

Bren moved forward and cupped my face in his hands; he stood rigid and hard and seemed so easily breakable to me. I felt so sad for the friendship that was lost between us. I grabbed onto his wrists and gently pushed his hands from my cheeks. "Bren, I don't want to be that messed up, loud-mouthed, hurt kid again. I was that way because I was *lost*." I stepped back, shaking my head and trying to make space between us. "I moved on with my life, let the crap go and things that were so important when I was twenty changed and aren't so important at twenty-four. Bren, I want to be put on a pedestal for being me and not because of what I can give you. Neither of us seems happy together," I sighed, rubbing the back of my neck. "I know you think I'm just a hopeless romantic, but I want more. I deserve more."

His hands were back cupping my face instantly. This time though, his grip was tighter, and his breath was shorter. "There you go again, living in the fictional worlds of those stupid romance novels you read. I'm sick of being compared to make-believe dukes, supernatural rock star angels, and fictional vomit. I'm in love with you, Sage. We are going to be married one day. We're going to put this shop on television and live like royalty. Mark my words, baby."

"Holy Hell in a hand basket, I just want to slap the crap out of your face for saying that to me. Brendan Gage Laux, my books have more substance to them than you have in your entire body. Hell, you make me so freaking sick some-times. What the hell happened to my friend, Bren? If I knew this was going to happen, I wouldn't have..." I didn't want to speak anymore. Instantly my brain planned on taking two distinct actions, in no particular order. One was to put a call in to Auburn's lawyer about the shop. I needed to know how tied up Bren was in the ownership with me, because I needed to get the fuck out of this relationship. And, the second was to one-click whore my way through a bunch of faceless book boyfriends that knew exactly the right way to make me feel good.

"Don't give up on me, Sage. I need you." His eyes looked haunted, but my heart just didn't care anymore. Maybe it never really did.

My phone chirped in my pocket, and Bren curiously watched me as I opened it and read the text message.

J: Big day tomorrow? Thinking 'bout you.

I rubbed my thumb over the screen. God, how much did it say about me that I couldn't care less about wanting to break up with Bren or leaving the shop, but my gut wrenched and my heart basically flipped its shit in my chest whenever I got one of my special texts?

"Who was that?" Bren asked gruffly.

Eff you, Bren. You've never earned the right to know. "Oh, it's just Goldilocks. She just got arrested, *again*, for burglary. Stupid kid."

"I'm serious," he said.

"Fine. It was the national children's book brigade; they just found Waldo."

"What the *hell* is wrong with you? Is it another man?"

"Truth? Prince Charming just texted me," I walked to the door and glanced back at him. "And he thinks I deserve my glass slipper back... Don't worry about my phone and my texts. Just spend some time helping yourself, Bren. Then, we'll see if we can make things work for us."

I walked through the door, leaving him standing there speechless, and I made damn sure I took all his freaking chocolate covered guilt with me.

By the time I climbed the back stairs to my apartment, alone, it was nine o'clock, and I was trembling with nerves. It wasn't the situation with Bren that had me on edge; it was the truth about what I would be doing the next day. Bren had no idea. He thought I was all talk, but I was actually scheduled to teach my first art history class in one of New York City's most prestigious art colleges; The School of Visual Arts.

My first class started at one o'clock in the afternoon. I was on the faculty, scheduled to teach two classes that semester. One, a lecture class for the history of tattoos, and the second was a studio class in theory and design. To say that I was scared *crapless* would be the biggest understatement of the century. I didn't want to put myself out there and fail; I wanted to shine and light up the sky like those fireflies all those years ago. My damn wings had been broken for far too long. I needed to learn how to fly again.

That next morning, bypassing all the chocolate-dipped goodness for breakfast, which was painfully hard, I ran through the shop to my studio. Still dressed in the small tank top and boy shorts I slept in, I attacked my punching bag and started hitting it as hard as I could, not even bothering with my gloves. I didn't care if anyone else was in the shop. I didn't care about anything but demolishing that bag.

A blinding rage took over as I hammered the bag with my bare fists. Bobbing and swaying to block invisible attackers (my demons), my fists pounded fast and strong against the thick canvas. For at least an hour, I fought. My muscles strained before they ached, and the skin of my knuckles burned and bled, until I dropped to the floor in surrender. Enraged, I blinked my teary eyes up at the ceiling and tried to get my breathing under control. I stayed on the floor until the anger drained from my body and seeped out of my pores in sweat and tears.

Thick drops of perspiration dripped off my skin as I stood up and thundered back into my apartment. It took all my strength not to devour all the chocolate in the place. I dumped everything in the trash and grabbed my phone, and thumbed through my contact list.

C: You there?

J: Always here for you.

C: I'm so damn scared about today.

J: Need to talk?

C: No just text. It's easier.

J: Yeah, for you.

C:!!!

J: Fine. Remember the first day we ever cut school and went to Rockaway Beach?

C: Yeah

J: You were terrified of the ocean

C: Effing ocean has slimy seaweed and jelly-effing-stingy-fish. Your point?

J: Feel me holding your hand?

J: Just jump.

Oh God.

It always killed me the way that he could make everything better. He always made everything better for me. Easier. Simpler. *Worth doing.* He never questioned my worth.

Just jump.

God, I wished I could just jump. Just jump and land right in front of him again, like nothing bad had ever happened.

🐚

AT FOURTEEN, I didn't understand what the big deal was about high school. To Joey, Jase, and me, high school sucked big, hairy moose ass. Maybe it was because of where we lived or the high school we attended, but it wasn't anything like the great time you read about in books.

It was like, well, *Dante's eighth ring of Hell*—a complete fraud and rip-off of everything I had read that high school *should have been.*

We went to John Adams High School in New York City. We took the public bus to get there, and then literally squashed ourselves into an overcrowded school with NO air conditioners. *Do you understand how horribly that could possibly smell?* No, I don't think you do.

Our textbooks were over thirty years old and so was the food in the cafeteria. The entire population of the student body, which was somewhere in the vicinity of 3,200 hormonal, sweaty teens, had to daily walk through metal detectors to get inside the front lobby of the school. Every ten minutes or so, students would randomly get patted down while they waited in line. Fun. Good times, I tell you.

Maybe it was the oppressiveness of the high school, or maybe it was what was going on with me at home, but I was a complete and utter disaster my freshman year. Okay, shut up, my whole high school career. We all can't be perky little cheerleaders, can we?

Honestly, I don't think my school even had cheerleaders. It didn't have much of anything, but science, math, and history. Even its art program lacked. Art was just an elective you had to take once in the four years you were there, and it consisted of drawing with broken bits of crayons and gossiping in class.

That summer before our ninth grade year started, Jase had to spend it in some sort of I'm-Gonna-Make-My-Kid-A-Lawyer camp that his father shoved down his throat. Joey and I hadn't seen him for four straight weeks, and we had seriously gone through Jase withdrawals. And that summer, Jase's father gave me the creeps. Every time I sunbathed on the roof of the tree house, I'd catch him watching me. Hell, once Joey and I even caught him with a pair of binoculars. We never told Jase; I didn't want him to hate his father even more. Joey and I hated him enough, anyway. When Jase wasn't around, we made up gruesome stories about horrifying ways his dad died. Of course, we never told those kinds of stories around Jase. It was his father. No matter how much Jase loathed him; it just wasn't right for us to agree with him. Even though we did. We so did.

Joey and I mostly hid in the tree house that summer and waited for Jase to come home. Everything was always fun with just Joey and me, but when Jase was around, things always seemed richer and fuller.

When the end of that summer came, he brought me home a pot-bellied pig. Who in the world got a pot-bellied pig from one of her best friends? *Me.* That's who! Jase supposedly saved it from a farm somewhere. At the time, all I thought was how very *Charlotte's Web* he was.

Joey? *He* got a dirty magazine. I, um, shared in the gawking and drooling of that too. I mostly giggled myself into a red-faced frenzy. Then later those nights, after the boys were long gone, I touched myself like a horn dog in that little special spot on my body that *Judy Blume* taught me about in *Deenie*. Again, need I remind you not to judge me? Because seriously, the hand reaches there for a reason and it's a good reason, too.

Anyway, I named my pig Bacon N. Eggs, and my mother cursed like a drunken trunk driver when I brought him into the house. I had Bacon N. Eggs for two weeks before my mother's newest paycheck, I mean *boyfriend*, was pissed off at me for something, and wanted me to be punished for speaking to him harshly.

I'm sorry, but when you ask a fourteen-year-old to, "Go get me a beer, baby, 'cuz I wanna watch those titties of yours bounce all the way back to me," when her mother isn't home, you should be prepared to be snapped at—teenage gangster style and all. The very next morning, after a huge fight between my mother and me about *my mouth* and *disrespecting my elders*, my pig was gone and *The Boyfriend* was cooking bacon and eggs in my kitchen, smiling like a damned, evil bastard. No, I don't think he was really frying up my damn pig, but the message was clear to me. Don't mess with him. I was devastated, but that was my life at home. Thank God, the majority of the time my mother just spent her time alone, asleep on the couch, with her eyes half-open, mostly comatose. I did my best to make sure that her cigarettes were put out while she slept, which allowed me to always have those little cancer sticks on hand to share with my best friends.

But when her boyfriends came around, in order for me to stay sane, I stayed in the tree house all the time and I read more books than I ever did.

Standing on the corner before first period on a hot, sunny, September day right after the pig-napping, I told my two best friends about Bacon N. Eggs, and the anger in both their expressions unsettled me. I knew they would never blame me, or be angry with me for anything my mother or her tribe of cavemen did, but I hated that I had upset them. I don't think that there was even a second of any day in our trio of friendship that any of us were ever *really* angry at each other. There wasn't anything ever bad between us, then. Yeah, all the darkness between our threesome comes later.

I was tense as hell as we walked into school, waiting in the line to get through the metal detectors. Jase and Joey both eyed me like they were afraid I would explode.

Then, one of the school safety officers pulled me out to pat me down. He was young and greasy looking, and I froze when he put his hands on me. His big hands slid down my sides, making sure his thumbs moved over my chest as he licked his lips. His eyes roamed hungrily over the front of my shirt, just like tons of other guys had since puberty smacked me in the chest. I cringed at the realization that my first feel up was with this loser, and I didn't even get a meal out of it.

"Hey, there, Officer Snapperhead, think that I got a gun or something hidden in my bra, or do you just want to lose both your arms?" I asked him, pushing myself away from him.

Jase grabbed my waist and walked me right back out the front door as he angrily eyed the jerk. Joey picked my book bag up off the floor and followed us.

Running his hand up my back and hanging his arm

heavily around my shoulders, Jase pulled me close. "Looks like a good day to cut classes, don't you think?"

Next to us, Joey matched our steps, looking up into the clear blue sky. "Yep. I see your logic in this situation, and I believe this calls for a vacation day."

Dorks.

I was sure glad they didn't mention what just happened. They always knew when I needed to talk about things and when I just wanted to pretend they didn't happen. No one knew me like those two did.

Jase squeezed my shoulder and nodded toward Joey, "And where would three extremely well-rounded misfits spend their vacation day?"

Joey's black hair flopped across his forehead as he leaned closer to me, "The Island of Misfit Toys?" He handed me back my bag.

"Too far," Jase chuckled. "But, it's definitely sunny enough for a day at the beach."

All it took was a two-minute walk to the subway station and a twenty-minute A-train ride across the waters of the Jamaica Bay to Rockaway Beach, and we had our beach vacation getaway.

That September day turned hot enough to go in the water, but I made my opinions about going into the ocean perfectly clear to both of them. I was scared of the things under the muck of the water: fish, seaweed, dead bodies held down with concrete blocks. Hey, this was New York, and I had seen a lot of mob movies, okay?

So instead of going into the water, we walked all the way down to the old pier that I always believed went half way across the ocean. Above us, the sky was a brilliant blue and only a dusting of feathery white clouds hovered almost invisibly over the horizon. "The ocean always looks so impossibly big to me."

Reaching out, Jase took my hand and entwined his fingers through mine. My heart beat a tiny bit faster and I turned toward him. The corners of his mouth lifted up in a stunning smile, "Nothing is too impossibly big to conquer." He leaned his head past me and eyed Joey, "What do you think?"

Joey reached out and grabbed my free hand and entwined his fingers in mine—the same way Jase had done.

Oh God, no.

"I say, let's just jump," he called.

And then, they were running, pulling me with them to the edge. They were both so strong and determined; I had no choice but move with them or fall flat on my face.

"No!" I screamed as we flew off the old wooden dock and jumped into the sky. Cold, salty water engulfed me and the sheer terror of what lay underneath the murky darkness with me caused me to kick and scream a profanity of bubbles into the pitch-blackness of the Atlantic Ocean.

As the taste of the bitter salt water filled my mouth, I felt both Jase and Joey's hands squeeze mine and tug me up. Gently, my body floated up through the rippling waves as my kicking and screaming stilled and complete awe and wonderment settled over me when I opened my eyes under the silent waters. Getting used to the stinging burn, I could see Jase and Joey with their goofy smiles and the sun hitting the surface of the water just above their heads, shining a halo over them like they were two angels.

Jase yanked my hand once more, and the three of us broke through the surface of the water laughing, gasping, and screaming. We swam back to shore, my legs kicking freely with my newfound accomplishment of conquering the scary unknown. Joey, of course, Mr. Captain of the swim team, reached the beach first and lay out on the wet sand with his arms behind his head.

Jase and I stumbled over each other, his dripping wet

body landing across mine. "Not so scary after all, huh?" he panted, taking his hands and softly tucking my wet hair behind my ear. His chest rose and fell heavily against mine, from the exertion of the swim.

The touch was such an intimate gesture that the trail of where his fingertips touched my skin tingled, and my heart hammered hard against the inside of my chest.

I tried to compose my thoughts into complete sentences, but all I could do was stare at his lips and wish I were back in Ava Marie's laundry room, so I could have another excuse to kiss my best friend.

The back of his knuckles rubbed over my cheeks, until his thumb softly touched my lips, "Well?" he whispered, his eyes focused intensely on mine.

I smiled shyly, terrified of the words that wanted to come out of my mouth. "I'm not scared of anything with you and Joey by my side, Jase Delaney."

Joey snuggled up in the wet sand next to us. The waves of the Atlantic lapped against our wet sneakers. "That was awesome, but I don't think we really thought it through. Like, how are we going to take the train home soaking wet?" he chuckled.

Jase lifted his eyes off mine and splashed the water that pooled around us into his lap, "You worry too much about shit," Jase said.

I laughed at the both of them, "Yeah, you guys both need to be more worried about how I will extract my sweet, sweet revenge for making me jump in the ocean."

Oh, and I did get my revenge too. In the sweetest way possible: dessert. You see, after spending the day lying in the sun and drying off our clothes, only to get thrown into the ocean once again, we took the A-train back into our neighborhood, dripping went. Walking from the train station to our houses, I said goodbye to the boys and made my way to a small deli. With squeaky wet sneakers and with the very last of my money, I bought a few ingredients to assist in my payback prank: a five pound bag of large sweet onions ($3.49), a jar of sweet caramel ($2.59), and a box of crafty ice-pop sticks for ($2.29). The sweet revenge of watching your best friends bite into the crunchy nastiness of a caramel onion thinking it was a caramel apple: PRICELESS.

❀

As THE ECHOES of my own giggles snapped me back into my reality, I hugged my phone to my chest, reveling in the sweet memory of being young. I missed being fourteen, and I missed my boys. My boys.

I texted a final thank you.

C: Thank you. You always say what I need to hear.

J: What about your husband and kids?

Don't make a strange, confused face reading his last text. Yes, he thinks I have a husband. And yes, I added in two kids and a cat for good measure. YES, it's a lie. Shut up. I told you not to judge me, yet. Don't call me a bitch, either. Because, I'm really not and if I could have any wish granted, it would simply be to never, never be apart from Joey or Jase.

But life happens and lies had to be told.

C: My husband and children never pushed me into the ocean.

J: Yeah, that's what you're going with?

C: Shut up

J: Lemme know how it goes.
C: You bet

Jumping up with a newer outlook, I ran the shower and started getting ready for my class.

As always, no matter how long I showered or primped or tried to pretty myself, I was never *ready*. I was never comfortable enough in my skin to be *ready*.

For the third time, I looked at myself in the mirror, and again smoothed down the material of my pencil skirt, erasing the non-existent wrinkles I worried would pop up. I slid my blazer on. Grumbling, I pulled it back off. Looking through my closet I groaned, grabbing the same blazer and shrugging it back on, turning in the mirror. I ripped it off and chucked it across the room. Maybe Bren was right. Professor? Who the Hell was I kidding? What the eff was wrong with me?

The fourth time I looked at my reflection, I threw my toothbrush at it and stuck out my tongue. I was 5' 1" and I wished...I wished I was one of those characters in a book that was 5' 8" and beautiful and perfect and tan and skinny and well, I'm just *not*. I'm real. I have stretch marks, cellulite, freckles, and I wear glasses; I'm like a frumpy librarian with a dirty imagination. I always have split ends, *let's not even talk about how big my ass is,* and as I stared at myself (still sticking out my tongue) I felt a lot like a little insecure kid and not at all like a professor in a college.

I ended up wearing the damned blazer, but leaving it open and letting the soft pink, silky, sleeveless shirt underneath show. Breathlessly, I caught a cab to East 23rd street before I could vomit all over myself.

The cab ride was short, just across town, but I sat in the back seat a frenzied, sweaty, nervous bundle of energy. I was excited and terrified. And in my heart, just as I always did when things were hard to deal with, I leaned back against the cool leather of the seats and imagined Joey and Jase on both sides of me.

The cab got there way too quickly.

Stupid cab driver.

I blinked my eyes closed for a few moments and inhaled deeply.

Then, I *just jumped.*

When I stepped out onto the sidewalk and looked up at the building, a legion of butterflies proudly swooped deep in my belly. I felt a smile tug at my lips, because *I could do this.* I could *jump.* I graduated from here, and they asked *me* to teach for *them.* I *could* do this.

Walking through the lobby of the school, the chemical smell of turpentine and thick, rich, oil paint hung faintly in the air. God, I *loved* that smell.

My heels clicked softly over the floors as I walked the expanse of the main lobby. Bright, white walls were graced with the brilliant oil and acrylic paintings of the most talented fine arts students in the city. I felt like I was home.

After greeting the faculty and mindlessly chatting with the president and others, I finally made my way into a small classroom to set up a projector and my slide presentation. Then nervously, I dimmed the lights down low.

At exactly one o'clock, the last of my fifteen students strolled through the door and quietly took a seat. I breathed in deep at the sight of the handful of students who gazed up at me with eager eyes.

I am not going to throw up.

I'm not going to throw up.

It's just talking to people.

About art.

My stomach rolled, and I smiled and started talking before I could think any more about throwing up. "I always thought art history was a boring class, unless it was your major, and I know this is just an elective for most of you. I fell asleep so many times in the seats you're in right now, but I'm hoping to change that a bit..."

Then, I began my presentation. The music started; their eyes widened and smiles grew. And *I knew* that I would be great at this. The fear of throwing up dissipated, and the excitement of the music, the pictures, and discussions, sent me into a wild, passionate high.

By the end of the day, after teaching both of my classes and eating in the lounge with a handful of excited students, the president of the college, Professor Lanes, asked me into his office.

My heart rate sped up, because I was well aware that he had slipped in to watch both of my classes and stayed until the very end. He also watched me eat dinner and discuss a dozen or so things that had to do with the current art world.

After the meeting, I decided to walk back to my apartment, and by the time I reached the corner of 23rd Street and 3rd Avenue, I had tears in my eyes. Within twenty minutes after the end of my studio class, I was moved to the amphitheater for the remainder of my lectures and the largest studio for my theory and design class. One hundred students had transferred into my class upon hearing about my lecture and who I was. The President of the college had never been so impressed by such a young teacher before. He asked me to think about teaching more classes for the next semester.

When I reached Fourth Avenue, I took out my phone and typed out a text.

C: I. DID. AWESOME!

J: Never doubted it. Going into work. Have a good night.

C: Stay Safe.

J: Always.

When I got home I leaned against my kitchen island and sighed.

I was completely alone. There was no one to share this amazing feeling with. The only three people in the world who would have cared about this (Joey, Jase, and Auburn) were no longer in my life. It was a sad, lonely fact that I knew I needed to change.

Determined to somehow celebrate this accomplishment of mine, I searched the cabinets for some ingredients and mixed myself a Mad Hatter shot, *a large one*, and drank it down.

Alone.

I heard the apartment door slam open before I saw Bren walk through. His eyes surveyed my small apartment until he found me cuddled up on my Lazy-Boy reading a book and gave me a smirk. "Still here? Your Prince Charming forget to rescue you out of the tower, Princess?" He kicked the door shut behind him, stumbled onto my couch, and kicked off his shoes.

His eyes looked cloudy and faraway. Damn it. He was messed up again. "Are you on something right now, Bren?"

Waving his hands at me, he gave me those stupid duck lips, "Don't get all motherly, I just had a few drinks, nothing else." Then, he shrugged. "I just wanna feel good. Don't you ever want to feel good again, Sage?"

"I feel fine."

"That's bullshit, Charlotte, you're more fucked in the head than me," he challenged, surprising me by using my real name—something he never did. He leaned forward, his bloodshot eyes blazing straight into mine. "You of all people know you can't pretend to be something you're not. You're always gonna end up where you belong. If you were born trailer trash, that's where you belong."

"I wasn't born in a trailer, Bren."

"I'm being rhetorical, Sage. Trash is trash, no matter how much you pretty it up."

"I think that's a crappy way to look at people. People can overcome the horrible hand they've been dealt in life," I argue, feeling no fight in me at all.

"Sure, keep telling yourself that."

"I do, every day."

But his words *did* cut me.

And just like everything good that happened in my life, there seemed to be some black cloud that hovered over me, waiting until the best time to rain down on me. Reminding me who I really was, where I came from, and all the shit I've lived through that was threatening to whip my emotions up into a storm of insecurity, pain, and heartache.

Just like the day we conquered the ocean. Just like the day we jumped into my fear.

The black cloud hung over our shoulders, not yet close enough for us to see it.

The day after our vacation getaway to the beach, Joey had swim practice after school and told Jase and me to meet him down by the pool after last period. Jase had a lab that day, so I knew he would be late.

Joey and three other boys were doing laps as I walked in. The humid chlorine smell immediately caused my eyes to burn and walloped me with a sneezing attack.

Carefully, I walked up to the side of the pool and got

Joey's attention by making seal sounds and clapping my hands at him like an idiot. Fourteen and idiot seemed to go hand in hand.

The shock of the cold drops of water he splashed at me caused me to yelp. He called me a string of silly names, which made me and the other swimmers laugh, until we heard the loud bang of the poolroom's door.

"Well, well, well," a deep voice echoed against the silence of the walls. Slate Marshall and a gang of wannabe-*Goodfella-guidos*, filed into the room. "If it isn't little Miss Hottie Stone," Slate sauntered over closer to me, licking his lips disgustingly.

I tilted my head to the side. "You got something wrong with your lips, Marshall? You keep licking them."

"I always loved your smart mouth, Charlie, and one day I'm going to shove my dick in it and you're going to suck me dry."

"I'm not too worried, Slate. I'm sure I wouldn't even realize it was there, because you're dick's so small."

"Get out of the pool, fags. I don't want any of you eyeing my dick in my swim trunks and getting all hot over me," Slate yanked off his shirt and stood there, flexing his muscles. God, he was huge, intimidatingly huge, *and watching me*. He pecked a kiss on his biceps and winked, "Like what you see?"

I gagged.

The three other students who had been swimming laps with Joey climbed silently out of the pool, quickly grabbed a few towels, and ran for the lockers.

Damn, I hoped they were getting the stupid coach.

Joey slowly made his way out behind his teammates, but stayed by the edge of the pool across from me. I knew he wouldn't leave me alone in here with Slate and his minions.

Spiky-gelled-haired-stupid-guido #1 walked behind me,

and Joey's eyes flared with anger. *Crap on a guido, I wish Jase was here.* I glanced up at the clock above the door; his lab was over two minutes ago. Where the heck was he?

Spiky-gelled-haired-stupid-guido #2 walked behind Joey and without warning, shoved him hard into the pool.

"Leave him alone, you piece of shit!" I screamed, moving closer to the edge of the pool.

"Hey, baby, we're just having a little fun is all," Guido #1 said as he grabbed me around the front of my chest and yanked me away from the pool.

I watched in horror as the rest of the guidos dove into the pool and swam for Joey. Slate stood at the edge and goaded them on.

"Let me go, or you're going to be sorry," I calmly told the son of a bitch behind me.

The idiot behind me laughed and held me tighter.

Joey was too fast for the greasy guidos, and he made it to the ladder. Must have been all that hair gel that made them all too slow. But, Slate was there to cut him off and shove him back in, slamming his body on top of him and pushing Joey under the water.

I could see Joey's arms and legs ferociously kicking and flailing and struggling to get free as Slate held him under and laughed.

"Let him go!" I screamed. He was going to drown him!

Instantly, my arms reached up, one grabbed the collar of the jerk behind me, the other took hold of the arms that he had tight around my neck. Pushing my jaw into the crease of his elbow, I whispered, "Goodnight, big boy," and did a perfect *ippon sainagi.* Kneeling and rolling forward, I threw the dumbass guido through the air and face first into the hard, tiled floor. He landed with a glorious wet smack, so loud it caused all the guidos to stop and stare at me.

No one but me saw Jase walk into the poolroom.

I lunged at Slate's arms, sliding along the wet edge of the pool, as Jase dove into the pool towards us.

Clawing at Slate's arms to free Joey until he finally let him go, Joey broke through the surface of the water sputtering and coughing.

Frantically, I yanked him over the side at the same time Jase caught up to us and helped me push him up and lay him flat on the ground.

I felt the tears spill out over my face, watching Joey throw up pool water, while desperately gasping for air, and I clung to his heaving chest, sobbing loudly.

The coach was beside us in seconds, and the school safety officers were pulling the sick guido pieces of shit out of the water.

They brought us to the main office and called Joey's mother and the police. I still clung to him. We sat shivering, soaking wet, until they brought towels and wrapped us both together to try to stop our bodies from shaking.

Jase sat in front of us on the wooden chairs of the office and silently watched us. His eyes never left us. They scanned back and forth over Joey and me, wide and angry, over and over.

By six o'clock that evening, Slate Marshall and the other four students involved in the attack were expelled from the school and brought up on charges. The words were said to me, and my statement was asked, but I couldn't focus on anything but holding Joey.

Even when we were driven home, they couldn't pry me off him.

That night, Jase and I took Joey back to the beach, and the three of us just sat silently watching the waves lap against the sand. We stayed and watched the sunset and looked out on the cold dark ocean we conquered just the day before. I could distinctly remember sitting there, the gritty sand against my skin, the smell of salty water, and thinking that one day soon the tide was going to come in and wash my friends and my life away from me, sweeping them all out to sea...

As the memory faded and I sat across from a passed-out Bren, I knew that I needed to go visit Joey. It had been too long since I was near him; he always had the ability to ease my heart without ever having to say a word. Then, maybe I could figure out what it was I needed to do with the rest of my life.

Because every time there was
Something good in my life,
It was always overshadowed
By the bad.

JASE

*B*rooke was in the locker room changing in front of everybody. The command didn't have separate rooms for us, and nobody ever gave a shit, but now she was using it to her advantage. She had an audience of men watching her taking off those painted on yoga pants she wore. Then, for good measure, to make a solid point, she bent over dramatically to pick up something out of the bottom of her locker. She even pretended to look around a bit, waving her ass with its lacy little panties in the air for the whole damn precinct to see.

She was playing some stupid mind game and trying to get me jealous; I snorted out a laugh and turned my back on her, letting her put on her show for whomever she wanted. I didn't care what she did. I threw my belongings in my locker, jammed my Glock in its holster, and left without her ever realizing it. She was too caught up in her "Brooke" show to even notice. Forget *that mess*. I'm a grown man; I don't play stupid high school games. *Well,* unless we're talking about naked Twister or something like that; I'm *always* up for those games.

I was only ever jealous with one girl.

I was only jealous when it came to Charlie.

🐚

EVEN WHEN WE were fifteen and all my thoughts were clouded with Charlie, the loser I was still hadn't told her how I felt. We were sophomores in high school. Both of us had a few dates with other people, but nothing serious ever happened with them.

Then spring came, and with it came the blossoming of hard-ons for every teenage boy in the vicinity of any girl, anywhere, but especially anywhere near, or around, Charlotte Stone. Hell, even the mention of her name or the thought of her in a T-shirt...

I watched Joey as he scanned the field for Charlie. His eyes widened when he saw that jerk, Mason LeDoux, talking to her. Yeah, it made my damn gut twist up, but what the hell was I going to do? All the guys in the whole damn school seemed to have it bad for her—except for Joey. He was immune to Charlie. It baffled me that he didn't spring wood every time she walked in a room. Everyone else did, and there was no way I could stop them all. And believe me, I wanted to. I even threatened a few, *but don't tell Charlie that.*

"Jase, you better step up your game and stop the stalling," Joey said, giving me a hard shove to the shoulder. "Mason LeDoux looks like he wants to eat *your* dinner."

"Shut up, Joey." I gave him a glare and a harder shove back.

"You shut up, Jase. You have had it so bad for her for so many years and now you're just going to hand Mason your girl?" He tossed me the basketball we'd been doing drills with in PE class as we watched Mason *La Douche* making time with my Charlie, *my girl.*

"I got it covered," I mumbled, bouncing the ball back at him, knowing full well I didn't have anything covered when it came to Charlie. "And you should talk! You've had a hard-on for Ava Marie since you felt her up at her thirteenth birthday party, but you can't even say 'hello' to her without turning all green."

His eyes narrowed and he hurled the ball back at me, slamming me in the side of the head with it, hard. I loved this kid like he was my brother but, damn! I could kill him some days. He always knew how I felt about Charlie, but the last few weeks he'd been giving me crap about it, calling me out on it, saying I needed to make my move before it was too late. The night before, he even went as far as unscrewing all the handles on every one my drawers, so that all my stuff fell all over the place when I opened them. Then, thinking he was so clever, he told me to *go get a handle on my love life.* So, after that, I flipped him on the floor and did a full nelson on him.

The problem was, I had too much crap going on in my head, and I was freaking the hell out about telling Charlie. I couldn't lose my best friend. That girl knew everything about me. She was my *anchor.* If I lost her... Just the thought of it made me feel like I was just going to die—or float away.

She was my family. She was my home.

It had gotten to the point where my father was never home, which was perfect for me, since then he couldn't tell me what a "waste of life I was" or call me by my favorite nickname he'd coined endearingly for me, "useless piece of shit." The man even set up a twenty-four-nurse service to take care of my mother; I swear I think he was screwing every damn nurse that came there. I had no clue how my old man's dick wasn't dribbling with pus and falling the hell off. I wished it would. I would've served him right.

It didn't matter to me, though; I didn't care about what

happened at home, anymore. There's only so many times you can try to help someone get out of a situation, like my mother, who refused to speak to anyone now. I just stayed the hell away. It worked for me—for them—for everyone.

Besides, it gave me more of an excuse to be with Charlie. Most nights, Charlie slept in the tree house just to get away from the pervy eyes of her mother's boyfriends. Jesus, that woman had a lot of them, too. Whenever I saw Charlie's little drawing light on, I'd sneak out my back door, climb up my garage, jump over, and sleep by her side all night.

She had to know how I felt about her, right? I mean, what guy would go to all that trouble to sleep next to a chick? And I do mean *sleep.*

Charlie waved goodbye to Mason and started walking toward us. Mason's gaze dropped to her ass and then the jerk adjusted his dick through his pants. I wouldn't have been surprised if he whipped it out and started losing his shit right on the field, while watching her ass sway as she walked away. Hell, I jerked off to Charlie every day. I kept a bunch of pictures of her in my nightstand, and I have one amazing video of her walking around in her little white bikini that I loved so much. I swear to you, when that tiny piece of material on a string was wet, you saw right through it. Yeah, I watched that video every damn day.

"Hey, guys. Wassup?" she grinned.

"Hey," I croaked, my voice cracking like I was twelve again. God, I was such a mess around her.

Joey, again, shoved me on the shoulder. Hard.

"What the hell, dude?" I snapped.

"Oh, sorry," he smirked at me and laughed. "I thought I'd try to push some sense into you, chicken shit." He turned to Charlie before I could say something back to him, "So what's up with that Mason dude? Your heads were stuck pretty close together."

"Yeah, he just asked me to that spring fling dance next week."

"*What?* What did you say to him?" I spat. A sudden burning sensation surged across my chest. *She said "no" to him, right?*

"Um, I said 'yes.' Girls like to get asked out to dances, you idiots. And I need the both of you to come to the mall with me on Saturday to help me find a dress," The girl was actually bouncing on the balls of her feet. *She was excited about this?*

"The hell I am," I snapped back, that burning feeling traveled down into my stomach and twisted in my gut.

"Yes. You. Are." She held her hands on her hips and smiled that beautiful smile at me, the one that raked at my insides. "You're both guys and know what guys think, so I'd like your opinion on a dress, okay. *Please*, Jase." Her long eyelashes batted at me. "This is my first real dance, guys. I don't want to mess it up."

Damn, she was going to kill me if she went with another guy. "Charlotte Stone, you could go to that dance with mud from head to toe, and you'd still be the prettiest girl there."

Her smile got even wider. "Thanks, Jase. But I wish you guys were coming with me too. Too bad you both can't dance."

Joey and I looked at each other, "Oh, hell girl. We can dance," Joey went all drag queen on us, pulling his shirt up over his head like it was long hair. Laughing loudly, we both started dancing around her, Joey busting out with the Charlie Brown dance and me doing the Airplane and dry humping her leg. She covered her mouth, giggling.

Mason was squinting his eyes in our direction, grimacing.

I stopped dancing and hunched down in front of Charlie, like I always did when we were messing around, and winked at her, "Come on, Charlie, hop on. I'll give you a ride back into school." I flipped Mason the finger as he watched us.

She jumped on my back and wrapped her legs around my waist as I carried her past the field and track, back into the building. I even tried carrying her right through the doors to the girls' locker room, but Ms. Hart, the girl's PE coach, stopped me.

Mason walked in behind us, smoke coming out of his ears, nostrils flaring. *Ha-ha, loser.*

The day dragged on after that. Seventh period literature was the last class of the day where Joey and Charlie usually sat on either side of me.

As soon as he walked in the classroom, Joey had this pissed off look on his face. Joey was always smaller than the rest of the kids we went to school with, and I guess that's probably why he was teased so damn much by the bigger dudes. Lately though, he was getting huge. He walked in the damn classroom and looked like some kind of menacing maniac, eyes all serious, demanding my attention. He had to be about 5' 11" now, almost up to my 6', and all the swimming and lifting weights we'd both been doing was transforming him into a monster. I was damn proud of him.

"Dude, you look all *Silence of the Lambs,* Hannibal Lecter; what the hell? You look like you're going to disembowel someone," I said, trying to ease his visible anger.

He gave me a hard glare and collapsed into the seat next to me. Leaning forward, he poked me hard in the arm, "I wouldn't have to feel like I wanted to make a skin suit out of somebody, if it weren't for your chicken shittedness."

Slapping his finger away from my arm, I deadpanned, "One, screw off. Two, Buffalo Bill was the sick freak who did that—NOT Hannibal. Three, shittedness is not a word and four, screw off again. Now, tell me what the hell is going on."

Joey threw his pen at me. "That Mason dude has been

walking Charlie to every one of her classes today. Plus, he asked her to hang out with him tonight at the weeds to watch him race his bike." He threw another pen at me, smacking me right in the head with it. "She said *'yes'* They're going out."

"Are you kidding me?" *The weeds* was an area that cut off our neighborhood from the waters of the Jamaica Bay. It was an expanse of land about a mile long, with dirt tracks that the neighborhood kids rode their dirt bikes on, without getting in any trouble from the cops. It was also filled with giant ragweed, taller than me, and at the farthest end of it was a rocky beach that we sometimes built campfires on at night.

I watched his gaze move toward the door. Nudging his head to make me look in the same direction, "Check it out for yourself."

There stood Charlie, clutching a handful of books to her chest, laughing at something Mason was dribbling on about. The whole scene cut me. My stomach churned and I jumped up out of my seat like a fool, making the whole desk tip over and crash to the floor. *Damn it.*

Charlie's full, pink lips smiled at me, and I wanted to immediately rip Mason's head off his body, thinking he might have touched them.

She gave Mason a wave goodbye and placed her books on the desk next to my fallen one. "Are you okay? Desk attack?"

Joey chuckled next to me. "More like a heart attack."

"Shut up, Joey," I hissed and looked at her. Damn, she was so pretty that it hurt. "I heard you're going to the weeds tonight? With Mason *La Douche.*"

Her eyebrows furrowed. "Yeah, *Mason LeDoux* asked me to. He said you guys should come, too. Didn't you say you were going racing tonight?" she asked, sitting down in the seat, her fingertips touching the edge of her books like they were some kind of shield for her.

"Well, I'm glad I got *Mason's* permission to go. And what the hell? He's walking you to every class now?"

She looked up at me with those deep green eyes, and I wanted to die. "Yeah, he just did it all day today. Why? What am I missing?" Her eyes assessed mine, looking for answers I didn't even understand the questions for. "Are you okay, Jase?"

"Yeah, Charlie. I'm fine," I said. "It's just that he should be holding your books for you when he walks you to class," I mumbled, grabbing my books off the floor. "I gotta get out of here...I'm going home. I feel like crap. See you later."

So, like a coward, I left. I didn't even take the bus; I walked and walked, and then after two hours, I went home. Like an even bigger coward, I walked through my front door with tears in my eyes. I was fifteen and my heart was crushed; it just never occurred to me that Charlie might like *someone else*. I just kind of thought she'd always be *mine*.

My mother was sitting in her chair in the living room watching soap operas; she was the biggest cliché of all mothers, I swear. She didn't say anything to me, just pulled her brows together, questioningly.

Her caretaker, Vicky, walked out of the kitchen holding a cup of coffee, sipping at it. "Hello, sweetie. How was your day?" She wore a tight, white blouse that was cut so low that her chest looked about ready to burst out. Her "skirt" barely covered her ass. She had my mother's diamond necklace around her neck with way too much make-up and way too high heels on for just being a caretaker.

What the hell?

I looked to my mother, who was squeezing her eyes shut tight, then back at Vicky.

"Did you just call me 'sweetie'?" I snapped.

"Yes, sorry. I guess you're too old for that, huh?" She

waved her hands in the air at me and giggled. "So, *Jase*...Your dad will be home soon. Will you be joining us for dinner?"

I'm in the freaking Twilight Zone.

I looked back at my mother again. "Is everybody in this house crazy? Is she actually wearing your necklace and dressed like a prostitute for a reason?"

Vicky started to interrupt me, but I cut her off. "I want to speak to my mother alone, *now*."

She cleared her throat and placed her coffee cup down on one of the tables next to the couch. The rim was stained with deep red lip prints. "Fine. I'll just be in the kitchen preparing dinner for your dad. If your mother needs me, you know where to find me."

I watched her walk out of the room and my head snapped back to my mother's embarrassed face. "Are you going to talk to me today? You wanna tell me what's going on?"

She blinked her eyes slowly and bowed her head, making a few strands of her hair fall in front of her eyes. Knowing she could barely use the muscles in her arms to lift her hands and sweep her hair from her face, I did it for her. She was so helpless that my heart ached. *I hated my father for what he'd done to her.*

"One of your father's many replacements for me, Jase. You know how he is," she whispered with a quivering lip.

"Don't put up with his shit. I'll get you out of here," I said.

"No."

"What? You *like* being the victim?"

"Jase, you will never understand. Not until you love someone more than you love yourself," she whispered.

"That's sick. You're sick. He's sick. And that nut in the kitchen is sick."

The front door slammed closed and my father's voice was a deep, low threat that slid over my skin. "Get away from your mother, and don't ever talk to her like that again."

Oh look, the jerk who thinks he's *God* is home.

"What? It's okay for you to disrespect her with your words, your cheating, and your fists, but I can't try to *help* her?"

He swallowed the distance between us in two huge steps, and I stilled myself to stand up to him and lifted my eyes to meet his ice-cold stare. His eyes were the same messed up whitish-blue as mine, and I hated that I looked anything like him. I hated anything that had to do with him. I knew what kind of evil he had inside him; that asshole is the reason my mother *was in* her wheel chair.

He swung hard and fast, knocking the air right out of my lungs with one quick punch to my chest. As soon as he pulled back for another swing, I blocked his hand and clocked him in the jaw. He tumbled backward with wide disbelieving eyes; I had never hit him back, *ever*.

Lunging at me, he struck me hard again—landing two jabs at my eye. My vision blurred instantly, and I quickly used my arm to wipe the warm drops of blood that fell down the side of my face. He took that reprieve to jab another two lightning fast punches, to my mouth this time, splitting it open. The taste of my own blood made me furious. He came at me one more time, but I blocked the advance and foot-swept him, making him crash hard to the floor.

I stepped over him, grabbed my helmet, and ran out the back door, slamming it hard behind me. I ran into the garage, gripped my dirt bike by the handlebars, and pushed it through the double doors. My father stood at the back door of the house, leaning against the doorframe, smiling. He was *smiling* at me.

"It's about time you learned to be a man," he mumbled.

"You are one sick son of a bitch," I said back, making my way out into the street with my bike. With my right foot, I jumped on the kick-start, bringing the engine to life, and without letting it warm up, sped away. I didn't even put the helmet on until I reached the corner of my street, and then slammed my visor down.

I rode like a demon through the streets to the end of the neighborhood where the weeds were. I didn't even stop for stop signs. I was too angry, and I was too reckless—that's how I always was. I never thought about the consequences for anything. And yeah, I thought about riding fast, head first into a brick building or off the Cross-Bay Bridge, flipping over my handlebars and dying some crazy-ass death. That's how pissed off I was. Don't you dare tell me that you've never thought crap like that, either! It's a human reaction, and we're not freaking *robots. Although I wished like Hell I was one, because then my heart wouldn't be aching so much. I could just shut myself off. Unplug myself so I could feel nothing.*

I rode my way down through the high weeds, along the dirt trail we all raced through, and over the sand to the beach. My red and black Baja Dirt Runner 125-motocross bike was the latest gift from Dear Old Dad after I walked in on him busting his nuts in the first woman he hired to take of my mother. I guess that was his way of bribing me to keep my mouth shut. I took the bike, but I didn't keep his secrets. I anonymously called the nursing service she worked for and got her fired, then told my mother. But again, my mother didn't mind, she already *knew*. Some people like living in Woe-Is-Me-Land, gives them a sense of worth—*being other people's doormats.*

Making my way over the rocky terrain, I searched for friendly faces. There were four other guys on bikes, revving their engines, just waiting for me to join them.

When I saw Charlie and Mason standing next to each other, I almost lost it. With everything that had just gone down, I'd forgotten what I was originally pissed off about. Staring at her, I realized I was spiraling into crazed territory.

Charlie had on a pair of low-rise jeans with torn knees and a tight white Avenged Sevenfold T-shirt that made her rack look un-freaking-believable. Her hair fell loose around her shoulders—her bangs cut long, letting her gorgeous green eyes play peek-a-boo behind her black-framed glasses. Charlie must have gone out of her way to dress herself up, because even her nails were painted a shiny black. Fuck, I could even tell her lips were painted with her favorite watermelon flavored lip gloss.

Mason was standing too close to her, and I didn't like the way she looked up at him. I revved my bike, and her eyes met mine through my visor. Her smile was genuine. I peeled out, and my tires crunched over the rocks and gravel onto the sand and dirt track to the starting line.

Was I finally losing my girl?

The race was about to start and my heart thudded hard in my chest. They had some freshman I never saw before waving the flag to start us off. We never raced for money or anything; we just raced for fun and did lots of daredevil freestyle jumps and stuff.

The second the flag was down, I popped a wheelie and took off like a rocket.

I flew past Joey, who leaned against his dirt bike with his arms crossed, scowling toward Mason. I mean, *damn it*, I didn't even know she liked Mason like that. And, she never once mentioned it to either of us that she wanted to go to a *dance*.

Other riders, who joined the track with me, tried to catch up, and I just tore ass and blew them all away. Five laps later, I crossed the finish line and didn't stop. Racing up the ramp to the beach, I sailed through the air and landed perfectly on the sand, blowing dust up everywhere. I heard the kids behind me screaming and whooping, but all I could think about was Mason standing next to *my girl*.

Wanting just a few minutes alone, I sped down the beach.

I was staring out over the water at the setting sun when Charlie and Joey tapped my helmet. *Mason* was with them, too. The little butt-munch.

I took my helmet off to talk to them, not thinking about how they'd react when they saw my face...I felt the swelling of my eye. I tasted the blood from my lips. I knew how bad I looked.

"Holy crap, Jase! What happened to your face?" Charlie yelled, shoving Mason out of the way to get to me. Joey was right behind her. She had her hands (God, those hands I dreamt about touching me) on my face, so soft and gentle against my skin. I had no choice but to lean into her and rub my cheek against the palm of the hand.

I shrugged my shoulders like I didn't look like I went for a round with a heavyweight champion, and lost. "Had a little tussle, that's all."

Charlie's eyes watered and her face twisted into a grimace as she ran her thumb over the cut on my lip. It took everything in me not to dart my tongue out and lick her. Mason *La Douche* walked up right beside her. "Whoa, Delaney. Who beat your ass?" Then he *laughed*. See how *La Douche* fits him better that LaDoux?

I ignored him and just kept my eyes on Charlie's. Her soft fingertips were doing a number on my insides. And, I sure as heck wanted them on other parts of my body. "Hey, Charlie. You wanna go for a ride?" I whispered, fiddling with the gearshift, revving my engine after my question.

"Charlie came here with *me*, Delaney."

I leveled my eyes on him, "Did I ask you who she came here with, Peckerbreath?" I had to hand it to the idiot; he only flinched a little. Most guys get one look at my eyes and back off. I was impressed, but I was still jealous as all hell. I

146

was actively plotting out ways to bury his body so no one would find all the pieces.

"Jase," Charlie whispered, stepping back and squinting her eyes at me.

"Fine, fuck off then," I croaked, and I peeled out, kicking up dust and sand in my wake as I sped away.

Ah, crap. What the hell did I just do? I never spoke to Charlie like that, well, not since I moved next door to her, and she stared at me with those impossibly beautiful green eyes and I threatened her life. I was *nine*; I didn't have a clue about how to act when I saw a pretty girl. All I knew then is that she made my heart race.

Skidding down along the beach, I rode through the wet sand, probably ruining my tires, but I didn't give a flying monkey's uncle about that. Everything inside of me felt twisted and wrong. The wind blowing past my face felt thick and pasty, making it harder and harder to breathe. My heart started beating out of control and my skin felt weird; all tingly and raw.

After a few minutes of pushing the limits of my bike, I saw a lone headlight behind me. In the twilight that had settled over the beach, the bright light came up from behind me, fast and steady. I heard the rev of the engine over mine as the rider tried to gain on me. I shifted into a lower gear and pressed my bike to move faster.

The pursuer continued after me, matching every jump I took and met my speed. Holy Hell, it was like the damn *Ghostrider*. From the corner of my eye, I could see the shiny white skull and crossbones that only decorated Joey's bike and mine. When I realized it was my best friend, I skidded to a stop, with the bike sliding out from underneath me.

Joey swerved, sliding his bike in a circle to face me and stopped in a spray of dirt and water. Jumping off his bike, he yanked off his helmet and threw it to the ground. The silhouette of long, gorgeous hair bounced free, and I couldn't catch my breath.

Pulling the helmet slowly from my head, I watched her form walk toward me. "What the hell was *that? You could have killed yourself driving like that! What are you, nuts?*" I yelled, falling to my knees on the cold, wet sand.

"You're the one who's freaking nuts, Jase Delaney! Why did you ride off like that?" she yelled, kneeling in front of me.

"Yeah, well I asked if you wanted to go for a ride," I mumbled.

"Yeah, Jase, then you told me to *EFF* off. You need *another* butt kicking? Because I think the one you got handed today, from God only knows who, looks bad enough," Then, before I could say another word, her fingers were on my lips again and skating softly across my cheeks to survey the damage.

"Is he your boyfriend now, Charlie?" my voice croaked.

Her eyes shined with tears, "You got the crap beat out of you, your face is covered with blood, and you're asking me if Mason is my *boyfriend?*"

"Yep. Now you know where my priorities lie."

"Jase. Come on, tell me what happened to you," she pleaded.

"My father."

"Crap, Jase, really?"

And then, she pulled me into her arms, and I held onto her tightly, breathing her in. Her hands were hypnotizing and instantly calmed my rage as she raked them gently through my hair, staying there with me on the gritty rock and sand until the sounds of the races faded and everybody left.

We found Joey a while later and the three of us walked the bikes home. I didn't let her go back to find Mason; she didn't even mention him, anyway. And my dad, he pretended like nothing had happened.

That weekend, Charlie dragged Joey and me for a forty-minute bus ride to get to the Queens Center Mall to search for the *perfect friggin' dress.*

The old prissy-ass saleslady led us to the back of the shop and sat us on these deep, red, lounge chairs, where she promptly told us to remove our drinks and walked away, grabbing tons of fru-fru stuff off hangers. Taking all the dresses in one hand, she threw them to Charlie in the fitting room in front of us.

"What the heck just happened?" Joey whispered.

I shrugged, "I don't know, but..." I pointed toward the fitting room doors and gave him a huge smile, "Charlie's getting *undressed* right behind *that* door." I sipped on my drink loudly. There was no way I was throwing it away just because the old hag thought she could tell me what to do.

Joey whipped his head around from the door to me and smirked, "Yes, Jase. Charlie *is* getting *undressed* right behind *that* door to get a *DRESS* to go with *ANOTHER GUY* to a dance!" Then, he shoved me in the arm, making me almost spill my drink all over myself.

Why couldn't he just let me have my fantasy?

After a few minutes, we heard the latch on the fitting door unlock and out stepped Charlie. And then I *did* spill my drink all over me. I didn't even move to clean it up either. I just. Sat. In. It.

She stood there with beautiful, blushing cheeks and this silky black dress that hugged every curve and line of her body. I couldn't swallow. I couldn't find my tongue. And, I couldn't look away.

"So, what do you guys think?" she said, blushing a deeper red. "I really like it, but I don't know what Mason will like."

"Whoa, she's smokin' *hot*, Jase," Joey mumbled under his breath.

"Ah," I agreed.

"Guys?" Charlie asked.

"I mean, like, she's hot-*hot*, Jase. And, she's *Charlie*," Joey whispered again.

"Gah-*ah*," I agreed, again.

"Guys, come on. Please let me know what you think," she said, balling her fists.

I mumbled something incoherently. I didn't even understand what the heck I was trying to say. Joey mumbled something back to me; apparently, we spoke the same language.

"Can you two speak louder?" Charlie hissed.

"Spin around," I said seriously.

She turned her body slowly around. She was *perfect*.

"Holy shit, even Charlie's ass is *hot*, Jase," Joey whispered.

"Okay, now shut up," I whispered back.

"Hurry up, guys! We're supposed to be going to Ava's after this, and I really want to have your opinion!" she huffed, folding her arms across her chest. My God, that just made her chest plump up more.

Couldn't focus. Could not focus.

Joey offered me a small nudge with his elbow, lifting a brow for encouragement. Standing, he said, "Charlie, you look really...*pretty...like a girl*. I'm going to wait outside. Jase needs to say some stuff to you."

What? What a dick move. How the *hell* am I supposed to get him back for that? I thought about telling Ava Marie every sappy thing he ever told me about her.

Then, my thoughts got all jumbled and confused, because Charlie was still standing there in front of me, wearing the sexiest dress I'd ever seen. Just watching me. Waiting for me to talk.

Fuuuck. My heart started hammering hard against my ribs. I think my tongue might have been dragging on the floor as I looked her slowly up and down.

Slowly standing up from the chair, I watched her eyes widen, and her hands dropped to her sides.

I didn't think. I didn't plan out what to say, or what I was going to do, I just went to her.

I calmly approached her and stood so close to her body that I could almost feel the cool silkiness of the material ghosting against my clothes. "Get back in the fitting room, Charlie," my voice rasped, hoarsely.

My body hummed with energy as I walked her backward into the small space of the room and closed the door behind us. Her back hit the wall gently and she took a long breath, making her chest almost spill out from the tightness of the dress.

I leaned my body against hers, taking both of her hands in mine and sliding them gently up the cool wall until they were on either side of her face. Her eyes looked up into mine, emerald green with flecks of blue and gold—our faces not even an inch away from each other. Her scent was heavy and thick, surrounding me, making me want to do things I had no clue how to do. *But, damn I wanted them.*

The warm breaths from her mouth fell against my skin and I closed my eyes, just to savor the intensity of her. Leaning my head closer to hers, I ran my nose along her jaw, nuzzling my face in her hair. Her breath pitched and quickened; her hands tightened in mine as her body arched off the wall to press against me.

"Jase," she gasped, in a low, husky whisper.

I lowered my lips to the base of her neck, pressing my body into hers. So close against her skin I felt every quick beat of her heart against mine. Brushing my lips along her skin made me high.

Breathless.

Her body shivered beneath my lips. Her movement made me yearn, wanting to touch her all over, cover her with my fingers, taste her with my tongue, and sink deep inside her with so many other parts of my body.

There was no control. I had none. *None.* I darted out my tongue and an explosion of taste and need erupted in my mouth. She gasped and her breaths came harder, faster. Her fingers squeezed mine as she leaned her head back, arching her body against my mouth. Her skin was warm and silky soft, and the low hum of beautiful moans rumbled deep inside her body.

I was doing that to her. *My body...my hands...my lips.* I wanted more. I needed more. Gently, I rolled my hips against her soft curves and heat burst low in my stomach. My hands tightened over hers; my entire body clenched in anticipation. Inside my jeans, I twitched and swelled, hardened to an almost painful ache. My brain fogged over, clouded with images of her lips on me, her hands touching and squeezing me. A deep growl rumbled from somewhere deep inside me.

A knock on the door interrupted us. *"YoooouWhoooo.* Hello in there! Did you find anything you like?"

Bad, bad timing lady. Come back in an hour, no two. Two hours. Please leave us alone.

"Heeellllooo," she sang, jiggling the door that I FORGOT TO LOCK. "Miss, are you okay in there? Do you need any help?"

"Ah, um. No, ah...thank you. I'm...I'm fine. I found the perfect one!" Charlie croaked, staring at me with those big green eyes.

Wait.

Was she talking about the dress or me? Because, she was looking at me when she said that.

"Okey dokey," the lady cooed. "Why don't you throw it over and I'll just ring it up for you? I'll meet you up at the register."

Um, I... Yeah, I think I loved that old wrinkly sales woman.

"Ahh, yeah. Okay," Charlie replied in a small voice.

Charlie exhaled and leaned her forehead into my chest. Warm puffs of her breath heated the skin under my shirt. Letting go of my hands with a shaky gasp, she softly placed her hands on my shoulders and gently pushed me back.

Excitement surged through my veins and left me gulping for air. I gritted down on my teeth, clenching my jaw, forcing my body to move away from her.

I staggered back, slumping my back against the fitting room door, body trembling. Warmth flooded across my skin and my hands turned clammy and cold.

Her eyes lifted and slowly locked on mine. They were a dark smoky green, sensual and lustful; they were made to look at me. Their gaze burned a trail of heat down the center of my body.

With hesitant, trembling fingers, she reached behind her head and slowly unzipped the back of her dress. The snap and the soft *zzzzzip* sounds of the metal teeth of the zipper and its fabric pulling apart, combined with both of our heavy breathing, filled the confined space.

She *didn't* ask me to turn around.

She *didn't* ask me to close my eyes.

She didn't. I was even listening for it. Waiting for it. *Expecting* it.

But, she didn't. So, I didn't.

God, *she was beautiful.*

My head thudded back against the wall as she stilled her movements. A soft sound fell past her lips—half sigh-half gasp. One hand held the dress in place across her breasts and the other came to meet it.

God, I wanted her to take off that dress.

I wanted to see every inch of Charlie.

My knees buckled and my body slipped down against the door until I was sitting in front of her—looking up. The skin covering every inch of my body tightened and hardened. My heart stuttered and stammered, and my eyes begged her to take off the dress.

Take off the dress.

Then, she slid the dress down her body, slowly, deliberately, letting it fall to the floor and pool in a silken heap around her feet.

She paused for a moment, standing there in a pair of panties and a matching bra; I swear she was letting me look at her. Her skin, my God, her skin was like ivory. Across her cheeks and across the plump rise of her breasts splashed a crimson blush, like a sunrise. I tried to talk, I did. I tried. I wanted to tell her how beautiful she was, how breathtakingly perfect, how much I loved her. God, I loved her. My mouth was filled with too much saliva and I couldn't seem to swallow fast enough.

I looked up, searching her eyes. She looked so vulnerable and so on fire at the same time. I wanted to say a million things, let her feel a million more, but I couldn't stop watching her. My chest tightened, drew together so strongly it choked the air from my lungs.

Bending down, she carefully picked the dress up off the floor and grabbed its hanger from its little metal hook just above her head. Then, *holy shit*, then she leaned her body over mine, stood *over* me on her tippy toes, and handed the saleslady the dress over the top of the door. The hammering in my chest started to hurt. Her skin was so close; I could just about taste her body lotion. She smelled of watermelons and Charlie and something so primal and hot, it made me want to plunge my flesh deep inside her. The lace designs of her panties were almost eye level with me and I caught a delicious glimpse of the dark patch of hair that lay just underneath.

"*Charlie*," my voice murmured, hoarse and low.

She backed up slowly, picking up her clothes along the way, watching me watch her as she lifted each smooth, perfect leg into her pants and pulled her shirt over her head, covering all that she had just bared to me.

I'm man enough to say that I almost cried.

She held out a shaky hand to me. "Come on, let's just go so I can pay for the dress—then we'll go find Joey."

Getting to my feet was a struggle, but she stood there and waited until I rose in front of her. We were so close that I could feel the heat of her body through her clothes. The way she looked up at me as I opened the door for her made me want to keep her inside that stupid, small room and kiss every inch of her beautiful face.

Of course *I didn't*. I was stupid and young and terrified.

Joey was standing in front of the fitting room, arching his head around, searching for me, probably. When he noticed us coming out together, he froze, did a double take, and shook his head, smiling. "Ahem," he said, pretending to clear his throat. "Find anything you like in there?"

Charlie glanced at me quickly, dipped her chin down, and answered, "Yeah, that black one. I have to go pay for it now," Rubbing the back of her neck, she left us and walked toward the register.

Tilting his head to the side, Joey raised his eyebrows. "Hey, Jase. Why is she still going to buy a dress to go to a dance with another dude? Didn't you talk to her?"

"No."

"You just came out of the dressing room with her," he stated.

"Yeah."

"What happened?" Joey asked, confused.

"I have no idea, but it was un-fucking-believable," I said, walking away.

The three of us walked through the mall in silence; the only sounds were from the crowds of families that strolled past us, and low rock music that drifted out from the stores. Even the walk to the bus stop was devoid of conversation; only the sounds of the cars driving past or their horns could be heard.

Joey kept a curious eye on the both of us.

And I was hoping Joey would be able to figure out what the hell was going on, because I had no damn clue as to why neither one of us said a word after what just happened.

The bus ride back home was worse.

She didn't even look at me once, and I just that there with my shirt sticking to my skin until the soda I spilled dried, which took the whole damn ride.

Sitting across the aisle from us, Charlie just stared out the window with her forehead smashed up against the glass.

"What the hell did you do to her?" Joey whispered to me.

"I didn't do shit," I whispered back.

Pursing his lips at me, he hissed, "Maybe that's the problem."

I shook my head, not wanting to share what I saw in the dressing room. I was taking that moment to the grave, and dying a happy man.

After the bus dropped us off, we went straight to Joey's house, where Charlie showed Joey's mom, Mrs. Graley, her dress. Both of them giggled and squealed like five-year-old kids as soon as the dress was out of the bag. While Mrs. Graley fixed us some dinner, she made Charlie try it on and walk around the room, bending every which way and pretending to dance around.

I was getting myself sick. *Why the hell was she still going to go to the dance with Mason? I didn't understand girls; I mean, didn't we almost kiss?*

Joey and I sat around the dining room table and watched the spectacle. Waiting for the girly crap to stop, we rolled an orange back and forth to each other across the table.

Then, when Mrs. Graley said in a dreamy voice, "So, tell me all about this Mason boy. What does he look like?" I squeezed the orange so hard in the palm of my hand juice squirted everywhere.

Joey howled in pain, "Holy shit, you shot that shit in my eye! Ah, that freaking burns!"

"Oh, my. Watch your mouth, young man!" Mrs. Graley came running at him with a kitchen towel and narrowed her eyes at me like I did it on purpose. Yeah, like I was the grand champion of orange squirters everywhere, able to hit any target I freakin' wanted from five feet away.

Charlie just sat herself down on the couch and looked at me with her eyebrows all squished together and raked her teeth over her bottom lip.

I sucked my cheeks in and stood up, flicking the juice of the orange from my hand all over the floor. "Yeah, let's hear *all* about Mason *La Douche*," I said through clenched teeth.

"Damn it! Does nobody care that I've been blinded by orange juice?" Joey yelped.

"Sweetie, you'll be fine. Just watch that mouth. Let's hear all about this young man while I clean this mess and set the table."

Then, I had to sit through an entire biography lesson of Mason La Douche. On and on, Mrs. Graley asked questions about him; I wanted to stuff an orange in her mouth to stop her.

"I still can't freaking see, dude," Joey mumbled.

"Hell, you think if I pour that crap in my ears I'd go deaf so I won't have to hear how perfect La Douche is?"

I barely ate any dinner.

Hell, I barely made it around the corner to Ava's house, because my lungs couldn't pull in enough air.

We hung out with a few other kids from school in Ava's backyard, all sitting on lawn chairs around a small, metal fire pit. Some of the girls were roasting marshmallows, and most of the guys were just throwing garbage in the flames to watch the burning embers burst up into the sky.

I sat and sulked.

Soon the conversation led to Mason and Charlie going to the dance together. Of course, one of the girls asked Charlie point blank, "Mason is a senior. He's going to want to do a lot more than just dance with you, ya know? What are you going to do?"

"It's just a dance," Charlie offered.

"Have you kissed him yet?" Ava asked.

Charlie's face turned bright red, but she didn't answer.

I leaned forward in my chair, rested my elbows on my legs, and clenched my hands together tightly; the searing heat of the fire fell harshly against my skin. "Yeah, Charlie. Tell us, did you kiss him yet?" I asked, glaring at her.

She said nothing as she stared at me wide-eyed.

My breathing grew ragged. My lips pinched and tightened against my teeth, and I felt my nostrils flaring as I tried to contain my rage.

Then, she shook her head and looked down.

"Hey, kissing is no big deal anyway," Rachel Jenson shot out, "not to a senior, anyway. And besides, how many times have we played those stupid kissing games between us? I mean, I think I've kissed every boy here."

Charlie's eyes snapped up to mine and narrowed.

"Bullshit," I said. "I never kissed you."

"That could easily be changed," she smiled.

"No, thank you." I snapped.

"Yeah, let's play something like we used to. Let's pair up!" Ava squealed.

No way.

Joey's eyes fixed on mine and nodded toward Ava.

I stood up, "Yeah. Sounds good. Rachel and Kevin, Tracy and Luis, and Ava and Joey should pair up. I *dare* you."

Joey stood up and crossed his arms and smiled at me, "Fine, then, Charlie and Jase. I double *dog dare* you."

I pretended to be shocked. This was working out great. Joey and I didn't even plan this out and we were seriously making this happen.

You could have said I was happier than a pig in shit.

That is, until Charlie stood up.

"I'm going home," she mumbled, and walked out of Ava's backyard.

Oh, my God. Charlie didn't want to kiss me? But, she wanted to kiss Mason?

Running after her, I silently followed her down the street and up to the roof of the tree house.

The sky darkened above us and the wind swept through the trees harshly, like a storm was approaching. The surroundings matched my mood; uncertainty, anger, *pure* jealousy. I just wanted her to be *mine*.

She was leaning back on her hands, eyes facing the sky, and tears streaked down her face. My heart stuttered, palpitated like I was having a coronary as I sat down on the roof next to her. Stretching my legs out in front of me, I leaned back on my hands just like her, our hands about an inch away from each other. I wanted to take her hand and hold it. I wanted to kiss her. I wondered what she would do, what she would say if I did.

I looked down at her hand, slowly sliding mine closer to hers, and then I chickened out and froze. *What the hell was I doing?* This was Charlie; I touched her all the time. I held her and hugged her. Why was this so damn hard all of a sudden? I looked up at her, but she'd already been watching me.

"You ever going to get enough courage to hold it?" she challenged me, and the air blew out of my lungs like she'd hit me in the chest with a sledgehammer.

"Come here," I whispered as I slid my hand underneath hers and braided our fingers together. She scooted up next to me and molded her body into mine. I buried my face in the soft hollow of her neck and breathed her in. After a while, she leaned back and searched my eyes, and it took everything in me not to kiss her.

I wanted to kiss her.

I really wanted to kiss her.

Screw this. I was going to kiss her.

My stomach went freaking haywire and my heart just about flew out of my throat. Charlie was staring at me like I was the next Messiah. Her lips were parted. Her breathing was heavy, and her fingers were sweating and crushing the crap out of mine.

Yeah, I was going to kiss her.

Slowly, I leaned in and lowered my lips to hers. She tasted like her watermelon lip-gloss and orange soda, and it got me instantly drunk. Letting her hands go, I pulled her gently against me. Her lips were soft and wet, and when she slowly started moving them against mine, I just about lost myself in her breath. Her head tilted slightly, and I slowly slid my tongue between her lips and touched her tongue against mine. I had never touched a girl's tongue with mine, and it was suddenly my new favorite taste in the world.

"Jase, what are we doing?" she breathed into my mouth, sliding her tongue over mine.

"Shh, don't stop."

"Why did Joey dare you to do this with me?"

I shrugged, kissing the side of her mouth.

"That's all you got for me? A shrug?"

"I *like* kissing you. God, Charlie, I *really* like kissing you. I want to be able to do it any time I want," I dipped my tongue into her mouth again and pulled back, "Don't go with Mason to the dance."

"Why?" she whispered.

"Because he's a dick," I said, kissing the other side of her mouth.

She scooted away from me and leaned back. "Maybe to you he is, but not to me. I need a reason, Jase. Give me a reason not to go with him."

"I said it, Charlie. He's a dick."

Staring up into the sky, she shook her head.

"What? You're *still* going to go with him?" I yelled. "Are you going to let *him* kiss you too?"

She looked so mad at me. I hadn't seen her look that mad since the last time Drake Fischer tripped Joey and she went all ape shit in his face.

"That's none of your business, Jase Delaney."

"Yeah, it is. You're my best friend. You're as close to me as a…as a sister."

"I'm like *a sister?*" she screamed at me.

"No, I mean… *Damn*, Charlie, he doesn't deserve you,"

Standing up, she dusted off her pants and looked down at me, "Yeah, well Jase, he was the *only one* who asked me. He didn't have to be **double dog dared** to do it, so I'm going."

"Fine then, I'm done with this conversation *and* with kissing you," I snapped, getting up and shoving my hands deep in my pockets. I jumped off the roof, walked through her backyard, back toward Ava's, and looked for Joey.

Weaving my way through our friends as they laughed and talked, not one of them realized that my insides were dropping from within me, and my heart was shattering against the ground.

Charlie was always good
At shattering my heart.
She was the only one
That ever could.
Even still.
To this day.

CHARLIE

lowers were delivered to my apartment at ten o'clock every morning. On Monday, it was five-dozen, deep-red roses. Tuesday, it was a slew of white lilies. Wednesday, it was pale, pink orchids. Thursday, it was enormous, bright yellow sunflowers, and on Friday, it was wild-flowers.

This happened for a month straight. A month straight.

Have I told you about my allergies? The one I have to flowers? An allergy Bren has known about for ages. Ages! Therefore, I had an intimate relationship with three bottles of Benadryl that month. Obviously, Bren didn't listen to my pleas to cease and desist the flowers, and I almost lost my mind on him.

First of all, he should have known I hated flowers, because I had used those *exact* words to him numerous times while we were friends and throughout this relationship *thing* we had going on.

Me: I *hate* flowers.

Bren: No woman hates flowers.

Me: Except for me. I. Hate. Flowers.

Bren: Bah, you don't know what you're talking about.

Me: Yes I do. *Flowers*! I hate them.

Bren: (Shrugging and smirking) Smell them, you'll love them.

Me: Odio las flores!

Bren: Excuse me?

Me: (Shrugging and smirking) Well, you're not listening to anything I say in plain English.

Bren: Stop being a bitch.

Me: (Seriously looking around the room for something to throw) Bren, trust me, you haven't met the bitch side of me yet, and I seriously hate flowers. 1.) They die overnight. 2.) They smell like funeral homes. 3.) They make me sneeze, make my eyes watery and itchy, and make my throat tickle and swell.

Bren: You're adorable, but all women love to get flowers. Just enjoy them.

If that crap wasn't bad enough, the afternoons were worse. Deliveries of more chocolate-covered guilty gifts inundated my shop. They were delivered directly to the shop, so I just shared them with the other girls and our clients. I didn't want to touch any of it, and Bren knew this about me. He knew I had a vice for sweets. I didn't understand what he was trying to do. I dunno, drive me insane with sneezing or maybe kill me sweetly?

However, with all that said, Bren was on his best behavior. He became attentive, loving, and here's the important part: *sober*.

We're talking about *weeks* here, too. Although, we didn't spend too much time together, every time I saw him he was sober, dressed to the nines, and *perfect*.

And, while all the girls in the shop fawned over his gifts to me and swooned over his visits, I knew bullshit when I saw it. I guess I'd been jaded by a lot in my life, but I knew this honeymooning Bren persona was just a fleeting phase. It wouldn't be long until I'd find him drunk in the back of a club somewhere getting a lap dance from some high profile celebrity.

I was impressed he kept it up well into autumn, and he showed no signs of stopping. He pleaded with me to hang out with him more. He had a few new guys he wanted to show me off to. Bren even begged me to move in with him and give up my little apartment, but something felt off. Really off. Maybe I was just too fed up with the way things had been. Maybe I was wasting too much of my hopes on imaginary characters and fictional plots, but I just felt like there had to be more. So much more. Was the grass greener someplace else, or was it fertilized with loads of bullshit like it was on my side?

I wasn't thinking clearly. I was being indecisive and annoying myself to all Hell. Did I even love Bren at all? I didn't think so. I knew very well what real love felt like, and this wasn't it. Not even close.

Time by myself was the best thing I could think of—time away from Bren and his stupid, stinky flowers.

I needed to clear my head.

I needed to stop stalling and being wishy-washy.

I needed my best friend.

Throwing myself in my Wrangler, I started the engine, filled the small cab with my special playlist, and pulled into the New York City traffic, making my way uptown to the Queens Midtown Tunnel and through the East River into Queens.

For the next seventy-five miles I screamed and sang and danced in my seat all along the Long Island Expressway toward Riverhead to Calverton. Songs we sung together filled me with nostalgia. Visions of us sharing my old Walkman, one ear bud for him and one ear bud for me, holding on to each other's pinkies, warmed my heart and watered my eyes.

One hour and thirty-three minutes later, I drove through a stone entrance, pulled over, and parked amongst the other cars that aligned the drive. Stepping out, I took a deep breath and tilted my head to gaze at the sky. The colorful autumn trees that reached far above my head were boasting their brilliant, fiery colors. Impressions of red, orange, and yellow flames licked the bright blue sky and feebly shook in the brisk, autumn winds. A few of the brightest ones twisted and tumbled, scattering onto the ground, leaving the trees bare, just to be trampled over or swept aside. The deep moaning of the branches overhead echoed the ache in my heart. The sadness of it all left me feeling a little broken inside.

Okay, maybe a lot more than a little.

With a heavy heart, I walked over the freshly mowed grass to find my oldest and dearest friend.

❦

BY THE END of May in my junior year of high school, I'd kissed a lot of frogs, hoping they'd magically turn into my prince charming. No such luck; they stayed as nasty, pimply, green frogs with major hand problems.

But I had bigger problems to worry about my sixteenth year of life. Stupidly, somehow, sometime along the way, I fell in love with one of my best friends. I had always known that I felt *differently* about Jase Delaney than any other boy. He was the first boy I ever kissed. He was the first boy I ever caught staring at me. He was the first boy I ever gave my heart to. As a matter of fact, that little thief stole it and never gave it back. Ever.

So I spent my sixteenth year of life secretly in love with a boy who wanted nothing to do with me—other than be his *buddy, or as he so eloquently put it—his sister.* I realized it the minute I went to that stupid spring fling dance with that jerk Mason *La Douche* as I was getting into his car. Before I got in, I chanced a small peek at Jase's house, just wishing he would run out and tell me that *he'd* take me to the dance, or fight for me, or I don't know, *something.* But all I saw was Jase kissing Rachel Jenson up against the side of his house. I knew without a doubt how trapped my heart was in his hands, the minute his lips left hers to call out, "Have fun Charlotte Stone! And, hey! Mason, make sure you kiss her real good, *I double dog dare you!*"

Because in that instant, that very second, which I can pinpoint with such clarity that it terrified me, I realized that I had fallen in *love* with Jase a long time before that. Whether you believe I fell fast and hard, or you think it was a slow build up over years, *it doesn't matter.* All that mattered was that I did, and now he was kissing someone else. Someone else.

That year, I watched Jase kiss a lot of frogs too (his frogs were always dressed like skanks), and every time, I died a bit inside when he did. But, I could never get enough courage to tell him how much I hated it. The only good part was that he never kept a girl around for very long. His average "relationship" was about a week, and then he'd be sucking face with some other girl and pawing at her boobs over her shirt.

So our relationship/friendship was strained and hard that year. Jase found himself a job at a local gas station, pumping gas and helping fix cars in their back garage. Joey and I barely ever saw him. He rarely crawled into my tree house at night—only once in a while when the fights with his father got too out of control. And even though I would cringe, hearing his father yell and scream or worse, I cherished those nights when I'd hear the loud thump of his sneakers as he landed on the wooden floorboards of the tree house. He'd just saunter in like he belonged there, take his sleeping bag off the shelf, and lie down next to me, talking and laughing with me until the sun came up.

In the beginning of spring that year, I found a frog that I didn't mind kissing too much. His name was Anthony Charles, and *yes*, Jase teased me mercilessly about me '*one day foolishly marrying him and becoming Mrs. Charlie Charles.*' Then, the teasing turned mean and hurtful. By Jase's seventeenth birthday that May, everyone was invited to the weeds for a bonfire to celebrate. He invited everyone—everyone except *me*.

Joey told Anthony and me to come to the party anyway.

So that night, holding hands, Anthony and I pushed through the crowds of drunken teens, trying to find Joey, or Jase, to wish him a "Happy Birthday."

"Hey, you made it," Joey said, grabbing me from behind and pecking a kiss on my temple. Holding me at arm's-length, he shook his head and eyed me from head to toe. "*Damn*. What the hell are you wearing?"

Anthony slid his hands around my waist and backed me up from Joey, "Pop your eyes back in your head, Graley. It's just a pair of shorts and a tank top. And keep your hands off my girl," Anthony joked.

But Joey kept his eyes on me, and his lips tightened into a straight, harsh line.

I was fully aware of how short my shorts were and how tight my shirt was. The thing was, I was dressed like every other girl at that party, and I was sick of being treated like Joey and Jase's little sister. "Where's Jase anyway? I haven't seen him yet."

Joey's eyes got real busy looking at something on the ground, and his hand was rubbing the back of his neck. "He went off somewhere with Kylie Simpson. Don't go looking for him, okay, Charlie? You won't like what you see…and he's definitely going to have something to say about your outfit."

My stomach dropped and my mouth became so dry it hurt when I swallowed. "What the hell does that mean?"

Joey darted a quick glance at Anthony and shook his head. "Just leave him alone, Charlie, okay?"

My body went rigid. "To Hell with this crap!" I snapped and turned to leave, storming past the drunken idiots and the roaring bonfire, and headed straight for the weeds.

"No, Charlie. Don't…" I heard Joey's voice as he caught up to me and swung his arms around my waist, pulling me back. His face was in my hair, his breath fanning across my ear. "He's really drunk, and he's with another girl. He heard some stuff in the locker room today and flipped out. And, Charlie, I don't want you to get hurt when you see him."

I stopped fighting and turned to look up into his eyes, "What stuff? Why would I care if he's with another girl, anyway?" I whispered.

His brows lifted, and his words drifted softly, in low whispers to my ear. "Because I know that you're in *love* with him."

I shoved his arms off me. "You're wrong. And besides, I have a boyfriend. I don't care what Jase does," I hissed back. I kept stepping back until I was a good five feet away from him.

Anthony's arms slid around my shoulders as soon as I backed away from Joey. "Everything okay?" he asked.

"Yes. Perfect," I lied.

"What the hell are they doing here?" Jase's voice growled from behind us.

Snapping my head in his direction, I found Jase stumbling out of the tall weeds, holding hands with a giggling, dark-haired girl. His shirt was off and his pants were unbuttoned;

seeing him like that made my heart ache in ways that I never felt before.

Hot tears blurred my vision as I watched the giggling girl wrap her arms around his waist. He lifted his hand and took a huge swig out of a half-empty bottle of what looked like whiskey.

I held my chin up to him. "I just came to say 'Happy Birthday' to my best friend," I said.

Dropping his hands off the giggling girl, he swayed toward me and laughed in my face. "Really, Charlie? I just got me a nice little birthday blowjob from Kylie over here. You up for giving me a better one? You know, since I've heard you're so freaking good at it," he leveled a challenging stare on Anthony.

"You better keep your mouth shut, Delaney!" Anthony lunged at Jase before I could stop it, but even drunk, Jase side stepped out of the way and laughed louder.

"How good of a fuck is she, Anthony? Huh? You told all the guys in the locker room at the gym how hard she sucks you off and how wide she spreads her legs for you" Jase gritted, his eyes narrowing. "That would be a great birthday present for me. Tell me how great *fucking* Charlie really is!" he screamed at Anthony, but as he said those disgusting words, his cold, blue glare was on me.

I backed away from him on shaky legs as my blood raced through my veins, pulsating in humiliation and anger. Why would he say that? *WHY would my BEST FRIEND SAY THAT? Why would he scream that in front of everyone?* I didn't even care what Anthony said about me to his friends. All I cared about was the crap that was falling from the lips of the boy I *loved.*

As calmly as I possibly could, I walked right up to Jase, looked up through my teary eyes, and whispered for only him to hear. "I hate you, Jase Delaney."

Turning around to lock eyes with Anthony, I asked, "Did you tell everybody that?"

The pure look of guilt on his face was answer enough, and I stormed off down the beach, screaming for everybody to stay away from me. I walked along the lapping waters and listened for the sounds of the party dying down the further away I walked. In the distance, I eyed the small, abandoned row boat we used to play in as kids and figured I would just calm myself down in there until I figured out what to do.

Just as I reached the boat, strong arms were wrapping around my shoulders and yanking me back, and Jase's cold, hard voice was in my ear. "Charlie, enough. Fuck! Charlie... shit...Charlie, I'm sorry!"

Turning around, I shoved him hard against the chest. "Don't you touch me! Don't you *ever* touch me again!"

Before I knew it, he grabbed me around my waist and slammed my ass down hard against the edge of the boat and positioned his body between my legs. I quickly leaned back to get away from him, and with the momentum of my movements, we both fell into the boat, his body crashing on top of mine.

"Get off of me!" I screamed, throwing out my arms, trying to find purchase.

Slowly, he leaned up on both his arms, his chest rising and falling fast as he hovered over me. I was trapped between both his arms and weighed down by the heaviness of his body that had fallen perfectly between my thighs. I tried to wrench my body and twist my way free, wiggling between the hard length of him and the wooden boat floor.

"Stop. Stop...just stop fucking wiggling like that under me, Charlie," he whispered as his eyes locked on to mine. A strange burn spread across my chest and heated my cheeks as our eyes, less than an inch away from each other, stared into one another's. Both of our bodies turned stiff and rigid.

"Charlie," he whispered my name. The way it fell from his lips sounded like a prayer, or a wish. My head spun and my heart fluttered with the ache of pressure that was building against his body between my legs.

His eyes searched my face, my eyes, my lips, my cheeks; like he was looking for me, but couldn't quite find me. "You don't hate me."

"Yes. I. Do." I insisted.

His body slid slightly against mine and I tried not to move, but the feel of him made my body throb and tingle everywhere I had skin—which was of course all over my body. My heartbeat started pounding in my ears, and the warm heat from his mouth as it landed against my skin made me want to move my body along his.

"Jase…"

Fight for me. Want me.

His lips collided against mine, devouring me, hard and strong. His tongue plunged past my lips and I took him in, kissing him back with everything I had. His body sank against mine, melting into me. Dropping to one elbow, he twisted his fingers roughly through the strands of my hair and his other hand, *oh God*, his other hand slid up the bare skin of my leg and gripped my ass through my shorts, pulling me harder against him. The pressure between my thighs tightened, and I could feel the hardness of him perfectly aligned with me—just his old, faded blue jeans and the thin material of my shorts keeping us apart.

What the Hell were we doing?

I didn't want to stop him.

I wanted him, my God, I wanted that boy more than anything in the world.

But Jase was drunk, wasn't he? I had a boyfriend, and he had Kylie. I knew all of this, and I didn't care. His hands and lips felt so good.

But truthfully, I did care. I didn't want him to kiss me because he was drunk. I cared so much that the tears started streaming down my face, mixing with our kisses.

"Jase," I gasped out. "Stop, this isn't right. You're...you're drunk. And you're going to be so pissed off at yourself when you remember this tomorrow."

I could barely catch my breath when he stumbled and twisted away from me as if I'd hit him. Backing himself against the other side of the boat, he froze, breathing hard and heavy, eyeing me like he'd never seen me before.

Sitting up on my knees, my head was spinning from the lack of his touch.

"I would never be pissed at myself for kissing you," he bit out.

"You're with Kylie, and I have a boyfriend," I whispered.

"Damn it, Charlie. You ever kiss that little turd like you just kissed me? Because I never kissed another girl the way I kiss you."

The snap of branches and sounds of footsteps silenced our conversation, but our eyes were still fixed together. I wanted to tell him the truth. That I'd never kissed anyone like I kissed him, that I never had that spill of warmth between my legs from anybody else but him. But I was so scared he'd laugh at me when he sobered up and then I'd lose my best friend forever.

"Hey, are you guys in the boat?" Joey's voice called out.

Jase's head thudded against the wood. "We *will* finish this conversation one day," he whispered.

"Fine. Just as long as you're not drunk when we do it!" I snapped back at him.

Joey's head peeked in over the side of the boat. Then Anthony's head followed. Then, a whole bunch of other heads popped in.

Anthony reached out his hand to me to offer me help. "Come on, sweetheart. I'll help you out of there."

My eyes shot to Jase. He had turned his face against the side of the boat, leaning his forehead against it. His arms were wrapped around his stomach, and he was breathing hard like he was in pain.

I ignored Anthony's hand. "Jase?"

He faced me again, and in the dim light I could see the shine of tears in his eyes. "Just fucking go. Your *boyfriend* is waiting."

There was an audience of people surrounding the stupid boat now, waiting to see what I'd do.

I snapped my head toward Anthony, who was still holding his hand out to me. I realized I didn't want it, because Jase was right. I never kissed Anthony like that. "I'm going to ask this again. *Did* you tell a locker room full of guys that I had sex with you, Anthony?"

"Shit," he stammered. "Charlotte, let's go somewhere else and talk, okay? Baby, this is a private conversation."

"Is it?" I snapped. I felt the heat of everybody's eyes on me. Little tiny prickles of heat spiked across my shoulders and chest. I couldn't let a boy talk about me like that, especially when it wasn't true. "Or is it because you don't want everybody to know how much of a disgusting liar you are? Because I don't know whose legs you've spread, but they sure as heck weren't mine."

Anthony coughed and cleared his throat, fidgeting and squirming. He still held his hands out to me. "I'm not angry with you, let's just go someplace and talk, okay?"

Moving closer to him, I leaned on the side of the boat and got in his face. "You're not angry *with me*? Well, isn't that a relief! And here I was thinking about how I should be pissed off at *you* for lying about sleeping with *me*. But, I'm just so glad you're not angry with *me*. It makes it so much easier to tell you just how over this relationship is."

I turned to Jase, who was smiling his stupid ass off, and asked, "Are you coming? I feel like having a few drinks for your birthday…since I'm single and all."

Laughing and stumbling, Jase jumped up and fell over the side of the boat. Jase made me climb onto his back for our usual piggyback ride. He turned to Anthony and said, "You don't deserve a girl like Charlie. Now get the hell outta my way, Assmunch."

He carried me to the bonfire, and Joey handed me a red cup filled with some dark liquid.

I looked at the inside of the cup, curiously.

"You don't have to if you don't want to, Charlie," Jase whispered hotly in my ear. "But, it'll make what just happened with your boyfriend go away."

"Okay," I said, taking the cup from his hands. I took a small taste. It burned the insides of my mouth and my throat, flooded warmth in my chest, and warmed the pit of my belly. I grimaced and almost coughed one of my lungs up. "That burns; what the Hell did you give me, gasoline?"

Jase laughed. "It's Jack Daniels whiskey. We all raided our parents' liquor cabinets and brought something. That's my father's. It's an acquired taste, but you get used to it."

Scrunching my nose up, I grimaced. "Why in the world would anyone want to get used to drinking something that tastes like burning gasoline?"

Joey bumped his arm into mine. "You'll see. After a few sips you're going to feel *nice*. And you're going to forget all about Anthony Charles."

I shrugged my shoulders and took another sip from my cup, feeling the burn slide down smoothly. "Who is Anthony Charles?" I laughed. Looking up, I noticed Jase's eyes on me, intently watching. I took a bigger gulp, the burn in my belly making me feel a little braver. "I'm more interested in trying to forget about Kylie Simpson giving a certain someone a blowjob."

"Come here," Jase demanded, pulling me gently toward him and wrapping his arm around my waist. The heat of his hands, mixed with the burn of my drink, made my head start to spin. Joey smiled next to us. "I forgot about Kylie the minute I zipped up my pants."

That made me take a bigger gulp of the burning gasoline. "Blah, you're making it worse."

Jase's eyes locked on mine and he pulled me tighter against him. "You don't think it affected me thinking that you were screwing Anthony? Besides, she was all teeth."

An array of loud giggles exploded from my mouth, and I was unable to stop them. "That's horrible." Laughing, I took another big gulp and spilled some all over my shirt. I looked up at him deadpan, feeling the bravest I ever felt in my life. "I'll make sure not to use any teeth, Jase. And I'm damn good at it, I've been told."

"*Fuck*, Charlie," Jase whispered into my hair.

Hours later, Joey, Jase, Ava, and I were stumbling around in my backyard, trying to climb up the tree house ladder. The swaying of it turned my stomach so violently that I ran to the bushes and vomited out whatever it was I drank that night. When I finally finished, and I looked up to see the dark sky spinning overhead, I realized that Jase had been behind me the whole time, holding back my hair.

"Feel better?" he whispered.

I giggled an answer. "Happy Birthday," I whispered back.

"Come on, Charlie, let's get some sleep," he said, pulling me to my feet.

Carefully, we climbed up the rope ladder; it took a few giggling tries and Jase's hands on my ass pushing me up the whole way. Joey and Ava were already asleep on the beanbags, and I tried to take a picture of them, but ended up tumbling over and falling into Jase.

Lifting me in his arms, he gently laid me down on my sleeping bag and positioned himself on his—next to me. I turned on my side to face him, snuggling into him while he stared into my eyes. I tried to keep my eyes on his, but my lids became too heavy and my world seemed to tilt into oblivion.

The last thing I remembered hearing was Jase's low whisper against my ear, "Stay in the rabbit hole with me this time."

I hoped it wasn't a dream.

The first thing I heard the next morning was someone moaning. It wasn't a pleasurable moan in any sense; it was a moan of pure, intense agony. And it seemed to be coming from deep within my aching throat. Slowly blinking my eyes open, my head seemed to torpedo into a million tiny pieces and hammer against my skull.

I tried to lift my head off the sleeping bag, but it was too heavy and thick. And dizzy—why was I so dizzy? And who in the world was snoring like that?

Peeking around the room, I was taking inventory in my brain of who came back up here with me last night, and what I might have done. My stomach rolled, and the tree house tilted and whirled around me.

Dark wisps of brown hair fell out of the sleeping bag next to me. Reaching out my hand, I pulled it down to sneak a look at who it was, and Jase's calm, sleeping face was hidden beneath. Feeling safe, I snuggled my body against his and fell back to sleep.

It was late afternoon when I blinked open my eyes again. The throb in my head was gone and the world stopped its crazy, jerky movements around me. Below me, under the heavy branches of the tree house, I could hear someone calling my name, pleading with me to come out.

Who the...? Was that...Anthony?

Lifting the sleeping bag off my body, I hauled myself into a sitting position. With just a hint of a churning deep in my belly, I smiled. I might have slept the entire day away, but I could drink like the boys!

Anthony's pleading voice was still calling my name. *Jerk.*

Looking around the small room, I noticed Joey sprawled out on one of the beanbags, watching me. Ava was gone; hopefully she hadn't gotten in any trouble for staying at my house all night.

Then, my eyes landed on Jase, who was rolling up his sleeping bag with a tight, angry scowl slashed across his face. He must have noticed me staring at him, because he stopped moving, just crouched over his bag for a moment, frozen. Finally, he turned his face toward me. His eyes were blood-shot and his hands were squeezing and twisting the material of the sleeping bag so tightly his knuckles were turning white. His teeth were clenched together firmly, and the pulse in his neck throbbed.

Damn, he looked like one of those crazy wrestlers on TV.

Anthony screamed out my name again, and something hard thumped against the side of the tree house, like he'd just thrown a rock.

That stupid son of a....

Jase's eyes darkened and his chest started heaving heavily as his eyes focused on mine. "Your *boyfriend* is outside with a handful of flowers for you."

I got to my feet steadily and walked to the window. Jase's eyes were on me the whole way. I opened it with a hard shove and stuck my head out, peering down.

Anthony was staring up at me with a handful of red roses, "Charlotte...Charlotte? Please, let me talk to you? I'm so sorry. I know I messed up. Please let me talk to you. Please let me explain," his voice cracked, like he was about to cry, "Charlotte Stone, I...I love you!"

From inside the tree house, somewhere behind me, Jase grunted and threw something hard against the wooden slats of the floor. Turning my head at the noise, my eyes met his icy blue ones, and I couldn't look away. I had no clue what was going on in Jase's head. However, with the intense way he looked at me, like he was some sort of wild animal, ready to devour me, I almost lost the ability to stand. I wanted him to look at me like that forever.

I searched those eyes long and hard in that brief moment, and in my head, I told him everything I ever felt for him. I lifted my voice and called out to Anthony, "Hey Anthony? I hate flowers. Giving me those stupid, nasty, smelling things isn't going to take your disgusting lies back!" I screamed, shaking my head. "So, I don't accept your apology. I will never think it was *okay* that you spread lies about me. Go home."

Slowly, Jase's expression changed. His scowl softened. His eyebrows lifted and his lips parted, revealing his surprise.

Suddenly, Jase was standing an inch away from me, tilting his head to the side; the heat rolling off of his body sent tingling waves against mine. His hands grasped my shoulders as he bent down and brushed his lips against my forehead, "That a girl. Don't let anyone walk all over you." His longs fingers softly squeezed my skin, spreading a surge of warmth across my chest. "And, don't forget, Charlie. We have a conversation to finish." The huskiness in his low whisper caused small sparks of heat to dance deep inside my belly.

I blinked my eyes rapidly, like an idiot.

Jase stepped back, letting his hands fall to his sides, and Joey was instantly next to us, placing a hand on each of our shoulders. Joey's lips twisted into one of his beautiful, goofy smiles. "I feel the need to celebrate, if I may be so bold to say that I am hoping to finally have my two best friends no longer at each other's throats."

Jase and I both nodded our heads.

"Good. We're getting drinks tonight...and I know just the place to go," Joey insisted. "Tooties. They don't card anyone. We've been inside there a few times, so they know us."

"Wait a second. You mean a bar? Like a *real bar*?" I asked.

Joey smiled a cocky smile at me. "Yep. The bartender who works there used to race in the weeds with us, so he lets us come in. Charlie, we've been going there for a few months."

"Seriously? To a real *bar*? Where the hell have I been?" I asked.

Jase snorted, "In Little Bumblefuck Dick Land, USA. Spending all your time with its King, the assmonkey, cock-waffle, dick-sneezing, fuckbutter, jerkass–Anthony Charles."

I stepped back and looked up at him through narrowed eyes and snapped back, *"Yeah, I did.* But, don't forget your hundreds of mini-vactions to Twatwaffle- Coochieville-Jiztit, USA. I hope you got your shots before visiting *all your vacationing areas,* because God only knows what nasty-diseased cooter roaches might have bitten into your dick!"

Joey groaned and dragged his hands down his face. "Holy crap. Can you two stop?" Stepping between us, he puffed out a loud breath and then smirked. *He smirked!* And then, you know what he said? He said, "You two are both still virgins, so get over yourselves!" Then he let go of us and walked to the door, "And...*we are* going out to Tooties tonight. Ava's going to be there with a few people, too. Go get showered and dressed, we're leaving at eight. *Idiots.*"

Jase was still a virgin?

My insides caught fire. Oh, sweet little baby Jesus. I wanted to be that boy's first.

I left the tree house with Jase Delaney biting down a

stupid, red-faced smile, as I wondered what in the world he could be thinking.

After showering and trying to dress myself like I was older, the three of us walked into the next neighborhood and strode right through the front doors of a little hole-in-the-wall bar. I'd never stepped foot in a bar before, and I gasped out loud as my surroundings came into sight. The walls were covered with photos, masks, baskets, and old retro advertisements. Bicycle parts and stolen traffic signs hung from the ceiling throughout the room. A long cluttered bar ran along one side of the wall and a few pool tables, ripped red leather booths, and tables and chairs, littered the back. It smelled like stale beer and pee. To be more specific, it reeked like a few of my mother's *friends*.

The place was crowded—stock full of kids from my school. How *illegal was that?* Everybody seemed to be holding a bottle of beer or small glass cups filled with dark liquid.

Jase tapped Joey on the shoulder and pointed to an empty booth in the back. "You two go grab that booth. I'm going to buy us a special drink I read about online."

Scared shitless, I grabbed Joey by the back pockets of his jeans and followed close behind him. I kept thinking that at any minute the cops were going to bust in through the doors, guns blazing, and arrest us all. I wondered if my mother would even come and get me from jail. I even wondered if they'd call my father, who I hadn't seen in four months, because he was traveling all over Europe with his new wife. *Crap, I had no one to bail me out if I needed it.*

After five minutes, Jase scooted himself into the booth across from me, placing three medium-sized, clear, plastic cups with an amber liquid inside, in front of each of us.

"What level octane of gasoline will we be drinking tonight, *Mr. Delaney?*" I teased.

Jase raised a dark eyebrow at me and lifted the corner of

his lips in a teasing smirk. "That would be a negative on the gasoline, *Ms. Charlotte*. Tonight, we will be drinking something called *A Mad Hatter*."

Joey chuckled next to me. "Hmmm. A Mad Hatter, huh?"

"Yep. It's made with vodka, peach schnapps, lemonade, and Coke." He held up the hand that was holding the glass, exhaled deeply, and quoted word for word from *Alice's Adventures in Wonderland*:

"'But I don't want to go among mad people,' Alice remarked. 'Oh, you can't help that,' said the Cat. 'We're all mad here. I'm mad. You're mad.' 'How do you know I'm mad?' said Alice. 'You must be,' said the Cat, 'or you wouldn't have come here.'"

Then he drank down his entire drink, and burped.

Joey laughed next to us and held his glass up, bumping me with his shoulder. "Have I gone mad? I'm afraid so, but let me tell you something, the best people usually are." Joey gulped down his drink next, and yelled, "Charlie, my sweet innocent Charlie, it's your turn! Drink up!"

Giggling, I brought my drink to my lips and sipped at my drink until it was empty. "Curiouser and curiouser."

After forty minutes of giggling, swapping seats repeatedly, and singing to each other in the booth, Joey stood up with his third (*or fourth*) Mad Hatter in his hand and cleared his throat. My head had started feeling a bit wobbly, and I seriously *loved everybody, even the scary bald man that sat in the corner staring at everybody.*

Holding his glass up, Joey's lips curled into another one of his goofy, beautiful smiles, "I think we need a *real* toast, don't you guys?"

"To best friends," I smiled back at him.

Jase softly nudged my foot under the table and pointed his finger past Joey to where Ava Maria sat alone in the corner. He looked at Joey and pointed him in the direction we were both looking. "To having the courage to talk to the girl you like!"

Joey stood up taller in front of both of us and let out a long, low sigh. Leaning my head back against the cool leather of the booth we were hiding in, I stared at him, at everything that was completely Joey. Something strange and unlike anything I'd ever felt passed between the three of us then, something that whispered our love and our friendship; in a thousand little words that never needed to be spoken.

Then Joey raised his glass higher. "Here's to falling..." He leveled his eyes on both of us. "...in love...and to the best example of it that I've ever seen, which is sitting right in front of me. And here's to hoping my two best friends finally find the guts to tell each other they've been in love with one another since the fourth fucking grade. Cheers."

Downing his drink, he slammed it on the table in front of us and walked away.

Here's to falling...

I sucked in a loud breath and almost started choking to death on my own saliva. Okay, that's a sorry-ass exaggeration, but that's what it felt like. "W-wait. Whooa...Hold up," I stammered.

Jase raised his head slowly, to meet my gaze. Stretching out his long legs under the table, he raised his feet up and planted them on either side of me on the cushions of the booth, trapping me in.

What? Did he think I was going to run? Well, I didn't want him to run, either! Grabbing both his legs, making sure he couldn't get away, I leaned forward. "You...you *love me?*"

He sat staring at me as if trying to decide what to say. Finally, as his teeth raked a hard line over his bottom lip, he spoke, "In millions of different ways...but the one that means the most to me you never knew about, did you?" He raked his hands through his hair. "Ever since the day I moved next door to you, and you stood up to me with that skull picture you drew...Joey's right. I've been in love with you since fourth grade, Charlie." He rubbed at the back of his neck and his voice lowered. "It's the only thing in this world that I've ever been sure of. When you went to that stupid dance with Mason a few months back, you took my heart with you. You ever feel like you wake up and part of you is missing? You were that part. Kinda been lost without you."

My thoughts scattered, exploded like a sky full of fireworks. My body quivered with the effort it took to control myself and not jump into his lap.

Running his hand through his hair, he looked at me with that confident grin of his. "What do you say, Charlie? Want to try jumping down the rabbit hole again? I promise I'll be better than any adventure you could ever read. The way I see it, Charlie, is that you've always belonged to me—"

"Jase Delaney, you make my freaking head spin, and I think I'm going to enjoy years of therapy because of you and *your adventures,*"

A loud crash broke through our conversation, echoing its sharpness against the heavily decorated walls. It sounded like someone spilled a ton of beer bottles on the floor, and then sheer pandemonium let loose as people screamed and a chair sailed through the air. Immediately, I thought it was the police raiding the bar for serving under-aged kids. People scattered and crowded around the entrance; my heart throbbed in my throat as I scanned the chaos, trying to find out what was happening.

Twisting back around to meet Jase's wide eyes, I watched him bolt out of his seat and run into the mass of people. My insides flipped as I stared after him.

Through the crush of bodies, I saw Slate Marshall, standing, hovering over a lump of someone on the floor. Everything in my head went dead silent when I saw the shaggy, jet-black hair that lay against the floor through the tangle of shuffling feet.

"Joey!" The scream ripped through my lungs and tore through my throat, but all I could hear was the deafening throb of my pulse in my ears. Lunging out of the booth, I struggled to get through the thick mass of bodies that surrounded my friend. Heads blocked me, all people I knew from school, with terrified expressions on their faces. A burning surge of adrenaline shot through my entire body, and everything—but me—seemed to move in slow motion. Movements stretched out awkwardly. Hands tried to grab me. The voices were garbled and sluggish. Everything seemed blurred and stilled, only my quickening pulse pounded faster in my ears, accelerating into a painful rhythm.

Joey's body lay limp on the disgusting bar floor; under his beautiful, soft hair seeped a thick puddle of dark red blood, spreading and stretching out sickeningly fast across the lacquered shine of the wooden floor. Red tears streamed down his swollen, battered cheeks. The streaks made him look as if he was beaten so hard that he was crying blood. Jase's arms grabbed onto me tightly, as if he were a human tourniquet, halting *my* blood, *my* life, *my* happiness from pouring out all over the bloodied floor to mix in with Joey's. If I'd had the energy, I would have stopped him. Let me melt into the piss and beer stained ground along with my best friend; let the three of us melt into everything and nothing all at once. Together.

The crowd shifted. The screams got louder, and Jase's hands let go of me.

Time sped fast in blurs of motion around me as I dropped to my knees. "JOEY! Come on, Joey! Get up!" I pulled at him, trying to grab his hands, but they were too slick and slippery with blood. I tried to crawl closer to him, but thick, rough hands were yanking me backward. Violently, my face was grabbed and twisted to look into the putrid, smiling face of Slate. I convulsed and gagged on hot vomit, realizing his dirty hands, the ones that just brutally beat my best friend, were now on me. And they were covered in Joey's blood. My body gave out, but I didn't fall far.

Yanking me off the ground by my chin, Slate forcefully pulled me against his chest and slurred through a puff of bitter whiskey breath. "I hope he fucking dies. Then, I'm coming after you. I'm gonna fuck you so hard you're gonna split in half, bitch."

Jase's arms savagely yanked Slate off of me and I fell back to the floor, grabbing onto Joey and wishing with all my might that he'd be okay. I heard the sirens in the background, but the sound of Jase's fists viciously hitting Slate's skin was the only thing I listened to.

The next thing I can vividly remember was being in the hospital, listening to the sounds of Mrs. Graley sobbing as the stoic faces of the doctors apologized for not being able to save the life of her sixteen-year-old son.

Slate Marshall had beaten my best friend to death.

After coming up behind him and hitting him in the side of the head with a glass bottle, Joey fell to the ground. While he was out cold, Slate Marshall kicked my best friend in the face and head until everything that made him Joey was gone, slipping out like red satin across the floor.

I stared quietly into the stark whiteness of the hospital walls, completely empty inside. A low buzz swam in my head. A small, yet growing pain curled out in waves from my chest.

Then, it hit me.

It hit me like two big pieces of shit in the face. Joey was never coming out of the doors I watched them roll his body through. He was never going to graduate from high school. Never going to get married and have a family.

He was never going to get past sixteen.

And it hurt, it hurt like the kind of pain that you don't truly feel at first, and then when you do get over the shock, it's the absolute worst kind of pain, the kind that literally takes your breath away.

I folded in on myself, wrapping my arms around my stomach, trying to hold in the explosion of pain that was threatening to shred me to pieces.

Screams tore from my lungs so loudly that they burned at my throat. I was sobbing so violently I couldn't catch my breath. I screamed for his mother, dropping to her feet as she held her head in her hands, sobbing into her palms. "Donate his heart *please*; don't stuff him in a wooden box. Please. Please. Please keep him alive. Don't put him in the ground. Let someone else feel the warmth of his heartbeat. Let others know Joey and how amazing he was. Don't put all the pieces of him in the dirt. *Please don't*. Please keep him alive."

My fists started pounding against the walls, and the vilest words came out of my mouth. *How could Slate Marshall's wish come true? Why would God do that? Slate said he hoped Joey would die. What about my wish, God? Why didn't my wish for Joey to live come true? Why was Slate better than Joey? Why would you do this to his mother? The mother who loved and cared about her kid is the one who loses him? My father wouldn't even know I was gone. My mother would have been too drugged up to notice, and how about Jase's parents? God, you took the wrong kid, you should've taken me.*

Not Joey. Not my Joey.

For days after, all I could see in front of my eyes was my best friend dying. The scene didn't stop rewinding itself in my head, rewinding and replaying the last things he said to us, the shatter of glass we heard, and the cold lifeless look in his eyes when I finally reached him.

If I closed my eyes, it only got worse.

During his wake, in the funeral home, crowds of kids from our school sat sobbing and wailing into their hands or each other's shoulders. Students from our school, who had never spoken to Joey, or worse, teased him along with people like Slate Marshall, hugged each other like they had lost *their* best friend, as if this tragedy somehow actually affected *them*. Whispers of their stories and memories of him filled the funeral room, making it twist repulsively with the decaying smell of flowers that had me running into the bathroom stall to heave up stomach bile. Their fictional memories of a boy they bullied or turned their backs on when the damage was being done by someone else. The boy everybody teased. Now they were all crying because he was gone.

Soon they were going to put him in the ground, I thought. My stomach coiled and rolled, and I heaved more. Six feet under the dirt with the worms and bugs and darkness. Joey was going to decay. Rot. Get eaten by bugs. Picked on nibble-by-nibble, like when he was alive. I was choking myself with tears, gagging at the disgusting thoughts and images that flooded my mind.

Having to view my best friend in a rectangular box, surrounded by white satin material, like a damn display doll, was one of the worst things I was ever forced to do. His usually tanned skin looked strangely porous and chalky, and it looked like someone had given him a freaking haircut. My fingers itched to touch his body, to poke him, caress him, kiss his cheek, and breathe life into him again. I was so stunned by the thoughts that I barely registered Jase clasping his hand in mine and lacing our fingers together.

"Who the hell is *that* kid?" Jase whispered, peering into the coffin alongside me. "What the Hell were these people thinking? That doesn't look like Joey at all. Did...did someone give him a haircut?"

"I think he's got lipstick on, too," I whispered back and tucked my head into his chest. "Do you think it hurt?" I asked, choking on a sob.

"Do I think what hurt?" Jase asked, giving my hand a squeeze.

"When he got hit. When he fell. When he hit his head. When he got kicked. When he died. I don't know what. I just want to know if he hurt."

"No, Charlie. I think it happened too quickly, and he was really drinking...so I don't think he felt anything," Jase whispered.

"I...I can't do this, Jase. I don't feel so good," I stuttered, wanting nothing more than to climb in that damn wooden box with him and snuggle into his chest, and have us take on the afterlife together.

"Come on," Jase murmured, pulling me into his arms. Standing in front of that casket with the body of a kid that didn't look like our best friend, with a line of people behind us ready to pay their respects, we sobbed the loudest.

At the gravesite, I tried to think about anything, anything else - dirt bikes, homework, books, so I wouldn't see the coffin being put into the ground. Or see the people sobbing and crying around me. So I wouldn't have to see my best friend being buried. But all I could think was that he's gone—like the light from a room when you flick the switch. Immediate. And final.

There was no going back and fixing this. I wished it was me instead as I watched the ground swallow the shiny wooden coffin that held the body of the best sixteen-year-old kid that ever walked the earth.

This is what I learned the day my best friend was buried:

There are sad songs that no one should ever have to listen to.

Goodbyes that no one should ever say.

Mothers should never lose children.

Forever is too long of a time. A part of you dies when you lose someone you love. Life is messy, it's never fair, and it's never pretty. And I will always ask God why, why, why, *why?*

And I'll never get an answer.

I'll never forget the exact way he looked and the sound of his laugh, and I will cry for him until the day I die.

There will forever be something missing in my heart, and I'd never be fully here without him.

Life was so different after, but only for Jase and me. Everything went back to normal at school; just a small area on the front lawn of the campus was set up with candles, letters, and flowers to remember him by. I didn't understand any of it, and I certainly didn't understand why the world just went on without Joey in it. To me, the earth had lost its sun.

Remember I told you about my BOOM? That was my first one. It wrecked me. My next BOOM, it completely destroyed me.

❀

MY CHUCKS CRUNCHED over the gravel and grass as I made my way through the cemetery, until I found the only thing left of my dearest friend—his cold, white, head stone. "I miss you so much, old friend. So much it hurts to breathe sometimes. Wish you were here. 'Cause I really need a friend, and I can't face Jase again. God, Joey. I want to so bad, so, so bad. But you know, don't you? You know why I can't ever look into his eyes again."

Tracing his name with my fingers and pressing my lips

against the chalky cool stone, tears spilled from my eyes. "As soon as I'm done here, I'll find my way to you. Both of us will."

I'll find my way
To you.
As soon as
I'm done here.
I'll shed a tear each day
Until then.

CHARLIE

For weeks after Joey's death I stayed in my bedroom, alone. Nightmares of Joey haunted my nights; images of him drinking a red solo cup that heaved with wiggling white maggots, while bloody red tears streaked his face. It was worse if I slept in the tree house. Besides, I couldn't stay in the tree house for more than a minute without busting out in tears or trashing the place in anger.

Slate Marshall was arrested on charges of manslaughter. That word, every time I heard it, made me gag. Manslaughter. *Slaughter.* That's got to be one of the most violent words in all the history of words. And, it happened to my best friend.

Jase was brought in for questioning and then his father hid him somewhere away for the entire summer, away from the whole situation, and away from me. I didn't get to see or hear from him for three months. So, I mourned for both my friends.

I only visited Mrs. Graley a few times; it was too hard for me to keep going. When you walked into her house, Joey's scent was all around you, and my heart would ache in *real* physical pain. His sneakers were still kicked off and laying in the corner of the living room. The book he was reading lay open on the coffee table next to a bag of half-eaten potato chips, as if he could walk in at any minute and continue on with the life that was so harshly stolen from him.

I ended up just staying in my bedroom; dealing with the hurt and the pain all by myself, by drawing thousands of pictures of Joey and devouring handfuls of candy bars for breakfast, lunch, and dinner.

And then, early in the morning of the first day of senior year, my doorbell rang, and I nearly fainted dead away when I opened it to find Jase standing on my front porch.

"Hey," was all he whispered, and my tears rained down.

He awkwardly pulled me inside and sat me down on one of the couches in my living room; I could barely see his beautiful face through my tears. But, I couldn't stop crying; and in my mind, I prayed to a God I was so angry with, to just let me drown in my own tears.

"I have something for you," he said, tucking my hair behind my ear.

I looked down, wiping my tears away to see him holding a small black box in his hand. His long fingers opened it to a short, thick, silver chain with a heart shaped locket that dangled from its center.

"It's for me?" I asked, hiccupping on a sob.

"Yes," he said, eyes blazing into mine. "It's a bracelet. You have to open it and read the inscription."

I leaned forward and softly placed my fingers on the heart and read it. The words, "Here's To Falling," were engraved into its front and "In Love" on the back. Unclasping it, my breath faltered as a picture of perfect, goofy-smiling Joey stared back at me.

I looked up at him through aching, teary eyes, and tried my best for a smile. "I love it, Jase. Thank you."

His lips were pinched in a small, straight smile, and months of sadness clouded his eyes. Releasing the clasp, he placed the bracelet on my wrist and fastened it. *I've only taken it off once since that day to move it to wear on my ankle, so it wouldn't dangle itself against my clients when I tattooed them. I haven't taken it off since.*

Jase looked so different that morning; older, more of a man. It was hard to look away from him. It was hard not to cling to him; yet it was awkward to be together after so long with the last time we spent together being when we buried our friend.

In complete silence, he drove us to school in his new truck, which was an old, beat up, white Bronco that he bought with his own money right after his summer stint in some Juvenile detention center that sounded a lot like a military camp.

For that twenty-minute ride, I knew we were both trying desperately to block out the sickening images that terrorized us each night we were away from each other. We made it to the school entrance without speaking a word about the things that haunted us.

Finally breaking the awkward silence, he pressed his lips to my forehead and said, "I'm here now, Charlie. Everything is going to be okay, I promise. I've missed you so much." I didn't even remember walking through the metal detectors or seeing any other students. All I could remember was the feel of his warm hand in mine as he led me through the doors and into my homeroom class.

By third period AP Literature, I was feeling the severe effects of all the tears from that morning and laid my head against the cool, smooth wood of my table and promptly passed out. I woke up with a start when someone jabbed me in the ribs with a hard finger and kissed me on the cheek.

Jase smiled and walked to the seat across from mine, where some surfer-looking kid sat drumming his pencils against a stack of books on his lap. "Your ass is in my seat. Get it off before I kick it into the next classroom."

Without saying a word, the kid leapt off his seat and sat himself down clear across the room. Damn. *Jase Delaney got more badass while he was gone*. For the first time in months, I think a real smile touched my lips.

Trying to focus my attention on our teacher, Mr. Falls, I sneaked a glance at Jase and caught him staring at me. It made my belly do all sorts of funny stuff, like riding on a roller coaster. And I couldn't wait until he kissed me again.

While we were supposed to be playing a cheesy icebreaking game of *'get to know each other'* with our tablemates, Jase nudged me under the table with his foot. "Bonfire tonight. You're coming with me."

"Alrightly there, Captain Caveman," I laughed. It was the first time in three months I had laughed; it felt foreign and wrong and disrespectful to Joey.

"Grrr," he growled low. "Me like cavewoman."

I felt my face blaze up on fire. Holy crap, we were supposed to be talking about our favorite colors, foods, and music with the people at our table, and all that was happening was the kids were gawking at Jase and me while we were laughing with each other. *Jase was back, and he was making my sorrow go away.* Tears stung at my eyes.

"Ugh. Caveman missed his cavewoman," he chuckled.

His? I was Jase's?

I *was* Jase's.

We laughed so loudly that Mr. Falls came stalking over to our table, "What's all the noise over here?"

"Um. Nothing sir. We were just doing the icebreaking exercises you asked of us," Jase answered, smiling brightly.

"*Really?*" he sneered, pushing his thick-framed glasses up the oily, thin, bridge of his nose. "Well, *do* tell me what you've found out about a few of your tablemates."

Jase leaned his elbows on the table and his smile got wider. "Sure, no problem. This here is Margo," he said, nodding towards some girl I didn't know. She was dressed head to toe in pink and had a giant New Kids on the Block pin that hung from her collar. "She loves the color pink, gets a kick out of boy bands, and loves a good romance story," His face turned to me and he gave me a little wink. "And, directly across from me is Charlotte, but she would rather be called 'Charlie.' Her favorite band is Avenged Sevenfold. She thinks their music is awesome, and she secretly has a crush on the lead singer." Then Jase points to the boy sitting next to him, "We were just about to get to this big guy over here. I believe I remember from last year, his name is Jonathan. Oh, and me? I'm Jase Delaney," he stood up to shake the teacher's hand, the rest of the class snickering low at his clowning around. "My favorite color is green, and I'm desperately in love with my BFF…"

"Okay," Mr. Falls clapped his hands together. "That's good enough, carry on class," he called out, walking away as he glanced around the rest of the room.

"Holy shit, dude." Jonathan said, "You got balls."

"Yeah, two of 'em," Jase answered with a straight face. "Why, how many do you have?"

Sliding down in my seat to try to reach him, I nudged his foot. "Hey, I thought your favorite color was blue."

"Not anymore. My favorite color is the exact shade of green in your eyes."

A low fluttering nipped at the bottom of my belly, and when I looked up into his eyes directly, the fluttering dropped to a dull throb in a very private place on my body. "Shut up, Jase!" I whispered, giggling.

"Nuh uh, Charlie. Tell me your favorite color isn't the color of my eyes."

Yeah, it was.

He chuckled, "Yeah." His hand raked through the layers of his dark hair and his eyebrows pulled together seriously. "And I promised myself, well I promised Joey, to never keep my feelings to myself again, to always speak my mind, and be fearless, especially about you. You never know how little time you have left with someone."

Oh.

Hell, he's right.

My hand shot up in the air to get the teacher's attention and I asked in a quick-snipped voice to use the restroom. Before I left the table, I stood up and leaned in close to Jase's curious face and whispered. "Second floor, girls' bathroom. Last stall. Five minutes."

He didn't even ask. Jase just pushed away from the table and jumped up, knocking the chair back, and ran out behind me. The murmurs and whispers of the classroom silenced as soon as the door shut behind us. I ran ahead, down the empty hallway, and turned into the back stairway, thinking the bathrooms were just too damn far.

Not caring one damn bit about where we were or who would be watching, I turned to face him; my chest hammered with thick, loud, heartbeats I swore the whole school could hear. Jase quickly devoured the distance between us, pressing my body with his up against the cool, tiled wall of the stairwell. The hungry, hooded look in his eyes made my knees tingle, and an explosion of sparks flamed between my thighs. His hands grasped both sides of my face, and like two magnets that had been held apart and suddenly let go, our lips collided together in need. His warm mouth covered mine; his wet tongue devouring my senses as my hands clawed at his shirt, pulling him closer. His hands slid into my hair, pressing my lips harder against his. Hard and fast his mouth moved with mine, like we were trying to melt into each other and sink into each other's skin.

A low, tingling pressure was building steadily between my legs as he pressed his body firmly against mine. Releasing my hair, he reached down, pulling my hips harder against his, and slipped his hands to grip my bottom, grinding himself into me.

Somewhere around us the sound of footfalls echoed against the stairs, and low voices fluttered through our minds. We were too consumed with each other to care—too overwhelmed with the taste and feel of each other after such a long time apart. Jase reluctantly pulled his lips from mine and his hands reached up from where they pleasantly were to cup my face. The heat from his mouth fanned across my skin, making it a struggle to keep my tongue and my mouth away from his.

His blue eyes met mine, our faces close to each other. "Every time I'm with you, close to you, my chest feels so damn tight." His voice shook and tears spilled from my eyes. He lowered his gaze to the floor and gently rubbed his thumbs across my cheeks, wiping the salty tears across my skin. "I'm so sorry I couldn't save him. I'm sorry I didn't kill Slate with my bare hands. You know I tried, and I would have if they didn't rip me off him." He stepped back, letting me go. and ran his hands along the back of his neck and over his face. "But the thing I hate the most, the thing I feel the most messed up about. is my father taking me away from you. And you dealing with this all alone. I am so sorry, Charlie."

"Stop, Jase," I whispered, grabbing his hands in mine and pulling him back against me.

Two students walked past us gasping, and gave us a disapproving look while shaking their heads. Jase blew them both a kiss and flipped them the finger.

I tugged on his hands to focus his attention back on me. "Jase, you did nothing wrong. This wasn't our fault; it's all on Slate. And the only way I've been dealing with this is by just saying to myself that Joey's away on a long vacation, and I'll meet up with him when I get the chance." Tears were pouring down my face now. "I know it's sort of crazy, but I just can't face the fact that I'm never going to see him again."

"No, Charlie. That's perfect. Joey *is* on vacation. And we definitely will see him again." His arms were around me instantly, and he crushed me into his chest. "Yeah, baby. He's just taking a little holiday, cutting a few classes. At the beach or something," he whispered in a hoarse voice.

We walked back to the classroom, hand-in-hand, and the rest of the day passed in a sad, hazy blur. Both of us missed him so much, and both of us suffered with the guilt of having to go on with the rest of our lives without him.

We never made it to the bonfire that night. Nope. We drove out to the cemetery and ate a picnic dinner of fast food with Joey and spoke to his gravestone like he was really there. You may think that we were both certifiable, but that was how we were dealing with our loss. We were young, we were devastated, and we were completely and utterly alone. All we had was each other.

Sometime after dusk fell over us, we walked side-by-side to his truck, our arms occasionally touching. Each time his skin brushed against mine, my entire body felt like it was engulfed in flames. Every time our skin made contact, he would glance down at me, like he was feeling the same strange inferno. After the third time, I reached my hand across and rubbed the area and wondered how I could possibly feel so much from such a small touch. After I climbed into his truck, he pulled me close to him, making every surface of my skin tingle and burn, causing flutters to roll through my belly. I wanted to keep feeling him, tattoo that feeling permanently on my skin. I wanted to surgically remove my heart and hand it to him wrapped in a little red box, because seriously, he had it already. And *that* feeling, that *need*, was the only thing that let me forget about Joey being gone.

The ride back home was full of songs and holding our hands out the windows, feeling the wind whip past us. He pulled his truck into a clear spot in front of his house and walked me to my door, placing a soft kiss on my lips. *God, I wanted more.* But, too nervous to tell him, I just opened my door and walked into an empty house, not even bothering to lock it behind me. No doubt my mother was with her newest sleazy boyfriend, the one that didn't mind when I walked in on them screwing on the couch. *Owen.* Owen just winked at me and held my mother's hips tighter and kept plowing into her. Vomit central. Honestly, I was pretty much used to it by now. It was like a college frat house around here, and my mother was the freaking slutty mascot.

Walking into the kitchen, I checked for messages and grabbed a bottle of water. Sipping it, I listened to two different, extremely drugged out, slurred messages of my mother telling me she'd be staying over at Owen's place. His own slurred, drugged out, laughter spilled out of the background, and she giggled uncontrollably into the phone. The third message was from my father explaining to me that he might be able to *pencil me in* for a visit on the fourteenth of October, which was over a month away. *What an ass.* He could shove his pencil right up his ass for all I cared. I hadn't seen him in over seven months. He was way too busy at the theater, watching the ballet, eating at the finest restaurants, or sailing around the world in his shiny new yacht with his shiny new plastic-*tittied* wife. Screw him and the Barbie doll he rode in on.

I kicked my chucks off as soon as I got into my room, and I yanked off my shirt and shorts that were full of grass stains from sitting on the cemetery lawn. Walking into the bathroom, I ran the water until it was the perfect temperature, stripped off the rest of my clothes, and stepped into the warm spray. Smoothing my body scrub into a lather all over my body, I couldn't help but think about the way Jase had kissed me in the stairwell that morning. That deep ache between my thighs throbbed again, and I wondered if he thought about things like this, too. Things like this with *me*.

I rinsed off and stepped into the steam of the bathroom, wrapping a soft, terry cloth towel around my body. When I walked into my room, the light from Jase's window caught my eye, and I slowly slid back my curtain to see what he was doing. My breath caught in my throat and heat exploded low in my belly.

Through the small opening of his blinds, I could see him sitting in front of his computer. Even from where I was standing I could tell what he was watching: that stupid video of me dancing around in my white bikini from last summer. I knew he had a ton of videos like that. I never thought anything of it, not until now. One of his hands was between his legs, moving quickly up and down, up and down. His body was tense and rigid and thrusting against his hand. My body shivered with a strange need. *Holy crap.* Selfishly, I wanted him to stop his private moment and turn it on me.

Without even thinking, I fumbled for my walkie-talkie and stammered a message into it, "Turn around."

His taunt body jumped up, facing the direction he kept his walkie-talkie in. I could see the stunned expression cross his face, eyes wide, and mouth open. With one hand still around himself, he shoved aside the blinds with the other.

His eyes met mine and I raised an eyebrow, daring him, daring him to continue to touch himself while watching the *live version of me*.

Please, Jase, please give me something to forget all the bad.

I took a deep breath and let the towel that was wrapped around me fall heavily in a damp heap around my feet. My heart thudded wildly in my chest and there was that strange ache between my legs again. It was like one of those aches when you saw a really sexy scene in a movie, but that kind was always in the pit of my belly. This ache was lower, much lower, and it was so intense. I felt like if I touched it, if I touched myself in that one specific spot, I would explode. His eyes looked everywhere at me, devouring me, and I shuddered with the need for him to touch me. Slowly, I slid my fingers down my belly and lowered them to the parts of my skin that throbbed the most. Instantly, my eyes squeezed shut tightly, too scared, and too terrified to see his reaction.

A few seconds later I felt something in the room *shift*; it was like the air became thicker and hotter. Blinking my eyes open, Jase was standing next to me, so close the warmth of his body made my cool skin prickle up with goose bumps.

I stopped breathing. I forgot my own name. I didn't know how to move. My cheeks flooded with warmth and my scalp tingled with heat, and that throb that was between my legs before, was pounding like it was my heartbeat. I was too frightened to look into his eyes, so I stared at his neck and watched it hammer with the pulse of his heart. I watched the rise and fall of his chest as it quickened.

Rise and fall.

Faster and Faster.

What am I supposed to do now? I never felt this much. The emotions, the need, the want–was overwhelming.

The rise and fall of his chest became even faster.

Then he stepped closer, lifting my chin to look at him.

Taking another step closer, he backed me up against my dresser. Sliding his hands up over my neck and grabbing a handful of my wet hair, he leaned down and opened his mouth over mine. When our lips touched my body went liquid. I thought my bones and muscles were going to melt into a thick, hot mass on the floor.

"Charlie," he whispered against my lips. "Do you want me to stop?" he asked, slowly skating his fingertips over my shoulders and collarbone.

"No," I whispered back hoarsely. "Don't stop. Don't ever stop."

"I've wanted you forever," he whispered as the heat of his warm breath brushed over my lips.

There were no more words.

When our lips touched again, there was more urgency, an uncontrollable need. His breath hitched as our tongues tangled together, and my hands were grasping at his shirt, clumsily lifting it over his head. I slid my hands to his waist, unbuttoned his jeans, lowered his zipper, and let everything that was keeping us apart fall to the floor. He kicked at his jeans, sending them flying across the room to land in a crumpled heap on my bed.

His fingers hesitantly curled around the weight of my breasts, caressing the rough pads of his fingers over my sensitive skin, touching, then tasting, licking, sucking. My pulse crashed in waves through my body; I'd never needed anything more in my life than I needed him.

I heard him hiss when I reached down and took him in my hand. Gripping him firmly, the smooth, taut skin throbbed and pulsed under my touch. Slowly, I moved my fist, sliding it up and down. Wrapping his hands around the back of my neck and kissing me deeper, he thrust himself against the palm of my hand, moaning into my mouth.

Still wrapped around each other, we stumbled awkwardly

to my bed, falling over the covers, laughing and giggling into each other. I was positive he had to feel the hammering of my heart as his hands and lips roamed my entire body. My head spun in circles. *This was my best friend. I was kissing and touching my best friend.* It was so utterly beautiful it nearly broke my heart.

My hands gripped the blankets that surrounded us as I watched him run his lips over me. When he reached the insides of my thighs, his dark, silky hair brushed along my most private area, sending shock waves through my body. A low moan escaped my lips and his mouth was on me, fingers inside me, as I franticly pressed myself against him, unable to control my hunger.

"Jase," I whimpered, pulling him up. His eyes were glazed over, a delirious smile on his face, lips glistening from *me*.

"I'm never going to get enough of you, Charlie," he said, looking into my eyes. "Even when we're old and gray, and back in diapers, I will never get enough of you." He captured my lips with his as I wrapped my legs around him. He lifted his lips from mine; his cheeks turned red with the question in his eyes. I nodded and smiled; my cheeks burning to probably match the color of his. He wildly grabbed at his pants that were on the covers next to us and pulled a foiled wrapper out of one of the pockets.

I yanked it out of his hand and ripped it open, giggling. "Let me," I whispered. And as he held himself over me, I slowly rolled it over the length of him with shaky fingers.

When I was done, he leaned his forehead against mine, gently laid himself over me, and grasped both my hands with his. Pulling them over my head, he entwined our fingers together, "Tell me what you want, Charlie."

"All I ever wanted was you, Jase," I whispered, lifting my hips to meet his.

"Then, I'm yours," he breathed, sliding slowly inside me.

"And, Charlie, you've always belonged to me." His forehead lifted off mine, our eyes locked, and the way he looked at me completely stole the air from my lungs. *I will never feel this way about anyone else in my life.*

His mouth claimed mine as we moved together. No, it was more than my mouth he claimed. He claimed my body, my soul, my mind; he claimed all of me. I knew without a single doubt in my heart, I would never love another person as completely as I loved Jase Delaney.

We slowly healed from our loss, wrapped in each other's arms. All around us, people were going on, living, breathing, working, laughing; whatever it was they did. But, we noticed nothing. None of it mattered, because we were the world to each other. Our kisses healed our tears. Our touches healed our sadness, and we healed each other.

There was nothing that
Could ever come between us.
We were each other's
forever.
But forever isn't real.
Is it?

CHARLIE

*D*uring our senior year, every moment Jase and I could steal for our own, we did. That Christmas we exchanged silver rings and vowed to never love anyone but each other. For Valentine's Day, we got fake IDs that said we were eighteen, so we could get half-heart tattoos. When we held hands, it made one heart. We slept in one another's arms every night in the tree house. Jase was there each time I cried over silly books in the middle of the night, or if I woke up, sobbing, with nightmares about Joey. His lips would find mind and we'd fit perfectly together—my lost puzzle piece finally fitting into place. His hands would slide across my skin in the darkness, pressing and shifting. I'd open to him each time, memorizing his breathing, his fingertips, his whispers, like every time would be our last, as if each time was our first.

And then winter turned to spring, and one day, when we were almost okay, the ground seemed to erupt beneath us. And within another few moments of violence, my life was changed yet again.

Jase was excited that night; he made reservations for us to

eat at a nice restaurant in the city and got tickets to see *Wicked*. There was no special reason; he just wanted me to get dressed up and feel special. He planned to take me to a bookstore after for coffee and dessert. It sounded like a perfect date to me. Anything to me was perfect where Jase was concerned—anything.

I even went and bought one of those little black dresses that all the glamor magazines swore you had to have. Better than that, I bought a pair of heels. High, like stripper high, heels. I even practiced walking in them.

I wanted to get ready as soon as I could, even if I was too early. My mother's boyfriend was over and she went out, leaving me in the house alone with him, which always creeped the Hell out of me. I had my curtains wide open, like I always did in my room, and so did Jase. We always seemed to need to keep in constant contact with each other, realizing it stemmed from what happened with Joey, and we never complained to each other. Neither of us felt suffocated; we just needed to feel safe. It was the only way we knew how. We spoke about it a lot and we never hid our feelings from each other no matter what the situation.

I ran from the bathroom with my robe on and a towel wrapped around my head, but Owen noticed me anyway. He always had a creepy way of standing outside of my bedroom door, offering me a smirk and a joint. "Mom's not home, precious," he said, chuckling.

"Jase is coming over *right now*. I have to get ready," I said, closing my bedroom door on him.

But of course, you could guess what happened. He wouldn't let me close the door on him. He kicked his foot out and slammed his big, beefy hands against it, knocking it wide open. I lunged for the walkie-talkies, but he got me before I could reach them. My robe was ripped, shredded, right off my body. I threw a punch at him, landing my fist against the bottom of his jaw, but he pushed me easily up against the wall with his body.

But I wasn't scared, because I could hear Jase as he tore through my front door. I could feel Jase as he yanked Owen clean off me and began pummeling and pounding on him with his fists. "She's mine!" I heard him scream, over and over. "You don't ever fucking touch her again, you hear me? You don't touch her!"

Owen tried to fight back. But Jase was an animal when he fought. I crawled away, still naked, trying to stay away from the two male bodies that were about to kill each other in the small confines of my room, while attempting to find something to cover myself with. Within minutes, Jase's father was there, separating his son from my predator. Jase's father tossed my tattered robe at my face, yelling at me to get dressed. And Owen, Owen was a bloody mess, threatening to sue Jase and his family.

I can still see him. Jase, panting heavily in the corner of my room with that crazed look on his face. *Unraveled.* I tried not to look directly into his eyes, the color intense and overwhelming. But they were my undoing; they unraveled *me* and trapped me, forever. They were stunning, yet intensely vacant, distant, and completely empty. *My beautiful monster.* He wanted to kill Owen, without even a thought, without regret, he would have. He would have done it for *me.*

Mr. Delaney was still holding him back when Jase's eyes zoned in on me. Both of his hands clenched on the edge of my dresser, his knuckles white with rage. "Let me go. Let me get Charlie. Let me see if she's okay," he begged through clenched teeth.

His father tightened his grip. "No, Jase. You went *too* far…"

"Move!" Jase shouted, his harsh growl cutting off his father's threat. The muscles of his jaw tightened and he pushed against his father's arms, cursing under his breath. **"Let me fucking see her!"**

"I'm okay, Jase," I said. My voice was a little more than a whisper. "He...he didn't touch me," I said, wrapping the torn robe closer to my skin. I tried to walk to him, but his father blocked my way.

"This is over," Mr. Delaney said. "The two of you, this *thing* you have, it's done." He grabbed Jase by the shoulders and shoved him out of my room toward the front door. Jase's eyes never left mine. Not until the door slammed in my face and Owen was standing alone with me, beaten to a bloody pulp.

I walked calmly to the kitchen.

"You touch me again," I said, pulling out a steak knife from one of the drawers, " and I promise you, I will carve my initials in your dick." Then, I walked backward into my room and locked my door.

Owen laughed at me for a good twenty minutes in front of that door, pounding and scratching at it just to taunt me.

Then, Jase's father did what he always did when he son acted out—he sent Jase away. I can still hear him screaming my name sometimes, the way he did that night when his father shoved him in the car. I wondered how long he'd be gone. It was April and there were only three more months until graduation. He'd be back soon, *right?*

I stood looking out my window for hours, staring out into the night, waiting for him to come back.... but he never did.

I stood there, wondering what I would possibly do, what *we* would possibly do, without one another. I counted my breaths since he'd gone: one thousand, eight hundred twenty-four.

I slept in the tree house alone, praying each night for the feel of him climbing into my sleeping bag beside me and curling around my body. But he never did. Seven thousand two hundred and sixty-two breaths since he left.

I waited for his call. An email. A text. Anything.

But I got nothing.

And I wanted my breaths to stop.

Breaths turned into hours, then days, and then weeks. At the end of April, a handful of shingles on the roof of the tree house ripped off in a strong thunderstorm, and the rain ran down the wall where Jase once wrote the silly words of my one-time favorite book. *Rabbit Hole* looked like it had melted and ran down the wood, and the heart next to it looked mangled and broken with its red ink seeping into the grain of the wood.

Then, two weeks after he left, I got a text message on my phone. *Jase!*

Come over

I'm in my bedroom

In the space between now and then, before and after, there's a *lifetime*. A lifetime of the choices you could have made, the paths you choose at the forks in the road, and the paths you never took. It's a lifetime full of wondering who you truly are or *who you could have been* if you had just taken that other path.

Sometimes, I cry so hard. Sometimes I scream so loud, just wishing for that heartbroken seventeen-year-old girl to take a different path.

But, she doesn't hear me.

Running at almost warp speed, I dashed through his back door straight into the kitchen. His house was eerily empty. That should have stopped me dead, but of course it didn't. Looking back in hindsight, everything could have been a path to turn back: *Why would he text? Why didn't he just come over? Where was he for two weeks?* I should have turned at every question I had. But none of it was the way I went, because all I thought about was Jase and running straight to him.

I would have never thought that he would hurt me.

The door to his room was half open and I busted through it excitedly.

You couldn't help but take a sweeping look around his bedroom when you first walked inside of it. His walls were painted an eggshell blue, and they were covered with heavy metal band posters: Avenged Sevenfold, Metallica, and Ozzy Osbourne. His computer was constantly on, playing a looped slide show, featuring pictures of him, Joey, and me—at school, riding dirt bikes, sitting in the sun. Scattered across his desk were a few empty soda bottles, an ashtray that he never hid from his parents, and dozens of books: Stephen King, Douglas Adams, John Green—all my idols. Leather bound notebooks filled with his writing and an empty bag of pretzels covered his bed. The smell that was only Jase filled the room; it was a mix between warm sunshine and his soap. It made my scalp tingle and my skin heat.

God, I'd missed him so much. I just wanted to be in his arms—safe.

A queen-sized bed took up the middle of his room, covered in a dark blue comforter. I had never sat on his bed; in all the years that I had known him, we rarely ever hung out in his room. And we had never been alone in it together.

I spun around in the middle of the empty room, confused. Then, the door clicked closed behind me. The lock snapped loudly into its chamber, and my heart swelled until it almost burst. I leaned in the direction of the door, ready to run to him, and swung my head around to face him. My cheeks burned from the wideness of my smile. I stumbled backward when my eyes discovered who was blocking the door.

It wasn't Jase.

It was not Jase at all.

Not even close.

Standing before me in his typical ominous and over-bearing disposition, was Mr. Delaney, Jase's womanizing, abusive, controlling father.

I stumbled and flinched back so violently in shock that I slammed into Jase's computer desk, causing his pile of books to fall and tumble against the wall and floor.

"I...I thought that...I just got a text...from Jase," I stammered, moving across the length of the desk to further myself from Mr. Delaney. The hairs on the back of my neck tingled, and everything felt wrong. *Why was Mr. Delaney in here? Was Jase in the bathroom? Was he going to yell at Jase and me again for what happened? Didn't he realize that wasn't my fault? Owen was a disgusting pervert!*

Mr. Delaney, dressed in one of his fancy suits, slowly walked closer to me. I leaned away from him, practically bending myself backward against the edge of Jase's desk. My hands, which were clammy with nervous sweat, slipped and slid over the surface of the desk, hitting into the computer mouse and grabbing onto the ashtray. If he tried to hurt me, then I was going to slam the damn ashtray against his head.

"Put that down, Charlotte. I don't want you to hurt yourself. The only one allowed to hurt you is going be *me*," he said, menacingly.

The words didn't register. They made no sense to me, as Mr. Delaney leaned forward, over my body, and grabbed for the computer mouse, sliding it over the mouse pad. "Turn around, Charlotte. I want you to watch something I found on Jase's computer." His free hand came up and pried the ashtray out of my grip. Tossing it onto the carpet, it made a loud thump against the wooden floor underneath, spraying a cloud of ash and cigarette butts across the room.

When I didn't move, he grabbed my shoulders and force-fully turned me in the direction of the screen. A still shot of me was displayed in an open file, standing in that stupid white bikini that Jase loved so much. Tears stung my eyes. Why did he want me to watch this? Did he want me to feel ashamed? *Embarrassed? Dirty? What?*

My knees felt weak; *all* of my bones felt feeble and shaky, like I was a person made of straw and one strong wind would scatter me across the earth. Then, he clicked on the play arrow, and the video of me dancing across the lawn in a very skimpy bikini started.

"You like making these movies? Letting him take pictures of you?" His voice was low and angry.

I didn't answer. All I could do was look down and let the tears fall, spilling against my shirt. I knew about the video. I knew Jase watched it...a lot. It never made me feel dirty or awkward. But, with Mr. Delaney standing over me, it was the first time I felt bad or disgusted about it. His father just made it filthy when all it ever was before was innocent and beautiful.

Grabbing my face, he yanked it back up to look at him. "I asked you a question. You're supposed to answer me when I do that," he growled, nostrils flaring.

"N...no..." I stuttered, trying to slide my body away from his, but he just gripped my face harder with his hand. What was I supposed to say to him to make him understand how much I loved Jase? It was just me in a bathing suit; I never took it off! It wasn't the start of some seductive striptease. That video was innocent. Why was he trying to make me feel guilty—and dirty?

"You're a liar," he spit out, pushing his body up against me, slamming me hard into the edge of Jase's desk. He was so close to me, bending over me, that the heat from his putrid breath was gagging me. I squeezed my eyes shut tight, but the smell of rotting alcohol and stale cigarettes seeped into my skin. I shivered from sheer disgust.

I tried to push against his chest with both of my hands, but he didn't budge. His hands dropped from my face and gripped both of my wrists so tightly I thought my bones would break. Tears blurred my vision as I looked up at him, and when my eyes fixed on his, I knew I was in trouble. My mind started freaking out, raw panic had my chest heaving violently, and my heart was hammering so hard I felt it in my throat.

His body was locked against mine; my hands were trapped in his. Not one damn part of my body would work to try to get myself away. In my head, I was this brave fighter, twisting and clawing my way to freedom, tearing his face off in my defense. But in reality, my body wouldn't move —*couldn't move.*

With one hand, he yanked the mouse cord from the computer and I started struggling to get free, thinking that he couldn't hold me with just one hand. But I was wrong. I dropped my body to the floor, trying to make myself heavy as he wrapped my wrists together with the cord.

He pulled me up and dragged me across the rug. My knees scraped and stung as I tried to pull back and escape from his grip. I screamed until my throat burned like fire, and his hands came up, muffling my mouth to silence me. "Shut up, Charlotte! You're going to wake my wife," My body shook violently from my sobs.

He threw me on Jase's bed and I tried desperately to kick out my legs, but Mr. Delaney just straddled them, pressing all of his weight on me, sinking me deep into the mattress. Yanking my hands above my head, he looped the mouse cord against the metal frame of the bed. He quickly yanked my yoga pants down, and I kicked at him violently when one of my legs broke free. Slamming his fist into my inner thigh, I cried out as the pain overwhelmed me. *I couldn't move.* Laughing, he tied one of my feet to the end of the bedpost with my own fucking pants and sat heavily on the other leg that was throbbing with pain.

Pulling up my shirt, he yanked down the cups of my bra, and sat over me, staring at my naked breasts. Then, his hands were on them, greedily touching what wasn't his to touch, and I cried out a loud whimper.

"Shut your fucking mouth!" he yelled, smacking one of his hands hard against the side of my head. He continued squeezing and touching my breasts. His harsh touches made me want to curl into a fetal position and disappear. Melt away and crumble into dust—blow away and evaporate into the wind.

His eyes traveled down my trembling body to my panties, and he licked his disgusting lips. "You're going to enjoy this, Charlotte. Just relax, okay?" he murmured, trailing his fingers hard against the skin of my belly and down over the cotton material of my underwear. Finding that special bump, he circled his thumb over it and brought his mouth down over my nipples and pulled at them with his lips.

My body started shaking in sheer horror when his lips and fingers started making things happen inside my body. This was a contradiction of what was happening to me. My head did not want his touches; my brain was screaming, "No!" But, the cotton material of my panties were slowly becoming damp from this man knowing exactly where to touch me, how to touch me. "Please, stop. Please. Please, stop," I cried.

Bloodshot eyes looked into mine. His mouth traveled down, meeting his fingers. Watching me, he pulled my panties to the side and took a taste of what he was *doing* to me.

I closed my eyes tightly and let my head fall to the side so I couldn't see him anymore. With the cord biting into my wrists, the resolve and fight drained out of me. I closed in on myself. It was bad enough I had to feel everything he was doing to me; I didn't want to freaking watch it too. He spread me wide and ran his tongue along me, sucking and nipping at my flesh.

Hearing him pulling his zipper down, a new wave of terror shot through me. Through my tears, I watched as he held himself in his hands and rubbed his head around my opening.

"Please don't," I sobbed, trying to hip thrust him off me.

And then the weight of him pressed heavily against my chest, and an intense burn ripped up from between my legs as he thrust into me with long hard strokes. He buried his face in my neck and whispered into my ear. "You like this, don't you?"

"No," I sobbed through clenched teeth. My bound hands tightened into hard fists, and I struggled violently to pull them free. His weight was so heavy against my stomach and chest, I felt as if I couldn't breathe. I closed my eyes tighter to the monster above me—a real-life breathing, panting, moaning, grunting, disgusting monster that was hovering above me, slamming itself inside me, over and over again. My mind took me to a safe place, and I was four years old again, sitting in my tree house for the first time ever, staring in awe and wonder at the castle in a tree that my father built for me. I remembered pretending to be Rapunzel, locked away in her tower, waiting for someone to rescue me. It was always Joey who pretended to be my prince, as long as he got to use his plastic sword or his Ninja Turtle nun-chucks; he always came to rescue me. Fuck those perfect, *untouched* Disney princesses and all their bullshit happily-ever-afters. To hell with those piece-of-shit useless princes, who never come to get you and just end up dead.

Reality was a cold, hard bitch, slapping my face. Mr. Delaney's laughter echoed through my happy place, his dirty words, his vile voice, making my safe imagination crumble into a harsh reality before my eyes. "Yes, you like this, baby girl, you like when I fuck you," he panted.

"No. I. Don't."

His raspy laugh puffed heat against my neck, "You're fucking lying to me again. This feels so good for you, doesn't it? I'm going to fuck you until you come so hard that you'll want to come back here tomorrow." Leaning his head back, he yanked me by the hair on the top of my head to force me to look at him. "Don't close your eyes, Charlotte. Look at me while I fuck you."

His hands clenched tightly at my esophagus, squeezing it until I did look at his crazed, wild eyes.

I didn't want to watch his face over mine—the sweat dripping from his brow, the bared teeth and tensed muscles as he moved inside me. So, I just pictured my Jase and how he always looked at me like I was his treasure when we were together. The beautiful image of his face was the only thing I saw as this man, *this sick, fucking, nasty, monster of a man*, ravaged and ruined me. And here, I thought stupidly that nothing could ever erase the worst event that ever happened to me. Here, I thought whenever I closed my eyes, I would always relive the moment my best friend was beaten to death less than ten feet away from me, and I could do nothing to help him. Finally, I found something else to repeatedly see on the back of my eyelids—the laser blue eyes of the disgusting man as he took everything from me.

Dipping his hand between our bodies, he rubbed against me until that low tension built deep inside, and no matter how hard I fought it, how hard I fought him, my body still ended up defying me. That pressure built and built, until I couldn't control the madness, and my body convulsed hard and pitifully around him. I wished I could bury my face and my shame, but I couldn't. He was still grunting and pumping relentlessly against me. His heavy body jerked violently, and with one last, loud grunt, he exploded painfully inside me, spilling what felt like fire deep within me. I never felt that before, none of it. Jase and I were always so careful, using condoms and now...now I was violated, defiled, and utterly destroyed. I turned my head and vomited against the blue comforter beneath me. The horrid smell of it made me heave more, and I spit remnants of my breakfast across the top of the dark blue blanket.

"Well, I'm unimpressed, honestly. That was a less than stellar performance from you. I don't understand what my son saw in you. Maybe because you were so easy?" he stated, zipping up his pants, tucking his shirt inside them, and straightening his suit jacket.

Quickly, he untied my leg from the bedpost and pulled my tied hands off their prison against the frame of the bed. "Get up," he demanded.

I don't know why, but I did what he said. I couldn't imagine him doing anything worse to me at that point, so I just followed his directions, hoping the next thing he would do was kill me. I wanted to die just from the feel of his semen running warmly down the inside of my legs.

Unlocking and opening the door, he shoved my body through the doorway into the hallway, pushing me hard into the bathroom. I stumbled, hitting my shoulder against the edge of the sink and falling hard against the hard, ceramic bathtub. He stood over me and turned the faucet on in the tub, touching the water with his hands to check the temperature. I silently cried and watched the steam rise up off the tiles. Yanking me up by my hair, he forced me into the tub. The water was scalding, but the burn of him rubbing the soap over my skin and deep inside me hurt so much worse. To this day, I can sometimes still feel the phantom sting and fire of that awful white bar of soap. That shit never leaves you, and *the smell of it*…the smell of that soap makes me want to peel my own damn skin off.

When he was done with me, I sat in a dripping heap of towels on the cold, tiled, bathroom floor. He threw my clothes at me and offered a smile. "If you tell anyone, I'll make sure to tell Jase how hard your little pussy came for me. I felt it, you know, when you came." He yanked my hair back until my eyes met his. "You came so hard it milked my cock dry." He smiled then and chuckled down at me. "I also recorded it on Jase's little camera; did you hear yourself moaning, Charlotte? If you want to come back I can teach you how to be a real woman…how to please a man. If not, this is me telling you, you will not ruin my son's life. He wouldn't want you now, anyway." He walked out, laughing, the steam of the hot water chasing him out.

Dressing as fast as I could, I ran out of the bathroom and down the hallway into the kitchen. My throat gagged back more hot bile when I saw Mrs. Delaney sitting in her wheel-chair next to the kitchen table. Cold, hard eyes blazed at me. Her head was trembling and her nostrils flared with loud, noisy breaths. "You're disgusting; you pathetic piece of trash," she growled, with the first words I had *ever* heard her speak.

My shoes became concrete, and my skin felt like stone. I had just been victimized in a room a few feet away from someone who could have helped me—his wife. Did she not hear me scream? Couldn't she have called the cops? Did she think I wanted that?

What the hell would Jase think? And then everything seemed to crumble and disintegrate around me, and I knew. *I knew* there was never going back from there.

Running out the back door, I couldn't even think a straight thought. My insides hurt; my thighs burned. But most of all, my eyes ached with the tears. I tore into my house, grabbed my purse, which had an extra set of Jase's truck keys inside, and stole his damn truck to take myself to the hospital. I would not let him get away with raping me. My body moved, pushing itself through the motions of taking me someplace safe.

Hospital.

Police.

Help.

I didn't remember the drive there. I have no idea how I came about slumped in the arms of a nurse in the middle of an emergency room in a hospital that was over twenty minutes away from my house, still clutching one of Jase's old T-shirts.

Hysterical and terrified, I was taken to an examination room to wait for a physician to administer a *rape* kit. The word suffocated me, cut off my oxygen, and my world turned black as I collapsed against the chairs and walls and whatever else I hit on my quick fall to meet the floor. The doctor watching over me held the police at bay, not allowing them to question me until she was finished.

Sometime later, when the sky outside the window was dark, I was awake enough for evidence to be *pulled from me.* Documents were signed. Questions were asked. Swabs of DNA were taken out of my private areas with long Q-tip looking things that scraped the Hell out of my insides. Urine was collected, and blood was taken. Everything was bagged and labeled in front of me. They offered me a morning after pill, and horrified by the chance of having a monster's baby grow inside of me, I took it.

I took it.

A pretty, dark-haired nurse held me until my trembling stopped.

"Miss Stone?" I looked up from behind the nurse's arms to the sight of an officer holding open a small memo pad. "Did you know the perpetrator of this attack?"

All I could do was nod.

The officer sighed and leaned at the edge of examination table I was on. "Can I have his name?"

"Michael Delaney," I said in a low voice.

The officer narrowed his eyes at me and folded his hands across his chest, rumpling his memo pad. "Really now? Judge Delaney?"

"Yes," I whispered, swallowing hard.

"Do you know false claims of sexual assault are punishable with jail time, Miss Stone?"

"I don't understand..."

"You don't understand? You're accusing a Supreme Court Justice of a felony, Miss Stone. Is there a chance you could be wrong about the identity or the actions...?"

"That's enough!" The doctor shouted over the questions. "I just examined her myself, Officer. There is physical evidence of an assault, and *I* want to press charges on her behalf."

The doctor physically escorted the officer out into the hallway. "That line of questioning is just victimizing her all over again."

Female officers spoke to me about Penal Laws and Rape in the third degree since I was only seventeen, and Rape in the First degree since I said it was forced. They warned me about a long backlog of rape kits and how sometimes kits don't get tested for years after the evidence is collected.

When I was escorted into the waiting area, my mother was standing with a scowl slashed across her bright red lips. I ran to her and threw my arms around her, but she didn't hold me back. She just stood there, still and hard. "How could you make up a story like this? Is it attention that you need? First you accuse Owen of something he would never do, now Mr. Delaney?" My mother. My own mother physically shoved me into the passenger seat of Jase's truck and then climbed into the driver's seat. Without even a glance in my direction she said, "I want you out of my house by tomorrow."

What?

Where the hell was I supposed to go?

In my wildest dreams, I had never thought about leaving that house. With all the shit that was said to me there, with all the times I had to stay in the tree house at night to hide from her and her drugged up friends, I never thought to leave. The only safe place I could think to go was to Joey's mom, and he was gone. Mrs. Graley couldn't look-me in the eyes without bursting into tears, remembering her son. I couldn't go there.

"And Charlotte, don't you ever come back."

"Sure, not a problem, *Mom*," I said, swallowing the lump of sorrow in my throat. I held my chin up, trying hard not to show her my tears. The rest of the drive home was my mother telling me how awful of a person I was and how much trouble it had been to raise a whore, a piece of lying, good for nothing trash daughter, who was just like my father.

The minute she yanked the truck into park in front of our house, I jumped out and ran inside. Owen was sitting at the dining room table with two big guys smoking a huge joint together. He laughed when I stumbled inside. Ignoring them, I raced down the hallway and into my bedroom, slamming the door behind me. From under my bed, I pulled out my schoolbag and dumped the contents all over the floor. Rummaging through my drawers, I grabbed a few days' worth of clothes, my deodorant, my albums full of photos, a few of my sketchpads, a shitload of my favorite books, and shoved them in my bag. Dashing past the high-as-hell assholes in the living room, I yanked Jase's truck keys out of the hands of the person *who spit me out of her womb,* and started loading the truck with everything I could that belonged to me. I made about five trips as those assholes rolled on the floor and laughed their asses off at me. I even took the damn ashtray I made for my mother in art class when I was in fifth grade, a box (yes, *box*) of her precious *white-trash* wine, and her most prized possessions: her *entire* collection of painkillers that filled up ten bottles along the top glass shelf of the medicine cabinet. *FUCK her.*

I took my bank account books, and the stash of rolled up hundreds my mother kept hidden from Owen inside her make-up case in the bathroom, shoved deep inside an empty bottle of wrinkle cream. I held on tightly to the cash and leaned against the cool, tiled wall of the bathroom as tears streamed down my cheeks. I forced myself to look at my reflection in the mirror behind the sink before I left. The person who stared back scared the hell out of me. It was the face of a complete stranger, with knotted tangled hair stuck against the sides of her face and giant, frightened, red-rimmed eyes with deep purplish skin below them. You couldn't see any bruises or cuts on my skin. The pain that ached and hurt in me was somewhere deep inside, far away from the surface. But the pain was pure and real, and mine.

I staggered through the rest of the house, sobbing. Without saying goodbye, I walked out the front door, hoping to God it was the last time I ever had to see those disgusting people.

I stumbled down the porch steps and fell to my knees on the walkway.

From the corner of my eye, I noticed Mrs. Delaney sitting just inside her entrance door, watching me. She was in the wheelchair, just like that first day, but now she was alone. There was no kid bouncing a basketball against her and no husband carrying her luggage.

"*You weak bitch!*" I screamed at her, grabbing a handful of her garden pebbles and hurling them against the glass door she hid behind. "You are going to live with this. What he did. What you let him do. You *heard* me screaming. *You heard me.* I hope you rot in hell." I crawled around the dirt and grass throwing whatever I could grab with my hands, and screamed until my throat was raw.

I was completely dead inside when I started Jase's truck and took off, peeling out and smoking the tires when I slammed my foot down on the gas pedal. Somehow, someday, I hoped I would be able to say I survived what had happened to me. But the truth was, at that moment, all I wished for was a quick and painless death. Something to just end all the chaos, end all the sorrow that was overwhelming me.

I drove to the only place I could think of....the cemetery. I needed my best friend.

I made it all the way there, crying and screaming at my windshield while taking huge gulps from the box of wine. Parking the truck on the side entrance to the cemetery, I hauled myself over the cement wall, clutching my wine and landing with a hard thud against the hard ground. Pathetically enough, even in the pitch dark of night, I knew exactly how to get to Joey's gravestone. I probably could have walked blindfolded and found it. I fell on my knees in front of his marker, praying, and talking to Joey.

"Please, just a minute," I cried, slurring my words. "Just talk to me for a minute. Tell me what to do to make this shitty life worth living. Tell me what I need to do. You were my best friend, and I lost you. I lost Jase, and I lost everything. Please talk to me one last time and tell me what to do." The silence that answered back almost killed me.

Alone.

I felt so *dirty.*

Helpless.

I felt so *ashamed.*

I'm so fucking scared.

I emptied the box of wine and I could no longer read the name on the gravestone through my blurry vision. Quickly, I forgot the hands that touched me and the lips that kissed me, but I still saw that cold, blue stare hovering over me when I closed my eyes. Slowly, the raw pain of my dirty shame got swallowed, along with the alcohol that surged through my system, and I floated along the dark sky of clouds above me.

I don't know how long I slept on the soft grass above the grave of my dead best friend, but I woke when the sun was warm and shining brightly against the front of my eyelids.

With throbbing eye sockets, I climbed back into the stolen truck and drove without a shred of direction.

When all was said and done, when it was all over, I was numb. Then, it rushed back in flashes. Minutes after, days after, months and years after. When I showered alone, when I was in a crowded room with people who thought they knew and loved me, when I was shopping for food. The flashes came and they reminded me, reminded me of who I am, and what was done, and what I've lost.

And every day after Mr. Delaney raped me, a little more of me died. It peeled away my layers of skin, little by little; my self-worth, my beauty, my innocence, my smile—until I was nothing but a bag of bones. The further the days got from what happened, the further I got from the seventeen-year-old girl I once was. It shredded me into fine, little pieces of thin tissue paper. He took everything that was *me*, and all I could wonder was *who would I be now?* I had no sense of self. I didn't know who I should be. What was the right me, because even though I knew it was wrong and I hated it, my body responded to him. Did I really want him? Did I ask for it?

How could I go back to being *me* now, after *that*? How could I face Jase after what I had done with his father? How could I ever let him see me again? His last name was like a poison to me. All these people poisoning my life; the bullies who thought they had the right to punch people and hurt them, call them names, scar them, kill them, touch them, all these people in my life who had made their poison seep through my skin. I was done with it. I couldn't be that girl anymore. I couldn't be Charlie anymore.

This wasn't how my story was supposed to be written.

This wasn't the way I wanted my story to go.

So I needed to rewrite it.

Word for word.

Rewritten.

Because, I was so young.

So young.

And utterly broken.

JASE

*T*onight's another routine *buy and walk*, picking up a bottle of a hundred Oxycontin for a supplier. It was supposed to take place on the corner as always, but the perp called my job phone to change plans. Doc, as we called him, the dealer, wanted me to hang out and meet a bunch of his friends at Club Underground. He explained that his girl was there and he had to watch her. He thought she was messing with some other dude. Wanted to know if I had the sort of friends that would see to it that she and the guy she's giving it to could permanently disappear.

"Of course I got those kinds of friends, if the price is right," I told him.

So it was Carter and I going as the undercovers, and Brooke was ghosting us. I was getting closer to Doc; real close to finding out who he got his pharmaceuticals from. Now he was asking to put a hit out on someone? I couldn't wait to put this asshole away for good.

The team parked the van by the side entrance of the club and the three of us jumped out, dressed to the nines for clubbing. And if Doc was being a little weasel tonight, Carter and

I both had a few placebo Oxycontin decoys in our front pockets, to prove we weren't narcs.

I hated clubs with half naked girls walking around drunk out of their heads, trying to find guys to buy them their next rounds, and the pumped-up testosterone of the juiced-up players ready for a fight.

We were in without a hitch. I thought it was thanks to Brooke since she was practically wearing an outfit right out of a Fredricks of Whoreywood catalog. She looked hot, though. I'd give her that. But that was all I was giving her.

"Beer?" Carter asked.

"Yeah, whatever. Let's get this shit done. I have a ton of paperwork to get to," I said, leaning myself against the bar and scanning the dance floor.

Carter ordered two bottles and slid one to me. Brooke was on the dance floor dead center, trying to dance provocatively and giving the head of a beer bottle a blowjob for my entertainment.

It wasn't very entertaining.

I brought my bottle to my lips to take a sip, when I spot a mass of copper-colored hair in the mix of sweaty bodies. As always, my gut wrenched. To me, every girl could be her. I *wanted* every girl to be her. She wouldn't be in New York though—in a club like this—surrounded by drugs and crime. She was probably lying safely next to the lucky guy who married her, somewhere in sunny California, with her two kids tucked into their beds.

I watched that mass of copper-colored hair though, captivated. Her body was moving enticingly to the rhythm of the song. The way her hips rocked and swayed was so hypnotizing. I took another sip of beer and warmth mushroomed like a strange poison across my stomach. This girl in front of me stood out like a rescue ship in a dark sea of waste. She wasn't dressed like the rest of the girls; she wore a simple, low hung pair of jeans and a plain T-shirt that revealed her toned back when her hands swayed in the air above her head. Her profile, the curve of her breasts, the round swell of her hips as they moved, and the contour of her ass just mesmerized me. Every move was like magic, causing my body to lean forward, craving something.

"Doc's at ten o'clock. Flanked by two. Dude, what are you staring at?" Carter hissed in my ear.

"Hmmm? What happened?" I snapped my face in his direction.

"Bro. Let's just do this buy and go. I gotta take a piss." Carter's eyes slid across the dance floor. "He's waiting on us, let's go."

"Yeah, sure," I said, my eyes drifting back to the girl dancing. She twirled around laughing, and suddenly my pulse was racing, the sound of it like crashing waves against my ears. No damned way.

It couldn't be her.

No way.

My steps faltered as Carter went forward clapping and shaking hands with the perp. I stood frozen, my eyes watching that familiar neck, the shape of her lips, the move of those hips.

When she turned completely around, it was like I'd been shot in the chest. Full force, point blank, dead. I couldn't fucking breathe.

The perp stepped in front of me, blocking my view. "Hey, JD, you okay, son?"

"Hey, Bren," I croaked. "What's up? Yeah. Yeah. I'm good. This place is just packed with some real beauties."

He nodded his head to me and offered me a pair of drunk-ass duck lips. Asshole.

We made the exchange, hand-to-hand. He pulled me in for a hug and dropped the pill bottle in my palm, which I stuffed into the pocket that held the placebo pills. Carter shook his hand next, went in for a hug, and paid him. I blinked my eyes a few times. I couldn't concentrate. If he pulled out a gun right now, I'd be dead. Forget that. I looked behind Bren's shoulder. A person who looked a lot like Charlie was still dancing. Was it her? My heart stopped instantly, and I was seriously freaking out that I might be having a heart attack in the middle of an undercover buy.

Panic set in.

Charlie was here? Am I seeing things?

"Try the merchandise, bro. You'll feel better," Bren yelled over the music.

Hold it together Delaney. Put the right pill in your mouth. You don't want to have a forced ingestion and get taken to the hospital for observation after this buy. My hands were steady, which surprised the Hell out of me.

"Gimme one too, bro," Carter said, rubbing his hands together. His head turned to Bren to get his attention away from me in case I screwed up our little illusion, "Damn, this place is full of sweet pussy. *Hooo-leee-shit.*"

As he had Bren and the others' attention, I lifted the cap off the bottle and pretended to pour out two in my hand and put the cap back on. But what was left in my hand were the placebo pills that looked exactly like the Oxycontin. Thank fuck they had no special markings on them or we would have been busted. Handing one to Carter, he smiled at me and we both popped them into our mouths and washed them down with our beer.

"Fuck yeah!" Bren yelled. "Hey, you think there's nice pussy here? Wait 'til you see the girls I have with me. Fucking golden." Then he was off. Carter and I stared at each other in dismay, and the next thing I saw was my perp with his arm around the shoulders of the only girl I ever loved. He pushed her forward, tucked tight into his side, and she looked mad as hell at him. She looked exactly the same. Her hair was longer than I remembered, but her face? Her beautiful face stole my breath away.

Bren pulled her closer, leaned over her, and placed an open-mouthed kiss against her temple. It was almost physically painful to watch it happen. I wanted to look away. Hell, I wanted to storm out of this club and take a shower to wash away the filth that suddenly felt two inches thick all over my skin.

Her green gaze snapped up and collided with mine. She flinched back as if something slammed her hard in the chest. *Good, I hope it hurt like hell.* I hope her fucking heart was racing—just as fast as mine. I hoped it was squeezing in her chest, throbbing, choking, and gasping for all that it's been missing. *Just like mine.* I tried like hell to drag my eyes off of hers, but I couldn't; they were locked on her like a vise grip.

Bren was talking to Carter about something and I was struck deaf and dumb. The only thing I saw was tunnel vision right to her. We both stared at each other. *Did she know it was me?* I stepped closer and searched her face. Her lips quivered the smallest bit, and she was sort of wobbling at the knees. She knew it was me. She knew she was caught. I knew her well enough to know exactly what she was thinking, and she knew—she definitely knew.

Suddenly, Charlie was a woman. Where did she learn how to sway when she walked? Who taught that little girl to bite down on her lower lip when she looked at a man? Where did my sweet girl go? God, did she always have such plump lips? Did her cheeks always blush such a beautiful pale red? Did she always look at me with those emerald eyes, like I was the freaking messiah...?

"Yeah...yeah, and this is my girl, Sage," I heard the words falling from the perp's lips. That scumbag just introduced her as his girlfriend, and she was supposed to be married with children and living almost three thousand miles away from me in sunny California. As an artist. Everything that she was supposed to grow up to be. But she was standing right in front of me, next to a piece of shit criminal that I'd been buying drugs off of for months.

I forgot how to breathe.

Her eyes got larger, rounder, and I swore, greener. A tinge of red splashed over her cheeks. I clenched my fists to my side so I didn't go yanking her away from him.

Bren was talking smack with Carter, who obviously saw I was floundering, and I cut them all off by asking her, "Do I know you?"

"No. I don't believe so," she whispered in a low, hoarse voice.

"Yeah, I think we've met before," I urged, stepping closer to her.

"Um, no. I'm certain I would remember you," she said, stepping back.

"Sage? Let me guess, is that a stripper's name," I taunted.

Her eyes narrowed and her beautiful face tilted up toward Bren. "Why is it every time I meet an asshole, the same shit comes out of its mouth?"

Yeah, that's Charlie.

"Well. Hello…Bren's girlfriend, Sage," I said. Leaning in, I whispered against her ear, "Sorry, I guess I was mistaken. You look sort of like the only girl who had ever gotten close enough to me to break my fucking heart."

I stepped away and watched her. She ignored me, looking at a girl with strange violet streaks in her hair standing next to her. "Hey, JD. We're getting outta here. Come party with us."

This was usually where we left the perps and went back to base to sit behind our desks writing reports about everything that was said and done. But I was standing in front of Charlie for the first time in years, and I wanted answers.

"Yeah, bro," I said, downing the last of my beer and wiping the back of my hand across my mouth. "I'm up for it,"

Bren smiled and led us through the crowd of dancing bodies; his entourage flanking the sides of him like he was a king. Her whole body cringed, and her eyes squeezed tight as she got pulled in with the tide. Scratch anything nice I'd ever felt or said about myself before. *I was a dick*. Looking at her walking away from me, looking at her, at those green eyes that looked flat and lifeless, I realized that something or someone hurt her. Something big. She was like a cardboard replica of the girl I once loved; stiff, hard, and empty. I messed up. Should I have looked harder for her? I should have fought harder against my father. Nah, maybe she just left. She never gave me the answer in her texts.

Carter pounded me in the arm when they all walked in front of us. "What the fuck? Are you crazy?" He clawed at my shirt, pulling me back.

I shoved my face into his. "That's Charlie."

Carter gave me a confused look. His mind was only on the case—then his eyes widened as it sunk in and his body stiffened next to me. "My Charlie," I repeated. It was all I needed to say.

"Ah, man. Seriously?" He stood there raking a hand through his hair. "We're going to get in a shitload of trouble, Jase. Let's just go."

"To hell with trouble."

"J, you need to walk away."

"Hey, I have a prescription for *Growacet*, testicular fortitude capsules, you could take one and then maybe you won't be such a pussy," I snapped in his face and walked after Bren. After a few feet, I stopped and glanced back at Carter over my shoulder. "That's *my girl*."

"Yeah. Okay. I'll meet you outside. Let me go give Brooke the heads up and have her tail us to be safe, yeah?"

"Deal." I called out to him as I chased after Bren and his gang.

I caught up to them outside the entrance. Bren nodded to me and asked, "Where's your boy?"

"He met a piece of ass earlier and he's getting her number before he leaves. He'll be out in a minute."

"No worries. We're going to take a cab to my place. I don't drink and drive. Always gotta obey the laws," he winked and started talking to one of his friends. I think his name was Jett.

Sage was standing against the wall with the strange haired girl, so I slid up next to her and pulled out a pack of cigarettes. I don't usually smoke while I work, but right then my nerves needed something. I pulled one out and offered one to her. "Wanna smoke?"

"I don't smoke," she whispered.

"When did you stop smoking?"

"When I realized the cigarette does all of the smoking and you're just the sucker." She pulled herself off the wall and looked up at the sky. "I really think you have me confused with someone else. I'm sorry for whatever heartbreak you had. But, I'm not the girl you think I am." She walked a few steps away, keeping me at a distance.

Suddenly, Carter was next to me with his arm around my shoulder, whispering in my ear, "She worth it?"

I just stared at her and nodded like an idiot, but answered, "Probably not since she's proved to be nothing but a messed up liar. But, I just need answers."

Bren hailed three taxis and walked up next to Sage. "You're coming, right?"

"I think Violet and I are going to head back. I'm really tired."

"Bull-fucking-shit! You ain't tired. You're either going to text your secret little prince charming or you're going to go home alone and read. What the fuck are you reading now? *The Great Gatsby*? I'll just buy you the stupid movie."

"The loneliest moment in someone's life is when they are watching their whole world fall apart, and all they can do is stare blankly," I remarked.

Bren just looked at me and stared—dumbfounded. I shrugged. "One of my best friends growing up got me hooked on reading and I never gave it up."

"Oookay," Bren turned around, shaking his head.

"Come on, bro." I laughed at him. "You gotta love a girl who reads...one of those girls that wakes you up at two a.m. clutching her books to her chest in tears."

"Bro, how many pills did you pop?"

I laughed and leveled my gaze back on Charlie's. "Nah, not the pills talking. I just love a chick who reads. They see things that other people don't." I gave her a smirk and a wink. "They can find magic in words and bring life into the mundane everyday things with their imagination. I'd just let her wake me up and give her a hug, pull her close. I'd let her tell me about the scene in the book that made her cry." I shrugged my shoulders and continued, "Then, to comfort her, I'd kiss the fucking hell out of her lips, make her want to read a book that I was the main character in. Be a man worth immortalizing with words."

Bren laughed out loud. "Yeah, you could be best friends with the nerd." He pointed to Charlie. "She used to be a lot more fun, though."

Two of the taxis were filled and left, leaving Violet, Sage, Bren, Carter, and me on the sidewalk. "Let's go, you fucking booknerds," Bren called out, climbing into the last taxi.

Carter slid in the front seat of the taxi, and the girls quietly followed Bren. I sat squashed between the hard stickiness of the taxi door and the soft heat of Charlie. The ride was silent and quick. We drove across town and then stumbled out onto the sidewalk in front of the building where I usually do business with him.

My eyes never left her as Bren pulled me over to the side and whispered, "That's her. I need her taken care of, bro. Not tonight. Not in front of me. We'll talk business tomorrow." He bumped shoulders with me and smiled maliciously, "Relax and chill with me and my boys. Get your dick a little wet tonight. I always have prime pussy with me—ass too if that's what you need."

I nodded, clenching my teeth.

Bren and his friends led the way through the lobby and into the elevator. Charlie held the door open for Violet. They looked at each other, silently passing secrets between them with their eyes. Carter walked in after Violet and I followed. As I passed, I turned to face her. I slid through the doorway purposely too close to her, gliding my whole body against hers, and she let out a small gasp. I could tell how it affected her by the way her face turned bright red, and she looked like she was having trouble breathing, limbs shaking.

"Hmmm," I hummed in her ear. "Sorry, *Charlie.*"

She shifted closer into me, fists clenched. "I told you, I have no idea who you are," she said through heavy breaths.

I felt the heat from her body against mine. It rolled off her like waves, and I wanted to dive into her ocean. Leaning my face closer to hers, I looked dead in her eyes. I could have stared into them for hours, days, weeks. No, I wanted to stare at them for forever. I wanted to stare at those green pools until the ivory smooth skin around them turned thin and wrinkled with lines from her laughter and not a second less. There was no way to ever describe the depth of green of Charlie's eyes. I'd spent years trying to forget that color, and now they were making me want to slam her against the wall and tell me what the fuck was going on. First, I had to prove she was Charlie.

I slid my hand to cup her neck, "Okay. But I got one word for you, ya know, to prove you're Charlotte Stone."

Wide eyes stared into mine.

Her lips parted,

And she waited.

"Joey,"

I whispered.

And then

The tears

Came.

CHARLIE

The whole world stopped and completely vanished the second he spoke the name. My eyes welled with almost a decade worth of tears, and my hands balled into a lifetime worth of angry fists.

Dressed all in black with those silent, watchful eyes, was Jase Delaney, and he was all man. There was no more roundness of childhood; just all hard, tight angles and ridges and muscles. His striking blue eyes studied me with the same intensity they held for me when we were kids, only now they seemed full of sadness and disappointment. So much disappointment. His eyebrows knitted together with thousands of questions that I would never want to answer. *We weren't seventeen anymore* I repeated in my head to save myself from wrapping my arms around him and clinging to him for the rest of my life. We weren't seventeen. I was different. He was different. And there were too many lies and secrets between us.

Yet, I couldn't move. I couldn't breathe.

For years I'd practiced in my head what I would say to the first boy I ever loved if our worlds collided again. What I came up with made me want to run away. Jump in front of a fast moving train.

I just told Jase Delaney that he didn't know me. I walked away from him without acknowledging him, without running and jumping into his arms and crying and gasping for air. I lied straight to his face and threw away any chance I ever had of him understanding.

I blinked back the tears and wiped at my cheeks, realizing for the first time how my life felt as if there were a thick layer of dust covering it since the last time I'd seen him. Its joints were rusted; its tears were dried up and stained along my surface, not having been truly alive since the last time I looked into his eyes.

Panicking, I wanted to leave. Run. Save him from all the pain that I held secret from him. Yet, I found myself following everyone up into Bren's apartment. I had worked out most of my demons in the last seven damn years of my life, and for the most part, I survived. I survived it all, right? I could get through this. He was my past. Past.

Past.

Past.

Over. Done.

Then why the hell? Why the hell did I feel like those blue eyes just yanked me out of the grave that I'd unintentionally dug myself into all those years ago? Why the hell was I freaking out about seeing him again? Why was my heart threatening to beat out of my chest at the mere thought of being in a room with him?

Goose bumps scattered across my skin and my lungs ached, realizing I'd been breathing shallow breaths of air since the last time I had seen him. That's right, I hadn't been breathing correctly since I was seventeen.

Everything I had built in the last seven years of my life completely shattered into millions of tiny pieces of dust the minute he walked through the door and his fingers touched my skin. Where his hands touched the back of my neck, I was on fire. How the hell did I ever think I could want anyone else, be with anyone else, love anyone else, was beyond me. There was never any other; there would never be any other. Everything since him was stale, make-believe, soft, nothing. And I hated Jase's father even more, for not only making my skin crawl from his touch, but also taking away the life I so badly wanted with this man.

I stormed into Bren's apartment with teary eyes. The chaos inside was nothing new to me. Bren would never change. There was a mountain of white powder piled on his dining room table, and Jett was cutting it into lines as Bren ran his nose along the wood.

I shivered in disgust. I needed to get the hell out of there.

Bren caught me as I walked toward the bedroom to use the fire escape. Grabbing me by the waist, he tugged me against his chest. "Why the fuck are you crying? You said it was over, right? That means, baby, that I can do all the blow I want." He bit into my shoulder, hard, then shoved me away. "You'll see; you're nothing without me, Sage. Nothing."

I stumbled away from him, throwing his hands off me. "Then I'd rather be nothing," I snapped.

Over my shoulder, I could see Jase right behind me, barreling through the apartment, hot on my heels. Bren grabbed a handful of my ass, hard. "This ass belongs to me, baby. I own you. I own that shop. If it wasn't for my mother, you'd be sucking dick on the corner."

I pushed off of him again and he and Jett stumbled into each other, laughing and falling over one of the dining room chairs. Panicking, I ran into the hallway. I didn't care about Bren. He could have the shop; he could have it all. He just couldn't have me anymore. But right then, I needed to get away from Jase. Lying to him was easy through texts, but having him look at me with his father's eyes—I just couldn't. In the hallway, I slammed into Violet and that guy that was with Jase. "Hey, what's going on? Are you okay?" Violet called after me.

"Yeah. Just going to climb down the fire escape."

Carter's eyebrows arched, "What? Where is JD?"

Then he was there, raw and angry, storming down the hallway after me. I ran past the bathroom, and he grabbed hold of my waist and pulled me inside. He pushed me roughly against the wall as he kicked the door closed and locked it. His hands slammed the wall on each side of my face and his eyes bore down on me with just enough anger to terrify the living hell out of me. It was like we were nine again, and he lived next door with those alien laser eyes.

He was panting. Leaning forward, his face tilted down so close to mine I could feel its heat. It burned through my clothing, marking itself on my skin. "Are you *positive* you don't remember me?" He pressed his body against mine and my pulse quickened as heavy, silent seconds stretched out around us. I couldn't move. He was a hot wall of hard muscles, and he was caging me in. It was devastating, tearing me apart inside. He still smelled the same. If I concentrated, just let myself think for one moment, I knew I'd be able to still feel the heat of his lips on mine from so long ago. I squeezed my eyes closed tightly and tried to focus on anything but the person I couldn't face in front of me. But his body shifted and slid against mine, dragging himself flush against me. And my body remembered him. Every nerve ending that had longed for his touch tingled and warmed and cried for him.

"Remember me?" he whispered, leaning in closer, lips hovering just over my skin, breathing fast and hard and hot against my mouth.

Don't do it, Charlie. Don't do it.

"Yes," I whispered.

"Do you belong to him?" he asked, as the pad of his thumb brushed gently across my cheek.

"I haven't belonged to anyone since I was seventeen," I said, opening my eyes and letting the tears spill.

Tension melted from his face. His eyes softened as one of his hands wiped at my tears. With the slightest movement forward, his lips just brushed mine—so close I could just about taste my childhood. My heart stopped and I closed my eyes. Warm lips teased the corner of my mouth.

But when my body arched forward to react, he turned his head away.

My heart shattered into a million little pieces.

Tears burst with renewed grief as I wrapped my arms around him. I clung to him shamelessly, breathing in the familiar scent of him. It wasn't even a second before he pushed me away.

His eyes slowly slid over my body, drinking me in. The way he did it was so full of hatred and anguish that my stomach twisted. Heat spread across my chest and plunged into my stomach as I struggled to breathe. *That's right, Jase, hate me. Hate me for breaking your heart, so you never know the truth.*

"You're right. You're not my Charlie anymore. You're used and broken, and I fucking hate you," he whispered. The words hit me hard, as if it were a real physical blow, sending my body reeling in its aftereffects. Sharp pain ripped through my chest, leaving me wide open and bleeding. I heard the whimper escape my mouth before I could even think to pull it back and mask my pain. It came out all the same. The intensity and hurt had me squeezing my eyes shut tightly, so that all I saw was spots.

I heard him step back, and my body melted to the floor. Clearing his throat, he lowered his eyes to mine. "You and your friend are going to leave this party quietly and come with me. I have questions about the criminal activity here."

That's it, Jase. Hate me.

Hate me.

Think I'm filth.

Think I'm bad.

One of your criminals.

Hate me, because standing here in front of you, I know without a doubt that I never stopped loving you. Not for one second.

"Am I being arrested?" I tried to smirk up at him.

"Did I read you your Miranda rights?" he snapped.

"No, but..."

"Just shut the hell up. I don't want you saying anything to me until we are in front of people. Don't make me cuff you," he hissed in my face then instantly backed away. "Carter and I will meet you and your crazy-haired friend outside. We're climbing out the fire escape so I don't cuff the drugged up shithead you've been fucking. *Yet.*"

We stepped out onto the fire escape and he was all business. No more intense glances, just bored, dead eyes doing their job, looking through me as if I weren't there. He brought his phone to ear as he pulled me down the metal steps. "Carter. Yeah. Going down the fire escape." His words were clipped and angry. "He'll be too high to notice if we left. Take Purple Hair out too. Make it look like you two are hooking up. Tell him I got some dirty skank riding me somewhere," his eyes flick to me. "Yeah... Yeah... Drop Purple Hair off. Great. I'll catch you back at base."

IT WAS my first time inside a police station.

"What are you doing, J?" Carter yelled, pulling at Jase's

arms, trying desperately to control him. "J, what the hell, man?" But Jase gripped me tighter and pushed me forward.

"Calm down! Dude, no..." Carter barked, as Jase opened the jail cell and yanked me roughly by the elbow into it.

It was my first time behind metal bars. My insides trembled. I knew I did nothing illegal, but I kept quiet. Whatever this was, this was what Jase needed to do. The bars of the cage slammed toward me and locked loudly into place. Staggering back, I sat slumped in the corner on a bench next to three other women. The smell in there was putrid. Leaning my head against the cold cage, I silently watched the turmoil of the room.

Carter stepped close to Jase, but he shoved him off like an animal and stalked back and forth in front of the bars that separated me from freedom.

"You can't leave me in prison," I said.

"This isn't prison; it's a holding cell. You watch too many movies," he snapped.

"I'm in here with prostitutes and strung out crack whores," I hissed, eyeing the three passed out women in the cage with me.

"Yep. Make yourself at home." He looked past me into the cell and smiled, "I'm sure you'll fit right in."

More chaos erupted when a huge guy stormed into the holding cell area and started screaming at Jase. "Do you want to lose your shield? Do you? Walk it off, Detective. Is she worth your pension? You can't just throw people into holding cells without..." his voice splintered off as he dragged Jase down the hallway into another closed off area.

Carter opened the cell and gestured for me to come out.

Hesitantly, I walked toward him.

Brooke, a girl who came into the tat parlor every once in a while, was behind him. *Why was she here? And Carter?* I've seen him inside Bren's apartment at his parties. What the hell was going on here?

I was given a hot cup of coffee and asked to sit in one of the interview rooms. It was definitely different than anything I'd ever seen on television or read about in one of my books. It was depressing. Long drawn out faces, little patience, and exhausted, haunted eyes were everywhere I looked.

After waiting alone for an hour, Jase and Carter walked in and sat opposite me at the metal table.

Both men had legal pads and pens in their hands.

I shivered. Truth was, I hadn't stopped shivering since I saw him.

"Miss Stone. What's your relationship with Brendan Laux?"

My eyes never looked up at either of them. I focused on the cup of ice-cold, stale coffee, and answered. "He *was* my boyfriend."

"Was?" Jase asked, angrily.

"Yes," I said quietly. "I broke up with him a few days ago."

"Oh, shit," Carter hissed, which made my eyes snap up— just as one of the metal chairs smashed into the wall.

"You were mine. *Mine*. Why the fuck are you with him?" Jase screamed.

"His mother took me in. I had no one," I yelled back.

"You had me," he said.

"No I didn't, I had no one," I whispered, shaking my head.

"I went back for you and you were gone," he said, standing over me.

"I stayed as long as I could for you, and you never came back. Auburn took me in, taught me everything, and even put me through school. She made me promise I would take care of Bren."

Carter pulled him away and threw him into one of the

chairs, almost toppling it over. "I need the name of his supplier," Carter said.

"His supplier for what? *I* get all the inks and *I* buy all the sanitizing supplies for the store. He does nothing! We get inspected all the time. I do everything by the book there, Detective. Everything." I balled my hands into fists and pounded on the table. "All the permits are in my name from the New York State Department of Health under the statutory authority of the Public Health Law Article four-fucking-A! My supplier, for all my equipment, is PermaInk Suppliers, right in Jersey City!"

Jase launched forward and both his hands slammed down on the table in front of me, "I'm talking about the pharmaceuticals that your boyfriend has been selling me for months!"

"One, he's not my boyfriend anymore. Two, seems like you have the drug problem, not me," I yelled back.

The large black coffee that was given to me when I first came in was thrown and splashed across the wall.

The woman, Brooke, ran into the room and tried to calm Jase down.

"Holy shit. You're a detective too?" I asked.

"Sage," she greeted, stepping in front of Jase, who was pacing back and forth.

"Brooke," I smiled tightly.

"Don't call her Sage! Her name is Charlie," Jase snapped.

Brooke's movements froze and her eyes went wide. "This is Charlie? I thought Charlie was a guy." She laughed thickly. "Nice reunion. Oh, Delaney. This just gets better and better."

What the Hell was she going on about? I narrowed my eyes at her.

"She's not much to look at, Delaney, I guess your tastes changed," she sneered.

I could see that she was jealous. I couldn't even look at

him. Here I was thinking I was brought into a police station for sleeping with an idiot, but he gets to sleep with her?

"You sound jealous," I smiled.

"Well, he's been over you for a while," she smirked.

"Let me guess, he's *your* boyfriend now?" I said, yawning.

"Don't fucking talk to her about me, Brooke," he rumbled low, eyes blazing into me.

"We've been together," she smiled, puffing out her tits.

I leaned back in my chair. "Nice, so you let him stick his dick in you? Congratulations, you must be special. A guy sticking his dick in a girl; must be love." I shook my head and looked up toward Carter. "You seem to be the only person here without a personal agenda in this, so please enlighten me as to why I was brought here."

"Did you know Bren was selling drugs from the shop?" Carter asked.

"No. No, nonono," I said, quickly shaking my head. "Detective, no, he wouldn't. He couldn't; that shop is all I have."

"He's going to kill you," Jase whispered.

"What?"

"Your little drug-dealing boyfriend? We've been doing surveillance on his drug operation for almost six months. Oh, and he was hiring me to kill you and whoever you're fucking behind his back," Jase spat.

I was floored. I knew Bren had been doing cocaine. That's why I broke up with him, but dealing drugs? I had no idea. I nodded my head and took a deep breath. "I can take care of myself, Jase. Thanks anyway."

"Who is the poor sap you're giving it to?" He slid a white pad topped with a pen across the table and pointed to it. "Write down his name, so we can send a patrol car to where he lives."

I looked at Brooke, her eyes intently watching Jase as he

watched me. I completely understood her desire for him. I'd never wanted to be in anybody else's shoes like I did at that moment. I looked back down at the pad and shook my head again. "I don't know who he could be talking about." I folded my arms and laid my head down on the table.

"You're a liar. What did he say tonight? What did he say?" Jase was pacing back and forth in front of the table once more. I fought closing my eyes and watched his strides. "Oh, right. He said you were either going to go home and read or meet up with your secret prince charming friend, so—"

"He's *talking* about you, *Detective*." I enunciated every word clearly and curtly.

Jase stopped pacing. The room stilled—quieted for a few heartbeats. Everyone was watching me. "Pardon me?"

"He sees when I text you."

Another chair gets thrown across the interview room, and suddenly another cop dressed in a crisp white shirt flew into the room and dragged Jase out of there, still screaming at me. "You were mine, always, Charlie. Since I was nine years old, you had me, had me right in the palm of your hand. *I never got over us! How the fuck could you hurt me like this!*"

"I'm so sorry," I whispered as soon as he got out the door.

Brooke bent down and picked up one of the chairs and dragged it across the table from me. Her eyes looked tired as she slumped heavily into it. "Never saw him like that before." She sighed and rubbed at her eyes. "So you're the one, huh? The Charlie that's tattooed over his heart? Did you *ever* love him?"

He has my name tattooed over his heart?

Her words broke the dam. Tears poured from my eyes. "Jase Delaney was the first and last boy I ever loved. I loved him a way that someone like you could never understand. It was one of those loves that only happens the first time, the kind that makes you dizzy and breathless. The one you compare all other guys to, and they never live up to it. But none of it matters now, right? He's got you."

Yawning, I gathered my stuff and got up to leave.

"Where are you going?" Brooke asked, following me out the door. In the hallway, Jase was leaning against the wall with his head up toward the ceiling. There were a few officers surrounding him, guarding him.

"Where do you think you're going?" Jase asked with a defeated look in his eyes.

"Detective, I know my rights," I sighed. "I haven't been arrested for anything. I was never read my Miranda rights. We all know from being in here for over three hours now that I have no clue what you're talking about when it comes to Bren. But by all means, arrest him for whatever crap he's done." I look directly at the cop in the white shirt. He looked like the head guy. "I will help in any way I can, sir. Despite the history between Detective Delaney and me, there is no way that I would allow the son-of-bitch to sell drugs out of that tattoo parlor. You need no warrants; you can look through anything and everything I have in that shop. It's all yours."

"Damn, Delaney. You just got lawyered," one of the cops laughed.

"Miss Stone," the white shirt called out, stopping me in my tracks. "Getting a warrant is the least of our problems. You need to have an unmarked car watching over you. He offered to pay Detective Delaney and Detective Mills to have you murdered."

I just nodded and looked down at my shoes, hugging myself tightly. "I'll wait outside then."

I let the tears fall as soon as I was outside. The sun was just rising, glinting off the steel skyscrapers and bending rainbows across the sky. I wanted to hail a cab and run for it.

But I could feel a pair of blue eyes watching me from the window. I didn't turn around to make sure. I didn't want to see the hate he had for me. I wanted Jase Delaney to forget me, be rid of me, and I'd succeeded after all these years.

Carter jogged down the steps after me, calling my name. "Hey. Stop. You can't leave. Your life is in real danger."

I stopped and pivoted around to face him, my shoulders slouched in defeat. "Yeah. I heard. What now? You guys going to use me as bait or something?"

"You do watch too much television."

"Yeah, thanks. I don't actually, but whatever."

"Just give me five minutes, and I'll bring you to wherever you need to go. Then, we'll get someone to look after you until we set up the money exchange with Bren."

I had no place left.

Detective Mills had me wait in one of the unmarked cars in the lot. It gave me time to think. I needed to just leave. Forget everything and find someplace new. It's not like I'd created any lasting, meaningful relationships in the last few years. Hell, I barely saw my father anymore. Once a year for the holidays. He had another new family to take care of now.

The only person I'd gotten close to was Auburn, and she was gone.

If it weren't for Auburn, then I would have probably died. It's still clear as day, the night I'd met her. I'd tried to live with my father and his new wife. I stayed with them for a few weeks, but I was too out of control. My stepmother was crazed with my hours and went through the guest room while I was sleeping and found an empty whiskey bottle; a few actually. They sat me down and told me I needed to leave. I was eighteen, an adult, I needed to go out on my own or back with my mother.

I left and spent the night walking the streets, until my legs were too tired to move. Crossing my arms over my stomach and hugging myself, I backed up against the gritty brick wall of a building, feeling terrified. My father wanted me to go back to my mother. My mother was useless. What kind of piece of shit parent throws her own daughter out on the street when she tells you she was…I couldn't even get my lips to form the word anymore.

Auburn found me on the street across from the shop. She gave me a cup of coffee and a stale candy bar from her jar; it was the first thing I'd eaten in two days.

Slowly, I put the broken shards of my life back together. I graduated from high school, enrolled in art courses at college, and worked every night alongside Auburn. When I saved enough money, I bought my own cheap computer, and the first chance I had, I logged onto my email. It was something I wished I'd never been curious about, but I missed him so much. I missed my best friend. I just needed to know if he was okay. Dozens of emails cluttered my inbox.

CHARLIE,

I don't know where you went. I came back and you were gone. Please call me. Please tell me you're okay.

It's hard to breathe without you.

Jase

CHARLIE,

My father said you left with some guy. Please tell me what is going on. Please.

Jase

CHARLIE,

Was it what happened with Joey? Did something happen

that I missed? I told you I'd come back for you. I promised. Was 4 months so long? When we'd been friends for years? I will never get closure from you. I will always look for you, always wonder where you are and what happened. And I hate you. I hate you for that. I hate you for not waiting just a little while longer for me.

Jase

CHARLIE,

I enlisted. Just like we planned. Except you changed your part. I will never forgive you for this.

Jase

CHARLIE,

The weather here is shit. It's fucking hot. Not the bipolar hot and cold, sunny and rainy of NY. Yeah, I got nothing else to say.

Where are you?

Jase

CHARLIE,

I had a dream about you last night. You were in the tree house and the walls were covered in your paintings...you looked at me through dead eyes. I've seen lots of that shit here, Charlie. Dead, glazed over eyes, just like Joey's. Do you still have nightmares about him like I do? I wake up covered in sweat, gasping for air. The guys here think I'm losing it. Maybe I am.

Jase

CHARLIE,

I'm here in the great Douchebagistan. "You never really get the smell of burning flesh out of your nose entirely, no matter how long you live." JD Salinger to his daughter about concentration camps when he was in the military in the 1940s - he was right. I really need my best friend to live through this.

Jase

CHARLIE

Okay so today I'm writing to tell you that I fucked another girl. Yep. I just went there. I hope you're having just as much fun as I am.

Jase

CHARLIE

Happy anniversary of the day you fucking broke my heart. I guess that's a little too harsh maybe. Nah, fuck you. Fuck you. I'm in the Middle East watching my friends die, and you fucking left me. You left me without any fucking clue.

Jase

CHARLIE,

How long will I love you? I can't choose between forever and always.

Jase

CHARLIE,

Fucking drunk as shit. Let me say this. Get it out.

You were wearing a little white T-shirt with something on it and a pair of jeans with a rip above your right knee. You were the prettiest girl I'd ever seen. I never needed anyone more than I needed you. You were always part of my heart, but that day you completely stole it from me. And it's yours Charlie, keep it, 'cuz I'm not going to need it without you.

Charlie, you're the best choice I ever made in my life. It was you that helped me through boot camp, it was you that helped me say goodbye to Joey, you who helped me through Afghanistan. It's always you. You're the girl I can't forget. Please tell me where you are.

Jase

CHARLIE

Don't ever ask me to stop searching for you, because I can't. Don't ever think I'll be able to forget you, because I won't.

Jase

CHARLIE,

Last night I fucked two girls. Two girls at the same time. But you don't care, do you? I hate that between the two of them, it was you I thought about.

Jase

CHARLIE

The first time we ever kissed, remember? The way you melted into me. Your lips tasted like watermelon lip gloss and blueberry bubblegum. Was it weird that I bought a pack of that gum and carried it in my pocket, just so I could taste you again?

Jase

CHARLIE

I swear I tried to move past this, but I can't seem to. My heart is stuck with you. You're gone. Vanished. I'm simply going through the motions. I look around and see everyone continuing on like they don't realize the sun has quit shining. It's just like when Joey died.

I can't stop thinking about you. How you felt in my arms, the taste of you still on my lips. It's pointless. I'm like a robot most of the time. Going through the motions, getting through life one day at a time.

Jase

CHARLIE,

It's been years. What can it hurt to email me back now? Just let me know you're okay.

Jase

CHARLIE

I miss the shit out of you, Charlie.

Jase

IT TOOK me two years to answer his emails.

Jase,

I miss you too.

Charlie

THE BOY I had loved so very much had done what he'd always set out to do. He joined the army and went overseas. He was a real life superhero. And when his tour was through, he became a New York City police officer. He was a real, true superhero, the one I always knew he'd be. And I could never find the courage to stand up for myself and tell him what happened. Simply because I loved Jase too much to ever let him know. I loved him too much.

In the beginning, we wrote emails to each other every week. I told him I was married. Over the years, we started writing to each other every day. Then texting. But, I would never let him call. He tried, but I knew hearing his voice would be too much. We never asked each other about families, about things that would hurt. We never talked about why; we just both pretended to move on. What could be changed? I told him I married someone. He was overseas for so long. I made a complete fantasy life up, so he could move on. What else could I have done? I wanted him to be there safe—not worried about how much I was hurting. I'd rather have him hate me.

Now we were face to face. He was on one side of the law and thought I was on the other. I was poison to him. I could make his world darker than it already was. I couldn't live with myself if that happened.

Let him think he was lucky to get away from me when he did. I'd be fine. I always was. I already knew what it was like to miss him. I was used to it.

I sat in the passenger seat of the car with my forehead against the dashboard. It was hot and sticky and all I wanted to do was forget everything that happened in the last twenty-four hours.

Jase Delaney needed to think I was no good.

He needed to think

It was all my fault.

Period.

End of story.

JASE

*T*his shit just got way too deep for me. I was at the door watching Charlie get into Carter's car and the lieutenant was pulling me back in. Carter will make sure she doesn't disappear on me again. He's got my back.

"I want you off this case. Take vacation time. Go somewhere. We'll put her up in a safe house if you really think your perp is going to hurt her."

I'm shaking from my lieutenant's words. "I can't let anyone hurt her, Lu. You know she was telling the truth. She has no idea what Bren does."

The clicking of Brooke's high heels came rounding the corner and a wad of paper got shoved into my chest. "Just got her history. They ran her name and she's clean. Not even a parking ticket."

The lieutenant nodded and leveled his eyes on me. "Have Carter take her to her family. Somewhere she feels safe. If he feels like she needs an unmarked car in front of the house, then he could come back and file the paperwork." I wondered if her mother still lived in the same place and what kind of relationship they had now.

"I want that cocksucker in jail. I want him away from her for good."

He glanced down at his watch. "What time is it? six a.m. …okay. Go home; get some sleep." He sighed and rubbed the back of his neck. "I'll have the team make a tact plan, and you set up a meeting with him to exchange words for money. You pick him up, and we'll set up a cam in the car tonight."

"Yeah sure. Sounds good," I said, nodding my head.

"I don't want you to take her home, Delaney. Have Carter do it. You need a clear head."

"Yeah. Got it," I said, walking to my desk to gather my things.

Brooke was a step behind me "You still have feelings for her?"

"You're talking shit, Brooke. You sound like you're jealous."

"I am, actually," she hissed.

I looked up at Brooke and stopped what I was doing.

"Delaney. Stop and look at how you reacted in the club. You could have gotten us all killed. But all you saw was her."

All I could do was give her a small, dry chuckle. "Drop it, Brooke. I'm not having this conversation with you. Or any conversation for that matter." I walked away from her. I needed a long vacation after this was all settled. Away from everyone and everything.

Outside, the sun was too bright, the sky too blue.

Charlie was slumped against the door of one of the unmarked cars in the lot. Her eyes were closed, but she didn't look peaceful. Not at all.

My chest tightened. Fists clenched.

It was like the minute I looked at her I had to remember I should hate her. Like some little punk, I wanted to say things that hurt her.

I yanked open the door and climbed in. She still smelled like watermelon lotion and I hated her for it.

Her eyes peeked up at me. They seemed empty, sitting next to me in this car, emotionless, while my life was a hurricane around me.

"I'm taking you somewhere safe," I said in a low voice.

"Hey," Carter's voice was instantly at my window, his hands banging at the top of the roof. "What's going on?"

I nodded up to him. "Get some rest. We're going after Doc tonight. Lu's setting it up now."

Carter's eyes narrowed into slits. *Shit.*

"Yeah. Okay, bro. So, why don't you let me drive her somewhere and we'll meet up later?"

"I got this," I said.

"No. No you don't," he said.

"*Yeah.* I do."

I started the engine as Carter's eyes widened. "Jase? Don't do anything stupid."

I pulled at my lips, biting them between my teeth, and nodded. "I got this," I growled, pulling the car away from him and out of the lot. A blast of gravel and dust made him barely visible in my rearview mirror.

I glanced at her still form next to me. "Your mother still live in Queens?"

"I don't know," she whispered.

"Well? How's your mother? Is that a safe place I could take you where he won't bother you?"

She cleared her throat, but her voice still cracked. "Lost touch with her."

"Yeah? Had a falling out?"

"Something like that." She didn't even flinch. She shrugged. Heartless. Suddenly, I realized that everything I thought I knew about this woman was a lie. Everything I remembered of her was just in my own damned imagination.

259

"Where do you live?" I asked her.

She stared out the window, watching the people outside. The wind from my window blew her hair across her cheeks. "Why don't you just say what you have to say and then I'll get myself home?"

My fingers squeezed the steering wheel; fireworks exploded through my bloodstream. "My lieutenant wants to put a car in front of your residence, just until we have Bren in. We could take him in now for selling, but I wanted to get his supplier. I also want to get him for setting up a hit on you. That'll be a nice little jail sentence." I smiled and couldn't help the venom in my voice, "Sorry, if that might hurt you."

"Tell your lieutenant I said, 'thank you,' but I'll be fine. Is there anything he needs me to do to help get Bren's supplier?"

"This isn't a request, Ms. Stone. I need your address. I'll drive you there now, and I will have twenty-four hour surveillance outside your front door," I snapped.

"I don't have a place. I live above the tattoo parlor," she whispered.

"Does Doc have the keys?" I asked slowly.

"Who's Doc?" she asked.

"Bren," I said, rolling my eyes.

"Unfortunately, yes he does. It's half his parlor."

Anger burned in my cheeks and I bit down, grinding out my jaw. Why the fuck would she be a business partner with a drug dealing asshole? "Fine then, where am I driving you? Your mother's? Your father? Your family? A girlfriend?"

She laughed. Not a sweet sound; a very hurt, bitter one. "I don't have anywhere or anyone. Just take me to a hotel or let me out here."

"How about your husband and 2.5 kids then?" I snapped.

She looked out the window, her lips trembling.

"I'm taking you back to my place, then. It's not up for

discussion." I was jeopardizing my job. What the hell was I thinking? I wasn't. I wasn't thinking at all.

That was a lie.

I was thinking.

All I was doing was thinking.

Thinking about why she lied to me. Thinking about the reasons she gave up on us. Thinking about wanting her to fight me. Fight with me. Thinking about the way those green eyes used to look at me and how no one ever looked at me like she did.

I couldn't stop thinking about my actions as I drove her across town to my apartment. She walked up the stairs to my place with the terrified look of a caged animal. I was defying every rule. I was supposed to do a job: get her to a safe place and arrest the guy who wanted her dead. *None of that was enough.*

She stood at the top of my stairs with her wide, green eyes, completely disarming me. Innocence and vulnerability. I couldn't take my eyes off of her. I couldn't drop her off somewhere. I knew getting in the car with her I was heading her back to my place.

I needed answers.

I needed closure.

I needed just one more day of her.

Then, I'd let her go.

We walked into my apartment and her eyes were taking in everything. I didn't even remember how we got there. I collapsed into a chair and watched her.

I wanted to ask her a thousand questions. I knew I needed to treat her like a stranger, but I couldn't. "Why did you lie to me all these years?"

Her eyes closed with what looked like overwhelming anguish, and she took a long, shaky breath.

I continued. "You told me that you were *happy*. Married

with 2.5 kids and a cat. A damn *cat*. I should have known you were lying; you always hated cats." I got up and walked straight over to her.

She turned her head around to meet my eyes, yet there was no reaction in them. No emotion and no answer. *I was going to lose my job. I was going to lose control.* I felt the fury build up in my stomach and climb into my chest, threatening to explode. "You're nothing but a liar."

"You're right; I'm a liar. And none of it matters. Get over it. We're nothing to each other now," she said in an even tone.

What the shit?

I stepped back and tried to focus, clear my thoughts. My eyes swept up and down her frame, assessing. Tight rigid back, stiff neck, hands balled at her side. Son-of-a-bitch! I needed to read her body language. She was lying to me. She was an emotional wreck inside. This was killing her, and she was pretending there was no effect.

I stepped closer, feeling my lips curl into a snarl. I wanted the confrontation. I wanted the fight. I wanted to see the real Charlie after all these years. My heart pounded hard in my chest.

I saw the moment she realized I knew she was lying. She was watching me, eyes wide, breathing hard, slowly backing away from me and hitting her back against the edge of my counter. It was my words that sent her reeling, no matter how much she tried to lie to me. "You were my world, Charlie. Losing you killed me." *Push her. Make her break.* My chest was ready to explode. "But all along you were nothing more than where you came from. You took right after your parents, didn't you? Just like your mother, who'd fuck anything for a good time. And just like your father, abandoning anything that was ever good in your life."

"Guess you're right," she said stoically. Yet, I could see the whites of her eyes reddening from holding back tears, desperately trying to look anywhere but on me.

I stepped closer—so close I could feel the heaviness of her breathing and the heat of the anger she was holding in. Her eyes, frantic now, lifted and met mine. Quickly, I lifted my hand and watched her flinch curiously as I reached to open the cabinet above her head. With a hard yank, I pulled open the handle and grabbed the first bottle of liquor my hand touched. As I twisted off the cap and took a few long pulls from the bottle, I watched as her entire body trembled next to me.

Wiping my lips with the back of my hand, I offered her the bottle and smiled, "Want to have a good time now?"

"I should leave," she whispered, tears welling in her eyes.

"Yeah? Why? Am I making you uncomfortable?" I said, leaning down and sliding my nose along the base of her jaw into her hair.

Her body shuddered violently. "*You* told me you'd never leave me."

There she was. Get mad Charlie. Fight with me. Tell me why you lied.

"Whatever, right? We mean nothing to each other now," I sneered.

"You told me you'd come back for me," she whispered. "I was long gone by the time you emailed me."

"You got that first email didn't you? You read it, and you chose whatever else over me," I said quietly.

"I chose nothing over you," she hissed.

"What the Hell are you doing with someone like Bren? You have nothing in common; you're like oil and stupid," I snapped.

"I worked for his mother at the tattoo parlor. She left me everything in her will. Before she died six months ago, she made me promise to take care of Bren and the shop."

"When did you work for her? You left me Charlie. When I came back for you, you were already gone. You left me," I said harshly.

"I never left *you*, damn it, Jase." She rubbed her hands over her face in frustration. "I brought you and Joey everywhere I went. I read every single word you wrote me. I cried when you went overseas." She fixed her eyes on mine and clenched a fist to her chest. "I prayed every day for you; you were on my mind always in here, always. I never left you. I just left that house."

"Tell me why you ran. What happened?" I asked, stepping closer.

"It doesn't matter," she sighed.

"I lost my best friend, my fucking best friend, Charlie, my world, and you won't tell me why?" I asked hoarsely.

"Is this why you dragged me here? To get some sort of answer? I have none. You left kicking and screaming that day. I was the one left behind to face everything on my own," she said, looking down.

"And who did you leave with? How long did you wait before you were wrapping your lips around some other guy's cock?" I snapped.

"Are you off duty?" she growled.

"Yes."

I saw the slap coming before I felt its sting, but I didn't move. Hell no. Let her break her damn hand on my face. I stood as still and as hard as stone.

Her eyes bulged with the impact, and she grabbed at her hand and cursed. She didn't back down. Her eyes spit fire and she panted for air. "There's not been a day that hasn't gone by that I haven't thought of you. You are a constant in my heart." She brought her hand up and poked a finger into my chest. "No one ever lived up to your memory. See, that's the thing Jase, that person you used to know, Charlie? She died, and the person standing here now, you wouldn't love her if you knew who she was–you wouldn't. So hate me all you want."

"Tell me why you lied," I growled.

"She kicked me out. I was all alone, so I left. There's nothing left to the story. I lied because I wanted you to move on," she said.

Once again, everything faded around us, like when we were kids and I couldn't focus on anything but her. I didn't understand what she was telling me.

My job phone rang, breaking the silent standoff. Bren's number flashed across the screen. "What up, boss?"

"Where'd you get to last night, son? Your boy told me you scored some party pussy," he laughed into the phone.

My fingers curled tightly around the phone, almost crushing it in my anger. "Best pussy I ever had," I said, staring straight into Charlie's eyes. "Call me next party. Yo, that blow was grade A."

Charlie's gaze flitted to the floor and she pushed off the counter, slowly making her way into the living room, practically collapsing onto my couch.

"Listen up; I'm calling to see if you could still pull off that job I was telling you about. Woke up and my girl is gone. She's probably with that dick she's been texting. She needs to go," Bren said.

Here it comes.

Somebody wants her dead. What happened to my sweet innocent girl? The one who taught *me* how to be a good kid? The one who never cursed? The one who made me believe I could be more than what everyone said I could be?

My body shook with rage. Through the open door I could see her sitting there with that gorgeous face in her hands. And every ounce of hate and anger just vanished.

"Yeah, bro. I hear you. I got this. What are you offering?" I asked, trying to sound excited.

"Five grand," he answered.

"Perfect number. They'll never find her," I said.

"Deal, bro. I got that cash at the parlor. When you want to do business?" He sounded as if he wanted it done as soon as possible.

"Tonight? I'll pick you up at nine. We'll go for a drive. That way, no one sees us talking. You tell me what you need. I'm your man. It ain't my first time, and I ain't ever got caught."

"Sounds good. Later," he said, disconnecting.

"Charlie?" My voice was nothing but a hoarse whisper.

She tilted her head up to look

At me

And I was lost.

*M*y secret. Just under the surface of my lips, like the beating of a guilty heart, I feared it was loud enough for him to hear. He'd hear it. He'd catch me. He already knew I was lying. He'd find the truth and that shitty life he complained about would be blissful compared to the hell of knowing.

Walking back into the room, he called my name in a low whisper. His eyes pleaded with mine. I didn't want to see him hurt.

"I'm getting as many answers as I can. Right now," he said, sitting down on the opposite end of the couch, facing me. "How long have you been messing with the drug dealer?"

"I worked for his mother. I—"

"You're living in the middle of filthy animals. Lower than life. Scum. *Why?*"

"I loved you so utterly and so completely, Jase. When you left it destroyed me." I ran my hands through my hair and stood up. I needed to leave. I'd take Bren trying to hire a cop to have me killed any time, but telling Jase what his own father did, I physically couldn't do it. I had cold sweats thinking about it, remembering it. "I need to go. I'll get a room at a hotel. I'm sorry, but I don't feel comfortable here. I feel sick, actually."

I walked over to the window and leaned my hands heavily onto the sill. My thoughts were fractured, snapping and splintering, and I needed to leave before I told the only person left alive I'd ever trusted how much I needed him.

Suddenly, there was a warmth behind me, and I whirled around the instant I felt the heat. Jase was facing me, so close I had to lean back on my palms to hold onto the last drop of personal space I had. But, he wasn't having any of it. His arms came around me and before I knew what was happening, he hauled me off my feet and slammed me down against the wooden edge of the window.

Oh, my God, no.

My throat seized and choked on a scream as he locked my wrists behind my back and shifted his brick shithouse of a body between my legs. Cold metal slid roughly along the tender skin of my wrists as he pulled me flush against his chest, trapping me. I heard the metal zip and click of what I could only guess were handcuffs. A desperate sob tore out of my chest and my focus blurred and whirled.

He cupped my face in his hands, tilting my chin up to see him. My vision worsened as all I could see were the streams of my horrified tears.

"Give me this one last thing, Charlie. Just tell me and you can leave me and never look back."

His touch was so gentle; contrary to the tight grip of the cuffs, it made me dizzy. I tried to twist away, only to thrash myself against the thick cold glass of the window. Pain shot up my forearms and into my shoulders. It was insane to rather slam myself through the glass of the window and fall to my death than to face what he wanted me to tell.

Insane.

And right about then, I was damn near certifiable.

My pulse raced through my veins, thrashing a thunderous heartbeat behind my inner ear. All I heard was the rapid, hard thumps of my pulse slamming through my body.

I couldn't get in enough air. There just wasn't any. Only a vacuum of nothingness threatened to burst inward and implode, folding in on myself—until I was nothing more than shadows and darkness. The only thing that held me in place were the metal clasps at my wrists that my shattered mind irrationally changed into someone's computer cord from so long ago.

Involuntarily, my body sank to the floor. Dark black spots darkened and bit at the edges of my tear-streaked point of view.

Someone called my name from far away. It sounded beautiful and safe and perfect, like the most precious of distant memories.

Haunting blue eyes pierced through the tears. The same color as those that had filled my nightmares for years, and I was back *there*.

The touches. The sounds. The sick, the filth and grunts, the rub of soap and the look in his eyes. The look in hers. The pity from the doctors. The suspicions from detectives.

"You *killed* me, Charlie. *You* left *me*. *You vanished*. You were my life. You were everything to me. Everything." Jase's voiced cracked through. A kaleidoscope of fleshy images and pain spun a design of madness before my eyes.

Jase's fist hit into the wall, "I couldn't breathe without you. So now, you tell me *why!*"

My head swam; my lungs ached. I threw my body weight at him. "Take them...take them...off...me. Can't stay like this. Jase! *Please*," I sobbed.

"Stop doing that! What are you doing?" He crouched down onto the floor with me and grabbed at my wrists. I didn't know what he was talking about. I didn't know what I was doing. I was just trying to get free. I felt a yank and my hands were free from the binds, only now they were held in front of my face, red and purple and raw.

"That's not normal. That's not what happens," he said, no louder than a whisper. "Innocent people don't react like that in cuffs!"

"Why are you doing this to me?" I cried through large gulps of breath.

"Tell me," he growled in my face. Relentless, he wouldn't stop. "Tell me!" he screamed.

"*Go ask your father*," I whispered, defeated, pushing him away with all the strength I had. He skidded back across the floor and landed on his ass.

Time stopped.

The air around us stilled.

Thickened.

My eyes stayed focused on the floor, but I knew he was watching me. I could feel the burn of his eyes.

His voice was harsh and mean when he spoke. "Charlie, my father's been dead for almost six years. He committed suicide when I was eighteen."

All of my muscles froze, tightened, and shriveled into dust. "What?" I sobbed.

Soft, warm hands gently pulled at my chin, slid over my jaw, and cupped my neck, pleading with me to look at him. He let out a long, sad sigh when I did. "He was the suspect in an alleged crime and was being brought up on charges of assault and rape."

Defeated.

Empty.

Numb.

I was done.

My body trembled; my bones and muscles were twisting

and jumping, trying to break through my flesh. "Yeah? Did...you ever see the...uhhh...victim's name?"

He leaned back and climbed to his feet. Scooping me quickly up off the floor and into his arms, he carried me to the couch, setting me down. He straightened up and with an exasperated expression, he raked a hand through his dark hair. "You don't give me answers, but you get to ask *me* questions? *Fine.* No. The report was closed because she was a...minor..."

The words hung in the air.

Heavy with implications.

After what seemed like an interminable silence, Jase's entire body stiffened, his head turned, and his wide-open gaze slowly locked onto mine.

"Charlie..."

"*Charlie?*"

As if I physically hit him, he staggered back, his head slowly shaking with its denial. His face blanched to a sickening white, and his stare turned vacant.

Immediately, his brain put the pieces together and he just knew. And I knew, there would never be a going back for us —ever. I had completely lost him. I was right to keep this from him all of these years. Now, every beautiful memory we ever shared would be tarnished with revulsion.

Then, there was that *moment.* The moment when someone's expression went from shock to pity for the *victim, and the victim's life before, whatever kind of amazing person she was, just disappears from their view.* I never wanted Jase Delaney to see me as a victim. It's not a part I play well. And the way his whole body reacted to the realization killed me.

His fingertips touched my face as tears slid down his cheeks. I'd never in my life seen a grown man cry. A fire spread across my chest and pooled up into my throat. I wanted to cover my face, curl up into a ball, and die, but he needed this. He needed to see me and forget all we ever were.

"No, Charlie. No, no. No, please, no." He fell to his knees in front of me. "How do I take that back? How? How do I erase that? How do I take that away from you?"

My chest convulsed with sobs and I shrugged. "I wanted you to just let me stay in your mind...perfect, Jase. Someone who once loved you, but chose to live a beautiful life in California with a man that loved her and their two kids. I never wanted you to worry about me. I wanted you to never know. I couldn't hurt you." My body collapsed back into the cushions of the couch in exhaustion.

I was so tired.

Of life.

Of feeling.

I had no more

In me.

JASE

*T*he thought that someone hurt her was excruciating. Adding the knowledge that it was at the hands of my own father was utterly unbearable. No one should know that kind of physical violation, especially not someone like Charlie.

It was a real physical pain, and it sliced me up the middle, making me stagger back. And through this all, she watched my reaction, and I knew I had just made everything worse.

Without thinking, I devoured the small space between us and reached out for her. I cursed under my breath at the way she tensed when I touched her. Those big green eyes looked up at me, and all the hate and rage fell to the wayside, shoved somewhere in the background for a moment, because that beautiful woman should never see an ounce of bad again. Never feel fear again.

Her breathing completely stopped when I wrapped my arms around her and gathered her into my chest. She shuddered in a small hiccup of a gasp, stiffened in my hold, and frantically wiped her eyes and cheeks free of tears.

"You were never supposed to figure it out," she whispered,

leaning her head against my shoulder and sniffling. "Now all you see is a victim. You can't see *me* anymore."

I carried her into the bedroom. *Damn it, the place was a mess.* I knew what she meant about seeing her as a victim. I understood completely, and I didn't want to say anything to mess up this situation any more than it already was. Silently, I pulled back the covers of my bed and laid her down.

"I have a big T-shirt to wear if you want to change. Get comfortable," I offered, quickly rummaging through my drawers. I handed her the shirt and turned my back to give her privacy, even though it just about killed me to allow her to think I wouldn't want to watch. But, now was not the time.

I heard the material shifting and folding. She still sniffled a few times before she whispered, "Okay. I'm decent."

I couldn't tell if she was though, since she'd tucked herself into my bed with the covers up to her chin.

It was the most gorgeous sight I'd ever seen.

I could remember the nights I sat and watched her as she slept in her tree house. I'd stay up until sunrise, tracing my fingers along her skin. I had never loved anyone the way I loved her and at that moment, I couldn't do anything but have incredible awe and admiration for the courage this woman before me had to go through—all she did alone.

"I've been in love with you since I looked up and saw the nine-year-old you standing next to Joey, and I flipped you the finger. I've been in love with you through everything and everyone I have ever spent my life with." I shook my head and sighed, "It was always you. Always. There is nothing you can tell me that will make me look at you as anything other than my Charlie."

A look of terror flashed in her red-rimmed eyes. She was exhausted and scared. I needed to give her some time to process me knowing her secret. *And I had to make sure it was true.*

"That call I got before...I have to go into work," I said.

"But you didn't sleep."

"I'm a cop; we don't sleep. Not when we can stop the bad guys," I smirked.

I backed away from the bed and tried to give her a comforting smile. "Sleep for a while. You're exhausted. I'll be back in a few."

She nodded her head and was out cold before I reached the bedroom door. A few soft sniffled hiccups slipped through her body.

I hated to leave her. But, I needed to make sure. I needed to make sure I wasn't going into this blind. I've been on the job for too long; I didn't trust anyone. The last person I trusted was Charlie, and before this, I hadn't seen her for seven years.

Walking into my kitchen, I pulled out my phone and found the contact for the lab. It rang four times before someone picked up.

"City of New York Crime Lab," a male voice greeted.

"Hey, how are you doing? This is Detective Jase Delaney, from Narcotics Division. I need to get a hold of an original case file of a sexual assault that happened a few years ago. The suspect's name was Anthony Delaney."

The douche had me on hold for way too long, and by the time he got back on, I was halfway there already. My hands slammed down on the dash and my fists smashed into the steering wheel at every light. If I only thought to get into the file as soon as I got on the job, I would have known all this time. But *if onlys* never help anything, they just drive you insane.

At seventeen, as soon as I'd heard the accusations against my father, I knew he was guilty as Hell. He had dragged me screaming away from Charlie and deposited me in Ivy Ridge, an *academy* for troubled teens housed in the remote Adirondack Mountains. My eighteenth birthday came, and when I still couldn't get in contact with Charlie, I enlisted.

They had evidence of the assault from some interview with the doctor that was in the hospital the night of the attack. My father killed himself just before the authorities got to question him. I was away at boot camp. I didn't even attend his funeral. I didn't care to. In my rulebook, rapists didn't deserve to be cried over, remembered, or mourned. He could rot in Hell for all I cared.

My stomach wrenched, thinking I might actually see physical evidence of the incident in the file I was racing toward, blowing stop sign after stop sign. Collecting evidence for a rape kit was such an invasive process. How the hell did she do it? How did she get through it all alone and only seventeen years old?

Jamaica Avenue was an absolute disaster to drive through. The morning rush of people heading out to work or school had me cursing all the way to the front door of the lab and slamming it open with a thunderous crash.

"Morning," I grumbled to the clerk, shoving my ID against the glass window that separated us. "I called about cold case file 32856."

He buzzed me into the office and I made my way down the corridor to the reports room, meeting another clerk in the back.

He handed me a thick, yellowed file that held the answers to every question I'd had for the last decade.

Stepping back, I gripped the folder, crunching the papers inside, and then I made my way to one of the tables set up for people to analyze data.

I didn't have to search long through the stack of papers within; Charlotte Stone's name was clear as the accuser against Anthony Delaney. My hands shook as I skimmed through the reports. The doctor in the hospital that night filed the claim. After her rape kit was done and all the evidence was collected, her mother signed her out. The victim was never heard from again. *Charlotte* was never heard from again. But, the charges still stuck. There was evidence, *specific DNA evidence,* against him. My father would have never been able to deny the claims. Semen stains sullied her clothes and hair. The evidence rocked me, hollowed me out, leaving me gulping for air. The pictures of her bruised thighs and welted wrists made me break down and cry in the middle of that office. No wonder she freaked out the way she did when I handcuffed her.

I'll never forgive myself for that.

Never.

"Hey, you got what you came here for? Anything else you need?"

All I could offer was a hard shake of my head. I couldn't speak. A primal scream bit at the back of my throat and threatened to explode past my lips if I did.

"You can keep the copies. Case was closed. Suspect offed himself a bunch of years ago."

I gave him another curt nod. My fingers twisted and wrung together as I silently stared down at them. I took a deep breath and lifted my head, easing my shoulders back, trying to calm the rage boiling under my skin.

There would never be justice served here. He took the coward's way out of trouble, and Charlie would never get her day in court. She hadn't even known he was dead. All this time, she just went on thinking that the monster that did this was still out there, but her only worry was about how it would *affect me if I found out.* All this time I'd wanted to be her hero, and she was already mine.

The whole drive back to the squad, I saw red. The inside

of my skin was seething and convulsing with rage. How would I ever get her to remember us after this? How would I ever be able to make up for the sins of my father?

It was just past noon when I walked into the precinct. Through the glass windows of his office, Lieutenant Masterson spotted me and came out into the hallway, heavy bags under his eyes. "You didn't sleep at all, did you?"

"When do I ever? Did *you* even go home?" I asked.

"No way. I have a two-month-old with colic; I'd rather be here right now."

"Hey, Lu, can I talk to you in your office?" I asked in a low voice.

"Yeah, come on in," he said, heading to his desk. "Close the door. Sit. Talk."

"Perp contacted me this morning. Wants me to get rid of her for five grand."

"Great. When? We got a tact plan ready for the cross street on the north corner of his block."

"Yeah. Perfect. I told him I'd contact him tonight. Pick him up. I'll wear the camera and wire," I said with a curt nod.

"You better about all this?" he asked.

"Nah." I tossed my father's case folder on his desk. "I have her with me, and that's where she's staying. That's what I wanted you to know."

There was something dark in his expression that I couldn't read—a hesitance, a trepidation that gave me the feeling that he thought I was losing my mind. Hell. Maybe I was, but I just didn't care anymore.

"Holy shit," he said quietly, scanning the first page of the report.

"Yeah."

"What are you going to do now?" he asked curiously.

"At least get this drug-dealing douchebag out of her life, tonight. Put him away for a long time. Then I'm going to do my damnedest to make her forget anyone who ever hurt her," I snarled.

THE STREET WAS DARK. Flashes of light and shadows danced along the edges of the sidewalk and crawled up the tall sides of the buildings. The car windows were open, and the air outside was still, cool. The trees above me were now bare, and the smell of food carts from somewhere down the block drifted through the air. They gave off a distinct flavor of chestnuts and soft, salted pretzel dough. Not five hundred feet away from me, in the dark shadows of an alleyway, hid a van of my teammates, listening in on surveillance. They had to know how on edge I was; usually, I would be singing off key at them into the mics.

My palms were full of sweat. I couldn't sit still. I rubbed my hands together and bounced the balls of my feet along the floorboards of the car. Damn, if I was standing, I'd be pacing, projecting to everyone the nerves that were coursing through my system. I wasn't worried about the deal about to go down. I was worried about Charlie.

Me and Charlie.

I thought knowing the truth would give me closure, stop me from measuring every girl to her. But her truth didn't set me free. Her truth weighed me down, sunk me deep under water, shackled to wrecked remnants of history on the bottom of the sea. It took time to learn how to brush away the everyday truth of this job. But when it hits home, when someone you love was subjected to the horror of violence, it guts you. It eats at your soul until you get lost in the darkness of it all.

Bren yanked open the passenger side door, snapping me from my thoughts. I needed to focus on him—on his hands, his forever bouncing eyes, his every tick, and everything around us. My firearm wasn't in the best place for me to get to. It was in an ankle holster, and my frame was way too big to maneuver around in the car.

"*Whaaaatup*, son?" he asked.

"Ima 'bout to make me some money. That's what's up," I feigned my excitement. "But, bro...You gotta tell me exactly what you need. There ain't no going back after this."

Bren smiled wide and scratched at the back of his neck. "Dude, she's been screwing around with this one guy she texts every day." He shrugged and looked out the window, "She's trash. My mom picked her up off the streets and we grew up together. My mom died and left almost everything to that girl. It's all mine, supposed to be. She's just in the way now. I need her gone."

"Gone how? What're you thinking?" I asked.

"Gone as in dead. I don't care how you do it," he said.

"You want her to suffer?" I asked coldly.

"No. Man, no. Shit, I didn't know you were that crazy," he laughed.

I drummed my fingers against the steering wheel. "I'm not saying I'm into that racket. But, you're the client. I could do her peacefully, like buy her a drink. Put something in it. Drive her body out to a place I know and dump it. But, bro...hey wait I got it..." I pulled out a small notepad and a pen and tossed it at him. "Write some shit down for me."

"Write what down?" he asked, confused.

"Where she hangs out. Where she works. Her address. What car she drives. I'm going to need to find her, right? Stuff that'll make it easy to kill her."

He wrote two pages full.

Dick. Bag.

"What about suffocation? I could get into her place while she's sleeping—"

"Dude, whatever. I don't need to know. I just need her dead," Bren explained heartlessly. "Two weeks ago she dumped a shipment of pills into the trash, because she has no clue what I do right under her nose. Cost me a ton of money. She's just in the way."

"And you said five thousand? Yeah?"

He pulled out an envelope and tossed it into my lap. "Count it."

I took out the cash and thumbed through it. "Hey, Bren. I was meaning to ask you. You need a bigger clientele? I got a ton of people looking to score off me. Maybe we could make some serious cash together."

Bren bobbed his head. "Maybe. I'll see how it goes with the shop. With Sage out of the way, I can bring in more merchandise and clean more money."

"Yeah, bro. Get back to me on that," I said.

"All right. When do you think you're going to...do it?" he asked.

"I'll have her out of your hair in the next twenty-four hours. Go celebrate. Make sure you go big. Have people take pictures of you, so everyone sees you. Secure an alibi."

His face paled.

"No worries. You're not going to need it. But it's always good to have in case one of her family members reports her missing."

Bren barked out a laugh. "Ah. That girl doesn't have any family. We don't have to worry about anyone looking for her. Nobody'll even miss her."

IT WAS after midnight when I stumbled into my apartment, body heavy with fatigue. I headed straight for Charlie.

She was asleep, curled into a tight ball in the middle of

my bed. Lights chased by shadows crossed the walls and blankets, illuminating her soft skin. I undressed in the shadows of the room and changed into a clean pair of boxers. I walked toward the bed, my heart in my throat, and pulled back the covers, easing myself next to her. The scent of my own soap filled my senses; she must have taken a shower, waiting for me. How in the world did she manage to make that manly smelling soap so damn sexy? Showers for me were never going to be the same again.

Charlie was facing the opposite wall, so I shifted closer to her and slid an arm under the pillow she was using and another around her waist. I buried my face in her hair. Her body stiffened, cringed. I could feel her hands fist the sheets and just knowing she didn't feel safe with me completely crushed me.

"Miss sleeping next to you," I whispered, moving my hand off her waist and into one of her tightly closed fists. Uncurling her fingers, I clasped our hands together, knowing damn well that the half tattoos we got as kids were now making one whole heart.

"This isn't a good idea," she whispered.

I tightened my arms around her. "Why?"

"Because I could so easily fall back into you."

"Please stay like this. I just want to feel your body next to me. Your warmth. After all these years, Charlie. Please give me this."

"Jase..."

"I can't get you out of my head. God knows, I've tried. But I just can't forget you. And I don't want to. Ain't going to happen. And I'm going to make you remember, too."

Nothing but silence filled the room.

"We did the *controlled meeting* tonight."

She still didn't answer, but her body slowly melted back into mine, which was answer enough for me.

"My team arrested him an hour later. Asshole has a ton of charges against him."

I felt her muscles unwind more, loosening up. Slowly, she shifted her body around to face me, eyes full of intensity.

There was only one thing left to ask.

There was more gravel in my voice than I wanted there. "Do you love him?"

"No," she answered without hesitation.

"He's going to go away for a long time. I had him charged with everything. He even wrote down directions to get to your place. That's premeditated evidence, right there."

Her eyes filled with something indescribable, and I leaned in, gently laying my forehead against hers. "How do I make this right?" I asked.

"It'll never be right," she said sadly.

"What can I do? I just..."

"Just let me *go*," she said, sitting up. Quickly, she climbed out of bed, out of my arms, and stood in the middle of the room, hands on her hips, defiant, brave, and beautiful. She gradually walked around and ran her fingers over the picture frames I'd placed around the room. Things I should have gotten to share with her. A thousand different lives we could have lived together. Then, her eyes landed on the pair of pink lace panties on the top of the laundry basket, and a tight, straight smile slashed across her face.

She walked over to the panties and scooped them up in her hand. Tossing them at me playfully, they landed on my chest, making my head thud back loudly against the headboard.

"Somebody will be mad if she finds out I stayed here tonight with you in your bed," she said.

I didn't even look at them as I tossed them to the floor.

"I don't even know whose they are," I said honestly.

"You don't know who you make love to?" she laughed, crossing her arms over her chest.

"I haven't made love to anyone since you. Fucking is a whole other story," I said, climbing out of bed and standing right in front of her.

"Stop. I can't breathe when you're this close to me," she said, swallowing hard.

"I can't leave you like this. I can't leave *us* like this," I whispered.

"Like what?"

"Unfinished."

"Jase, we've been finished. You gave me the best years of my life so far. You taught me to be strong before I ever knew there were things in this world you needed strength for. You prepared me. You taught me self-perseveration. You taught me to love myself." She stepped back from me, inching closer to the door. "So this is *me*, Jase, being strong. This is *me* not letting anyone ever hurt me again."

"You leave, Charlie, and I will chase you. I will chase you until I am old and gray. I want my best friend back. I want the best thing that ever happened to me back. And I promise you I will make you fall in love with me all over again. This time, it'll be the forever kind," I promised.

"Jase. I've messed up so much..."

"I've messed up too, Charlie. This whole time. Without you. I just couldn't feel anything...for anybody," I said quietly.

"I tried to love Bren. I tried to love everybody. Anybody," she said, sitting back down on the bed.

"How'd that work for you?" I chuckled.

"It didn't; none of them were you." Her cheeks darkened with her admission, then her eyes turned concerned. "Jace, sleep, you're exhausted."

"But I'm not finished with you. I need to..."

"Sleep."

"You'll leave," I growled.

"I'll stay," she lied.

"I know what to do to get you to stay!" Exhausted, I stumbled into the living room and came back with my iPad and collapsed next to her on the bed. "My kindle app. I have books."

A lock of cinnamon hair escaped from her ponytail and fell into her eyes as she opened my reading app. I reached out and curled it around my finger, running it over my hand. There was always something about the way she looked with a book in her hand, complete chaos surrounding her, while she just sat, in her own little world...reading.

I slid my hands away, into the covers, and gripped at the sheets, hoping like hell I could keep my hands off of her.

Her head tilted up, green eyes sparkling at me, her face full of excitement. "Have you read all of these?"

I still love you.

I love you.

I love you like we were never apart.

Her eyes blinked, and her bottom lip pulled in between her teeth. "Jase..."

She said my name as more of a plea than a question, and all I could see were her lips. The way her eyes looked into mine was what I'd been missing all this time. Slowly, I reached out and cupped her face in my hand, running the pad of my thumb along her bottom lip. Her pulse raced under my fingers and her breathing quickened.

"Oh, God, Jase," she whispered, as her eyes closed.

"Stay with me," I said, covering her mouth with my lips, leaving a soft kiss.

Her lips immediately parted and she gasped. The sound was soft and sensual, a surprised breath full of promises and want.

I pulled my hand back and pressed my temple to hers. She

clutched my iPad to her chest as I slid my hand down her arm. The feel of her skin made me delirious with want, but my body was shutting down from total lack of sleep. "I'm going to remind you how much we loved each other."

She pushed my chest down into the bed and nuzzled into me. "I never forgot, Jase."

Charlie didn't leave.

She couldn't actually. The Lieutenant told her she could either stay with me or in witness protection until Bren's court date.

She chose me

To keep her safe.

She chose

Me.

CHARLIE

Soft music played in the background; I loved to listen to music while I read. I loved keeping it low, letting it rumble just below the whispers of words and scenes that formed in my head.

I stood in Jase's kitchen, dressed in one of his button-down shirts, cooking a pot of chili. The smell of burning beans brought me to my senses, and I finally put down the book I was trying to finish and lowered the flame on the stove. I couldn't focus on anything I was doing when the fate of one of my fictional characters hung in the balance. There were only twenty pages or so left, and I was in desperate need of a happily-ever-after.

I deserved one.

"You're so beautiful," Jase's voice rasped from somewhere behind me. I froze in surprise, the spoon in my hand splashing into the pot and splattering sauce across the shirt I wore. The stinging burn of the steaming food made me curse as it landed against my skin where the huge shirt had fallen off my shoulder. A swarm of butterflies tore through my belly. He had come home early. I wasn't dressed, and I just ruined his shirt.

The ankle bracelet, the one he'd given me so long ago, clinked musically against the locket that hung from it as I whirled around to face him. I watched his gaze fall toward the noise.

How long had he been standing there?

He was leaning against the wall with one of those slow, uneven smiles that always made me melt, hands jammed into his pockets, watching me. Crap, I was talking to myself there for a minute, growling about the stupid heroine of the book. Why couldn't she just realize how much the hero wanted her? Why play coy? Because then there'd be no story? *Stupid fictional characters.*

Jase raked his teeth over his bottom lip and slowly slid his gaze up my legs until he tilted his head and locked his stare on mine.

He hesitated, taking a stuttered step, cautiously. Then, a steel band of determination crossed over his expression, and his strong, heavy strides devoured the distance between us.

My stomach flipped, and my heart did a strange rhythmic dance inside my chest. I closed the open parts of the shirt and tried to hold his stare. It was terrifying. There was so much intensity to it—it was breathtaking.

"Don't, Charlie," he said, his voice low, husky. I fisted the material a little tighter.

We stared at each other for a few quick heartbeats before his gaze fell to my mouth. I pulled the shirt tighter around me, hiding myself. "Don't cover up," he said.

I thought about the heroine in the book I'd just put down and how I was complaining about her actions. I thought about how people should never hide from their feelings and truths—how so much time always gets wasted. If this was the book of my life, I wanted to skim all the way to the good parts.

So, I dropped my hands to my sides.

The huge shirt slowly slipped from my shoulders, leaving me almost bare in front of him.

He stepped closer, eyes never leaving mine. His head tilted as he brushed past me, reaching behind me to shut off the burner on the stove. I wanted to tell him not to. I was making dinner for him. But those blue eyes had me wondering what was in his head, and I was desperate to know if it was the same thoughts that were in mine.

"What song is this?" he asked low, leaning his body closer to me, yet not touching me. The slow, sexy melody floated through the air, surrounding us.

"*Take Me To Church*," I answered, unsteadily. "By Hozier."

"I like this song," he whispered into my hair, warm breath fanning gently across my neck. His voice drifted softly and slowly, gently taking hold of my heart. And for the second time in my life, I could remember with clarity the moment I realized I was in love with Jase Delaney.

"Yeah...it's good," I said, lifting my face closer to his.

"Being this close to you always made it hard for me to breathe, Charlie."

Tears burned at my eyes; the bridge of my nose stung as I held his steady stare. "Being this close to you, Jase? It makes me feel like I haven't taken a deep breath in seven long years."

"*Take me to church, Charlie*. You were the only place I ever worshipped," he said, as he dipped his face toward me, brushing his lips against mine. His hands reached up and skimmed my cheeks, trailing down my face and neck, touching me like I was a long lost treasure. The soft touch was almost unbearable, a small whisper of a touch that moved over my skin—his eyes still fixed on mine.

"Can I kiss you?" he asked with a deep whisper.

I gasped out a sob as I nodded my head, too afraid to speak for fear my words would tangle with tears. The feeling in my chest was overwhelming.

Slowly, deliberately, he lowered his lips to mine. I could hardly breathe. My chest tightened, heart beating fiercely against my rib cage.

He stilled, just over my lips, and breathed me in. Anticipation and need wrestled between us. His chest moved faster, a quick rise and fall as he still kept his eyes fixed steadily on mine. He was making sure. He was making sure I saw only him, making sure I was okay.

And I was.

All I saw was him.

And then, his lips brushed softly over mine, and I melted into him.

"*Amen*," he whispered against my lips. "Charlie...been all over the world, seen so many places, but I swear my favorite place is against your lips."

A wild, breathless gasp escaped my lips as his hands pressed down around my face and his mouth crushed against mine. My hands flew up to his chest, fisting into his shirt, pulling him closer, greedily grasping, unable to get enough. There was so much sensation from such a simple kiss. It was staggering, disorienting. I hadn't been kissed like that since the last time his lips were on mine. Whatever anybody else had offered me with their kisses was nothing more than a shadow of feeling compared to Jase's.

Our lips moved hot and wet over one another's, his tongue dipping into my mouth, shooting fire across my chest.

His hands traveled up, threading his fingers through my hair and he broke away from our kiss. His hands fisted my strands of hair and pulled back until my face tilted up and our eyes were back to being fixed on each other. His warm breath blew across my cheeks; the rise and fall of his chest was wild as he gripped my hair in his fists. Sky blue eyes darted back and forth between my eyes and my mouth, and his jaw clenched tightly. I felt his chest shudder and inhale deeply against mine.

"Here's the twist to your story, Charlie. You ready for it?" he growled and nipped at my lower lip. "Breathe me in deep. Hold your breath. I *will* make you fall in love with me again. Because I sure as shit didn't think I'd ever see you again, and I sure as shit didn't think I could fall in love with you again, but I did." His hands gripped me tighter. "Like I was falling from a cliff, Charlie. Then...*then*...I realized when I hit the ground; I've been in love with you this whole time. It never stopped. I'll never stop. I will *never* stop, and I will never give up on you." His voice lowered, "It was you from the beginning, the minute you taped that skull and crossbones to your window wearing those baggy jeans, that Nirvana T-shirt, and those God-awful chucks, you were my horizon. Everything I could ever see."

The tone of his breathless words coiled heat through my belly. My heart went wild. God, I never thought I'd hear those words from him.

"Too much? Too soon?" he shrugged and smirked.

I shook my head. A few tears escaped down my cheeks. His fingers were quick to wipe them away.

"Way I see it, it's not about the time we spent away from each other. And it's not about the time that we have left. It's about the moments—the moments that we shared. Every moment with you was an adventure, Charlie. Every one. You are my moments. And I'm not spending any more without you."

I opened my mouth to speak but it got drowned away with a kiss–slow and languid, causing the slow burn in the center of my chest to ignite into an inferno.

"The rest of your moments belong to me," he whispered between my lips. "From now on, we go through everything side-by-side. Together, like we were always supposed to." He tilted his lips away and held his right hand up to mine, threading our fingers together. The two broken halves of our tattooed hearts became one. "You have the other half of my heart. Can't live without it anymore."

I smiled back, and I swore my cheeks hurt. It was the first genuine smile I think I had in the last seven years.

"I like the ending of this story," I whispered. "But...there are a few pages left, and I'm hoping there's a heavy sex scene before I hit the end."

"Missed you so much, Charlie." His voice was soft, yet heady and gravelly. He slid his hands slowly up my arms and cupped the back of my neck, pressing his lips back against mine. A throaty growl tore past his lips as his tongue dipped past mine. Bursts of soft, sweet sensations filled my mouth. The taste of him, the feel, made me delirious.

I closed my eyes, letting the heavy drugging feeling of his lips pull me under. My hands pressed against his chest and his heart thundered beneath my fingertips.

My lips slid across his, our tongues slipping and dancing slowly, making me remember how he used to move deep inside my body. *My God*, I wanted him inside my body again.

His hands slid down my back and wrapped around my waist, pulling me in closer. He broke off the kiss with labored breathing and murmured, "Can I touch you?"

"God, yes." My voice sounded raspy and breathless. An explosion of flames erupted low in my belly.

Please touch me.

Lowering his hands, he tugged at the hem of the shirt that had fallen off my shoulders. It fluttered down my arms and pooled into a wrinkled lump around my feet.

"So beautiful," he murmured, sliding his hands slowly up

my sides. His fingers grasped softy at my skin, a touch that I fought years against remembering. The moment his fingertips met my bare skin, I sank into him, and all my emotions bubbled to the surface in tears from the perfect beauty of how it felt. Goose bumps spread like wildfire over my skin. My flesh only felt alive where his fingertips touched down; the rest of my body was just shadows and memories of us.

But God, his kisses were better than I'd ever remembered.

Then suddenly, his lips were gone, and he was sinking to his knees in front of me. His hands slid like silk over my breasts, across my hips, and around to the small of my back, drawing my body closer. I grabbed at his dark hair as he nipped and licked his way across the expanse of my breasts.

I choked back a gasp when his mouth closed over a nipple and sucked hard. A surge of warmth flushed down the center of my body and throbbed hard against the apex of my thighs.

His hands pressed at my back and finally, dropped to my hips, hooking his thumbs into the sides of my panties and twisting them tightly.

I moaned and tugged at his hair as his hot mouth and tongue made their way over my belly. The anticipation of feeling him inside me again was unbearable. I never wanted anyone, never needed anything so much in my life. My body ached for him.

Coarse, hot fingers slid across my hipbones.

My eyes were locked on his movements. I couldn't stop watching it; the way he worshipped my skin, teased my body.

His blue eyes shot up to mine as he looped his fingers into the middle of my undies and slowly dragged them across my wet flesh. Immediately, my knees bent, buckled, and I was melting, slowly spreading my thighs to him.

Begging to be touched.

Begging to be filled with him.

"Can I taste you?" he whispered, nudging his lips against

the front of my underwear. The heat of his mouth made my clit throb wildly, and I gasped, arching forward.

He bit at the material, scraping softly against my skin, and the need to press myself against his mouth was maddening. *But he's asking permission. He's asking permission for everything. Every beautiful step he took, he wanted me to be sure.*

And still, his fingers brushed over and over my flesh. He sucked at the front of the material, latching onto my clit and tightening his lips over me. The sensation was exquisite, the slow, hot pulls of his lips over the fabric and gentle long strokes of his fingers. My hands clutched onto the counter; dishes and silverware clattered behind me.

He pulled his mouth away and I moaned from the loss of pleasure. Raking his teeth over his bottom lip, he smiled up at me. "The smell of your skin is sinful, Charlie." And then my panties were being tugged down my thighs, past my knees and calves, in agonizingly, slow pulls. Spikes of heat tingled all over my body as I stared down at the man kneeling in front of my naked body. My breathing faltered. My lungs couldn't get in enough air.

His eyes filled with emotion as he dragged them slowly up and down my body, taking me all in. "Damn, Charlie. You're...you're perfect. So beautiful." His hands dug into my thighs and tightened their grip on me. Jase softly kissed the tops of my thighs, and then pressed his mouth between my legs.

"Oh, sweet Jesus," I cried.

His hands gripped me tighter as his tongue explored, licking wildly against me. I swore he trailed it along every inch of me, leaving nothing out of bounds. Tension twisted and built, pressure pounded against my insides and tore down my legs. My knees buckled, and I tumbled to the floor with him.

"You're making my knees weak, Jase."

He crawled over my body, chuckling. "Mmm-hmm. Can't wait to watch you come apart for me." He scooped me into his arms. Suddenly, I was airborne, and he was carrying me through his apartment and into his bedroom.

His lips attacked mine as he walked. My fingers raked through his hair, pulling and yanking. I could taste myself on his mouth and it drove me insane. We fell onto the bed together, his body landing over mine, and I automatically wrapped my legs around him. With his tongue still dipping into my mouth, his hands pawed and pressed at my flesh. Fingertips pressed down and dug their way over my arms, my waist, my legs, until both of his hands were cupping my bottom, grasping at my skin. His mouth continued to slide over mine, his chest panting hard against mine, his heavy weight pushing me into the mattress. His fingers slid along the crease of my bottom, moving it upward in slow lazy circles. "So wet," he mumbled between kisses. "Need you."

Then, his movements stilled. His forehead dropped against mine and his eyes looked into mine. His breaths were heavy; his heart crashing against my chest. "Need you, Charlie."

He was asking if he could.

His blue eyes pleaded, begging for it to be okay. It'd been so long, so very long since someone looked at me like that— so long since someone touched me the way he did. The intensity of it all brought tears to my eyes.

"Yes, God yes, Jase. Please, don't stop," I whispered. "Don't ever stop, Jase. I want *this*. I want *you*."

He backed away slowly, reluctantly pulling himself from my body, and leaned back, sinking his knees into the mattress. Gathering the material at the hem of his shirt, he lifted it above his head and tossed it off to the side.

Oh, my God.

My name was written besides Joey's across his chest,

splashed in thick, dark ink across hard, twisted, tight muscles. His body was ripped. Tight. Flexed. Ready to pounce.

My mouth hung open. I heard myself gasp and my cheeks heated. *He was stunning.* Ten times broader and stronger than the last time I'd seen him shirtless. He was all man. Fire ignited deep inside me, the sweet sensation of its heat mushroomed throughout my body.

Somewhere in the background of the apartment, the song played again. I had it on loop while I was cooking. It intensified the way he looked at me. The sound of the singer's slow, deep voice was sexy and desperate. What was it about the song that made the moment feel so sublime? As if we had our own soundtrack to our story? Or maybe it wasn't the music at all. Maybe it was just the way Jase stared down at me while the music played. It was as if all my senses were heightened, just because those blue eyes were watching me. Every sound, every touch, everything was just more. He looked at me as if I were something precious and I realized at that moment that Jase had always looked at me like that.

Standing up, his fingers tugged slowly at the buttons of his pants. Then in one smooth movement, he slid them down. Jase was gloriously naked in front of me, and I was practically breathless, panting desperately with need and want.

For a brief moment I froze, utterly paralyzed, watching the impossible beauty of the man standing in front of me as he stared back down toward me with a look of the most untouchable emotion I swore I'd never know again. His gaze locked on mine and it burned through me. I was lost, deeply and completely.

Crawling onto the edge of the bed, his hand skimmed over my ankles, slowly up to my knees. My skin awakened and screamed for more.

He lowered and gently ran his tongue up my calf. A low moan escaped my lips, making me clench my fists at the blankets beneath me. He continued the slow assault up my flesh and I got lost in the sensations of his tongue and lips—his fingers and skin.

Then a sharp thrill coiled deep inside me as both of his hands pushed at my inner thighs, spreading me wide open before his eyes. Cool air touched and tingled along my skin with the heat of his breath. I fisted the sheets tighter in my hands; the anticipation of his touch made me want to push myself into his mouth.

Delicately, he slid one finger over me, stroking me; everywhere he touched made me gasp out a small, low moan. I lifted myself onto my elbows to watch. God, he was sexy. Blue eyes stared up at me, his face between my legs, breathing his heat against me. His hands pressed my thighs wider and I wiggled and squirmed in want. He dug his fingertips into the tops of my legs and pulled me into him.

Then his mouth was on me, licking and sucking. I arched toward him and moaned loudly as his tongue stroked and nipped.

"You taste sinful," he growled, voice thick and hoarse, full of desire.

"Oh, God...yes," I whimpered, rolling my hips to match the exquisite motions of his mouth. Every hot, wet, thrust of his tongue deep inside me sent me closer to the edge.

Then, his fingers joined in pushing deep inside me, and pleasure coiled and twisted wherever he touched. My stomach muscles clenched; my breathing accelerated until my lungs burned. Wet heat gushed through my core, meeting his mouth, and a hum of delicious sounds fell past his lips.

His fingers stroked and curled again and again as his tongue lashed and sucked on my clit. The sensation was torturous. Each touch was promising to send me closer and closer to the edge. The sweet rhythm of his wet mouth had me soaring higher and higher. I felt as if I were a small spark ready to explode, burning everything around me.

Abruptly, his movements stopped, and I was left aching and clenching.

He pulled his face up, his breathing ragged and panting. His wicked eyes traveled up the rest of my body as he slowly began teasing and kissing the sides of my inner thighs, moving his way up toward my belly.

"Oh, my God, Jase. I think you're trying to kill me."

A small chuckle rumbled through his chest as he crawled up my body until his mouth latched onto my nipple, sucking and pulling at it so hard I could feel the tightening pull deep in my belly.

I needed him then. I couldn't wait any longer.

I wanted him to stop. The sensations were too much. I needed him inside me, filling me.

I pushed up to sit; his mouth lifted, meeting mine. Our tongues twirled and slid against each other.

One hand cupped my face as both of mine ran over the hard muscles of his chest. As I did, I could distinctly feel the hard, strong beating of his heart, pounding against his chest.

I inched closer, wanting to feel my chest against his.

Then, everything stilled.

We both stopped, eyes locking.

I could feel him. The heavy heat of him—right at my opening.

The way his eyes were fixed on me, the way his lips parted and his breathing came out gasping; I knew he could feel it too.

He was right there, almost inside me, skin to skin.

We both looked down between us. His fist was wrapped around his length, exactly where it needed to be, exactly where I wanted it to be.

My body trembled with want; the feeling of him laying against my entrance was maddening. I heard him gasp, watched him squeeze tighter around his shaft. I looked back into his eyes. His expression was heady, desperate; he had no control. Finally, I felt the smallest rock of his hips against me.

I matched his gasp.

"Please..." I begged. My voice shook and cracked, "Oh, my God, Jase...please."

The hand cupping my face slid around my neck and twisted a fist into my hair. My eyes met back with his.

Then, the feeling of hot pre cum slid over my clit, making it pulse and throb.

I could have come with just that sensation alone. Tingles and tiny sparks of something danced deep inside me.

I wanted to move, but his hand dropped to my hip and held me still. My body shuddered with need, aching and pulsing.

He gripped my hip tighter, but I rocked into him, sliding the head of his cock over my wet skin.

"Fuck, Charlie. You feel...so good. I need...I need..."

His hands clamped down over my hips, and without either of us being able to speak, I slid down over his length, stretching over him. His gasps and moans were the most beautiful sounds I'd ever heard.

He tightened his grip on me, digging his fingers into my skin. And then he was pushing and plunging into me. Long, slow, hard strokes. My head dropped back and his mouth latched onto my neck.

"Feel so good, baby." His voice rumbled as he pushed my body back into his mattress and buried himself deep inside me.

Our lips met again, and a deep pleasure began building slowly, intensely. A rush of pure, unadulterated pleasure bubbled low as the sensations tightened and climbed.

The orgasm hit me so fast and hard that I cried out his name as my body shook and clenched around him. He rode wave after wave, thrusting through it, spilling his own release with a sudden shudder.

We laid there, him still inside me, until our breathing slowed, both staring into each other's eyes.

His fingers traced slowly over my skin. "I'll never let you go again, Charlie." His lips touched down against the tip of my collarbone. "Can't get enough of you."

I smiled, pulling him close, "Don't. Don't ever let me go."

"Charlie, I want to feel this forever."

"Forever, Jase."

EPILOGUE

Today
Charlie

hese old bones of mine feel tired I think as I sway myself softly on our old porch swing. It's just touching down on dusk, the fireflies have come to visit, and a cool, salty breeze blows through my hair.

"I broked my lightening bug, Great-gramma," my youngest grandchild cries softly. It's Cassie; she's the most sensitive of the whole lot of them. She collapses onto the swing, causing me to hold on tightly to its rickety old sides.

"Let me take a look, sweets."

She hands me over her mason jar and plops it into my lap.

My stiff fingers twist open the top and free the poor little scared bug onto my palm.

"I love my bug. I don't want it to be broked." Her three-year-old body shakes with sobs.

The bug's wings lift and flitter.

"Blow a kiss on her, Cassie. Let her know how much you love her. She'll fly again when you do," I say.

Cassie's eyes go wide and she blows the biggest kiss over the palm of my hand. The firefly takes flight in its soft innocent breeze and rises up with a great swirl into the darkening sky.

"Yay! You saved her." She twirls around and jumps off the porch, dancing through the grass. The rest of the children join her in her joy.

I watch them run back through the yard and climb up the short ladder of the old tree house my husband and I built when we first got married.

God, I miss him.

I lost my beloved Jase shortly after our fiftieth wedding anniversary. It's been hard to wake up every day since then. But I know it won't be for much longer. My moments without my two boys won't be much more.

Jase made good on all of his promises to me. All of our moments were together from that day on. Every single one of them. And oh, my, were those moments glorious.

We shared a long, beautiful life, until the day my Jase finally left to meet up with Joey again.

I know it's just a matter of time, now.

I won't be long until I'm back with my boys, the three of us hanging our legs off the edge of a tree house, swinging in the summer sun, waiting for the sunset and fireflies. Won't be long until we're licking our fingers clean of cheesy Doritos and chewing on blueberry bubblegum, watching out over Heaven, down through the wispy clouds, watching over all those we love below.

Until then, boys.

I'll miss you.

Years of dirt under our nails
After we've said goodbye to all those we love

We cling to the smell of earth and rain
Not me
I've waited
To evaporate with the rain and pour down again
In memories and dreams
Save a place for me
Next to you
I've waited
You know all my secrets
My body's tired
I can't wait to see you both again
Until then
I miss you every moment.

HERE'S TO FALLING PLAYLIST

Conversations With My 13 Year Old Self by Pink
Just Give Me a Reason by Pink
Life After You by Daughtry
Here Without You by 3 Doors Down
When I'm Gone by 3 Doors Down
Take Me To Church by Hozier
Dancing in the Sky by Dani and Lizzy

ALSO BY CHRISTINE ZOLENDZ

If you want to read more of my books, below is a list of my other titles.

Mad World Series

Fall From Grace (FREE!)

Saving Grace

Scars and Songs

Romance Suspense

Brutally Beautiful

Cold-Blooded Beautiful

Hilarious Chick-Lit

#TripleX (co-written with Angelisa Stone)

Contemporary Romance

Here's To Falling

Best Man

Contemporary Romance/Erotica

Suite 269

Behind Blue Lines Series

Resisting Love

Searching for Love

Finding Love (Coming Soon!)

Missing Love (Coming Soon!)

Journals

Check out my Journals, sketch pads, and planners. They make AWESOME gifts!

Signed Books

Newsletter Sign Up

ACKNOWLEDGMENTS

Thank you to all my readers. Without you, I wouldn't be here. Thank you for sharing in my imagination and falling head first into my many different worlds.

A special thank you to Carol-Angelisa-Deena: Thanks for pushing me to finish this story. Thank you for straightening out my tenses, yelling and cursing at me, driving me around South Carolina to hang with stoners, hanging out in biker bars with me, and being my friend. There's a lot more you've done, but we'd be here all day, so thanks for everything.

Thank you to Dan, Hailey, and Emily: I love you more than anything in this world.

Finally, thanks J. It should be our turn to sit around eating donuts while our kids play under the table. You were the only one who knew my secret, thank you for taking it to the grave. I miss the shit out of you.

SNEAK PEEK 1

HOW A PREVIEW OF SOME OF MY OTHER BOOKS?

uite 269

"I'm getting drunk, where you at?" @**Kavon** #**SeeingDouble**

Damn it! My pink penis-shaped water gun was almost out of water. Tossing it over to Mandy, she fumbled for it, and of course, missed the giant rubbery monster. It wobbled through the air, landed hard, bounced twice, and skidded across the dance floor. Everyone howled in drunken laughter. "You gotta fill up the balls for me," I screamed in a fit of giggles. "It's all out of juice."

I couldn't believe those words came out of my mouth. I couldn't even believe I was *there*. It was all too surreal. Because right at that particular moment, it was closing in on midnight and an extremely *hard*, mostly naked stranger was *humping* my backside in hard, quick thrusts. A sexy song thumped through the speakers, his quick movements matching the rhythm of the bass. A low, white, smoky mist rolled out across the floor; it tickled my throat, and sent icy chills up my arms. Okay, okay—maybe it wasn't from the mist, maybe it was from *Mr. Jack P. Hammer*.

Ordinarily, I'm not the kind of woman who gets herself into these sorts of predicaments. No, not me, I'm pretty much an easily embarrassed, one-man, only-in-a-bed, lights off, average kind of girl. I may talk the talk, but I'm too damned chicken to walk the walk. However, this night was a bride-to-be's rite of passage, and it definitely called for a stripper. Pardon me, *strippers*; there was a definite need for more than one.

Luckily, we were surrounded.

Let's see. There was the cowboy, gangster, soldier, cop, and superman. Oh, and the guy trying to jackhammer his screwdriver into me was a construction worker.

So, there I was in the middle of them wearing the obligatory bride's tiara with glow in the dark rubber penises jutting out of my head like a pair of horns. *Literally,* I was in the middle of them, getting shoved into a chair decorated like a throne with the entire club of salivating woman watching. Women, from all lifestyles, grabbing hungrily at the dancers, while money flew up to the overhead rainbow-colored disco lights. The music kicked up faster and the MC was announcing yet another dancer; some other poor bride-to-be was going to be getting dry humped alongside me. A handful of desperate middle-aged women shrieked in the corner, wads of singles in their hands, as *Thor the god of Thunderfucks* came out dancing.

Then Mandy was back, dancing across the floor, waving my penis above her head and thrusting it into my chest. She flopped past my stripper and giggled. "Here you go, can never have enough cocks if you ask me," and pinned a corsage of rubbery, bouncing penises to my shirt. A shirt that was all wrinkled because Jack Hammer was half octopus, hands all over as if he owned me. I shot my penis water gun at him but he kept on humping. I guess that only worked on dogs.

Behind the bar, bartenders dressed like sex slaves, all leathered, laced, collared, and spiked, mixed drinks. They whirled and danced, pouring without missing a glass; it was mesmerizing, hypnotic. Everything seemed shiny and dreamlike and the volume of alcohol I drank made everything look as if it were melting; the colored strobe lights bled into the crowds of people, blanketing them with strange dancing shadows. The temperature of the room rose higher, thicker, and humid. My dancer—the one sliding his groin all across the back of my pants—was *hotter than Hell* and slick with sweat. Oh yes, a perfect male specimen: tall, chiseled body, blond hair, who-cares-what-color-eyes, and arms full of tattoos. As he grinded to the music, I wiggled a hand free and wiped the drool off the corner of my mouth. I covered my face from embarrassment, cheeks scorched with flames.

Someone yanked my hands away. "Shhhtop blocking your face, how am I sssuppposed to take incriminating pictures?" Mandy squealed in laughter. *Son of a bitch!* Beads of sweat burst out across my upper lip and chest, a gush of fiery waves tumbled and rolled low in my stomach. My pulse raced, heart thudding in my chest. *Oh, my God, I would just die if anyone saw pictures of this.*

The music pounded faster. Confetti-like neon lights drew out a strange, erotic, almost primal feeling along my skin. Jack P. Hammer spun around me, hands grasping my shoulders, squeezing, kneading, and looked into my eyes. *Brown... his eyes were brown.* Sexy brown eyes that slowly crawled up and down my body unapologetically. One of those indecent looks that made you feel like you were the only woman in the room...a wolf and his prey. I melted into a wet puddle of stripper goo. That's probably the reason why strip club floors feel so sticky; the women melt from the heat, just liquefy from the sexiness and end up stuck under a stranger's heels. It doesn't seem like the worst way to go, actually.

Arching one eyebrow, he cocked his head to the side and slid his lips along my jaw, my neck. *Oh, my God, were strippers supposed to do that? Where the heck were all my bridesmaids?* My hands squeezed down hard on the arms of the chair. The band of my engagement ring clinked against the wood as I tried to gulp in air. It felt as if I was stealing a deep breath, someone else's, and I ended up coughing out a bunch of nervous giggles. Around us, the crowd went wild. I was completely flushed, drunker than I'd ever been, and there was a gorgeous man licking my face. And neck. *And, oh God, he can't do that, can he?*

Mandy's flushed face was next to mine instantly. "This guy is *soooooo hawt.* Do you *see* him?" *He's freaking slathering his man stuff all over me, how could I not see him?* Drunk as hell, she couldn't focus on my eyes and her forehead knocked hard against mine. Suddenly, a loud slap erupted from behind her, causing her eyes to bulge out in shock…giant brown and white ringed saucers. Her lips burst into a perfectly shaped O. "Ohmyfreakingword! He just shhhh-panked me."

We slid off the chair in a heap of giggles, Mr. Hammer crawling on top of us, mock humping our laughing faces. This was all Mandy's fault. I blame everything on Mandy—taking me to a shabby little strip club and getting a face full of humping junk all night.

Mandy was a wild one.

If anything ever happens, everyone just looks to Mandy; she's always the one guilty of something. Everyone has one crazy friend like her; the one you really shouldn't take out in public, because when you do, someone is getting arrested. Although, at that particular moment, it was *me* thrusting a fistful of sticky dollar bills in a strange man's G-string thingy. *This morning I would have never said my night would end like this.*

The women in the crowded bar, *all of them my friends,* began screaming and clapping when the stripper grabbed onto my hand with its fistful of money and started grinding into it. *Oh Lord, I didn't know they came in that size!* My stomach muscles ached from giggling so much. Even my cheeks hurt from the constant laughter. My bones felt rubbery and numb.

All this insanity was because I was supposed to get married in three weeks. The thought made me smile and giggle more.

"Do you want a private dance?" the stripper's deep voice whispered into my ear, his lips warm and wet. Two strong hands slid up the back of my neck, the rest of his body gliding all around me so fast my drunken brain couldn't keep up with it. "Come to the VIP room with me, baby girl," he groaned, thrusting against me, "I got what you need."

This just got weird.

I laughed nervously, my voice struggling with my brain. *Okay then, I think it's time to head on outta here, back to the hotel.*

"Yessssh!" Mandy squealed, pointing a drunken, crooked finger at me. "He's got what you need," her eyes blinked spastically and her eyebrows arched up high. She completed the look with duck-shaped lips. "You get yourself in that Very Important People room and ride yourself a Hammer. *Ish on me.*" She stumbled back, laughing.

"Nope. Not me. Not going to happen. No way."

"Yessshhh. You have to go and get the Hammer; it's all good. Go. Now. Shoo, shoo," Mandy slurred, shoving me towards the back rooms. Mr. Hammer grabbed onto my hand and pulled, leading me through the crowd and into a dark corner with a red glowing hallway attached to it. It looked like the gates of Hell.

The room spun around me, the thump-thump-thump of the music vibrating through the floor. I leaned back and yanked my hands away from him. It was easy to slide through the sweaty grip. "Um, no thank you," I yelped, breaking into a fit of nervous giggles. I couldn't do it. I couldn't go in a back room with a strange man three weeks before I was supposed to get married. Was he crazy? I backed away carefully onto the middle of the dance floor, my stilettos wobbly stilts underneath me. Disappointment flashed across Mr. Hammer's face.

I just couldn't do it.

Then I was airborne, hanging upside down, hair dangling towards the dirty floor while two new strippers mock-pose my body in various sexual positions so far from anything I had ever remotely imagined *could be* sexual positions.

From there, I watched as the Hammer pounded against another bride-to-be, who within the first five minutes, happily skipped towards the back VIP room with him. Wow.

Just wow. That took guts and probably a crap load of douche. *And,* probably a medicine cabinet of antibiotics and creams a few days from now, but who was I to judge.

An hour later, the limo my bridesmaids rented for me dropped me off in front of my apartment, completely forgetting the plan was to go back to our hotel room at the Marriott downtown. I tumbled out of the car, sprawled out on the grass, my *Buy me a shot, I'm tying the knot!* T-shirt wrapped around my head, a white cotton bra out for all my neighbors to see. Not that anyone would look, because at the same moment, Mandy was completely topless, her full bare torso jutting out of the sunroof of the limo. And she was bouncing.

Laughing, I crawled across my wet lawn and fell against

my front door. My fingers fumbled with the keys as I waved goodbye to the back of the limo as it sped down the street.

I might have fallen asleep for a few moments, but when I finally remembered how to use a lock mechanism correctly with my questionable slippery key (when in doubt, slowly get on your knees, give it a little blow, and firmly push it in), I walked (okay crawled) inside to all the lights in my apartment on.

Every single luminescent bulb in the apartment: on.

So even though I was in the most inebriated state I'd ever been in my life, I clearly saw one of the top contributors for *InTrend Magazine, Sophia Willington,* having sex with Trager the Mailroom Guy, smack dab in the middle of my living room. Sex being a questionable word for the act I stumbled upon. She was riding him like a racehorse. My drunken brain could not wrap itself around the fact that *thee Sophia Willington* was in *my* apartment with Trager the Mailroom Guy. That's what we called him too—everybody who worked at the damn magazine—*Trager the Mailroom Guy.*

Who incidentally, was supposed to be marrying me in three fucking weeks.

BUY NOW: Suite 269

319

INTERESTED IN SOME MORE OF MY STORIES?

LIV

It was a butt dial that changed everything—stunning me awake from some obscure unsettling dream—scattering it into a kaleidoscope of colors and emotions. My eyes snapped open, my breath sucking back into my throat so violently fast my lungs almost burst.

An icy layer of sweat broke out across my skin as I clawed senselessly at the tangled sheets around my legs. For a moment, I sat, panting, stomach twisting sickly, peering into the dark, wondering where I was.

A sliver of pale yellow light poured in from the window, falling softly against my desk. My eyes traced its path to my cell phone just under its glow, buzzing with lights and sounds.

I ran my hands over my face and took a slow deep breath.

Cursing, I climbed to my feet and staggered over the soft rug, my hands fumbling for the phone.

My mother's face popped up on screen.

"Hello?" I said, quickly answering the call, stomach rising to my throat.

A blur of noise and music spiraled out from three hundred and two point eight miles away.

"Hello?" I asked, louder. "Mom?"

On the other end, glasses clinked together, and my mother's voice muttered incoherently about tequila and the greatest love of her life. Someone laughed deeply and answered her. Muffled voices in the background cheered and someone asked for a cigarette as my mother slurred a sad rendition of what she always thought should have been her wedding song.

"Mom? Hello?"

She was still singing.

I pulled the phone away from my ear and stared at it, exhausted and angry.

My mother was drunk. Drunk—in some crowded bar mumbling unintelligibly to some poor sap about how much she still loved my father—a man neither of us had seen in years.

"Mom!" I shouted into the phone.

She slurred the chorus to the song, mixing up the words pitifully.

"Mom?" I said more softly, squeezing the phone against my ear. "Mom, *please* go home."

Memories ricocheted through foggy fragments of my childhood—playing all the same images—a broken story that was once my life. Olivia Rhys was a mistake born to a sixteen-year-old with two drinks in her hand and the older boy who broke her heart. The greatest love story that never got finished, she would tell me, her breath the flavor of cheap tequila. It was a love that was so consuming, you couldn't tell where he ended and she began. Except, he ended it by leaving her with *me*, and she never began anything, but another bottle of whatever she could get her hands on.

Maybe she was right about love, who knew? I certainly didn't.

"Mom?" I asked into the phone again.

Someone answered her song with some drunk pearl of wisdom that had something to do with a fish and a telephone pole. I sighed heavily and cut off the call.

My mother and I were as emotionally distant as the miles we put between us. For the last few years I'd been gone, we'd seen each other less than a handful of times, each visit ending in tears.

I was probably the worst daughter in the world. But I figured it would equal out in the end somehow, since I practically raised myself, and the mostly unconscious woman hovering over the toilet every night.

The dim colors in my room blurred, dissolving into a teary darkness. Something with her always tugged at my insides. No matter what the past was and how much I'd tried to forget my lonely childhood, I couldn't shake the fact that something was always pulling me back home.

That, and her ass called me four more times.

She always needed someone to take care of her. She always made the wrong choices and never worried about consequences for anything. What she really needed was a full time babysitter.

Guilt kept me up for the rest of the night—it took over my body—my mind. My arms and legs became puppet limbs, packing an over night bag, dragging my exhausted body down the steps of my apartment, and into the car. Five hours and four spilled coffees later, I found myself walking up the overgrown pathway to my childhood home wishing I'd just stayed in my own damn bed. This was supposed to be my winter recess from work. For twelve days, the schools were closed, and I planned a staycation that included books, parties, and sex with strange men. Yet, there I was, back at my horrible childhood home on a guilt trip for one.

I hesitated at the bottom step, hands wrapped around the rusted railing, tired eyes squinting into the bright morning sun. *Why was I even there?* Thinking I could do anything there to make a difference was absurd. I'd spent my childhood trying; it was never good enough. She loved her broken heart and her sad life more than she ever loved me.

My insides knotted with nerves, fighting the urge to turn around and drive all the way back home. Surprise visits never ended well in the Rhys house. Trying to calm the tension in my shoulders, I leaned back against the rail and took in a slow deep breath. It puffed back out in a pale mist; the air tasted like sea salt and filth, New York style. From the porch, I could hear Jamaica Bay a few blocks away, dark and violent, beating at the sand with its high tide.

Even though I had my own key, I rang the bell and peeked through the smudged-glass panels of the door. I couldn't see past any of the grime, but I could hear the television clearly through the thin wooden door.

After pushing the buzzer a few more times, I rummaged through my bag and pulled out my keys. "Mom?" I called as I opened the door. "Don't get scared. It's me, Liv." And just so she remembered correctly, I added, "You know, your daughter."

She didn't answer. There was nothing but the loud voices of a bunch of women on some morning talk show discussing some new political catastrophe. I tossed the keys into the small basket on the table in the foyer, and leaned my bag up against the wall. "Mom?" I called again, walking deeper into the house. The stench of stale cigarette smoke and burnt fried onions hung heavily in the air. It was enough to make me swallow back a gag. I held my nose and called out to her again.

Still no answer.

Glancing toward the living room, a hot flash of nostalgia hit me—the house hadn't been changed in years. The same worn brown couch sat forlorn up against the far wall decorated with the same old mismatched pillows. One sole picture hung crookedly on the wall, taken when I had to be about six, my two front teeth missing. The curtains were open, a fine grayish dust covering the tops of them. They probably hadn't been cleaned since the last time I was here. The only difference I could see from my childhood was the small water stain on the ceiling had grown into an enormous discolored lumpy mess that offered a steady drip across the now peeling linoleum floors. She didn't tell me about it; I was going to need to call a plumber for her. Again. There went any vacation ideas I had for next spring break. My money would once again be handed right over to my mother.

Sighing, I walked toward the windows and opened them wide, letting some fresh air in. The screens were torn, but the breeze was cold and clean. I could even smell the big old pine tree from the neighbors' yard—a yard I spent more time growing up in than I did in my own house. Next door, the Fury family had been my refuge from loneliness—a sister who was my best friend, an older brother who was my secret crush, and parents who held hands and took their kids to the movies in a big suburban. My mother was always just some shadowy silhouette at my door at three in the morning. My father was just a story to me, told in late-night drunken monologues that would make Shakespeare cry. The Furys sort of pulled me into their home and made me feel like I belonged. They tried to, anyway.

It had been years since I lost touch with them. Every few

months, Brooke and I emailed or messaged each other on social media, but I moved on, left this place and made a life for myself that was a great deal more stable than the one I was brought up in.

I let the curtain fall back in place and wandered my way into the kitchen. My chest tightened as I stepped through the doorway. It reeked of cheap whiskey and seared onions—a charred pot sizzled loudly over a low flame on the stove—thick gray smoke billowed out around it.

Something lay still on the floor in front of the stove.

I stepped closer.

It wasn't a *something*.

It was a *someone*.

My heart thudded hard across my chest. I heard it, thick and wet, slamming around inside me.

Utterly still and limp, her legs at a curious angle, dark dried blood and vomit haloed around her head, lay my mother.

I stumbled closer, collapsing my body against a table piled with jagged sharp edged bottles and ashtrays overflowing with cigarette butts.

Bloody, bleached-blonde hair knotted across her cheeks. Tiny shards of glittery glass reflected swirls of light across the floor. A broken bottle—a quarter full—still clutched tightly in her hands and dark brown urine colored her creamy white leggings.

Nope, surprise visits never ended well at the Rhys house.

BUY NOW: <u>Resisting Love</u>

THIS BOOK IS FREE EVERYWHERE!

all From Grace (FREE!)

WHAT WOKE me was the insistent beep-beep-beep of the little machine that was monitoring his dying heart. I opened my eyes slowly, and as always, he lay there watching me.

I got up from where I was sitting and leaned in close to him, placing my hand on his cheek. "Let go. I understand."

He struggled for breath and mumbled something I couldn't hear. I smiled anyway. "Go, Jake. I'll be fine, don't hold on for me."

A lone tear escaped from his eye and his breathing stilled. The monitors screamed their piercing sirens.

I stepped back as nurses and doctors flooded the room, but I knew it was too late. He was gone and I was completely alone again.

Voices blurred and time seemed to slow down as I made my way towards the hall. God, I don't belong here anymore. This is my own personal hell.

Someone cut off the horrific screams of the heart monitor and the sudden realization that Jacob was dead shot waves of horror through me. Does life ever get any easier?

For so long, I helplessly watched as a vicious disease sucked the life out of his once strong spirit. Jacob's trembling hands, and jaundice skin showed his inability to fight the invisible murderous enemy. How much more powerless and insignificant can a person feel when watching someone they love slowly die? I wished each night to take his place, yet I was still standing there and Jacob was gone. I never believed in wishes anyway.

I placed my hand on the doorframe and looked back once. Do not resuscitate. Do not grieve for me when this cancer wins. Do not give me a funeral to remember what killed me. They were calling the time; it was 3:16. The numbers made my frown tighten, or maybe it was just the knowledge that Gabriel would be standing right outside the door.

"Hello, Gabriel," I whispered, even before I stepped through the doorway. My insides twisted themselves into knots as I stood before him.

"Grace."

I looked up and tried my best to smile; trying to hold in the tears that I knew would soon flow like a great flood from my eyes. Gabriel was always so beautiful to look at. No matter when or where he showed up, he was perfect. He was leaning against the white walls of the hospital hallway and his perfection made them seem dirty against his bronzed flawless skin.

"What is your plan now, Grace?"

"Oh, Gabriel, it's the same as always. Just keep breathing and put one foot in front of the other. Now, if you would please excuse me, I just lost my brother and I'd like to be alone." I brushed past him, accidentally touching the edge of his arm, and I shivered.

Gabriel reached out his arm and gently touched my shoulder. "I'm sorry about your brother, Grace. I'm sorry about all of this."

I stopped and turned towards him. Even though his voice had sounded full of tenderness, his ice-cold blue eyes held no emotion. "Thank you, Gabriel. I'm sure that one day, I'll meet up with him again. After all, we all gotta die sometime, don't we?" My sarcasm dripped thickly off every word. I couldn't say what I wanted to. How many times can you say I'm sorry? How many times will I watch death take everyone, leaving me here? How much more can I endure when I've endured so much more than others have? How many times have I wished death would come for me? Even in death, I would not be allowed to rest, would I? Sorrow seeped through my veins. This is all I knew; all I'd ever know; an eternity here on earth.

His long elegant fingers brushed up against my cheek. "I really am sorry about Jacob, Grace. I wish I could do something. I know how special he's been to you." For a single nanosecond, or maybe even less, his eyes offered a smoldering glance, as if they were trying to tell me something separate from his blank expression.

He turned to leave, but I felt his halfhearted attempt at being able to do something, hang heavy and linger in the air between us.

"This has nothing to do with Jacob, Gabriel. Yes, my brother is gone now, and I will miss him, but this has to do with my being here, still alone. I'm relieved Jacob is gone. He's been dying for years with that cancer. No human being should suffer as he did. Being here is excruciating, Gabriel, but I'm still here! So please, do not patronize me. Do not visit every so often, glare at me with those cold dead eyes, and tell me how you wish you could do something, when I know for a fact that you could. Unless you have something to offer me in way of advice or counsel, I'll be doing what I've always done, putting one foot in front of the other and moving on." My eyes welled up when I turned from him. Of course, I would miss Jacob. Someone like Gabriel would never understand any of these horrible human emotions and all this pain. I just wished it would end; I would just like not to exist in this world anymore or in any world. I just wanted, well, it doesn't matter what I wanted, did it?

In one quick movement, Gabriel grabbed me and spun me to face him. His stern fatherly expression dissolved into a tender smile. The behavior startled me in such a way that my knees gave out from underneath me. I had never seen Gabriel smile like that. He embraced me in his huge bronze arms and whispered into my ears without saying a word.

"You are the strongest person that I have ever known. You've been broken more times than anyone, and yet you keep...I want so much to save you..." His embrace calmed me. I slowly pushed myself off and out of his arms, trying to distance myself from him.

The tenderness was gone and the stern father figure was standing before me as if that little slip in time of encouragement and tenderness never happened.

"Thank you, Gabriel." And, that's where I left him. Standing in a hospital hallway, in the middle of nowhere, thinking that I was the strongest person he'd known. As if, I had a choice in that.

GET NOW FREE! Fall From Grace

Thanks for reading!
XOXO